A **KNIFE** to the **HEART**

By Barbara Nadel

The Inspector İkmen Series
Belshazzar's Daughter
A Chemical Prison
Arabesk
Deep Waters
Harem
Petrified
Deadly Web
Dance with Death
A Passion for Killing
Pretty Dead Things
River of the Dead
Death by Design
A Noble Killing
Dead of Night
Deadline
Body Count
Land of the Blind
On the Bone
The House of Four
Incorruptible
A Knife to the Heart

The Hancock Series
Last Rights
After the Mourning
Ashes to Ashes
Sure and Certain Death

BARBARA
NADEL

A **KNIFE** to the **HEART**

HEADLINE

First published in Great Britain in 2019 by
HEADLINE PUBLISHING GROUP

1

Cataloguing in Publication Data is available from the British Library

ISBN 978 1 4722 5457 3 (Hardback)
ISBN 978 1 4722 5458 0 (Trade Paperback)

Typeset in Times New Roman by Palimpsest Book Production Limited,
Falkirk, Stirlingshire

Printed and bound in Great Britain by Clays Ltd, Elcograf S.p.A.

HEADLINE PUBLISHING GROUP
An Hachette UK Company
Carmelite House
50 Victoria Embankment
London EC4Y 0DZ

www.headline.co.uk
www.hachette.co.uk

To Deniz
Rest in Peace

Cast List

Çetin İkmen – former İstanbul detective
Çiçek İkmen – Çetin's eldest daughter
Bülent İkmen – one of his sons
Hülya Kohen – a younger daughter
Samsun Bajraktar – İkmen's cousin, a transsexual
Dr Arto Sarkissian – police pathologist, İkmen's oldest friend, an ethnic Armenian
Inspector Mehmet Süleyman – İstanbul detective
Sergeant Ömer Mungun – Süleyman's deputy
Peri Mungun – Ömer's sister
Inspector Kerim Gürsel – İstanbul detective
Sergeant Elif Arslan – Gürsel's deputy
Suzan Tan – Hülya Kohen's friend, an historian
Tayfun Yıldırım – Suzan's step-uncle, a property developer
Admiral Alaaddin Tonguç – elderly disgraced military man
Halide Tonguç – his wife
Timur Tonguç – the couple's elder son
Aylin Tonguç – a daughter
Zeynep Tonguç – a daughter
Ateş Tonguç – their younger son, a publisher
Berfu Hanım – Tonguç family's neighbour

Mustafa Ermis – husband of Tonguç's deceased daughter Deniz

Hayrünnısa Hanım – the admiral's mistress

Angela Aksoy – wife of artist Burhan Aksoy, friend of Timur

Ali Ok – kapıcı of a Tarlabaşı illegal brothel/drug den

Haluk Andıç – landlord of Tarlabaşı brothel/drug den

Güneş Sağlam – resident of Ali Ok's building

Yeliz – another resident, a prostitute

Numan Osman – heroin addict, another resident

Branko Topaloğlu – another resident addict

Tansu Barışık, aka Sugar Hanım – an ageing prostitute and police informant

Metin Demir – an imam; also works as a tailor

Selçuk Çeviköz – Metin's assistant

Serkan Asal – bonzai addict

Abdülmecid Killigil – aristocrat

Büket Teyze – a fortune-teller

Rosarita Elias – Syrian child refugee

İlyas Müslim – works for social services

Hüseyin Sağlam – son of deceased pathologist Orhan Sağlam

Fılız Aksoy – escort girl

It had been when she had been sorting through a pile of water-damaged photograph albums on the top floor of the yalı that she'd come across the ouija board that had, indirectly, led her to this stifling apartment listening to the sobs of a woman old enough to be her mother. Not for the first time, she wondered what she was doing. Especially when Aylin Tonguç scuttled towards her in the darkness and whispered, 'Does anyone know you are here?'

Aylin sounded like a little girl. And in the thick darkness of that oven-like room, she could have been a child, had Suzan not known better. Aylin Tonguç was fifty-six and she was drowning in tears. Now that she was here, Suzan just wanted to get up and go, but how could she? She'd asked for this meeting. It had taken her weeks to arrange. If only she'd never seen the amazing villa known as the Kara Lale Yalı! If she hadn't, she wouldn't be sweating herself dry in this creepy apartment in Nişantaşı. But the architect of her discomfort was neither this keening woman nor even the yalı; it was the man who had become her uncle.

Suzan had always liked her mother's younger sister, Aunt Nalan. Nalan had always supported her; in fact she was in her car downstairs right now, ready to whisk Suzan away as soon as this meeting was over. But Nalan's latest husband was another matter. Tayfun Yıldırım, on the face of it a pious government supporter, was actually a ruthless property developer, not a

1

million miles away from a Mafia boss. When Suzan had heard that Yıldırım had bought an historic wooden villa in the Bosphorus village of Bebek, she had been horrified. He'd torn down historic houses and apartment blocks all over the city of İstanbul. Now he was going to replace a nineteenth-century wooden summer house in what had once been an idyllic village with a monstrosity in glass and steel. She had begged her aunt to ask her husband to let her make a record. At least if the yalı and its contents were properly documented, the fact of its existence wouldn't be lost. Reluctantly he had agreed. But only when Nalan had explained to him the kudos he would gain from allowing an actual historian to investigate his property. Maybe Suzan would even write a book?

Suzan didn't know what to say. The woman's face, hairy and scented with musk, brushed against hers. Then a tiny, thin hand held her fingers.

'I keep everything closed so it can't get in,' she continued.

'What?' Suzan asked. No one had told her the woman was actually mad. Maybe her aunt should have come in with her.

Aylin Tonguç's cheek pressed into Suzan's and she smelt her sour breath.

'Kismet,' the woman whispered. 'Kismet.'

Chapter 1

Marlboro the cat wouldn't sit on Çetin İkmen's lap when he chose to rest out on the balcony. He also wasn't keen on the kitchen these days.

Ever since his wife Fatma had died, İkmen had become almost a stranger to himself. Alone in his apartment with his unemployed daughter and, when she deigned to turn up, his transsexual cousin Samsun, he lived in near silence, smoking furiously and talking mostly, according to his daughter Çiçek, to the ghost of his dead wife. All his friends, both inside and outside the police force, worried about him. Fatma's death had been a bolt from the blue.

'I know you'll say it's because of the djinn,' İkmen told his wife. 'Animals are sensitive. And yes, I know, I know, an exorcist. But I can't face getting one of those in. Either some crypto-businessman who will also want to sell me some bloody amulet that's been made in China, or a half-mad illiterate who stinks of goat.' He smoked, then he said, 'Yes, I know it's been there for well over a year. I'm not entirely indifferent to it. Angels and demons, like that bloody djinn, have always followed me about one way or another.' He turned his head away. 'I've had better things to do.'

Retirement had never been on Inspector Çetin İkmen's agenda. With a forty-a-day smoking habit, plus a liking for alcohol, he thought he'd be dead long before that happened. But circumstances had dictated otherwise, and so, after almost forty years

3

on the İstanbul police force, he had finally gone. It had been that or be thrown out. It had left a bitter taste.

'Anyway,' he said. 'I must try and put on a happy face when Çiçek gets in. She didn't get that job at the Four Seasons and so she'll be depressed. I don't blame her, but I need to try and keep her spirits up. She says she'll never work again, and I know that's a possibility these days. But I can't say that to her, you know. How can anyone think that a girl like that, raised by me, would follow some mad sheikh who lives abroad? I mean, I know you wanted all the children to be religious, but it never happened. How can they think my Çiçek . . .' He shook his head. 'They think it because they choose to. Because they want scapegoats . . .'

'Dad!'

She was back. İkmen walked through the French windows and into his vast, messy living room. His daughter, an attractive woman of forty, wasn't alone.

'I met Hülya in the Hippodrome,' she said.

'I was coming to see you,' Hülya added.

İkmen kissed both his daughters and sat down.

Hülya, the younger of the two, sat next to him. He took her hand.

Çiçek said, 'I'll go and make tea.'

She looked crushed, and although in a way İkmen wanted her to talk about her fruitless interview, in another way he didn't. After leaving her job as a flight attendant at Turkish Airlines, Çiçek had worked for budget carrier Marmara Air. But after the failed military coup in July 2016, they had dismissed her for having the same messaging app on her phone as the religious organisation that had apparently instigated the putsch. The difference being that Çiçek had never belonged to any shady religious group and she'd never actually used the offending app. But she was marked, which meant she had lost just about everything, including her apartment.

4

'We saw Samsun outside the Mozaik,' Hülya said. She gave her father a cigarette and then lit one for herself.

'Yes, it's now her local watering hole,' İkmen said.

'Used to be yours.'

'Yes, well,' he said. 'Samsun has her own friends and Resat Bey is entranced. I believe he thinks she's good for tourist dollars.'

'I'm sure Samsun would be delighted if you joined her . . .'

'Please don't push me to go out, Hülya, there's a good girl,' İkmen said.

And so his daughter became quiet. The thing she'd come to see her father about still trapped inside her head.

Street brawls were not Inspector Mehmet Süleyman's purview. In his role as an İstanbul homicide detective, he didn't usually get involved unless someone died. But this was different. This was Cihangir, his home turf.

'What he does is his business!' he yelled at the frothing middle-aged man he held by the neck against a wall. On the pavement, a young man with dreadlocks groaned. He nursed a broken beer bottle against his chest, and his face was covered with blood.

'He and those other devils were breaking the Holy Fast!' the older man cried.

'As I say, his business,' Süleyman reiterated. 'His choice, his soul. What's it to you?'

'I find it offensive.'

'So go and complain to your friends in your local coffee house. Tweet about it, mortify your own flesh for all I care, but don't attack other people.'

'His drinking is like a slap in the face . . .'

'No it isn't,' Süleyman said.

He didn't know the older man, although the youngster was familiar to him. He worked at a tiny bar on Akarsu Caddesi, one of liberal and trendy Cihangir's many alcohol-serving establishments.

'Where do you come from?' Süleyman asked the older man.

'What's it to you?'

'I'm a police officer.'

'Then you should be on my side!' the man wailed.

'No he shouldn't.'

The unfamiliar voice didn't come from the man on the ground, who had just discovered he'd lost a tooth, but from a smartly dressed man probably in his forties.

When he saw him, the older man hung his head. 'Metin Efendi . . .'

Süleyman said, 'What's going on here? Who are you?'

The man smiled and bowed slightly. 'I am Selçuk's imam – and his friend. He also works for me; I'm a tailor by trade.'

'Selçuk?'

'Me,' the offender said. 'Selçuk Çeviköz.'

'We come from Gaziosmanpaşa district,' the imam said. 'Selçuk's brother has not been too well; I accompanied Selçuk here in order that he could visit.'

'This part of the city makes me nervous,' Selçuk said.

'Makes *you* nervous!'

The young man who had been on the ground stood up. 'I'm the one who lost a tooth!'

'Metin Efendi, he was drinking beer. In front of my eyes!'

The imam put a hand on his friend's shoulder. 'Selçuk, you may mean well—'

'Mean well!' The young man looked as if he was about to explode. 'He came out of nowhere! I was having a drink, minding my own business—'

'You shouldn't drink during Ramazan. It's an abomination!'

'Shut up, all of you!'

They looked at the policeman and then at the ground.

6

'You,' Süleyman said to the injured man. 'Do you wish to press charges?'

The youngster sighed. 'What's the point?'

'The point is that you've been assaulted.'

'You know what I mean.'

And Süleyman did. Under the tutelage of the ruling party, religion had become much more visible in everyday life. In fact many secular Turks felt oppressed by it. Some, like this man, felt powerless to live their lives as they saw fit. Many believed that not even the police would stand up for them.

'Well?' Süleyman asked.

'No,' the young man said. 'The dental work will cost me a fortune, but if I have to wait for him to pay, I suspect I'll be an old man by the time I get reparation.'

'You have the right.'

But the young man was already walking away. Süleyman let go of Selçuk Çeviköz and said, 'Seems like it's your lucky day.'

'I give my thanks to God . . .'

'Yes, right. But if you assault anyone again, you won't be so lucky.'

The imam began, 'Officer—'

'Inspector Süleyman.'

'Inspector Süleyman, I can assure you—'

'Just take him back to Gaziosmanpaşa and get out of my sight,' Süleyman said. 'I'm sick to death of people throwing their weight around in this city. There is something called tolerance, you know. I believe God is quite an enthusiast.'

He walked away.

Aged fifty, he remembered a time when the observance of Ramazan had been a choice. Although if he were honest with himself, back in his childhood, most people didn't observe the fast. Hard-line secularists saw it as reactionary. And that had been wrong too.

7

The smell of the beer the young man had spilled when he'd been hit made Süleyman want a drink. In the old days, when İkmen had still been grumpily walking the streets of İstanbul, he would have called him up and they would have met at the Mozaik and probably got drunk. But that wasn't going to happen. İkmen didn't go to the Mozaik any more. In fact he hardly ever left his apartment.

Süleyman put a cigarette in his perfectly shaped mouth and lit up. A man across the road glared at him. Süleyman muttered, 'Fuck off.'

'Suzan Tan.' İkmen smiled and shook his head. 'Was she in the same year as you?'

'One year above,' Hülya said.

Four of İkmen's nine children had attended the prestigious İstanbul Lisesi. It was a selective school, and they had had to compete with children from all over Turkey. But then the İkmen children, like their parents, were bright.

'Didn't her family live somewhere posh?' he asked.

'Kadıköy, just off Bağdat Caddesi. So her mum could be close to Gucci and Prada.'

Bağdat Caddesi was probably the most glamorous shopping street in the city. Even those who, like İkmen, lived on the European side would go to Asia to sample the delights of Bağdat Caddesi.

'Didn't Suzan become an academic?' İkmen asked as he took a glass of tea from his older daughter.

'An historian, yes,' Hülya said. 'And that's why I'm here, on her behalf.'

'Oh?'

'Yes,' she said. 'She's been compiling a history of a wooden yalı in Bebek. Her uncle's bought it or something. I don't know, she witters on, and I was trying to get Timur to go to bed when

8

she phoned. Anyway, this yalı was the scene of a murder back in 1976. She wondered whether you'd remember it?'

İkmen lit a cigarette. 'I don't know,' he said. 'I was a constable back then. Little more than a kid.'

'You had three children already,' Çiçek said.

He shrugged.

'Well anyway,' Hülya said, 'according to Suzan, a young woman called Deniz Tonguç was found dead in the garden of the yalı, which belonged to her parents. At the time, her husband was the primary suspect, but that didn't come to anything. Don't know why; maybe he had a good alibi.'

İkmen frowned.

'I don't know what the outcome was in the end,' Hülya said. 'But Suzan says that this event is still having repercussions in the Tonguç family now. Long and short is that she wants to talk to you.'

At first İkmen said nothing. Talking to people was something he'd rather got out of the way of.

'She'll come here if you want,' Hülya continued. 'But then she'd be equally happy to take you for a drink.'

'Do you know how this woman died?' İkmen asked.

'Oh yes,' Hülya said. 'Sorry, I left that out. She was stabbed through the heart.'

Although she still liked to refer to herself as a 'party girl', İkmen's cousin Samsun Bajraktar was nearly seventy and would soon be home wanting food. Then she'd fall asleep in her chair, snoring like a rhino. Unable to afford the bills on her old flat in Beyazit, Samsun had moved into the İkmen apartment shortly after Fatma's death.

And because, left to her father, no one would ever eat again, Çiçek went into the kitchen to begin preparing the evening meal. It was a sort of İftar meal – the breaking of the Ramazan fast – but not, as no one in the İkmen apartment was fasting.

Her sister, Hülya, had had an agenda with their dad. Not that her story about Suzan Tan wasn't true; it was. But it had been Hülya and not Suzan who had suggested that he might be able to help. Anything to get him out of the apartment and involved in life once again!

Çiçek cut four aubergines in half and sprinkled them with salt, then began chopping onions and garlic. She knew she was being watched, even though she could only see it out of the corner of her eye. It had started about three months before the failed coup, according to her father. Only Çiçek, her dad and her brother Bülent had ever seen the djinn. And her mother, of course, briefly, in the weeks before her death. Because that was what djinn did.

Beings of smoke and fire, the djinn were situated in Islamic mythology somewhere between humanity and the angels. More often than not demonic, they often presaged a death in the family. Living mainly in dark corners and behind pieces of furniture, they watched, only sometimes revealing themselves in all their snaggle-toothed, fur-covered glory. They could be tiny or enormous. İkmen had once seen one grow so tall, its head popped out through the roof of a house. They were always a problem.

Çiçek muttered under her breath, 'Go away.'

But nothing changed. Nothing would until her father resumed his life.

'There was a seance,' İkmen said. 'The mother was a spiritualist. I don't know how or why. I heard all of this second hand, you have to remember. I was walking the streets telling kids to get to school and picking up dope-heads at the time. The seance was before the girl died. I don't know how long. But apparently someone asked the spirits, or whatever you like to call what may or may not exist, who was going to die first. I don't know if it was just the family in the room or whether others were present, but the thing spelt out the eldest daughter's name.'

10

'Deniz?'

'If that was the girl's name, yes,' he said.

He could hear Çiçek chopping vegetables in the kitchen. He could feel her anger at being watched by that bloody djinn.

'I think if I remember correctly her death was declared a suicide. A classic case of a self-fulfilling prophecy.'

Hülya said, 'Isn't it difficult to stab yourself through the chest?'

'One would think so, yes,' he said. 'But don't take my word for it. Your uncle Arto would know better than I.' Not that İkmen had seen his oldest friend, the pathologist Arto Sarkissian, for months. He'd kept him at arm's length, like he had everyone.

'So, will you speak to Suzan?' Hülya asked.

'For what it's worth, yes.'

The silence between them became painful. Hülya was struggling to know where to go next, and İkmen felt her anxiety.

'She can come here,' he said.

He watched as Hülya looked around the chaotic room. You didn't have to be a mind-reader to know what she was thinking. And the awfulness didn't stop at the look of the place. The whole apartment reeked of cigarettes and Samsun's heavy Arabian perfume.

'Or not,' he added.

Hülya breathed in deeply. 'Dad, Suzan lives in Galata now. I know it's not far, but she's really busy with this project and doesn't get much time to herself. She'd really appreciate it if you met her over there.'

He didn't say anything, mainly because he knew she'd be disappointed if he said no. But also because he feared saying yes. To be out would not just mean leaving the apartment to the tender mercies of the djinn in the kitchen; it would mean leaving poor Fatma too. Feelings he didn't want to acknowledge jangled for position in his head, rendering him mute.

Eventually Hülya spoke. 'Dad, I know you don't want to leave because of . . . Mum . . .'

11

He watched her lower her head. Hülya, in common with all of his children except Çiçek and Bülent, had never understood. It wasn't her fault. He put a hand on her shoulder and smiled. He knew what she was going to say next.

'It's been nearly a year since Mum died,' she said. 'You have to start letting go.'

Chapter 2

Back when you couldn't see the high-rises of Esenler cluttering up the skyline, Karayolları mahalle had been a good place to live. Everyone had been poor back then, but there had been a sense of community. Back in the sixties and seventies, although there had been political unrest, it hadn't been the same. Only last week, the police had raided the apartment above the pharmacy and taken away a rocket launcher. What was wrong with people?

Imam Metin Demir smiled when he recalled the dried peppers his school friends used to grab from their roofs before heading to school. Usually they'd give him some, unless of course his dad had been in a fight with one of their dads. It couldn't have been easy for Regep Demir trying to bring up his son on his own. But he only had himself to blame. A bully, a drunk and a thief, Regep had beaten Metin's mother so hard that one night she had left the family home never to be seen again. At least that was what Regep told people. There were those who were convinced he'd killed her and then dissolved her body in acid he'd stolen from one of the chemical factories on the Golden Horn. Metin always gave his father the benefit of the doubt.

Suhoor had been hours ago and Metin had stuffed himself fit to burst, but he was already hungry again and wondered how he was going to make it through the day. He certainly wasn't going to venture back into the city, especially not with someone like Selçuk Çeviköz. Metin felt sorry for Selçuk because one of his brothers was sick, but that didn't excuse what he'd done when he'd attacked that young man the previous day. They'd both nearly ended up getting arrested. Such lurid religious fanaticism was concerning and saddening. As both his imam and his employer, Metin had spoken firmly to Selçuk on the way back to Gaziosmanpaşa, but he knew his words had not sunk in.

Metin glanced at his father's old lokum box and wondered, not for the first time, whether he should look through it properly. Apart from a house and his now broken old watch, which Metin always kept in his pocket, the only thing Regep had passed on to his son was this old sweet box full, as he had told Metin, of 'treasure'. Probably stuff he'd robbed from houses and handbags, Metin suspected. He didn't really want to look too closely at what the box contained. If he did, he'd feel duty-bound to get those things back to their owners, and that was potentially a very big job.

Another day without food or drink was a daunting prospect, particularly for a man with a big appetite. Dr Arto Sarkissian wasn't even a Muslim, but as principal pathologist for the İstanbul city police department, he felt obliged to support his staff. An ethnic Armenian Christian, Arto dreaded Ramazan and lived for the few moments when he could escape from his laboratory and hide behind the dustbins with a bottle of water and a tiny sigara börek. Not that anyone, apart from people he didn't care about anyway, would blame him even if he was caught.

Now he leaned on one of the stainless-steel dissection tables and breathed out. Thank God for air conditioning! Ramazan falling in June meant it was hot, which meant dehydration. The last thing an overweight man in his sixties needed. That morning's entertainment was to involve a man his own age who had died while in sexual congress with a prostitute in one of Karaköy's last remaining legal brothels. Arto wondered whether

14

this unfortunate incident – probably a heart attack – would be used by the local authority as a pretext to close the place down. He smiled briefly when he tried to imagine what his old friend Çetin İkmen would have said about it back in the day. Something along the lines of 'Fucking puritanical bigots, they're probably all screwing little girls!' Even when he'd first retired, İkmen had still retained his fire. But not now.

The night of the coup, 15–16 July 2016, had been a confused and terrifying time. The plotters had bombed the parliament building in Ankara, blocked the Fatih Bridge over the Bosphorus and attempted to assassinate the president. İstanbul had been fired on. As soon as he could, the president made contact with the people and urged them to fight back. Thousands took to the streets, including Fatma İkmen. A ruling party loyalist, unlike her husband, Fatma had run out on to Divanyolu at five o'clock on the morning of the 16th, ready to do her bit against the coup, and had been struck by a car. It had been an accident and the driver had been inconsolable. Luckily Fatma had died instantly.

In common with many things she'd found in this house, Suzan came across the little gold cross by accident. Ornate and delicate, it was clearly a khachka or Armenian cross. She wondered whether it had belonged to one of the old family's servants.

A voice over her shoulder made her start.

'That gold?'

She turned. It was Tayfun Yıldırım. Her uncle had a habit of turning up unannounced. Suzan failed to keep the contempt off her face.

'Hello,' she said. 'Yes, it is gold.'

'Take it to the bazaar, see what price you can get,' he said.

'No!'

'Why not?'

'Because it probably belonged to a member of the Tonguç

family, or their servants,' she said. 'I'll send it on to one of them.'

'You don't want to get too close to that family,' Yıldırım said. 'You know why.'

She did. The ancient head of the family, eighty-eight-year-old Admiral Alaaddin Tonguç, was currently in prison awaiting trial on charges of treason. Another adherent, it was said, of the shady religious organisation and its sheikh.

'Halide Hanım isn't implicated,' Suzan said.

'How do you know?'

'Just because she's the admiral's wife doesn't mean she's necessarily involved.'

Yıldırım was fifteen years younger than Suzan's aunt. At forty-three, he wasn't much older than Suzan herself. In what many considered the prime of his life, he wasn't unattractive if, as Suzan had once remarked to a friend, you liked that sort of thing. And by that she meant a man with a short, brutish neck, a chest like a barrel, and eyes that never contained emotion. If he had been a house, Tayfun Yıldırım would have been empty.

He said nothing. He enjoyed being close to power. It meant he could make veiled threats. Not that anyone seemed to know how close he was to anyone with real clout. He was rich and he liked to give extravagant warnings on behalf of those with influence. But whether he had influence himself was another matter.

Without warning he ripped the small cross out of Suzan's hand. As she tried to cling on, one of the arms of the cross cut into her hand.

'Ow!'

He took it and put it in his pocket. 'This is my house now and so I own everything in it. Including you. Do as I say.' And then he left.

For a moment, Suzan didn't know what to do with her anger. She wanted to shout down the narrow stairwell, calling him

16

the most offensive names she could muster. But she was pretty sure he wasn't above hitting her, and because Auntie Nalan was so besotted with him, she'd be on his side in any resultant argument.

Suzan sat down on the floor and performed some breathing exercises she'd learned at her yoga class. But they didn't help. She wasn't just angry, she was livid. First, because that thug had bought this beautiful yalı just so he could knock it down, and secondly because her aunt had allowed herself to be suckered into marrying the evil bastard.

Her old friend Hülya İkmen, the policeman's daughter, had offered to help her. But she'd not got back to her. Suzan felt completely deserted.

Çetin İkmen didn't believe in djinn. Not really. Even when this one looked up at him from the space behind the cooker, he felt compelled to say, 'You're just concentrated bad thoughts.'

Then he usually remembered his mother. A witch from the mountains of Albania, Ayşe İkmen had possessed the ability to read the future and speak to the dead. The memory would make him apologise to his mother, if not to the diffuse fur-covered being that inhabited his kitchen.

Had it presaged her death? Who really knew? Some people said that djinn enabled ghosts. But the nature of djinn was to be mysterious, and though it occasionally growled, this one never spoke. It was always up to mischief, moving things around and occasionally curdling milk, because that was what djinn did. That was while he was in the apartment. If he went out, who knew what it would get up to? And so when Hülya had asked him to go and meet Suzan Tan in Galata, he had refused. How could he leave Fatma alone in the house with *that*?

He didn't want to make Çiçek have to stay in, and Samsun was a force of nature who did whatever she pleased anyway. He was stuck. He lit a cigarette and wandered into the living room. He put the TV on and then turned it off again. *The Valley of the Wolves* he could do without. As patriotic as the next Turk, he didn't need it rammed down his throat. He went out onto the balcony, where Fatma was waiting.

Inspector Mehmet Süleyman was accustomed to being called out to the rougher neighbourhoods of the city. And so when he received the request to attend a murder scene in a semi-derelict house in the district of Tarlabaşı, it had come as no surprise.

'I don't know who she was,' said the woman standing in front of him, still in her dressing gown. 'I keep myself to myself; we all do.'

Süleyman had been in houses like this hundreds of times. He knew what it was.

'I only called Ali Bey, the kapıcı, when water started to pour down on the TV,' she said. 'Replacing that'll cost me.'

Süleyman looked at the old man standing behind him and said, 'Who's your landlord?'

He shrugged. 'I'm just the kapıcı. I collect the rent,' he said.

'Who do you give it to?'

'Haluk Bey.'

'Who's he?'

'He comes once a week,' the old man said.

'I didn't ask when he came . . .'

'I don't know. When Osman Bey left three years ago and the house was sold, that was when Haluk Bey started to come.'

Finding out who owned some of the houses in the district of Tarlabaşı was no easy task. Much of the area, famed for its high proportion of residents engaged in either drugs or prostitution, was in the process of being demolished prior to redevelopment. This picture was further complicated by the fact that a lot of Tarlabaşı's residents were foreigners.

'The woman must have spoken to you when she rented the room. Didn't you take her name?'

Ali Bey shrugged. 'She had an accent,' he said.

'But she spoke Turkish.'

'Yeah.'

Süleyman walked upstairs and went back into the tiny room the dead woman had apparently shared with a child.

'I don't for a moment think that Samsun has met anyone,' İkmen said. 'Not in a romantic sense. Though I may be wrong . . . She's always had lots of friends, you know that. And as Sultanahmet has become more conservative, I don't blame her for wanting to spend more of her time in Beyoğlu. Most of the trans girls congregate in Tarlabaşı, which, in spite of redevelopment, still clings to its old raffish ways. The last remaining syphilis sore on the face of Beyoğlu municipality. God bless it! I know you don't approve.'

Marlboro the cat looked at his master through the French windows but didn't attempt to approach.

'Yes, I know you want more food, so go out and catch something,' İkmen said. He turned his attention back to his wife. 'I was so rarely at home in the past. You looked after all of us single-handedly.' He shook his head. 'I took you for granted. And now what am I? I won't clear the place up myself and I won't let anyone else do it. I just don't have the energy to either do it or watch it being done. Drives Çiçek mad living in this tip. Samsun's all right; if she can't find any clothes, she just goes out and buys more. It's messed up, and I know it must be a huge disappointment to you.'

The midday call to prayer interrupted his monologue. Living as he did almost opposite the Blue Mosque, the call was always too loud to make conversation easy, especially out on the apartment's balcony.

When it was over, he said, 'I know I could vacuum.'

He looked at her. When she appeared, she was always silent and still, always in that same chair on the balcony. Just very slightly see-through.

'Yes, I go out for cigarettes,' he said. 'Uğur Bey at the kiosk needs my business and I'm at the most a couple of minutes, unless someone talks to me, which doesn't happen often. It's nice when it does, but . . .'

He began to cry. Utterly spontaneously. Choking with sobs, he was unable to speak. When he'd sobbed what felt like every drop of water out of his body, he poured himself a glass of brandy and lit a cigarette. For a few minutes he said nothing. He just looked at the magnificent skyline in front of him – the Blue Mosque, Ayasofya, and beyond, the Sea of Marmara. His city, battered and bruised by time, poverty and, latterly, urban development, was still the most fabulous place in the world.

When he did speak, his voice was hoarse.

'I know I can keep nothing from you,' he said to what he now saw was an empty chair. 'I know you know it's not just guilt that keeps me here. I have loved you since I was seventeen years old. Death doesn't end that. I don't want to leave you.'

He drank. She came into focus again. Small, round, her long grey hair hanging down into her lap.

'My fear is that you will want to leave me,' he said. 'Sorry, I put that badly. My fear is that you will have to leave me because I am not ready. Selfish, isn't it? But then I always was. Back to guilt.' He smiled, and so did she. 'Every bone in my wrecked old body screams to go out. But then I'm not telling you anything you don't already know, am I?'

The woman had been beautiful. Even with a ligature round her neck, her eyes bulging sightlessly at the ceiling, even soaked in stone-cold water, it was clear she had not been a run-of-the-mill streetwalker. Naked, she was slim and pale and had long, glossy black hair.

When Süleyman walked into the squalid little room, his sergeant, Ömer Mungun, stood up a little straighter. His boss could be a difficult man sometimes, and so it was always sensible to keep in his good books by exhibiting respect.

'Sir.'

'Where's the child?' Süleyman asked.

'Downstairs with Constable Alpay,' Ömer said.

The old kapıcı, Ali Ok, had broken down the door of the victim's flat in response to a complaint from the woman who lived in the room below about water pouring down onto her TV. He'd found a room awash with water from the sink, and a dead body on the bed. But he hadn't, so he said, found the child. She'd only appeared, from a cupboard, when the police arrived. The old man had said he hadn't even known the woman had a child. Like the woman who lived below the victim, he had been barely aware of her.

'Do you think she was on the game, sir?' Ömer asked.

Süleyman squatted down beside the pathologist, who was making a preliminary examination of the body.

'You've seen some of the other residents, Ömer,' he said. 'What do you think? She had an accent, according to the kapıcı. Could be Syrian. There are plenty of them round here. She probably thought this was the only way she could make money. Did you try to speak to the child?'

'Yes, sir. I tried Turkish, then Arabic, but she didn't respond to either.'

Ömer Mungun came from the eastern Turkish city of Mardin, where many residents were of Arab origin. And like a lot of people in that city, he was multilingual.

'May be in shock.'

'Yes, sir,' Ömer said. 'Not surprising.'

'No. And one of the reasons I don't want the press to know about the child at this stage. We need to try and minimise gossip coming out of this place. Until and unless we find some relatives, she'll have to be put in temporary care,' Süleyman said. 'Do you know if Constable Alpay has managed to get anything out of her?'

'I don't think so, no. Maybe a woman out of uniform may have more success. The poor little thing must be traumatised. I know Constable Alpay is concerned to get her some food and drink. She's like a tiny stick.'

The pathologist, a protégé – almost a doppelgänger – of Arto Sarkissian, joined the conversation.

'If the child's malnourished, she'll need to be seen by a doctor before you give her anything to eat,' he said. 'Sudden exposure to food after a long period of starvation can be dangerous. Consider admitting her to hospital.'

Süleyman nodded. The little girl had looked thin, but clearly he hadn't really taken in quite how dangerously underweight she might be.

'Oh, and on preliminary examination the woman seems to have died from asphyxiation caused by strangulation,' the pathologist said. 'Let us see whether Dr Sarkissian concurs. So, ghastly murder in Tarlabaşı, gentlemen. Depressing.'

'They'll cut her open and put her heart in a refrigerator,' Güneş Sağlam said.

The woman who had lived underneath the dead woman shook her head. 'You watch too much *CSI*,' she said.

They were part of a group of residents watching the body being taken out of the house.

The woman downstairs, who was called Yeliz, tipped her head towards Inspector Mehmet Süleyman, who was walking behind the stretcher bearing the body. 'He's an arrogant bastard,' she said to Güneş.

'Yes, but you wouldn't say no, would you,' Güneş replied.

Yeliz shrugged. 'That type I can take or leave.'

Güneş nudged her in the ribs. 'Liar.'

'Fuck you.'

Old Ali Ok made a fuss of clearing litter on the steps leading down to the street, and Branko the junkie, who lived in the basement, laughed as he disappeared into his room.

'Respect for the dead.' Yeliz shook her head. 'Pity these men don't show any of that to living women.'

Ali Ok heard her. 'You should shut your dirty mouth!'

'It's my dirty mouth as keeps you in rakı!' she countered.

'I do not drink! I respect God, and anyway I can't, I'm ill. Don't you dare say that I drink, you disgusting—'

'Shut up, all of you!' Süleyman roared. 'If you can't behave yourselves, you can all come and spend a night in my cells!'

The crowd fell silent. Only when the body and Süleyman had departed did Güneş say to Yeliz, 'I'd bet good money he likes being tied up.'

Chapter 3

Tünel Pasaj had never been one of Çetin İkmen's favourite places;
it had always been a bit upmarket for his taste. In its favour, the
small cafés inside the gates leading into this elegant nineteenth-
century enclave served alcohol, the pasaj was full of stray cats,
and the human habitués were somewhat louche.

Although he didn't notice her, Suzan Tan recognised him
immediately.

'Çetin Bey!'

She got up from a small table between a minuscule café and
an antique shop and went to shake his hand. Grown up, Suzan
still retained some of the nervousness he remembered her having
as a child. Her mother, to İkmen's recollection, had been something of a diva. Suzan, he had felt then, existed only in her
shadow.

'I'm so glad you agreed to see me,' she said as they both sat
down. 'I had a terrible day yesterday and Hülya's call really
cheered me up. Would you like tea or coffee?'

Hülya had been so pleased when he'd asked her to contact
Suzan for him. She'd cried.

'Coffee, please,' he said.

'What kind?'

'In recent years I've developed a liking for espresso,' he
said.

'Not a million miles from Turkish coffee.'

'No.'

For a moment they sat in awkward silence until eventually Suzan said, 'I was so sorry to hear about Fatma Hanım.'

He shook his head. 'Thank you. An accident . . .'

'Yes, I know, but still hard to bear.'

He turned away.

Suzan called a waiter over and placed her order. A large ginger cat, completely unbidden, came and sat on İkmen's lap, breaking through the topic of Fatma's death.

'Oh, hello!'

Suzan said, 'You've made a friend!'

İkmen stroked the cat and smiled.

'God, that's what I always remember about your apartment,' Suzan said. 'You had a cat called Marlboro. I thought that was hilarious.'

'Ah, we still have a cat called Marlboro,' İkmen said. 'Not the same one, of course. All our cats have been called Marlboro because I am too lazy to think of another name. The current one, like all his predecessors, is a vast, ragged street animal with bad breath. I adore him.'

Their drinks arrived, and once they'd talked about how much they missed the historic trams that used to run from Tünel Square to Taksim, Suzan began her story.

'I'd been working on a project down in Izmir,' she said. 'Documenting stories about synagogues. When that finished and I came back to İstanbul, I discovered that my aunt Nalan's new husband had bought a house called the Kara Lale Yalı in Bebek. I went to take a look and was captivated, especially when I discovered it had been sold with its contents. The previous owners were a family called Tonguç.'

İkmen lowered his voice. 'Admiral Tonguç and his wife needed to sell quickly . . .'

'I know. My aunt's new husband is the sort of man who, shall we say, takes opportunities. Anyway, with his agreement, albeit reluctant, I began cataloguing the contents of the yalı two months ago. It was only a week into my investigation when I found the ouija board, in the big salon at the top of the building. It was hidden in a pile of old clothes, covered by a load of damp photographs. I didn't know what it was at first. I'd never seen one before. I asked my old supervisor at the university, Dr Erbaş, for advice, and he told me not just about the ouija board, but about the story surrounding the Kara Lale Yalı too.'

'Deniz, the eldest Tonguç daughter, asked the ouija board to tell them who the next person to die would be,' İkmen said.

'Yes. It spelt out her name, and within a year of that seance, she was found dead. What I didn't know until I went to visit Deniz's younger sister Aylin was that Deniz then asked the spirits to tell them who would be the second to die, and the board spelt out Aylin's name.'

İkmen sighed. He recalled thinking at the time just how stupid the Tonguç family had been. Playing with the dead was not for the faint hearted.

'She now lives as a recluse in Nişantaşı, her doors and windows sealed against the fate that she has feared will come for her ever since. I found her through the second Tonguç sister, Zeynep, whose number I got from their mother. Zeynep lives in Izmir with her husband and son. She too was apparently marked for death, after Deniz and Aylin, but she doesn't believe in it. She doesn't come to İstanbul very often and really rather likes it that way.'

'You can see her point.'

Suzan leaned across the table towards him, fixing him with her eyes. 'Çetin Bey,' she said. 'I felt for Aylin Tonguç when I met her. She's never married, had children, had a career . . . Her entire life has been ruined. Her sister died, just as the spirits had predicted, and to make matters worse, nobody was ever seriously implicated in her death.'

'It was judged to be a suicide.'

'It was. But do you know how much force you need to exert to stab yourself through the chest? Especially if you're a slim teenage girl? I've thought about little else since I discovered this story, and I tell you, I don't buy it.'

'I know many felt it was unlikely at the time, including me,' İkmen said. 'But remember, we had very little technology available to us then.'

'I'm not blaming the police. It is what it is. But if we could somehow find out what really happened, if indeed Deniz didn't commit suicide, then maybe Aylin Tonguç could get her life back. Honestly, Çetin Bey, you have to see her to appreciate how bad she is.'

He lit a cigarette. 'So what do you want me to do?'

'I'd like you to work for me,' Suzan said. 'Reopen the case. Not officially, of course. But I'll pay you.'

'No, no!' He waved a hand at her.

'Yes,' she said. 'I'll be honest with you, Çetin Bey. I intend to write a book about the Kara Lale Yalı. It's like a time capsule. I don't think the Tonguç family did a thing to it after the admiral's father bought it back in the 1920s. It's a treasure house of nineteenth-century ephemera.'

'What does your aunt's husband think about your project?'

She frowned. 'All he wants to do is knock it down and put some glass and metal monstrosity in its place.'

'So he's a property developer.'

'Yes. He's called Tayfun Yıldırım.'

İkmen finished his coffee and said, 'Oh.'

The bed, devoid of the body, was a filthy mess of unwashed sheets and a few items of underwear. Now that the water had been pumped out, it reeked of damp plaster.

'You'll have to repair this room and the one underneath it

before you rent them out again,' Süleyman said to the man who claimed to be the landlord, Haluk Andıç. Although quite how a man with a long record for petty theft, who lived in a room underneath a massage parlour, came to own property was a bit of a mystery. But then, as Süleyman knew only too well, the life of Tarlabaşı could move in some extremely mysterious ways.

'Yes, efendi.'

'I will liaise with my scene-of-crime officers and let you know when you can clear the place,' Süleyman said. 'And remember, no gossip about that little girl.' Then, with a wave of his hand, he added, 'You may go. For the moment.'

The man bowed his way out. When he'd gone, Süleyman said to Ömer Mungun, 'I need to go and speak to Sugar Hanım, find out what the real story is about Haluk Bey.'

Sugar Hanım was an elderly prostitute who lived near Tarlabaşı's Syrian Orthodox church. She knew everyone and everything about Tarlabaşı. And she had a soft spot for Süleyman.

'You don't think he owns this place?'

'I doubt he owns a decent suit much less this house and the two next door,' Süleyman said. 'Wheels within wheels in a place like this, especially now that it's up for redevelopment. The real owner's probably in Dubai or Monte Carlo. Did Forensics get back to you?'

'Nothing much to report yet, sir,' Ömer said. 'Although that letter they found could be significant.'

Despite the deluge, a one-page letter in Arabic script had managed to survive on the table beside the bed.

'How so?'

Ömer said, 'It's not Arabic.'

'No? What is it then? Farsi?'

'No, sir, it's Aramaic. They're sending it over so I can translate it.'

Aramaic, the ancient language of Syria and Palestine, was

Ömer's native tongue. Apart from a few members of the Syrian Orthodox clergy, no one else in İstanbul except academics would, Süleyman imagined, be able to do this translation.

'That's good,' he said. 'Now, how do you fancy a trip to old Sugar Hanım's lair?'

'He's never been convicted of anything, and that includes traffic violations,' İkmen said. 'So my assertion that Mr Yıldırım is a crook is something he could challenge in court.'

Suzan nodded. 'I can't stand him,' she said. 'He's one of those people who, if they end up in prison, are called "victims of misfortune" by certain interested politicians.'

İkmen smiled. Some of the biggest gangsters in the country were known to be 'victims of misfortune'.

'Doesn't make him a villain, though,' he said. 'Even though he is.'

Suzan smiled too.

'He's a classic example of the similarities between a businessman and a thug. A businessman has friends in high places. And Mr Yıldırım has a lot of those. I know this might sound rude, but what did your aunt see in him?'

Suzan shrugged. 'He's younger than her. And he's her type. My late uncle, her husband, was a former oil wrestler. Mind you, he was really nice. And he was well off, so Auntie Nalan didn't need Yıldırım's money. I love my aunt, but she is a vain woman, and he flatters that vanity. Does Yıldırım being involved mean you don't feel able to help me, Çetin Bey?'

'Oh no,' he said. He lit another cigarette. 'But I need the full facts.'

'Of course.'

'And you must know that I won't be able to reopen this case officially. I can call in favours and I'm fairly sure my old colleagues will help me. But it won't be straightforward.'

29

'I'll pay you,' she said again.

'No you won't. Private investigation hasn't always been legal in this country, and I am, I must say, still uneasy about it. Pick up my expenses and I will be more than happy.'

'So you are intrigued?'

'Who wouldn't be?' he said. 'You know I've come across many reclusive people in this vast city of ours, but never one who tries to hide from her own fate. That piques my interest and, like you, my compassion. Wherever one stands on spirits, the life that Aylin Tonguç is leading is no life at all.'

'No.' Suzan smiled. 'Oh, I'm so excited,' she said. 'This is great.'

İkmen lifted his empty coffee cup to her as if to make a toast. 'I imagine step one is for me to see this wonderful yalı of yours.'

Tansu Barışık, known to people in Tarlabaşı as Sugar Hanım, lived in a tiny basement flat underneath a sex shop close to the Syrian Orthodox Church of the Virgin Mary. Diabetic, crippled with arthritis and monstrously overweight, she had once been a prostitute of rare sexual skill. Even at the age of something between seventy and eighty, she still had an eye for a good-looking man.

'Ah, Prince Mehmet Süleyman!' she said when Cenk, the pornographer who ran the shop upstairs, let Süleyman and Ömer Mungun into her flat.

Sugar Barışık was one of many people who never let Mehmet Süleyman forget that he was distantly related to the long-deposed imperial Osmanoğlu family. It wasn't something that he himself pushed in people's faces, though he was unlikely to allow others to treat him with anything but deference.

'Sugar Hanım.' He bowed low and kissed one of her fat, greasy hands. Although he hadn't seen her in probably three

30

years, he noticed that her flat had got no better. There were still only wisps of carpet on the floor, all her tea glasses looked filthy, and mangy cats, many of them gnawing on dead mice, roamed around her enormous feet like a tribe of unruly street kids. Ömer Mungun, who had only been in the flat once before, was shocked by all the dusty sex toys and skimpy lingerie that still lined the walls.

'Normally I don't welcome the police,' the old woman said. 'But I always make an exception for you, Mehmet Efendi.'

'And I appreciate it, hanım,' he said.

'Sit down! Sit down!'

There were three chairs in the small space, all of which had, to some degree, collapsed. The one the old woman sat in was basically a cushion on the floor. The two men made themselves as comfortable as they could, given the circumstances.

'So to what do I owe the pleasure?' Sugar said.

'I imagine you heard about the death of a woman in a house on Kalyoncu Kulluğu Caddesi?'

'Oh yes,' she said. 'A foreign working girl, I heard.' She shook her head. 'This city gets worse. Especially round here.'

'We've been told that a man called Haluk Andıç owns the property as well as the houses on either side.'

She laughed, a hoarse, grating yelp. 'That's a good one!' she said.

'You don't think he does?'

'Haluk Andıç is a junkie,' she said. 'Couldn't find his own arsehole if you gave him a map. He doesn't own so much as a pair of shoes. You'll find he's being paid to say he's the landlord – enough to get himself high once in a while.'

Ömer said, 'Why?'

'Why, the boy asks!' She laughed again. 'Darling, this area is being redeveloped, if you notice. There's a lot of money involved in these old wrecked houses. And not just for

31

government-backed development companies either. Some of these old places officially belong to Greeks and Armenians who left the city decades ago. But until now, no one's bothered if some chancer comes along, takes over and calls himself the landlord. Some of these characters have made good money out of what they don't own. But those who have replaced them, well, they're different. Historic buildings these are, and so strictly they can't be knocked down to make way for new-builds. And waiting for them to fall down can take time.'

She shuffled in her broken seat and took out a cigarette, which Süleyman lit for her.

'Thank you, young man.'

'My pleasure.'

'God, if I were twenty again, I'd eat every centimetre of you!' She shook her head. 'So this is how it works. You're a gangster and so you have men on the payroll who are not above breaking someone's legs. Your men persuade a local landlord to "sell" his property to their boss. However, not wishing to attract attention to themselves and their interest in what has become a very lucrative market, they employ airheads like Haluk Bey to act as a front for their activities. The Haluks of this world deal with dirty things like rent, and when the time comes, they will evict the tenants and thereby invoke their anger. Mr Gangster meanwhile will do a secret, private deal with those we know are the big players in the construction industry, make sure those buildings collapse in short order, and walk away having done little more than beat a few people up and pay for a couple of grams of heroin. Our homes are being subjected to a feeding frenzy. Tragically for us, we still remain hungry.'

Süleyman had suspected something like this. He said, 'Do you know who really owns the houses on Kalyoncu Kulluğu Caddesi, Sugar?'

32

'I don't, but I can probably find out quicker than you can.'

'I've no doubt,' Süleyman said.

Tarlabaşı was one of those places that, in spite of encroaching gentrification, kept itself to itself.

'And so . . .'

She smiled. 'A man of your calibre will, I know, make it worth my while.'

'Of course.'

'Not that I want money,' she said. 'But the occasional visit from some of your colleagues would be really comforting to an old woman living alone.'

'I'm sure I can arrange that.'

'All the better if they're in that lovely uniform some of your young men wear.'

'That will, I'm sure, be no problem.'

After several glasses of tea and a petting session with a couple of moth-eaten cats, the two men left. Out in the street, Ömer said, 'People round here don't generally welcome us, much less ask for us to visit.'

'No,' Süleyman said. 'But Sugar Hanım owns the building where she lives. Cenk, the maker of sex movies, is her tenant, and there's also an old man who lives in the attic. She's one of the few residents of Tarlabaşı to own their property. My guess is that she's being leaned on by some of the big players who are buying up around here. She may even already know who the landlord of the Kalyoncu Kulluğu house is but wants to make sure we will protect her when she tells us.'

İkmen had a term for houses like the Kara Lale Yalı: 'architectural confectionery'. Although made of wood, the entire facade of the five-storey building was decorated with intricate filigree work. Every floor had an enclosed balcony from which, in Ottoman times, the women of the harem would have looked out at the sea traffic going into and out of the capital. Ornamented with a profusion of arabesque designs, these small enclosed platforms had once provided fresh air and light to the exalted residents.

'It was built for an Egyptian princess,' Suzan said. 'It's said she came to the city to marry Sultan Murad V, but he succumbed to alcoholism and so the wedding didn't happen.'

Rather than being topped off by a flat roof, the Kara Lale Yalı was surmounted by a small black onion dome, which gave it the appearance of a Russian Orthodox church. The yalıs on either side were, by the look of them, in much better condition; one had a very modern large glass balcony on the third floor. To İkmen – and, he imagined, to Suzan – this was an abomination.

The garden was at the front of the building, which had once looked straight out onto the Bosphorus. Now the coastal road cut the yalıs off from direct access to the waterway. A bit of a wreck, the small space was surrounded by a line of scrappy mulberry bushes.

They went inside, where the intense sunlight from the street became muted as a result of the wooden fretwork covering the windows.

The ground floor – what had been the reception area – looked like an antique furniture shop. Sofas and chairs, all opulently upholstered in red or gold, stood in no particular configuration beside dark, heavy wooden writing desks, china cabinets and round copper braziers once used to provide heat on cold winter evenings. In common with all but the most prestigious yalıs, the Kara Lale's rooms were small, typically one in each corner, arranged around a central staircase.

'I've gathered a lot of the furniture down here,' Suzan said. 'I've left the huge bed in the admiral and his wife's bedroom, and there's one other small bed in a tiny room on the first floor. Most of the paintings, books, papers and God knows what else are on floors two, three and four. There have been some casualties, sadly. There was a massive dining table on the first floor, but as soon as the removal guys tried to shift it, it just fell apart. Floor five consists of one large salon, but the roof leaks, so I've had to clear it. That was where I found the ouija board.'

'Carpets?'

'Second floor. Mildewed, most of them,' she said. 'The kitchen, as you'd imagine, is down in the basement, where you can really appreciate just how damp this place has become. The walls are soaking. And it's things like that which give Yıldırım ammunition for his demolition plan. His pitch involves the idea that the place is dangerous.'

They walked up to the top floor. Not a natural climber at the best of times, İkmen wheezed and coughed his way up. His daughters would have used his discomfort to speak to him about his smoking, but luckily Suzan was not his daughter.

When they arrived on the landing, he looked out of the window at the garden. It was a mess. Overgrown, full of random items of rubbish, surrounded by those straggly bushes.

Suzan put the ouija board she'd found into his hands, and İkmen felt an instant rush of adrenaline.

'I'm not asking you what the place is. I know that,' Süleyman said.

Haluk Andıç looked down at the floor. He hadn't managed to score that morning. He'd still been in bed when Asena the gypsy had yelled in his ear that the police were on Kalyoncu Kulluğu Caddesi and wanted to speak to him again. He'd gone over, and the next thing he knew he'd been loaded into a car and taken to police headquarters. Now, just to make his day complete, he was coming down and he didn't like it.

'Men were still turning up when we arrived,' Süleyman continued. 'Straight after the body had been discovered.'

'I just own the place,' Haluk said. 'Ali Bey is the kapıcı; he collects the rent. I was at home when all this started. I've shown you the TAPU; what else do you want?'

The TAPU, or title deed of the property, was in the name Haluk Andıç.

'You live in one room on Kapanca Sokak,' Süleyman said. 'You own, apparently, the three properties on Kalyoncu Kulluğu, two of which are tenanted. And not just tenanted, but stuffed full of women and junkies.'

Haluk shrugged.

'You own, if not run, an illegal brothel, Mr Andıç. Not that I am bothered about that at the moment. I want to find who killed this apparently unknown woman who died on your property, and put a stop to his or her activities. Now look, we're both men of the world,' Süleyman said. 'Men come to that house for sex. I don't know why, given the number of women in that house, you choose to live in one room . . .'

'I've got expenses,' Haluk said. This Inspector Süleyman knew what he was, he could tell.

'Let's not talk about gear then either,' the policeman said. 'I want to know about the house and how the men who come to use it comport themselves.'

'You what?'

'Who takes the money, and does anyone – I know this is unlikely – look at ID? Ask people who they are?'

'I don't know,' Haluk said. 'Ali Bey is the kapıcı, ask him.'

'I have. He told me that he just collects the rent.'

'So what's your problem?'

'My problem is that you appear to be the owner of an illegal brothel where money clearly changes hands but without a recognisable audit trail.'

'A what?'

'The women in that house are all but destitute,' the policeman said. 'Where's the money, Mr Andıç? Even you can't, surely, be sticking it all in your arm.'

Haluk felt blood drain from his face. This Inspector Süleyman obviously didn't know him very well. Or at all.

Chapter 4

Ömer Mungun poured himself a drink and then flopped down on the sofa.

'The child was terrified; she couldn't even look at a woman, much less a man,' he said. 'Can you believe they sent a male social worker?'

'Yes.'

Ömer's sister, Peri, was a nurse who had worked in the city's hospitals for the past twelve years.

'I wish that were uncommon, but it isn't.' She sat in a chair opposite her brother, her long, slim legs tucked underneath her.

'We couldn't question her. It's likely she saw whoever attacked her mother, but if she won't speak . . . We think the woman might have been Syrian, so I tried Arabic, but that didn't work. I think it's possible she may have been a Christian, one of the people known as the Syriani.'

'Why?'

'Scene-of-crime officers found a page from a letter in Aramaic.'

Peri raised her eyebrows.

'Once Forensic have finished with it, I'm going to translate it.'

'Maybe she isn't a refugee at all,' Peri said.

'Maybe. But if she is, I don't know her,' Ömer said. 'Of course she could be related to one of the Mardin Christians. But I know all the families, just like you do. She's no one I've seen before.'

'And how was Ramazan?' Peri asked.

38

Neither Ömer nor his sister were Muslims, but they both practised restraint when they were amongst those who were.

'We had to go and visit this old woman, who gave us both tea.'

'Süleyman doesn't fast?'

'No.'

The Munguns were a very old Mardin family, part of a small community of people who worshipped a snake goddess called the Sharmeran. An ancient pre-Islamic cult, Sharmeran worship had been almost wiped out since the coming of the war in nearby Syria. The Mesopotamian plain, the goddess's traditional home, was now a no-go area.

Both Ömer and Peri often felt they wanted to go home and look after their ageing parents. But neither of the older Munguns would allow them to return, except to visit. They felt that their land and their way of life were dying, and they wanted their children to make their lives elsewhere.

'Çetin?'

There had been a time when finding İkmen sitting outside his laboratory would have been a common event. But Dr Arto Sarkissian hadn't seen his friend for a good six months, and was surprised.

'Wondered if you fancied a drink?' İkmen said. 'My place?'

It was typical of him to behave as if nothing had happened. The months he'd spent as a recluse just melted away, and Arto knew, furthermore, that he couldn't allude to them.

'I just need to tidy up . . .'

'No problem. Mehmet Süleyman and Kerim Gürsel can't meet us until eight.'

It was only just after six, and even taking into account the ghastliness of the traffic, there was time to spare.

'Give me five minutes,' Arto said. He went back into the lab.

Intrigued by his friend's sudden reappearance, he did think about calling Mehmet Süleyman or Kerim Gürsel to see what, if anything, they knew about this. But one look at the body on his bench was enough to remind him that Süleyman was probably drowning in things to do. So was he. The Tarlabaşı body, a once beautiful young woman, lay in a refrigerated drawer awaiting his attention.

And maybe Kerim Gürsel was involved too. When İkmen had retired, Kerim, once his sergeant, had been promoted to his friend's job. Back in the olden days, İkmen and Süleyman had frequently worked cases together. Maybe it was now Gürsel and Süleyman?

It was a good minute before Arto noticed that Çetin was looking at him from the doorway. He tipped his head at the covered corpse and said, 'Who's your friend?'

'Oh, sudden death in Harbiye,' Arto said. 'They just keep on coming . . .'

'Mehmet Süleyman Bey . . .'

The girl, who was standing in the doorway of a wig shop, crooked a finger at him and giggled. Across the road from the shop and right next to the howling traffic of Tarlabaşı Bulvarı, Süleyman got into his car and began to back out of the tiny road where earlier he'd managed to find a discreet parking space.

He knew the girl; she worked as a dancer in several of the city's more downmarket strip clubs. She was a good girl with a nice body, but she was rather too keen on him. Needy was not a feature he looked for in a woman these days, and that included those who claimed to adore him.

His glamorous Ottoman forebears helped, especially now. Since the election of the Islamically inspired AK Parti in 2002, it had become acceptable, almost chic, to come from a venerable Ottoman family. Süleyman was distantly related to the sultans themselves, and so his pedigree could hardly be better. But he didn't personally approve. Although he retained the bearing of a monarch, he knew that his ancestors had presided over an empire that had ended up mired in corruption, cruelty and political insanity. Only the founding of the Republic under Mustafa Kemal Ataturk had saved the country from being broken up by the Allied forces after World War I.

Süleyman, like a lot of secular Turks, still saw Mustafa Kemal as the father of the nation, and was horrified by the way the life stories of his Ottoman ancestors were being distorted by those who knew nothing about them, in the service of political populism. Not that he often gave voice to such opinions. He could only do that with close friends, like Çetin İkmen, whose apartment in Sultanahmet he was driving to now. İkmen had been lost in his own grief for so long that when Süleyman had heard his friend's suddenly cheerful voice on the phone earlier in the day, he had almost cried.

If Çetin was back to being Çetin, then maybe the world wasn't such an alarming place.

The Western Prayer, the last but one prayer of the day, signalled the end of the fast. Kandil lights would be lit, illuminating the beautiful imperial mosques of the Old City; people would begin to eat, drink and be relieved. Ali Ok of Tarlabaşı ate one date for the sake of his health, then lit a cigarette and drank rakı straight from the bottle. He fasted, yes, but that was over for the day.

With what some of the old whores were already calling the 'death room' cordoned off by the police, no one was actually working. That bottle-blonde bitch Yeliz had moved those of her possessions not ruined by water into her friend Güneş's room, where a load of the younger kids had gathered for İftar. He could hear them talking in low tones, the occasional giggle. Of course they were all shocked by the woman's death. Some of them had asked him about her, but what could he say? He hadn't known who she was any more than they had. And Ali was accustomed to not asking Haluk. Like most junkies, he never knew anything even if he purported to own the place.

Ali took another swig from his bottle. The dead woman hadn't ever worked in that room. Not to his knowledge. It happened. Girls were brought in to use the house to sleep in and then shipped out to men across the city as and when they were needed. Haluk brought them in, but who he was working for was unknown. The real owner of the house, maybe? Or some other thug you wouldn't want to meet or get on the wrong side of. Ali didn't ask questions. He had a job and a roof over his head. Unusually, that woman hadn't been brought in, though. She'd turned up. That happened too.

He'd said nothing to the police. He knew that his ignorance smelt bad – even brothel-keepers knew who worked for them – but he'd genuinely known nothing about that woman, which meant that he could say nothing.

In the meantime, he'd drink, eat a bit and make plans for moving Yeliz back into her own room once the police had gone. To hell with repairing the place! Haluk wouldn't give a shit and neither would the owner, whoever he was. As for Yeliz, at forty-five she was well past her sell-by date and would put up and shut up if she knew what was good for her.

It was so good to see her father talking to the living. It had been especially edifying to see him walk in with his arm around her uncle Arto. It was nice to see Kerim Gürsel too and, of course, Mehmet Süleyman. Çiçek had once had a fierce crush on him, years ago.

The djinn rose up to some ridiculous height, its head jammed against the ceiling. Çiçek ignored it. She took a large tray of iftariye, a traditional selection of snacks with which to break fast, into the living room.

'I know you don't all fast,' she said as she placed the tray on the coffee table, 'but Mum used to make this every night during Ramazan, and so I do it to honour her.'

Arto Sarkissian patted her arm. 'It's a lovely idea,' he said. 'Your mother would be proud.'

Çiçek sat down. 'Mind you, she used to always make her own Ramazan pide. But I'm hopeless.' She pointed to a round flattish loaf with a weave pattern cut into the crust. 'Shop-bought.'

'It's perfect,' her father said.

Süleyman, although far removed from his religion these days, went straight for the big pile of dates in the middle of the platter. In traditional emulation of the Prophet, he ate three.

'So, Dad . . .'

'The gentlemen know the task will not be an easy one,' İkmen said. He didn't touch any of the food, but he poured himself a measure of rakı, which he topped up with water, and lit a cigarette.

'A possible murder committed forty years ago won't have a very big footprint now,' Kerim Gürsel said. 'But if your sister's friend is right about how the incident is still affecting the Tonguç family today, I feel, like Çetin Bey, that we have to try and help.'

'Ideally I'd like to have a conversation with Admiral Tonguç,' Süleyman said. 'But with him incarcerated in Silivri . . .'

'Difficult though it is these days, we must at least try to be apolitical,' İkmen said. 'As far as I know, as well as the dead woman, Deniz Tonguç, the only other people present at the notorious seance at the Kara Lale Yalı were other family members: Admiral Alaaddin Tonguç, his wife Halide, son Timur and daughters Zeynep and Aylin. These people are all still alive, and as we know, Suzan has met Aylin Tonguç. I am going to try and make contact with the others, with the exception of the admiral.

43

Arto, can I ask you to see if you can find the medical report on Deniz?'

'Yes,' the pathologist said. 'It won't be easy after all this time, and of course I didn't perform that investigation myself because I was still at medical school in London. If I'm right, I think it would probably have been performed by Dr Sağlam.'

'I remember him,' İkmen said. 'Didn't he have a drink problem?'

'Yes, he did,' Arto replied. 'But he was a good pathologist who must have had a reason for deciding that Deniz Tonguç's death was suicide.'

'You doubt it, Doctor?' Kerim said.

'I am dubious. It's really difficult to stab yourself through the chest.'

'What about the Japanese practice of seppuku?'

'Well,' Arto said, 'apart from the fact that it's a technique that was only ever applied by Samurai warriors, seppuku involves cutting the abdomen. Stabbing oneself through the bones of the chest is a much more difficult operation. And to actually get the heart . . .' He shrugged. 'Deniz Tonguç was a young girl. I may be underestimating her, but to me, until I see some evidence to the contrary, her death looks suspicious.'

Çiçek tore herself some bread and took a few slices of pastırma. She wasn't hungry, but it seemed rude not to join their guests. She looked at her father and caught him peering into the kitchen. Looking for the djinn, she imagined, but it seemed to have gone.

'Kerim Bey and myself will do our best to get hold of any records that remain about the incident,' Süleyman said.

'Don't put yourselves at risk,' İkmen said.

Since 2015, Inspectors Kerim Gürsel and Mehmet Süleyman had been obliged to work under a new commissioner of police called Selahattin Ozer. Unlike his predecessor, Hürrem Teker, Ozer was a man, he had no discernible sense of humour, and he was a staunch supporter of the ruling elite. And although the latter quality didn't always mean that a person was necessarily unable to see the world from anything but an Islamist viewpoint, in Ozer's case that was the reality. This made his thinking, and his personal rules, rigid. Fortunately for İkmen, he had taken retirement before he would have been obliged to get to know Selahattin Ozer well.

Süleyman smiled. 'I think we can handle Ozer,' he said.

'As long as you always behave respectfully, adopt a pious demeanour and send him all the requisite paperwork, he's happy,' Kerim said.

'But no fool,' Süleyman added. 'We will be careful, Çetin Bey, but be assured that Kerim Bey and myself have the measure of the man.'

İkmen doubted that. Selahattin Ozer, despite the fact that he'd come out of retirement to take the job, had a reputation for preference and, some said, corruption. İkmen knew that neither the attractive Ottoman Süleyman nor the caring, professional Gürsel were finding it easy to work with him. When they could, they were ignoring him – or so he'd heard.

Later, when he was alone on the balcony, in the dark, İkmen said to his wife, 'I do these things and then think them through afterwards. I was so taken with this old mystery I forgot it wasn't just about the Tonguç family and me. By asking for help, I make it about others.

'And yet, as you say,' he continued, 'it is their choice.' He nodded. 'Just as it is my choice to do this for absolutely no money whatsoever. But how could I take Suzan's money, eh? The girl's an historian. Probably just about makes her rent. No one who does a job that means anything gets properly paid or respected these days. If you're a gun-toting gangster everyone wants to throw cash at you, but . . .' He smiled. 'I'm ranting again. I expect I always will, and you know why and I'm sorry it upsets you. But this investigation will keep me occupied. I know that is what you wanted. And yes, I will get to grips with the djinn, but in my own time and my own way.'

Süleyman hadn't seen Samsun Bajraktar for over a year. Not since Fatma İkmen's funeral, when, out of respect for her cousin's pious wife, Samsun had cut her hair, put a suit on and attended as a man. It had been an awful day. İkmen had been like a thing made of stone. Samsun had even confided to Süleyman that the family were afraid he might die.

Now she lifted her gin and tonic to her lips and drank. 'If Çetin Bey is working, he will survive,' she said. 'Although quite what he'll do with that old story, I don't know.'

'The Deniz Tonguç case?'

Once the meeting at the İkmen apartment had broken up, Süleyman had taken Çiçek for a drink down in the Mozaik, where they'd met Samsun.

'I remember it,' Samsun said. 'Good family, as they were at the time, it was a scandal. The girl hadn't long been married, and so the in-laws weren't happy. They felt slighted. Especially when their son was briefly in the frame. Can't remember his name, but I expect his family were somebody, if you know what I mean.' She looked at Çiçek. 'You say the person your father's working for is a friend of Hülya's?'

'Yes,' Çiçek said. 'They went to school together. Suzan Tan. Her aunt's new husband owns the yalı where the supposed suicide happened. He's called Tayfun Yıldırım.'

Samsun scowled. Now that she was old, making faces did her no favours.

'Him,' she said. 'Pulls down people's houses while they're still inside. Bastard.'

'And yet he's squeaky clean,' Süleyman said.

'Aren't they all?'

46

The big nightly İftar in Sultanahmet Square was coming to an end now and people were beginning to walk home. Soon they'd be trying to get some sleep before getting up to prepare the Suhoor meal just before sunrise.

'He's one of those who plays the game,' Samsun said. 'He'll be fasting. Putting pictures of himself on Facebook refusing sustenance, then shuffling off to visit Russian hookers.'

Çiçek said, 'Life at the top of the food chain was always thus.'

'Yes, but we should be better than that now,' Samsun said. 'Your father has always known that and fought for it. Just because a person is "someone" has never made any difference to him. A thief is a thief even if he wears bespoke suits.'

'Mmm.' Çiçek looked sad.

'What's the matter?'

She lit a cigarette. 'I'm glad that Dad is coming out of his shell, but I'm worried too.'

'What about?'

'I know he's not investigating Tayfun Yıldırım, but just the fact that he'll be in his vicinity bothers me. You know what he's like; if he finds anything out about him in the course of his investigation, he won't keep it to himself.'

'I wouldn't expect him to,' Süleyman said.

'Nor I. But in the past he had the protection of his colleagues. Now he's on his own.'

Süleyman put a hand on her shoulder. 'He's never on his own, Çiçek,' he said.

Chapter 5

In order to translate the fragment of a letter found in the dead woman's room, Ömer Mungun needed to be able to concentrate. This wasn't easy in the never-ending sound and activity show that was police headquarters. But to make things as easy as he could for Ömer, Süleyman gave his office over to his inferior and went to share Kerim Gürsel's.

Gürsel's sergeant, Elif Arslan, was currently working on what could be a suspicious death in the village of Kanlica, across the Bosphorus, and was at the site with scene-of-crime officers.

'Yalı seems to be the word of the day,' Süleyman said when Gürsel had finished telling him about the discovery of a body in a run-down seafront property in the popular and attractive village. 'Çetin Bey's Kara Lale Yalı, this Kanlica place . . .'

'The Fındık Yalı,' Kerim said. 'Wooden, rotted beyond repair apparently. When we got a report of a body *in situ*, I thought it would be some old aristocrat. But it's a woman of no more than thirty. Expensively dressed, coiffured, plastic breasts . . . Someone I'd expect to see in a fashionable apartment.'

'Maybe she had an illicit meeting with someone.'

'Or maybe she was doing a bit of urban exploring and had some sort of seizure. There's no sign of violence. Mind you, if she was an urban explorer, she was wearing very unsuitable clothes.'

Süleyman frowned.

'What Sergeant Arslan assured me was a Valentino dress. That's apparently a very expensive design label,' Kerim said. 'I've a feeling this is maybe more than it seems. Don't ask me why. I just sense that it may lead me down some strange paths . . .'

Süleyman smiled. 'You sound like Çetin Bey.'

'Talking of which . . .' Kerim looked around to make sure no one was in their vicinity. Then he said, 'I've put in a request for any physical documents that may still exist about Çetin Bey's cold case.'

'How did you present it to our esteemed commissioner?'

'I distracted him so he couldn't concentrate on what he was signing,' Kerim said.

Süleyman looked at him doubtfully. 'You think?'

'No, not really. I'm sure he saw something, even if he didn't know what it was. But he didn't comment. It'll come back to bite me, but what can you do? When everything is examined and explored to within a centimetre of its life . . .'

The two men sat in silence for a moment, and then Süleyman said, 'We can only do our best, Kerim Bey.'

Gürsel sighed. 'But this is Çetin Bey we're talking about here. He needs a win to get him back to himself. If he doesn't work, he doesn't live. Especially with Fatma Hanım gone.'

'I know,' Süleyman said. And in lieu of lighting a cigarette, he chewed one of his thumbnails. He knew that more than anyone.

Before he left, he said, 'Keep me up to date about your body in Kanlica. Çetin Bey taught me many years ago to take feelings like yours seriously.'

Suzan Tan had never met Halide Tonguç in the flesh. When she'd contacted her initially about the Kara Lale Yalı, it had been by phone. Less fearful than her daughter Aylin, and not nearly so friendly as her daughter Zeynep, she had not been particularly forthcoming. And so it was a surprise to Suzan when Halide

Hanım agreed to see both her and Çetin İkmen. Where they found her, however, was an even greater surprise.

'This is my sister's apartment,' the old woman said as she showed them into a small, dark room furnished with heavy green armchairs.

They were in what was now a very trendy part of the city, Hoca Tahsin Sokak, in the central district of Karaköy. It was home to many high-end lofts and apartments. But this was not one of them.

'I came here when my husband was taken,' Halide Tonguç said.

İkmen, breathless and therefore speechless after climbing five flights of stairs, said nothing.

'My sister's up at the church,' the old woman continued.

It had been impossible to miss the bright green cross-topped cupolas on the roof of this and the apartment building next door. There were two Russian Orthodox churches on these rooftops, one directly above the apartment.

Halide Hanım gestured for them to sit down. 'Barçın, my sister, married a White Russian,' she continued. 'He worshipped at St Panteleymon.' She pointed upwards. 'Barçın still goes to help with the cleaning and the flowers. Not that she ever changed her religion, you understand.' Then she added, 'No one can accuse us of that.'

Now able to breathe again, İkmen said, 'Thank you so much for seeing us, Halide Hanım. I apologise in advance for bringing up a subject—'

'The death of my daughter Deniz is something I thought I came to terms with a long time ago, Çetin Bey,' she said. 'But to be honest, I never really accepted the verdict that was given. Which is why, when Miss Tan contacted me, I agreed to help. And of course when I heard that you had an interest . . .' She smiled. 'I have followed your career over the years. I was saddened when I saw that you had retired.'

He smiled.

Suzan said, 'To be truthful, Halide Hanım, I don't think I would have pursued this matter had I not met your daughter, Aylin Hanım. Her fear, even now . . . it wrenched my heart.'

Halide's eyes became wet. 'If I had known where my silly pursuit of the occult would lead, I would never have meddled. That was what Alaaddin Bey called it: "meddling".'

'And yet your husband was at that seance,' İkmen said.

'Laughing behind his hand, yes,' she said. 'When the spirits spelt out Deniz's name, my husband remained sceptical. Even after her death. Alaaddin Bey has always been, and remains, an atheist. He feels that should he confess to a crime he didn't commit and pretend to a faith he doesn't possess, things might go easier for him. I don't know whether this is true or not. But what I do know is that he won't do those things. He is too honest.'

The arrest of Admiral Alaaddin Tonguç two months after the attempted coup of July 2016 had shocked the nation. He was accused of membership of a religious organisation trying to wrest power from the government, but no one who knew him could believe it. As his wife had said, Alaaddin Tonguç had never had any time for religion.

İkmen said, 'Halide Hanım, could you please tell us what happened during that seance?'

She smiled. 'I can. Ah, but would you like some tea or . . .'

'No thank you,' İkmen said.

Suzan shook her head.

'You are busy.' Halide smiled again. 'So . . . I bought the ouija board in an antique shop on İstiklal Caddesi. Long gone now, it was a few doors down from St Antoine, towards Tünel. Since my husband and I had moved into the Kara Lale Yalı, I had become fascinated by stories about the lady for whom it was built, Princess Fawzia of Egypt.'

51

'By Sultan Murad V,' Suzan said.

'No. It is true that she was supposed to enter his harem as his wife, but this was in 1876, which was the year he was deposed, on account of his madness, and then incarcerated in the Old Çırağan Palace. The yalı was built for the princess by the Egyptian royal family during her long betrothal to the sultan. It was thought for a while that Fawzia might marry Murad's brother, Sultan Abdul Hamid II. But it didn't happen.'

İkmen speculated that the insecure and fearful Abdul Hamid II would probably have felt threatened by a foreign princess.

'As things turned out, Princess Fawzia never married,' Halide Hanım said. 'Neither did she go back to Egypt. She retained a small retinue of servants and eventually became acquainted with members of the Young Turk movement. Although royal herself, she developed a view that democracy was the only rational way forward for mankind. Eventually she grew close to Halide Edib and other female revolutionaries. It is said that just before her death in 1919, she met Ataturk. It was also said that her spirit lived on in the Kara Lale Yalı. My husband's relatives were always seeing her, even if he did not.'

'So you wanted to make contact with the princess?'

'Yes.'

'And did you?'

'I thought so at the time,' she said. 'Now? I don't know. Something came through, or someone managed to manipulate the board.'

'Any idea who might have done that?'

'No. Each of us put a finger on the planchette – that's the arrow-shaped piece of wood that the spirits use to spell out their messages.'

'Who exactly had a finger on the planchette?' İkmen asked. 'Your husband?'

'No,' she said. 'Nor my younger son, Ateş. He was in bed. It was myself, my daughters Deniz, Zeynep and Aylin, and my elder son, Timur.'

'What happened?'

'I asked any spirit resident in the yalı to make contact. Princess Fawzia came through almost immediately. By this I mean the planchette moved to spell out her name. I can remember feeling elated.'

İkmen looked at Suzan, whose face was white.

Halide Hanım continued. 'I remember I asked her about Ataturk and she said he was very charming. She said they often danced together in the afterlife.'

Had Mustafa Kemal Ataturk even believed in an afterlife?

'It sounded like a . . . nice place.'

'The afterlife?'

Halide nodded. 'It was Deniz who asked who, of those present, would be the first to die.'

'And it spelled out her name?'

'Yes.'

'How did she respond to that?' İkmen asked.

'She laughed,' Halide said. 'Then she asked who would come after her. I didn't for a moment believe that Aylin would take the spirit's prediction as badly as she did. Even after Deniz died . . .' she wiped her eyes, 'we all tried to persuade her it was just co-incidence. But what could I do? After that, Zeynep went to Izmir to marry her husband, my sons pursued their careers, and Aylin . . . The apartment where she lives belonged to my husband's mother. I could live there myself if only Aylin behaved normally. But I can't talk to her. Her life revolves around her obsession.'

'With some cause,' İkmen said.

'I agree. But even if you manage to discover the truth about Deniz's death, if such a thing exists, Aylin will still see herself as being at risk.'

'If Deniz's death was unnatural, maybe she won't,' he said. 'Halide Hanım, can you remember who else knew about this seance between the event and Deniz's death?'

'I can try,' she said. 'It's a long time ago now. Of course I don't know who, if anyone, my children told. You would have to ask them.'

'Do you think they would be willing to speak to me?'

'If I can remember who I told, I will ask them to do so,' she said. Then she was quiet for a few moments.

İkmen looked around the walls of the small room. Every centimetre was covered with ikons. Dark, forbidding images of saints and gods . . .

'The servants were out that night,' Halide Hanım said. 'My husband insisted they be out of the way in case the seance unnerved them. Such people tend to be very religious.'

And so, even in the Turkey of the new Islamic elite, the old secular narratives persisted. But İkmen didn't comment.

'Halide Hanım,' he said, 'in order to gain access to whatever official documentation still exists about Deniz, I am going to have to liaise with ex-colleagues. These are trusted people with whom I have worked for decades. However, I know that, due to your husband's current situation, you may feel nervous about any police involvement.'

'To be truthful, I *am* afraid, Çetin Bey,' she said. 'But I also need to be at peace with my daughter's death. Had I not felt this way, I would never have allowed Miss Tan into my life.'

He smiled. 'That's good. But we want to keep my colleagues' involvement to a minimum, so if you still have any documents relating to Deniz's death, it would be incredibly useful for me to have access to them.'

'I will see what I can find,' she said. 'Sadly, since I moved in here, much has been discarded. Although my husband at first believed that Deniz's husband, Mustafa, killed her, he was content

54

with the eventual suicide verdict. A strong, pragmatic man, Alaaddin. Not a man one could easily oppose in his pomp. And so I didn't.'

'And you?' İkmen asked. 'What do you think about your daughter's death?'

She paused for a moment. 'I have always, in my heart, believed that Deniz was murdered. I don't know why. She was a lovely, placid, clever girl.'

'What did you make of Zeynep Tonguç when you spoke to her?' İkmen asked Suzan as they sat outside a trendy Karaköy cafe.

Halide Tonguç had given them addresses and telephone numbers for all her surviving children, including her daughter Zeynep.

'We didn't speak for that long,' Suzan said, 'but I got the impression she was tired of the whole thing. Rather than feeling sorry for her sister Aylin, she appeared more irritated than anything else. She told me she didn't believe in the seance. She's certainly not unnerved by it.'

'So Aylin and Ateş live in İstanbul, while Zeynep is in Izmir and Timur in Artvin, where he has a hotel. Do many people take their holidays on the far reaches of the Black Sea coast?' İkmen said.

'It's supposed to be very beautiful.'

'And,' İkmen said, 'it has a reputation for insularity. The back of beyond, I always thought.' He visibly shuddered. Rural places where old, often conservative religious values held sway always made him uneasy.

He looked at the list of contacts Halide Tonguç had written down for them.

'Ateş Tonguç is a publisher. Offices in Beyoğlu,' he said.

'They've all done well, except for Aylin, although with their father now in prison, who knows how long their good fortune will continue,' Suzan said.

'Indeed.' İkmen turned the list over. 'And then there is Mustafa Ermis . . .'

'Deniz's husband.'

'As I recall, he was in the frame for a while,' İkmen said.

'Was he detained?'

'I don't know. Hopefully my ears in the police force will be able to find out. In the meantime, I will make a start on these family members. I know you're busy with the Kara Lale Yalı . . .'

'My so-called uncle is champing at the bit to get the place destroyed,' she said. 'I'll stall him for as long as I can. Do you want to come back to the site, Çetin Bey?'

'I will need to, yes,' he said.

'Anything I can do?'

'I would like to talk to Aylin Tonguç at some point, if you could take me to her.'

'I'll try,' she said. 'To be honest, after my last visit I left her in a bit of a state. Myself too.' She smiled. 'You know she's not that old. I feel she could do something with her life if only she could get over this . . . horror.'

'Well, we'll have to see what we can do about that, won't we,' İkmen said. 'I have seen families atomise after an event like this. You know, Suzan, I do believe that at times, the dead do speak to us. But I don't believe they can predict our futures, just like I don't believe that anything is "written". My dear wife was a devout and passionate Muslim who did believe such things, but I never could, much as I sometimes tried . . .'

Surviving is all there is. Remember that. Our people have lived in these lands longer than those who oppress us. And we will return. Our children will come back. I have to believe that. Whatever you have to do, and much as I love you with all my soul, remember that only Rosarita matters. Do what you must.

It wasn't signed. A letter from a ghost. An instruction to take care of a girl. But was it the girl found with the dead body of the woman in that squalid room in Tarlabaşı?

Ömer Mungun rubbed his sleeve across his eyes and breathed in deeply to calm his emotions. If the child was this Rosarita, was she the daughter of the dead woman? And the writer of the letter? Penned in Aramaic, it seemed to suggest that the woman, the girl and the author were all Christians. Christians had inhabited Syria prior to the Muslim conquest. They had been the subject of numerous purges by groups like IS. Christians, Yezidis, his own people . . .

The child had said nothing. She'd eaten everything they had given her, slept in the clean, comfortable bed she had been allocated and watched cartoons on television. But she still hadn't spoken.

The couple caring for her were nice people. The husband worked for social services, while his wife, an author, worked from home. Their small apartment in Nişantaşı was clean, bright and comfortable. But when Ömer Mungun approached the girl, he could still see the marks of death in her eyes. He'd seen eyes like that all his life.

While a group of household pets dressed in superhero outfits attempted to save the world on the TV screen, he spoke to her in Aramaic, the language of the Christian Jesus. Did she like cartoons? What was her favourite? He told her about his house back in Mardin, where he'd lived with his parents and his big sister. From his bedroom window, he said, he could see Syria.

But she didn't even flicker. Whether she didn't understand or wouldn't respond was impossible to tell. It was only when he said the name 'Rosarita' that she reacted. A tiny twitch of her left eye told him that he'd finally, if only marginally, made a breakthrough.

Chapter 6

İkmen, in his prime, had appeared on television more than once. Amongst certain groups in İstanbul he was well known and loved, and amongst others he was well known and reviled. Those with liberal tendencies – often with a somewhat artistic bent – were generally fans. Long-haired, pipe-smoking Ateş Tonguç was, it turned out, a big fan.

'I'd publish your memoirs like that,' he said, snapping his fingers under İkmen's nose.

The two men had met in the small garden of a vegetarian restaurant just around the corner from the offices of Akrep Yayıncılık, Tonguç's publishing house on Zambak Sokak. At his mother's suggestion, Ateş had called the ex-policeman himself.

İkmen smiled. Buoyed up by how easy it had been to get an appointment with the youngest Tonguç child, he was nevertheless having some difficulty getting him to concentrate on his sister's death.

'I fear any memoir of mine would be somewhat contentious these days,' he said.

Ateş Tonguç shrugged. 'I know.' His face became grave. 'But indulge me. Sometimes I just have to pretend I can publish whatever I want. I know I can't. I know I've never been able to do that.' He puffed on his pipe. 'You want to know about my sister, Deniz.'

'As much as you can tell me, yes,' İkmen said. 'I understand from your mother that you weren't at the seance.'

58

'I was still at school,' he said. 'So I was in bed. My siblings and I, Çetin Bey, were very clearly divided when we were children. There was "the big two", the eldest, Timur and Deniz, then there were "the girls", Aylin and Zeynep, and then there was me, little Ateş, the afterthought.' He laughed. 'The last gasp of my parents' passion – if that ever really existed. In 1976, I was eleven. Zeynep, at fifteen, was the nearest in age to me, but she spent all her time with Aylin, who is only eighteen months older. The big two were basically grown up. Deniz was nineteen and Timur twenty. I can't tell you why they had a seance that night. My mother was fascinated by spiritualism at the time, so seances were not unusual events in our house.'

'I would have thought,' İkmen said, 'that an eleven-year-old boy would be curious about such peculiar goings-on. Did you never sneak out of your bedroom to see what they were doing?'

'When it started, yes.'

A waiter approached their table, and Ateş ordered coffee. 'It's very good here,' he said. 'The vegetables I can take or leave.' Then he leaned forward. 'More to the point is that this is a good place to talk freely.'

İkmen didn't comment. It was said that government informants were almost everywhere since the failed coup.

Ateş continued. 'To be honest, the one time I did see my family use the ouija board, it freaked me out. As I always did back then, I went running off to Aliki, who simply underlined my notion that what my parents was doing was bad.'

'Aliki?'

'Our nanny,' he said. 'Old by the mid seventies. She'd been our mother's nanny. I loved her. She was Greek, superstitious, judgemental, and she gave me everything I asked for. Sweets at midnight, skateboarding in the kitchen. Total indulgence.'

'So the night of the seance, Aliki had put you to bed?'

'Oh no,' he said. 'She had died by then. Had to be about six

59

months before. It's why I didn't know anything about that seance until Deniz died, when it all came out. Aliki would watch them, tutting and disapproving, and tell me in the morning that they'd been "at the black magic" again. No, I had no idea my family had a seance that night. Aliki's death had hit me hard and I was spending a lot of my time on my own. Coming from wealth and privilege, no one ever thought I could possibly have problems. But money doesn't stop your family from being fucked up, and mine was fucked up. Still is.'

'The official verdict on your sister's death was that it was suicide,' İkmen said. 'Can you tell me what you think? Or what you thought at the time?'

'When I was a kid?' Ateş shrugged. 'I was upset. I wasn't close to Deniz, but she was my sister and I loved her. Unfortunately my parents didn't see fit to tell me what the verdict was, but the kids at school had no such compunction. I was shocked. That my sister could do such a thing was unimaginable to me, even though I knew she wasn't right by that time.'

'Wasn't right? How do you mean?'

'Deniz married a few months after that seance.'

'To Mustafa Ermis?'

'Yes,' he said. 'They'd known each other since they were kids. Mustafa went to the same kindergarten as all my siblings. They were sweet together. But after the wedding, I felt that things changed. Deniz didn't look happy, she came home all the time, she cried. I don't know what I felt about it at the time. I wasn't close to her. I knew Mustafa had taken over his father's company when he got married, so maybe he wasn't around much. His parents bought them a massive great apartment in Şişli, so she would have been there on her own – just with the servants. She wasn't used to that. The Kara Lale Yalı was always teeming with people – family and friends.'

'Spiritualists?'

'Some. And other wackos. My mother needed constant stimulation.' He said it bitterly. 'Still does.'

'You said that Mustafa Ermis inherited his father's company,' İkmen said. 'Do you know what that is?'

'Tea,' Ateş replied. 'Ermis's people are originally from Rize.'

İkmen nodded. The Black Sea region was well known for its abundant tea plantations.

'One of those families whose holdings just got more and more extensive with the passing years until, sometime in the fifties, I think, they could leave the back of beyond, move to the city and let their peasants do the hard work.' He shook his head. 'Mustafa was a nice man, as I remember – still is. But his father was stuck in the past. Worshipped the Ottoman Empire . . .'

'He must've liked the yalı,' İkmen said.

'Oh yes, he did, although he disapproved of the alcohol that was consumed there.'

'He was religious.'

Ateş shrugged. 'He did the "I'm just a simple man" act. Even a kid like me saw through it. Treated people like shit, and that included Mustafa. Spent most of his time in Rize. Died years ago. Mustafa divides his time between his apartment in Şişli and the family estate in Rize. We talk occasionally. I always liked him, even though my father didn't.'

'Why didn't Admiral Tonguç like him? He allowed his daughter to marry him.'

'Because the Ermis family had money,' Ateş said. 'I heard my parents arguing about it. My mother liked Mustafa; my father called him soft. Mother told him not to be rude, but then you might as well tell the clouds not to rain . . .'

'And when your brother-in-law came under suspicion?' İkmen asked. 'What did your mother say then?'

'Nothing,' he said. 'Not that I can remember, anyway. My

61

father gloated. Told my mother he'd bury Mustafa for what he'd done.'

'What's the matter with her?'

Ali Bey had been to the bakkal to stock up on bulgur. It got underneath his dental plate, but he loved it so much he put up with the inconvenience. Bulgur with a plate of stewed mutton. Ah, that was an İftar meal to die for! But now he'd come home to find one of the old whores weeping on the pavement outside the building, another prostitute comforting her.

'She's seen a ghost!' Güneş Sağlam said.

'A ghost? What nonsense is this? Ghost of who?'

'That women found dead in the room above hers,' Güneş said.

Two young police officers stood guard at the entrance to the building. Ali looked at them and then said in a loud voice, 'How did she know it was her? She told our gallant police officers she didn't know the woman.'

One of the officers moved forward. 'What's this?' he said.

'She didn't know her, Ali Bey, you stupid old goat!' Güneş said. 'She saw a . . . What was it, Yeliz? What did you see?'

Her friend lifted her head. 'It was a shape,' she said. 'Grey. A woman.'

'Like a shadow?' the officer asked.

'Well, yes, I suppose . . .'

'So, a shadow?' he smiled. Then, shaking his head, he returned to his post.

Güneş moved close to Ali Bey. 'A ghost. You know they exist. Don't try and pretend you don't. Your family comes from a village, just like the rest of us.'

'Ah, but in the city, I am a man of business,' Ali said. 'I left such silly notions behind many years ago.'

Güneş shook her head. 'No you didn't. You saw that djinn in Vahap Bey's room the same as the rest of us.'

62

He waved her away. 'That was years ago.'

'Yes, but you saw it,' Güneş said. 'We were all there, we know.'

'Yes, well . . .'

'So don't try to deny it! And don't try to deny Yeliz's ghost either. There are places in this city, Ali Bey, where people get their rent reduced for having a ghost.'

The old man pointed at the construction site across the road. Only weeks ago, once-elegant Ottoman houses had graced that wasteland. Bought by a large house-building conglomerate years ago, they had finally collapsed into the ground back in April. 'So go and live over there if you don't want ghosts,' he said. He lowered his voice. 'We'll be lucky to have a tarpaulin to live under at the end of this, so shut your yap. One word from me and you're gone.'

Güneş curled her lip. 'And one word from me and you're in one of Inspector Süleyman's cells,' she said. 'I've seen how you look . . .'

'But only look,' he said. He moved closer and added, 'Only looking is not a crime.'

I hope you die, he thought. Whoever you are, I hope you die in pain.

Dr Arto Sarkissian turned to his assistant. 'Close up for me, will you, please, Meral?'

'Yes, Doctor.'

The pathologist walked away from the body, discarded his disposable face mask and gloves at the door, and walked into his office. With weary hands he removed the plastic cap that had covered what remained of his hair and sat down behind his desk. The woman, in her mid twenties he had estimated, had been stunningly beautiful. Not even the post-mortem bulging eyes could ruin what had once been a sweet and delicate face. What on earth had such an exquisite little creature been doing in a filthy brothel in Tarlabaşı? Poverty, of course. She, like the little girl she had been found with, was malnourished; in addition, there were signs of drug use. A few recent, maybe even experimental, track marks on her arms. He picked up his phone and called Süleyman's number.

When the policeman answered, Arto said, 'Good afternoon, Inspector. Thought you'd like to know my findings re the Tarlabaşı woman right away.'

'Yes, thank you, Doctor.'

'All right.' He sighed. 'Well, as we suspected, cause of death was asphyxia. Confirmed by the *in situ* leather ligature, turned once, secured with a reef knot and then pulled upwards in order to compress and break the hyoid bone. Usual signs I would expect – bruising around the trachea and larynx, haemorrhages in the strap muscles under the skin . . . She was a slight woman and so her assailant wouldn't have had to exert a lot of pressure to kill her.' He closed his eyes for a moment. 'She was a mother. I've taken samples for DNA.'

'The child was given a cheek swab yesterday,' Süleyman said.

'Is she talking yet?'

'No. But we think we know her name and she seems to respond, albeit minimally, to Aramaic.'

'Gives a new meaning to the word "niche" . . .'

Sometimes he sounded like Çetin İkmen, whose stock-in-trade had always been grim humour.

'Indeed.' Arto could hear the normally urbane Süleyman smiling. 'But we'll do a comparison and see what comes up.'

He paused, then asked, 'Sexual activity?'

Here the doctor baulked, as he had done in the lab. 'Oh yes.'

'Useful samples?'

'No. There is evidence of sexual intercourse and I've good reason to believe that it was non-consensual.'

'Evidence?'

'Bruising around the tops of the legs, defence bruising on her arms, internal vulval bruising and contusion. Whoever he was forced his way inside her. He raped her and then killed her.'

'But no semen?'

'He must have worn a condom,' Arto said.

'Mmm. Unusual in a punter,' Süleyman said. 'The antipathy of some men towards the use of condoms is generally why such people go to prostitutes. Pay extra and you can ride bareback.'

The doctor flinched. 'What a very colourful term,' he said. 'But I take your point and concur.'

'Use of a condom implies a man whose fear of sexually transmitted disease is greater than his need for sex. That, or he thought ahead. Knowing he was going to kill the woman, he was anxious to leave no trace. Anything under the fingernails?'

'No,' said the pathologist. 'That too is unusual.'

'You say the ligature was leather . . .'

'A strap, yes. Like the sort of thing one might use to tie up a parcel.' Then he said, 'How are you getting on with Çetin Bey's little conundrum?'

'Badly. Just don't have time. I'm back in Tarlabaşı in a few minutes. We're all stretched to the limit here.'

'We hold our old records in a storage facility at the Forensic Institute. I'm going to try and get out there today if I can. Once I've written up my notes.'

'We can't let him down,' Süleyman said. 'This is the first time I've seen a light in his eyes since Fatma Hanım died.'

'I know . . .' Arto changed the subject. 'Something I have done is make contact with my predecessor Dr Sağlam's son. He was a student in 1976 and was working for his father as a part-time porter. I don't know if he will remember anything, or even if he'll speak to me. He wasn't exactly keen to meet when I contacted him.'

'You think he might know something we don't?'

'I don't know,' the doctor said. 'He is a man of some influence now. An architect responsible for the design of some of the new housing we see around us these days.'

He heard Süleyman snort.

'Yes, that's what I think too. Whatever mess his father may have made of his work in the past, his son has surpassed him. And unlike poor old Orhan Bey, Hüseyin Sağlam is, apparently, sober.'

Anything could be a trap these days. Just because the man was Armenian didn't mean he was necessarily to be trusted. Not even his work with his father counted. Nothing did.

Hüseyin Sağlam's father, Orhan, had been dead for thirty years. But people still talked about him. The son of a hard-line Kemalist from Izmir, Dr Orhan Sağlam had been a well-known functioning alcoholic. Hüseyin had spent much of his early life listening to half-whispered jokes about his father and the fact that it was lucky for everyone he was just a pathologist. The dead were always very understanding about the odd slip of a scalpel. Still, it had taken the Sağlam family some time to come out from under Orhan's slightly wobbly shadow, and for Hüseyin to reinvent himself and, to some extent, his past.

Now an enthusiastic member of the ruling party, he used his skills as an architect to design new buildings for İstanbul's pious elite. Offices that incorporated small mosques and prayer rooms, places where women could find privacy. His father had no place in his world, not even as a memory, not even as a question on the lips of Dr Arto Sarkissian.

However, if Sarkissian wasn't checking up on him, then where was the harm? And why would he be doing that anyway? He wasn't a party member. He probably wished the party nothing but ill will; most of those secular types did. And so his desire to speak to Hüseyin about one of his father's autopsies performed in the 1970s was probably genuine. Hüseyin had been working part-time at the laboratory back then in order to make some money while he was at college.

But what if Sarkissian was looking not for information as he said, but for evidence of his father's malpractice? If he was, then why? Was it to get at Hüseyin through his father?

Secrets could be destructive, but they could also be benign, and sometimes they could actually be useful. Kerim Gürsel wasn't the sort of man who liked to keep secrets, but during the course of his life, it seemed that secrets and those of a secretive nature had followed him around.

One such individual was Constable Ahsen Palavan, a lowly and ageing officer whom Kerim had once bumped into in the Aquarius Sauna – a place where lots of gay men went. Not a word had passed between them on that occasion, and in fact, they had only spoken once since, when Kerim asked Palavan if he could borrow his pass to the case file archives.

Records from the 1990s and even some from the 1980s had been digitised, but the older records remained on dusty shelves in what was often rather loose date order. Kerim knew he had no legitimate reason to be there, but he had a story ready. The case he was working on, the death of a woman in the Bosphorus village of Kanlica, had provided him with a weak excuse. Had anyone ever died in that ancient and venerable house before?

Kerim knew that had he waited for his information request on the Deniz Tonguç case to be fulfilled, he could have perused any resultant case file at his leisure. But he also knew that such things could sometimes take months to materialise. Not that he'd told any of his colleagues about his plans. Ahsen Palavan and what he liked to do with young men in bathhouses was his secret.

Kerim walked amid the racks of files until he arrived at the one labelled 1976.

Mustafa Ermis looked at the rosy colour of the tea in his glass and thought: It's not all about tea. It never had been, but until he'd come of age and taken over his father's estates and businesses, Mustafa hadn't known anything but tea. His father's other pursuits – his hand in the glove of a man in Trabzon who could get hold of drink, cigarettes and other things for a price, his involvement in the movement of such goods into what had then been the Soviet Union – had resulted in Mustafa and his brothers being sent with their mother to live in İstanbul. Because that was somewhere the families of Black Sea gangsters went in those days. Far from the border with Russia, far from the competition, perfectly positioned to challenge the powerful presence of the state-owned tea company, Çaykur. Thank God the industry had been opened for private competition in the eighties, or the family would have sunk without trace. Making up for his father's illegal activities, Mustafa had turned Kızıl Ağaç Tea into a major brand that now sold across the world.

Sometimes he wondered what would have happened had his marriage to Deniz Tonguç lasted more than a few months. Mustafa's father had been almost delirious with joy when he discovered his son wanted to marry the daughter of an admiral. He'd been less impressed by the Tonguç family's lack of money, but he'd dined out on the status, and anyway, money hadn't been an issue back then. There had been plenty of that until the old man suddenly gave up his subsidiary business pursuits in the early eighties. With the military running the country, he just couldn't risk it, and so he went legit, rediscovered his youthful atheism and died in 1995, just before Kızıl Ağaç really took off. In the new, more pious Turkey, he would have had to change his beliefs again if he wanted to be in with the movers and shakers.

68

Mustafa had been married twice and had four children since Deniz. It was a long time ago. But occasionally, like now, the fear he'd felt when he was taken into custody the day after her death came back to torment him. But then the post-mortem had come in and her death was declared a suicide. That had been a relief, though according to Ateş Tonguç, some members of the family never believed the verdict. And now, apparently, neither did a former police officer.

Ateş, in his usual casual way, had phoned Mustafa out of the blue and behaved as if they were best friends. But Mustafa knew his brother-in-law well enough to know that he probably wanted him to take part in this new investigation into Deniz's death. Mustafa, however, was not so sure.

'I went to see my mother.'

Branko Topaloğlu was one of a large cohort of timid Tarlabaşı heroin addicts. Not one to hassle people in the street, he would however regale people in cheap bars with stories about his gangster past. None of the tales he told was true, just like his name wasn't really Branko. It was Nedim. When pressed, he told Süleyman that he reckoned Branko sounded harder, more Slavic.

'And what,' the policeman said, 'does your poor old mother make of a son who aspires to be a Russian mobster?'

'She doesn't know!'

Branko was agitated. Kept walking backwards and forwards to the one window at the front of his room. He needed a fix.

But that wasn't Süleyman's problem. He said, 'So, Mr Topaloğlu, where does your mother live?'

'Kasımpaşa.'

This district was down the hill that sloped from Tarlabaşı to the Golden Horn.

'So you went to see her on the day the woman died?'

'I was there for a week,' he said. 'Didn't want to be, but the old girl takes me to see all these holy men, trying to cure me, you know . . .'

'Get you off the gear?'

'Yeah. But once I'm there, it's hard to get away. I came back yesterday.'

'I saw you.'

He shrugged. 'I don't know who that woman that died was,' he said.

'People come and go?'

'Some do. Some, like me, have been here years.'

'Why have you stayed?'

The house was a dump. The hallway stacked with rubbish, holes in the walls, rats. Süleyman imagined it was freezing cold in the winter.

'Cheap,' Branko said. 'And I've got friends round here.'

'What do you know about your landlord, Haluk Bey?'

'Nothing.'

'I mean, it's quite clear he's on the gear . . .'

'Nothing to do with me!'

'This isn't a drug-related investigation, Mr Topaloğlu,' Süleyman said. 'I don't care what you take or why you take it. I simply want to find out who killed this woman. In order to do that, I need to discover what goes on in this house. Specifically I need to know who was here two days ago.'

'Can't help you. I told you, I wasn't here.'

The building had one of those ever-open doors typical of the unofficial brothel. People came and went at will. No ID checks, no real names, just customers of either prostitutes or casual drug dealers and, of course, that ubiquitous Tarlabaşı resident, the whacked-out bonzai user who needed somewhere to crash until the hit wore off. So far none of the working girls on the site could remember who they'd been with. But that

70

probably also applied to men they'd seen less than an hour ago.

Apart from outside the Syrian church, CCTV cameras were few and far between, and those that did exist rarely worked. In many ways, although so many of the residents knew each other, Tarlabaşı could be a very anonymous district.

Chapter 7

There were a lot of things people thought they knew but didn't. Many people from the Western world, for instance, still thought that İstanbul was the capital of Turkey. When told it was actually Ankara, they would look confused. Another well-known fact that wasn't was the position of the heart in the human body. It wasn't bang in the middle of the chest, but slightly to the left, behind the sternum or breastbone. And so aiming to kill someone, or oneself, by plunging a knife into the chest might or might not result in piercing the heart. And even if the heart was pierced, there was a chance of survival due to its ability to repair small wounds.

Arto Sarkissian laid the slightly yellowing documents out before him and read through them again. Poor old Orhan Sağlam had been in the final stages of liver disease when he'd composed this report, and so his writing wasn't easy to decipher. But Arto persisted. For Çetin İkmen, and also, now that he was in touch with the case notes, for Deniz Tonguç.

According to Sağlam, the body he'd been given to examine had been that of a healthy nineteen-year-old woman who had died from exsanguination – she had bled out. This was not because she had been stabbed in the heart, as the popular story went, but because the aortic arch, part of the major artery through which blood was pumped away from the heart, had been pierced. This would have caused a sudden and catastrophic drop in aortic pressure, resulting in almost instantaneous death. Photographs of the corpse *in situ* confirmed this massive exsanguination. They showed a slight, bikini-clad woman lying on a sunlounger, her body red from the chest down. Blood had soaked into the lounger and pooled around the metal legs of the chair. There was also a smear of blood underneath her chin.

The aortic arch was actually above the heart, also behind the sternum and the ribs as well as the tough connective tissue that connected the chest bones. Penetrating all those structures was, as Arto knew very well, difficult. It would require considerable force and was not a commonly favoured method of dispatch. It was an even rarer method of suicide. Typically, in his experience, which consisted of one case back in the eighties, stabbing oneself through the chest usually involved falling onto a knife held in place somehow near the ground. Incredible nerve as well as iron control of one's own reflex to pull away from such a threat would be needed to do this. That and utter desperation, maybe even insanity.

Sağlam had identified what he described as 'hesitation wounds' around the site of the fatal incision. Typical of someone with not quite sufficient resolve to plunge a knife into their own chest with the requisite force, these could also have been caused by the ineptitude of an assailant.

Except there were no defence wounds. Even if Deniz Tonguç had been assaulted in her sleep, there would have been something, mainly because her assailant would have had to hold her to make sure she didn't move, which would have woken her up. Her attacker would also have been covered in her blood as he or she drove the blade home, and yet there was no evidence that anyone had been with her when she died. That said, back in 1976, forensic technology had been rudimentary. Arto wondered what the results of a full forensic examination of the site would have yielded had Deniz Tonguç died in the twenty-first century.

The blade used in the incident had been recovered from the ground beside the sunlounger; it had apparently dropped from Deniz's hand as she died. Described by Sağlam as a 'wide-bladed chopping knife', it had come from the Tonguç kitchen, which could feed into either a verdict of suicide or some sort of attack by an outside actor. Except that the Kara Lale Yalı showed no sign of having been broken into. And Deniz Tonguç's prints had been present on the blade.

'Doesn't Yıldırım own that yalı where Çetin Bey is investigating his cold case?' Ömer Mungun said.

'He does,' Süleyman said. 'Which is why we will have to proceed with some caution.'

'We will anyway, won't we? I mean, given that this is information supplied to us by Sugar Barışık . . .'

'Sugar Hanım is a very reliable woman in my opinion,' Süleyman said. 'More to the point is that Yıldırım, it seems, is hiding behind this Khachaturian family.'

Sugar Barışık had called Süleyman when he'd got back to his office. She'd told him that the house on Kalyoncu Kulluğu Caddesi, plus its neighbours either side, was actually owned by property magnate Tayfun Yıldırım. However, in order to get to Yıldırım, one had to apparently go through or around the original owners, an Armenian family called Khachaturian with whom, it appeared, Yıldırım was in partnership.

'It'll be easy enough to find out whether a family called Khachaturian did actually own that house in the past; probably less easy to find out what involvement they have with it now,' Süleyman said. 'Anyone can summon up an old name and use it for their own purposes. The fact is, as we suspected, Haluk Andıç doesn't own that house and clearly fails to maintain the building. At some point, therefore, Yıldırım will either sell it on or develop the site himself. There's so much potential money sloshing around in Tarlabaşı these days, almost any scenario is possible.'

The sun was beginning to set, and all across the city, people were rushing to get home for İftar. Süleyman switched on his office light.

'There's a core group of eight people who have lived in that house for years,' he said. 'I heard one of the women refer to a man called Osman Bey as the landlord before Andıç. I think tomorrow I'll go to the council offices and see if I can find out who he is and how much money he got for his properties.'

'You think it's some kind of scam?'

'Of course it is. Why put a junkie in charge of your property if it isn't a scam? But it's interesting because Yıldırım usually keeps his record clean. Mind you, he sort of has here too . . .'

'Land is not becoming easier to get hold of, sir,' Ömer said. 'Not unless one has the right connections.'

'Maybe he hasn't,' Süleyman said.

'He used to.'

'Yes, I heard that too. But then things can change, can't they? In fact, since last year's attempted coup, things have been changing a lot . . .'

'I do know a man over in Üsküdar who used to live in a place Yıldırım demolished last year. He's a bit of a bonzai casualty.'

'Go and see him,' Süleyman said.

'Bülent is coming for İftar tonight,' Çetin İkmen said. 'Not that he keeps Ramazan. I could lie to you and tell you that he does, but . . .'

He saw his wife smile. Bülent was his fourth-born son and the only other child, apart from Çiçek, who could see what İkmen saw.

'He reckons that if we ignore that thing in the kitchen it will melt away,' he continued. 'Djinn were in the world long before we were, so why do we think our "holy" men can get rid of them? Exorcism isn't always the answer. Sometimes just ignoring or co-existing is the way forward. I don't mind it. It bothers Çiçek from time to time, but not constantly . . .'

'Hello, Dad!'

Bülent was the son who was most like his father, even down to his smoke-scarred voice.

'Hello, boy!' İkmen replied. 'Be with you in a minute.' He leaned forward and whispered, 'I hope you'll keep being here for as long as I love you, and I'm sorry for that. But what can I do, eh?'

Bülent İkmen even leaned in the same way as his father. Slouching against one of the kitchen doorposts, smoking a cigarette, he said to his sister, 'It's a bit boring.'

Çetin İkmen smiled. He loved his children so much.

Çiçek shook her head. 'Not when it's staring at you while you try to peel vegetables it isn't,' she said.

The kitchen table groaned underneath the weight of the bread, fruit, pilav, bulgur, vegetables and fish she had prepared for İftar.

Her brother shrugged, but his eyes never left the djinn's fur-rimmed face. 'I'll grant you it's ugly, but if you ignore it, it'll go away.'

'Says the expert on djinn!' his sister said.

İkmen joined them, 'Let's eat.'

Then his phone rang.

He hadn't eaten or drunk anything all day, so why didn't he feel hungry? Imam Metin Demir, the tailor, was very grateful to the family of his neighbour the pharmacist for inviting him for İftar. The man's wife must have been cooking all day to put on such a feast. Laid out on a blindingly white tablecloth on the patio out the back of the pharmacy, the food looked and smelt inviting. As he'd sat down on one of the cushions at the edge of the cloth, Metin had been certain he'd gorge himself. After all, he didn't, for once, have Selçuk wittering in his ear, which was a relief. But then that story he'd read in *The Star* had come back to haunt him.

A woman had been found dead in a multiple-occupation house in Tarlabaşı. This was code for an unofficial brothel. The story had brought to mind Metin's father. He'd gone to brothels all the time. He'd done a lot of bad things. Metin always thought about his father when he heard about prostitution – or murder. The old man was long dead, but that lokum box full of his junk was still in Metin's home. Metin knew, as he attempted to put food in his mouth without gagging, that he would have to take his courage in his hands and look at it properly one day. For years, some people in the quarter had whispered that his dad had killed his mum. He'd never been convicted of her killing, but he'd been to prison many times and had a reputation for being violent towards women. And there were still people around who held grudges against him.

However, by the time Metin left the pharmacist's garden to make his way home, he didn't feel so sure about opening the box. Did he need that kind of hassle in his life? But when first one man, then another appeared to be following him and his heart beat so fast that by the time he got inside he was exhausted, he wondered about it again. The area was getting worse all the time. People of all sorts just fetched up from who-knew-where. People who were rarely good news for the impoverished district. Maybe even people who had once known his father . . .

Or was that just paranoia talking?

'The body was discovered by the woman's younger sisters, Aylin and Zeynep Tonguç.'

İkmen felt that explained at least some of the behaviour Suzan Tan had observed when she had visited Aylin Tonguç.

'The father made the formal identification,' Dr Sarkissian continued.

İkmen had told his children to eat while he took the doctor's call. Sitting in the living room, he smoked as he listened to his friend on the phone.

'As we know, the verdict on Deniz's death was suicide. But now that I've seen Sağlam's report, I'm even less convinced. The weapon used was entirely unsuitable for the job. A flat-bladed kitchen knife, admittedly long enough to be able to penetrate the chest and reach the heart – yes, I have been reading up on this. But it wasn't the right tool.'

'Which implies an unplanned act . . .'

'Or a very highly planned one.'

'I was about to say that.'

'If we assume, as Sağlam did, that Deniz stabbed herself through the aortic arch above the heart, whilst lying on a sunlounger, she would have had to have arms like a wrestler. And she didn't. What she did have was a smear of blood underneath her chin, which, if we assume she killed herself, just isn't possible. How did it get there, and more to the point, why was that very unsuitable knife on the ground and not still stuck in her chest?'

'It was on the ground?'

'Beside the sunlounger.'

İkmen ran his fingers through his hair. 'She would have been . . .'

'Dead, yes,' the doctor said. 'And yes, of course this is wrong. It's actually as wrong as a post-mortem can get. But whether it is suspicious or not is another matter.'

'How can it not be suspicious?'

'If poor old Sağlam was too drunk to know what he was doing,' Arto said.

'Do you think that's possible?'

'I don't know. I didn't work with him. But his son, Hüseyin, was his porter. He may remember. When I contacted him, he wasn't keen to speak. We all knew that Dr Sağlam liked a drink, and there were stories about his, shall we say, more lurid behaviour from time to time. But how much it affected his work, I don't know.'

'But could you say there is a question mark over this PM?'

'Oh most certainly, yes,' Arto said. 'It's not suicide, Çetin, not by any stretch of the imagination.'

It had to have been at least ten years since Ateş Tonguç had visited his sister Aylin in what had once been their grandmother's apartment, in Nişantaşı. He knew he should have been to see her more than he had, but he comforted himself with the fact that Zeynep hadn't been either. Not even their mother came that often.

A maid let him in. A thin, silent little thing who looked as if she was still living in some dirt-poor southern Anatolian village in the middle of nowhere. She wasn't even wearing slippers. And her feet were dirty.

Aylin had shrunk. Always small, and never one to eat if it could be avoided, she now looked skeletal. And mad.

Ateş kissed her. She smelt of camphor, that mothball odour he remembered from his youth. From the Kara Lale Yalı. The maid brought tea, which tasted stale. But he didn't comment.

After an awkward silence, Aylin said, 'I suppose you're here about the woman who came to see me. Zeynep sent her. I didn't want to talk to her.'

'You could have refused,' he said. 'Why did you let her in?'

She turned away. Aylin's response to Deniz's death had always irritated Ateş. Rather than evoke sympathy, her terror that she would be next had consistently repelled him.

'What did you think it would achieve?' he asked.

'I don't know.'

'From what I hear, you rolled out the seance story and launched straight into your own fears. She must've thought you were mad.'

And this, of course, was why he didn't visit his sister, because when he did, he berated her. He felt bad about it, which was why he said, 'I know I wasn't at the seance. I'm sorry that you were and I'm sorry Deniz asked those bloody ridiculous questions . . .'

'We all wanted to know,' she said. 'Except Father. Even me.'

'Father should have stopped it.'

'Yes, but Ateş, given who had come through . . .'

'I don't care!' he said. 'It's all nonsense, Aylin! The fact that Deniz died within months of that seance is a coincidence if you believe she was killed by someone other than herself, and a self-fulfilling prophecy if you think she committed suicide.'

'It *was* suicide. There was a doctor's report . . .'

'Yes, except that some people don't think that's right,' he said. 'That woman who came to see you? She's got a retired detective to look into it.'

'Oh.' Her face lost what little colour it had possessed.

'If he comes to see you—'

'I don't have to see him. I won't.'

'But if he does, I'd think carefully about what you might say. Especially about Mustafa.'

She turned on him, eyes blazing. 'What about him?' she said.

'About how you felt.'

'I felt nothing for him! I never did! He married my sister!' She began to cry.

Ates said, 'But who knows what he'll find?'

'I don't care,' she said. 'I just want to live.'

'So you sit here in the dark, waiting for the Ferry of the Dead to pass you by . . .'

'You know it's real!' she said.

'I know nothing of the sort!' He took a deep breath to calm himself. 'I don't even know where the notion of a death ferry comes from.'

'Yes you do!'

He lit his pipe. He knew that Aylin didn't like people smoking, but he'd lost the will to live. 'No, I don't, or rather I do, but . . .' He sighed. 'The notion of a ferry that appears once a year on Kadir Gecesi . . .'

'Which means it will come soon.'

'No,' he said, 'it won't come at all. It doesn't exist.'

'All year, souls are gathered for the Ferry of the Dead to take them on the Night of Power to the other side . . .'

'You know, I was always grateful that we weren't raised to be practising Muslims, but when I talk to you, I wonder,' Ateş said. 'At least if one has a religion, one can't be at the mercy of every crank notion that comes along. Aylin, you got this ferry idea from Aliki. Much as I loved her, she was a cranky, superstitious old woman. It's a twist on a classic Greek myth. It doesn't actually happen. There is no ferry full of dead souls that appears only on the Night of Power. And even if such a thing did exist, quite how you think you're going to avoid it by living in the dark and never going out, I don't know.'

As soon as he'd said it, Ateş wished he hadn't. Of course it didn't make sense. His sister had lost her mind when Deniz died. He remembered that well. She'd even had to go away for a while, as he recalled. Their mother's spiritualism fad as well as the strange beliefs of their Greek nanny had rendered what had probably always been a delicate mind a wreck. That and her unrequited passion for Mustafa Ermis. Part of Aylin's problem had always been the fact that she'd never, to his knowledge, been laid.

He leaned forward in his chair and took her hand. 'Look,' he said. 'I'm not here to torment you. Believe it or not, I'd like to help you; we all would. But you won't listen. I know this; I even, in a way, respect it. The reason I've come is because Deniz's death is going to be reinvestigated and I want to know that you are prepared for that. Specifically, you mustn't let them think that Father had anything to do with it.'

'Father didn't kill Deniz!'

'I know that,' he said. 'But we must be careful. His enemies are always waiting for an opportunity to blacken his name. We don't want to give them any more ammunition.'

'But Father hasn't done anything wrong!'

'No, he hasn't. We all know the charges against him have been made up . . .' He stopped to collect his thoughts. 'If you are asked about your childhood, don't allude to Father. You had a nice childhood, in a nice house, amid a loving family . . .'

'I did.'

'Yes, good,' he said. And then he smiled. 'Say that.'

'I will, because it's true.'

And Ateş had to be content with that. He also hoped that it *was* true. Because it didn't reflect the silences, the ill feeling and the tension he had always felt back in the Kara Lale Yalı. Nor did it reflect what Zeynep had once told him.

Haluk Andıç picked up a handful of dates and shoved them into his mouth. Lip service to İftar paid, he sat back against the wall and watched Ali Ok make a pig of himself.

After the traditional three dates, the old man stuffed in bulgur, cacık, köfte and two different types of fasulye, with bread and a liberal libation of rakı. He'd prepared the bulgur himself, but all the rest had been given to him by some ancient Somali woman who lived up by Tarlabaşı Bulvarı. Probably because she wanted to marry a Turk, any Turk who'd get her a passport, she'd been pandering to Ok's 'poor little old man' act for almost a year. This included cooking for him from time to time and plying him with booze.

Haluk let the man chew on in peace. He himself was high and so perfectly content. That was, until Ali Ok stopped eating and began to speak.

'Some of the old tenants, particularly the whores, are seeing ghosts,' he said through a spray of bulgur wheat grains. 'They've asked for a reduction in the rent.'

Haluk laughed. 'Nice try.'

'Ah, but you know there are places where people get reductions for djinn.'

'Where?'

'Gaziosmanpaşa. My nephew told me. He has a friend who lives over there.'

Haluk shrugged. 'Gaziosmanpaşa is full of Alevis; they'll believe anything.'

A form of Shi'a Islam, Alevism was practised by many people in the district of Gaziosmanpaşa. It was something that some members of the Sunni majority found unpalatable. A lot of lurid stories circulated about Alevis, most of which were completely fabricated.

'Djinn come because people attract them with their evil deeds,' Haluk said. He didn't believe what he was saying; he was just making it up. If the tenants wanted a rent reduction, they could sing for it. 'And ghosts only appear to people who want to see them. Who cares about some old whores? Tell them to shut the fuck up or get out.'

'I have. Not in those terms, but . . . Maybe you should consider, under the circumstances . . .'

'Look, this building is finished,' Haluk said. 'It can't go on now someone's been murdered. New people won't come here. The area's getting worse. Until Tarlabaşı has all been replaced, nothing will change. Even the new houses won't sell until we knock places like this down and get the scum off the streets.'

'Scum? You and I live—'

'I bought this building.' He was careful not to say that he owned it. 'And you've done your job well. We'll be fine.'

'You can't know that.'

'Oh I do.'

'How?'

'I just do.'

Ali Ok had tried various ways to get Haluk to say how he'd got the money to buy the three houses. He'd told him he'd got them cheap, and the old man had no way of knowing whether that was true or not. Osman Güler, the previous landlord, had just disappeared. But as Haluk recalled, Güler too had boasted that time for his tenants was almost up because of the new development. He'd thought he'd make his fortune out of it. Not that Haluk had told Inspector Süleyman when he'd asked. He'd actually told him very little, and so far he'd had no comeback on it. Which was good.

İlyas Müslim had been diabetic for as long as he could remember. When he'd been very young, his mother had given him his insulin injections. But when he started school, he began doing them himself. Now, at thirty-five, he was an old hand. The only thing he did insist upon was privacy. Just before a meal, as now, he would go into the bathroom or the bedroom he shared with Zehra and do what he called 'the necessary'.

He didn't hear the silent little girl come in behind him. Later, he would think about what she'd wanted. But when she started to scream, he simply dropped the syringe and ran to her. But the little girl cringed away from him. One of the problems of being a foster carer, often for really damaged children, was that you never knew how they were going to react to anything. This poor little girl had been found in a brothel with the body of a woman who could have been her mother. İlyas tried to comfort her, but as far as he knew, she didn't speak Turkish. He felt so sad for her, and helpless.

Chapter 8

At one time the small garden in front of the Kara Lale Yalı had
been a well-looked-after green space stocked with flowers, trees
and marble water features. But that had been before the coastal
road had been completed, cutting off many of the very best
Bosphorus properties from direct access to the water. And so
Çetin İkmen, while screened from the endless stream of passing
vehicles by some somewhat tragic mulberry bushes, was dis-
inclined to stay outside once he had finished his cigarette.

He'd only just got out of bed when Kerim Gürsel had arrived
at his apartment carrying a bundle of paperwork.

'This was all I could find that refers to Deniz Tonguç,' Gürsel
had told him. 'Can you get them back to me this evening?'

İkmen had said that of course he could. Then Suzan had called
to say that Tayfun Yıldırım was out of town for a few days, and
did he want to come and spend some more time at the yalı. It
was an opportunity not to be missed.

The door from the garden led down to the kitchen and up to
what would have been the yalı's reception hall, back in the day.
Traditionally designed to keep men's and women's apartments
separate, it made what was a considerable building feel smaller
than it was. Heavy Ottoman furniture didn't help to dispel this
illusion.

İkmen sat down behind a large, dusty coffee table and began
to read. Upstairs he could hear Suzan moving around on the

creaking floorboards. Wooden yalıs like this were not places where privacy was easy to obtain.

'I've felt for a very long time that we need to clear this up. That was why, when Dr Tan contacted me, I spoke to her.'

Halide Tonguç sighed. Zeynep had always been the most outspoken of her three daughters.

'I agree,' she said. 'There are still questions that remain about Deniz's death. But did you have to pass on Aylin's details to Suzan Tan?'

'Mother, I live in Izmir. The poor woman is working to a deadline to preserve what can be preserved of our house. I personally feel grateful, which is why I've taken the time to come here and hopefully see her. At the time, I gave her your number and Aylin's, and Aylin agreed to speak to her.'

Halide shook her head. 'I should've done it.'

'Yes, you should. But you didn't.'

'I've met her now, and the ex-policeman who is helping her. They're very nice.'

Zeynep sat down opposite her mother. 'But now you're worried, right?'

'Of course I am.'

'Because of Father.'

Halide leaned forward and held her daughter's hands. 'You know how those who oppose him seek to blacken his name!'

'He had nothing to do with Deniz's death,' Zeynep said. 'He was at the Gölcük base.'

'Yes, but just raking all this up . . . Our enemies don't have any regard for the truth!'

'So why did you let Dr Tan—'

'Because you had already spoken to her!' Halide put her head in her hands. 'And because I want to know.'

'We all do.'

The day Deniz died, 6 August 1976, Zeynep had taken Aylin with her when she went to visit her friend Selina Gabras in Yeniköy. It was a Friday, but because it was the school holidays, children all over the city were out playing in the streets, in the parks and along the shores of the Bosphorus. Because Selina was Greek, however, the girls spent a lot of time indoors that afternoon, eating far too much chocolate cake at a name-day celebration for the Gabras family's priest. When they returned home, they were relieved to see that their mother and brother Ateş had not yet returned from visiting relatives in Sarıyer, as both girls had dropped chocolate on their dresses.

They cleaned themselves up as best they could in the bathroom and then went out to the garden with a view to drying off. It was then that they saw her.

'I don't know exactly what I saw that day,' Zeynep said. 'Not really. I saw blood, I saw Deniz not moving. Aylin was just screaming. I couldn't get her to stop. I think if Daddy hadn't arrived then, I might have gone closer. But I didn't.'

Admiral Tonguç had called the police. Newly arrived from the naval base at Gölcük, he was in full uniform, which, Zeynep had later thought, made the policemen who attended the scene cringingly deferential. Had it also made them inattentive to the crime?

'Your father wouldn't let me see her,' Halide said. 'Or Ateş. When her body was brought through the house, he made us sit in Aliki's old room with the blinds drawn.'

'I remember Timur coming home later that evening,' Zeynep said.

Both women became quiet. Timur Tonguç, the eldest sibling, had been a student at the naval academy on the island of Heybeliada when his sister died. He left the academy that day and never went back.

'I put Dr Tan and the policeman in touch with Ateş. I don't know if they've spoken to Timur. He's not always at that pansiyon he owns,' Halide said. 'Do you have any idea where he is?'

'No,' Zeynep said. 'He's still basically a hippy at heart. He comes, he goes. None of us know where.'

'I see,' her mother said.

Zeynep added, 'That's how he wants it to be, Mother, you know that.'

The silence returned.

Deniz Tonguç had been found dead by her sisters at approximately 16.45 on Friday 6 August 1976. Their father, Admiral Alaaddin Tonguç, just returned from naval headquarters at Gölcük, had called police at 17.00. The scene had been attended by Constables Özgür Ayhan and Faruk Eski from the nearby Akıntıburnu police station, who had then passed the case over to officers from police headquarters. Inspector Hakan Köse had attended together with police pathologist Dr Sağlam. The body had been laid out on a sunlounger in the garden of the family's yalı in Bebek. The dead woman had been wearing a green bikini.

İkmen sat back in his chair and looked at the ceiling. Sağlam, according to Dr Sarkissian's evidence, had done a very poor job of coming to a conclusion about Deniz's death. He wondered what Inspector Hakan Köse had thought. He remembered the name, if not the man. He'd been beyond retirement age then and so maybe he just hadn't been that bothered. Or perhaps he had been leaned on to support the pathologist's findings.

From the small amount of information that Kerim Gürsel had managed to unearth, it seemed that Deniz Tonguç's death had been solved and filed away very quickly. But it had made the papers. One cutting, the only one in the file, from *Cumhuriyet*, showed a picture of a fresh-faced, light-haired girl, underneath the strapline 'Newly-wed found dead'. Published prior to the

89

verdict, the story gave a bald, factual account of an incident that police had been called to in Bebek. İkmen wondered how the ever more lurid reporting of the twenty-first century would spin such a thing. Deniz, bikini clad and sunbathing, would probably have been presented as some sort of loose woman, while at the same time, her physical assets would have been described in some detail. Damning whilst titillating. He hated it.

The noise of movement upstairs had stopped. Suzan was in the process of cataloguing the small library on the first floor, and so he imagined she was probably reading. She'd told him she'd found an Armenian cross made of gold during one of her investigations but that Tayfun Yıldırım had taken it. She'd wanted to give it to Halide Tonguç but he'd said that since he was now the owner of the yalı it belonged to him. He was right, even if his action over the cross was not.

İkmen looked back at the documents in front of him and wondered where the story about the seance at the Tonguç yalı had actually come from. There was nothing about it in the *Cumhuriyet* report. Maybe some of the other papers had carried it. How had he known about it? He really couldn't remember. It was just one of those stories that he somehow knew. Had Suzan known about it before she went to visit Aylin Tonguç? He'd have to ask her.

He wanted another cigarette. He got up and went outside. As he walked past the kitchen door, he saw something move very quickly across the threshold.

His mother had seen things that some would call ghosts. His father said it was because she had come from Albania, a country not entirely Islamic, imbued with the supernatural beliefs of both Catholic and Orthodox Christians. But İkmen's mother had understood the Islamic supernatural world too. It was she who had once told him: 'Ghosts are always controlled by djinn. They will always inhabit a house together.' And so of course İkmen didn't want rid of the djinn in his kitchen even though he knew that his wife did. How would he cope without seeing her sweet face?

And now this.

What had moved across the entrance to the kitchen had been nothing beyond a thickening of the air. A small aggregation of darkness. He'd looked for a cat or a rat, but found nothing. And it had made him feel bad, which had led to guilt. Holding on to Fatma was laying him open to things he had always tried to keep in check. As a working police officer he had used what some called his 'witch's senses', inherited from his mother, only as a last resort.

'Çetin Bey . . .'

He looked up and saw Suzan walking towards him holding three cardboard boxes, stacked up on top of each other.

'What have you got there?' he asked.

'Very old sugar cubes,' she said. 'I found them in that tiny bedroom next to the library.'

'Do you know who slept in the bedrooms?'

'Only the one the admiral and his wife used,' she said. 'All the children had gone by the time they sold the house. As you saw, many of the rooms had been converted to storage.'

'This is the little room on the first floor?'

'Yes, it's the only one that still contains a bed. There's not much in there, but I found these on the dressing table,' She opened the lid of the first box to reveal the dusty sugar lumps.

'Maybe someone took them from the kitchen for some reason,' İkmen said. 'Or . . .' A very old memory came back to him. 'Maybe that was Aliki's old room.'

'Why do you say that?'

'Because the Greeks always hand out sugar lumps during the feast of St George.'

'Do they?'

'At the Church of St George on Büyükada, pilgrims are offered sugar lumps when they reach the top of the hill where the church is situated. It's a very old custom.'

Suzan shrugged and went back inside. Just before she reached the kitchen door, she said, 'Would you like tea, Çetin Bey?'

'Yes, thank you,' he said.

He let his mind wander back to what he had seen in the kitchen. A place like the Kara Lale Yalı, where an unexplained death still lingered . . .

İkmen hadn't sought out company for a long time. He'd heard, mainly from his children, that many of his old contacts missed him. Not just his former colleagues and informants, but also people he just knew. Individuals who lived at the margins, mainly, men and women devoted to a life between the ancient cracks in İstanbul's long, long story. He thought about one in particular.

'I have to inject myself with insulin three times a day. I try to do it away from others. It's not pleasant. I honestly thought I was on my own.'

İlyas Müslim, the foster carer of the girl known as Rosarita, was a pale, slim man in his thirties. A social worker, he and his wife had been fostering children in trouble for the past five years. In that time he'd come across some bizarre behaviour amongst those for whom he cared, but he'd never heard screaming like it from such a small child.

'It chilled my blood,' he told Süleyman. 'And when I tried to go and comfort her, she threw herself under the bed and stayed there. We only managed to get her out in the early hours of the morning. My wife slept on the floor in her room because we didn't know whether she might try and run away. I know it was foolish not to shut the bedroom door, but Zehra, my wife, had just called up that dinner was ready and so I wanted to do my injection and then go and get the girl from her room. I can't imagine what possessed her to come in behind me. Why did she do that?'

'Sergeant Mungun will try to find out,' Süleyman said. 'From the little we know, it seems she understands Aramaic. Is it all right for your wife to bring her downstairs so that he can talk to her?'

'Of course.'

After some persuasion, they managed to get the little girl downstairs. Ömer Mungun smiled at her.

'I am not a Muslim,' he said. 'I don't think you are either.'

The girl said nothing, but her hands worked, clutching and unclutching the hem of her T-shirt.

'We have that in common in this country,' he said. 'But I have always been here, whereas I don't think you have, have you?'

He'd eventually, after some persuasion, managed to get the couple and Süleyman to leave him alone with the girl. He knew why they wanted to stay, so that the girl wouldn't feel intimidated by being alone with a man, but so far she hadn't spoken with anyone else around. He had to see whether she would open up in Aramaic.

'I come from a city in the east of Turkey called Mardin,' he said. 'Where do you come from?'

There was a very long pause, which Ömer had expected. What he hadn't been ready for was that she would talk.

'Mardin.'

Her voice was husky and oddly deep for one so young.

Ömer leaned forward and smiled. 'Yes,' he said. 'Do you come from Mardin too?'

Again he had to wait, but when she did speak, he knew for sure that she had understood his Aramaic.

'No,' she said.

He smiled. 'So where *do* you come from?'

'Syria.'

'That's good, that's really good,' Ömer said. 'Look, first tell me your name. I think I know what it is. Is it Rosarita?'

She nodded.

'You're in no trouble at all, Rosarita. All we want to do—'

'When the man came to see my mother, Takla, he put a needle in his leg before he made her die.'

Ömer felt his heart pound.

'Will the man here kill me?' she said.

It was always the same three people. Two young men and a middle-aged woman. Every other day they came, talked to the site foreman, looked around what had been built, looked at his houses, briefly, and left.

Haluk Andıç had been told they came from the construction company, and that the woman was the architect, the two men her assistants. He'd also been told that the owners of that site wanted his properties too. After all, who would buy their properties, once they were finished, if the ones opposite were full of whores and junkies? Nice people wanted to live in Tarlabaşı, but not until it had been altered out of all recognition.

But Haluk Andıç also knew that the developers could wait, because he had been told that too. And when the time came to sell, it wouldn't be he who would do it. Hopefully he'd be getting high when that happened.

'You got anything?'

He hadn't noticed Branko Topaloğlu flop down on the steps up to the doorway beside him.

'Yes thanks,' Haluk replied.

'Sweet. Can I pay you Thursday?'

Haluk looked down at him. Thin and pale, Branko smelt of body odour and piss. As junkies went, he was a couple of levels lower down the scale than even Haluk.

'You haven't paid your rent yet.'

'Yeah but you know I'm good for it.'

'I don't,' Haluk said. 'What makes you think that?'

Branko said nothing. Like a lot of drug users, like Haluk himself, he was hopeless at paying his way. Unless he'd just got some money from somewhere, he was always broke.

'I'm getting money Thursday,' he persisted.

'So if I've got anything by Thursday, you can buy it then.'

'I need it now.'

Haluk didn't reply. Branko was young and could be volatile. His family came from the Black Sea, where lots of the people were the descendants of Georgians and Armenians. Haluk thought they were scum – and he wasn't alone.

For a while, Branko fiddled with his fingers and chewed on his nails. Then he said, 'Just have to get my money early, then.'

Which Haluk felt was probably code for Branko planning to snatch a bag. But then if he got the money to do a deal with him and pay his rent, what of it?

'Rosarita didn't see his face, but she knew it was a man. She saw him inject himself in his leg, from her hiding place under the bed,' Ömer Mungun said.

'And what about the water?' Süleyman said. 'Did this man turn on the tap?'

'No, she did. She tried to wash her mother, she thought it might make her better. Then she couldn't get the tap to turn off. She hid in a cupboard. Can you imagine?'

The image of that small child alone with her dead mother, trying to wash her better, was almost unbearable.

'She's from Syria,' Ömer continued. 'I don't know where, I didn't like to push her too hard. But I did get the mother's name. It's Takla Elias.'

'Forensics have confirmed they are mother and daughter, yes,' Süleyman said. 'But given their lack of papers, I doubt they entered the country legally. Does the child have a father?'

'Still in Syria, apparently. They came here to be safe.'

Süleyman shook his head. 'We seem to be fast becoming a place of broken Syrian dreams.'

Ömer didn't reply. He'd watched the Syrians arriving whenever he went home. There were vast refugee camps in the east, but who wanted to stay in one of those? Takla Elias and her daughter, like thousands of others, had obviously headed for the city and the faint possibility of work.

'All right,' Süleyman said, 'issue the woman's name to the press and let's see if we can find anyone who knows anything about her. But not the child. Whoever killed Takla wasn't aware her daughter was in that room or he would have killed her too. If he knows of her existence, he may try to find her.'

'Yes, sir.'

'That house, in fact the whole of Tarlabaşı, is full of intravenous drug users. Our man could be any one of them.'

Halide Tonguç missed her elder son, Timur. After Deniz had died, he'd become a beach bum for a number of years, hanging out around the Mediterranean coast doing any job he could get. The pansiyon in Rize had come later. But he wasn't always there. In fact whenever she called, he never picked up, and he rarely got back to her. She felt his isolation from the family was his way of coping – with Deniz's death and the fact that he'd disappointed his father by dropping out of the naval academy. She called anyway, and left a message.

'I don't know where you are, as usual, but I just thought I should tell you that you may be contacted by this ex-policeman. I left you another message a couple of days ago, concerning Deniz's death. You may already have spoken to this man for all I know. But if you haven't, just be aware that you must be careful what you say about your father. Given his current situation, people who oppose him could be using this investigation to implicate him in Deniz's death. You know how the military have been purged since the coup – whether they were involved or not. Maybe avoid talking to this man, I don't know.'

She ended the call. Of course Alaadin Bey had had nothing to do with Deniz's death, but in the current febrile political atmosphere anything was possible, and Timur had hated his father. He could easily say things, while not lies, that did not show him in a good light. And if anything even more appalling happened to her husband, Halide didn't know that she could bear it.

Chapter 9

Ever since his landlord had sold the house he shared with a load of other bonzai addicts to property developer Tayfun Yıldırım, Serkan Asal had been on the streets. But because he'd always lived in Üsküdar, he hadn't gone far. He spent most of his days hanging around the Üsküdar ferry terminal, with occasional trips across the road to a small büfe outside the Mihrimah Mosque. There he'd beg for cigarettes, and occasionally the owner of the büfe would give him the odd damaged orange he couldn't use for juicing.

Ömer Mungun had come across Serkan when he'd been in uniform. Back in those days, when Serkan was just a pot-head, Ömer had picked him up a couple of times for shoplifting. An educated man, Serkan chose the life he lived and didn't complain about it, which was one of the reasons why Ömer liked him and tried to help him when he was evicted. Even though Serkan was by that time on bonzai, Ömer knew he was basically a decent man. But Yıldırım had got his way and the quaint old wooden house with a well in the cellar where Serkan and his mates had lived was pulled down to make way for a mansion of glass and steel.

Serkan was sitting on the ground, leaning against the side wall of the ferry terminal, when Ömer found him. The men exchanged greetings and Ömer gave Serkan a packet of cigarettes. He wouldn't pay for any information Serkan gave him, as it would all go on bonzai and Ömer didn't want to actively contribute to his death. But he would buy him a meal – provided they could eat outside. Serkan, homeless, was a bit ripe. And it was Ramazan.

But before that, he wanted to talk about Tayfun Yıldırım.

Serkan, as was his custom, was straight to the point. 'He's a cunt,' he said. 'He doesn't care about anything but money. My house was historic. A hundred years old. We had a natural spring in the cellar.'

'I remember it,' Ömer said. 'A wooden villa.'

He'd been told once that Çetin İkmen had been born in a wooden villa on the slopes of Çamlıca Hill, which was where Serkan's place had been.

'Yıldırım used that new mega-mosque they've built up there to justify it,' Serkan continued. 'Said a house like ours was a disgrace so near a sacred place like that. But he made money off it.'

Çamlıca Republic Mosque had been completed in 2016 and was the largest mosque in Asia.

'Old Ahmet Bey died the day we left there.'

'I'm sorry.'

'You would be because you're a decent man,' Serkan said, 'but him, Yıldırım . . . All holy, holy so he can suck up to the people who give out the building contracts, but I know what he is.'

'What do you mean?'

'When he came to look at our place, he treated us like we weren't there,' he said. 'I know we were just a bunch of bonzai addicts, but that was our home! Landlord was no use. Just rubbing his hands about the money he'd make. But he didn't make what Yıldırım did. Millions he charged for that thing he built. When he finally got us out, I watched to see what he'd do with the place. Hung about the streets up there. I had nowhere else to go. Gagging to knock the old place down, he told the landlord, but it just sat there.'

99

'What did he do with it?' Ömer said.

'Nothing at first,' Serkan said. 'Until he started to bring women there.'

'What, he used it—'

'Handy place to fuck girls,' Serkan said. 'I mean, you can even tell your wife you've been at work if she asks – and with a straight face. And of course, these days, with everyone watching everyone else's morals, it makes sense to be furtive. I mean, people in hotels talk.'

Zeynep Tonguç was, she said, staying at the Four Seasons Hotel in Sultanahmet.

'Why don't you join me here for lunch?' she'd said when she contacted Suzan Tan. 'And bring your policeman with you.'

It was a short walk, even for İkmen, from his apartment to the hotel. When he'd been a youngster in the 1960s, the place had been known as the Sultanahmet Jail. Built as Turkey's first modern prison in 1918, with fearsome lookout posts and screeching peacocks on the roof, it had been a place of fear and ill repute. İkmen always felt uneasy walking through its smart doors into what had once been home to hard prisoners and even harder guards. It was well known that murders had happened there back in the day.

He met Suzan at reception and then walked with her through the restaurant and out onto the terrace. A smartly dressed woman with expensively bobbed red hair came towards them. She shook Suzan's hand.

'You must be Dr Tan,' she said. 'I'm Zeynep.'

'Suzan.' She introduced İkmen, then Zeynep Tonguç led them to a table.

'They do a wonderful barbecue lunch here. I do hope that you're both meat-eaters.'

'I am,' İkmen said. Suzan nodded in agreement.

'Me too,' Zeynep said. 'And I hope you don't mind eating outside either. I have to be able to smoke, you see.'

'I don't know who he is, but I thought I'd better tell you about him,' Selçuk Çeviköz said.

Imam Metin Demir looked up out of his basement workshop and into the street. When he wasn't at his mosque, he was almost always in his tailoring workshop, sewing and being talked at by Selçuk. The man he found himself looking at was tall, grey haired and dressed in camouflage trousers and a T-shirt.

'And you say he was asking about my dad?' the imam said.

'Yes. Do you want me to beat him up?'

'No!' Metin shook his head. 'Why do you always have to resort to violence?'

He went out into the street and walked over to the man, who smiled.

'I hear you've been asking after my father,' Metin said. After possibly being followed home the previous night, he was nervous.

The man, who was indeed very tall, bent down and looked at him closely. 'You're Regep's son?'

'Yes. May I know who you are, please? And why you have been asking after my father? I don't remember your face.'

A small crowd had gathered around the two men. Visiting strangers did come into the mahalle from time to time, but they always caused a stir. As Metin knew only too well, it was because many of them were unemployed.

'Is there anywhere we can talk more privately?' the man said.

Metin didn't know him, but he took his point. Trying to talk in the street with ten people gawking at you wasn't easy. Also, Selçuk was in the workshop should this character prove to be one of his father's old criminal contacts.

'Come with me,' he said. 'What is your name, by the way?'

'It's Cengiz Bey,' the man replied.

Had his dad ever mentioned a Cengiz Bey? And even if he had, would Metin have known?

Regep Demir had been in prison with lots of men. Every time he'd gone away, Metin had been looked after by an old widow called Tansu Hanım. She'd been kind and gentle, and in fact Metin had always preferred living with her than with his father. It had been Tansu who had awakened his interest in religion.

He took Cengiz Bey into his workshop and asked him where he'd met his father.

'Maltepe. The prison.'

'Yes, I guessed that,' Metin said. 'My dad was in and out many times.'

Cengiz Bey shrugged. 'We were the same. Thieves and house-breakers. When did your father die?'

'Ninety-nine,' Metin said.

'I'm sorry.'

The man looked as if he was about the same age now as Regep had been when he died. Although Cengiz Bey appeared far healthier and more prosperous than Regep ever had.

'I'm assuming you don't . . . pursue your previous line of work,' Metin began.

'I left town after my last sentence,' Cengiz Bey said. 'Went to the country, found myself a good woman. I'm a bus driver.'

'An honest job,' Metin said, although most of the bus drivers he knew looked more battered than this man. But then maybe driving buses in the country wasn't so stressful as it was in the city.

'I like it.' Then, 'So your dad, he ever . . .'

'Oh, he was a rogue until the end,' Metin said.

Cengiz Bey leaned back in the chair Metin had given him. Selçuk watched him closely, which was embarrassing.

'I came to your house a couple of times,' the visitor said. 'A small house . . .'

'He built it himself.'

'Yes. I thought it was in this street.'

'No.' Was he trying to get Metin to tell him where he lived? Why?

'Oh, I must've misremembered.'

'Yes.' There was an awkward pause, and then Metin said, 'So why are you in the city, may I ask?'

Cengiz Bey smiled. 'To visit.'

'Ah.'

'I was born here. In Beyoğlu. I wanted to see my home again before I die.'

Back in the eighties, when travel across the country was either by arduous but cheap bus routes or expensive flights, Metin would have understood that statement. But everyone travelled these days. Unless, of course . . .

'I have cancer,' the man continued. 'I'm perfectly well right now, but I know I'm on borrowed time. Felt I should come home for a few days now while I could.'

In spite of counselling the sick and the dying for years, Metin was suddenly lost for words. He felt both guilty for having suspected the man of something nebulous and also extremely uncomfortable in his presence.

There was yet another awkward pause, and then Cengiz Bey said, 'Well, I'll leave you in peace now, Imam Metin.'

Flustered, Metin said, 'I'm sorry. I'm sorry too that you've had a wasted journey.'

'I'm sorry your dad died,' Cengiz Bey said. 'I always thought that old Regep Bey might sort himself out one day. But . . .'

'Dad wasn't bad, just weak,' Metin said.

'Yes . . .'

'My mother has always been a snob,' Zeynep Tonguç said. 'Her grandfather worked at Yıldız Palace when he was a young man, and so Mother's always had a bit of a thing about royalty. You can imagine how delighted she was when she moved into the Kara Lale Yalı, the home of an actual princess!'

İkmen smiled. Zeynep Tonguç's mother sounded a bit like Mehmet Süleyman's mother – an ordinary girl who had married a prince, albeit a deposed one, and turned into a full-on royalist.

'So of course when my mother became obsessed with spiritualism, it was to Princess Fawzia that she turned,' she continued. 'But that wasn't the case on the night Deniz asked her stupid question.'

'You don't believe in spiritualism, Zeynep?' Suzan asked.

'Nonsense for the feeble minded,' she said without hesitation. 'And destructive. It frightened me as a young person. When Deniz died, I was as sure as Aylin was that the spirits had been involved. But then I grew up. I left home and have never been back. But I do want to help. I understand my mother told you that during that seance, the planchette made contact with the princess.'

'Yes.'

'Well, it – we, whatever – didn't,' she said. 'That night it was supposedly the spirit of our old nanny Aliki Xipias who came through. Although I'm fairly sure we children influenced that. Aliki was a funny, superstitious old thing, but our younger brother, Ateş, was devastated when she died. We all tried to comfort him, but what he really needed was more attention from Mother. I know I felt that if Aliki told Mother to spend more time with him, she would. I'd no idea it would go the way it did. Aliki was clearly in a playful mood when we contacted her, and didn't want to talk about Ateş at all. That was when Deniz decided to ask her damn-fool questions.'

'Do you know why?' İkmen asked.

'I haven't got a clue,' she said. 'Deniz was always a bit peculiar. She'd do things unexpectedly. Go out without telling anyone, suddenly announce she never intended to have children. In retro-spect, I imagine she was seeking attention. Our parents weren't what you'd call naturally nurturing. I think Mother got over Deniz's death more quickly than any of us.'

'Why do you think your mother said that the princess and not Aliki came through that night?' İkmen asked.

'I don't know,' Zeynep said. 'But I can speculate. Now that Mother doesn't believe any more, she finds the whole idea of contacting an old servant distasteful. I mean, anyone can try and contact a princess because that is really quite interesting, even if it is nonsense. As I told you, she's a snob.'

İkmen ate the last of what had been a really beautiful piece of barbecued lamb and then said, 'Your mother gave us an address and phone number for your elder brother Timur in Artvin. But I can't seem to get hold of him. I've left messages.'

She shook her head. 'Timur doesn't really maintain contact with the family. He fell out with our father just after Deniz died. Probably because he used Deniz's death as an excuse not to go back to the naval academy. That's what I think. I know he hated it there. He only went to please Father. But then again . . .' She shrugged. 'There were other issues between my father and Timur.'

'What?'

Zeynep Tonguç lit a cigarette. The sun was now beating fiercely down on the terrace outside the Four Seasons. İkmen poured himself another glass of sparkling water, glad not to be fasting.

Zeynep said, 'I'd rather not say, given my father's current situation.'

'Neither Çetin Bey nor myself will pass on anything you tell us,' Suzan said. 'We just want to get at the truth.'

'I know, but . . .'

'If this is anything to do with your father's personal life, we will certainly keep that quiet,' İkmen said. 'I am one of the last people to want to endanger a man I feel has not been treated fairly.'

Zeynep thought about it for a few moments. İkmen knew it was hard for her to speak candidly given her father's imprisonment. Lurid stories, most so wild they couldn't possibly be true, were already circulating about Admiral Tonguç. The last thing the family needed was more of them.

She cleared her throat. 'Timur told me he thought Father had a mistress,' she said. 'I don't know how he knew that. I never asked him, because I didn't believe him. I still don't.'

'Do any of your siblings believe it?'

'I didn't tell Aylin. It would've upset her too much. I told Ateş. He just laughed. Couldn't understand why anyone apart from our mother would find Father attractive. I don't know why Timur said what he did, but it was just before he left home and he was absolutely mad to get away.'

'Why do you think that was?' İkmen asked.

She shrugged. 'He wasn't what Father wanted him to be at all. Rather than be in the military, Timur wanted to have free love, drop out and "find himself". You have to understand that although our mother was flaky, our father indulged and pampered her. But he wasn't like that with us. His children were required to conform to the highest moral and behavioural standards. We were drilled like soldiers, and if we failed to live up to his standards, he beat us. Between our mother's woolly-headedness and Father's discipline, there was only Aliki, our nanny, and she indulged us, especially the boys. They could do exactly as they pleased. I remember being quite jealous at the time. But we all enjoyed her stories.'

'What were they about?'

Zeynep smiled. 'She was so very Greek,' she said. 'Stories from the *Odyssey* and the *Iliad*; heretical tales, to Turks, about once and future Byzantine emperors. The one that both frightened and fascinated me was the Ferry of the Dead. A twist on the Greek myth of the land of the dead and the ferryman and all that, but for Turks. Every year on the Night of Power at the end of Ramazan, a ferry will cross the Bosphorus from Europe to Asia carrying those souls of the dead who have unfinished business with the living. God, that used to terrify me! Every year on Kadir Gecesi when I should have been eating too much and having fun, I was with my sister in her bedroom, terrified.'

'Which sister?' İkmen asked.

'Aylin,' she said. 'And she's still hiding.'

'From the Ferry of the Dead?'

'Don't try to make sense of it,' Zeynep said. 'Because Deniz is dead, and Aylin is doomed to be next, she's somehow decided that this Ferry of the Dead will be the cause of her demise. She is mad. There's no getting away from it. She needs help. She always has.'

İkmen said, 'When you found Deniz, you and your sister were together?'

'Yes,' she said. 'We'd been eating chocolate cake and so when we got home we had to wash ourselves before Mother got in. Then we went out into the garden.'

'Together?'

She thought for a moment and then said, 'Actually Aylin left the bathroom before me. I needed to use the lavatory.'

'So Aylin found Deniz before you?'

'Only a minute or so before, but yes, I suppose so,' she said. 'She was screaming.'

'It's an interesting angle,' Kerim Gürsel said.

Now back at headquarters, Ömer Mungun had joined Kerim in his office for a furtive glass of tea.

'Serkan Asal clearly hates Tayfun Yıldırım because he turned him out of his house,' Ömer said. 'But I don't think he'd lie. I think that if he says he saw Yıldırım go into that house with various attractive young women, it probably happened. What I'm not saying is that that is what happened at your crime scene in Kanlica. But I just thought – young woman, well dressed, empty building . . .'

'You may be right,' Kerim said. 'I appreciate it. I know you've got quite enough on with the death of that Syrian woman over in Tarlabaşı.'

Ömer smiled. 'Do you know who owns that yalı?'

'The Fındık Yali? Yes,' Kerim said. 'The family who've always owned it.'

'But it's a wreck!'

'Which they can't afford to repair. The holder of the title deed is a man called Abdülmecid Killigil. He's your typical, although now almost extinct, impoverished aristocrat. Related to someone from the Ottoman Empire, he lives in Kadıköy in a small apartment with his wife. Like most us, he just wants to make next month's rent.'

'So why doesn't he sell the yalı?' Ömer said. 'I know it's a wreck, but nobody cares about that. The land is what's valuable.'

'Yes, I know. But Mr Killigil seems to believe that if he holds on to it for just a little bit longer, he'll get more money for it. He's probably been saying that for years. Truth is, he doesn't want to break with his past.'

Ömer shook his head. He knew that Mehmet Süleyman's mother was in much the same situation, except that she still lived in her ancient unkempt villa.

'He's had offers,' Kerim continued. 'Although none from Tayfun Yıldırım. Or rather, he didn't mention him.'

Ömer sighed.

'Bit of a breakthrough on the victim, though,' Kerim said. 'Twenty-nine years old, originally from Rize. Came here to become a model, according to her landlady. Name of Fatima Akopoğlu. Her brother is on his way here from some village in the middle of nowhere.' He shook his head. 'Speaks with a very strange accent. Didn't make it easy finding the right moment to tell him his sister was dead.'

Çetin İkmen got a tram down to Kadıköy and then rode the Tünel funicular railway up to Beyoğlu. Unlike Sultanahmet, where most people were fasting, Beyoğlu was very much open for business, with modern coffee shops vying for trade with small, traditional lokantas and büfes. There was a smell of cooking meat in the air, and some of the faces of those simply strolling and not eating or drinking looked strained. Only two more days remained before Kadir Gecesi, and people were becoming desperate to celebrate the end of what had been an arduous Ramazan in the humid midsummer heat.

But even if his stomach hadn't been full of Four Seasons barbecued lamb, İkmen hadn't come to Beyoğlu to eat. Turning right out of Tünel, he made his way on to Galip Dede Caddesi and into an unfashionably down-at-heel coffee shop called the Kervansaray. He'd been there before, not for the coffee, which was good but not *that* good, nor for the fact that the depressed-looking man behind the counter let people smoke, although that helped. No, he was there for Büket Teyze.

He'd first heard about Büket Teyze from İrini Mavroyeni, a Greek alcoholic who had been involved in his last case on the force. He'd been having difficulty knowing where he was going amid a welter of competing evidence and so İrini had suggested he consult a falcı or fortune-teller. And because his mother had practised that very art, he had given it a go, which was how he'd ended up in the Kervansaray.

As usual, he had to wait. Büket Teyze was not a young woman and probably needed her rest, particularly if she was fasting – although he strongly suspected she wasn't. She was probably having a little rakı brightener.

İkmen had smoked two cigarettes and finished his coffee when she came out from behind a tattered curtain. When she saw him, she smiled. 'Çetin Bey.'

He stood up and bowed. 'Büket Teyze,' he said. 'I find myself in need of your help once again.'

'Oh no, not my help,' she said. 'You need the help of the dead.'

She was hugely overweight and everything about her appearance was fake – hair, eyelashes, jewellery, silk scarves . . . And yet because of what she did, Büket Teyze epitomised the ordinariness of magic. Like his mother, like the djinn, like the way he sometimes just *knew*, Büket was part of that thin ribbon that threaded its way through most people's lives completely unrecognised.

She turned his cup over, pointed the handle towards his chest and looked. The grounds on the right-hand side showed the present; the left, the future. She murmured, 'I am sorry for your loss.'

'Thank you.'

He let her peer at his present and his future in silence. Word travelled fast in the mega-city made up of a thousand villages. He knew that. But he also knew she didn't necessarily need the İstanbul grapevine.

She said nothing, and he waited. Then she put a fat hand into the grubby patchwork bag she kept on the chair beside her and pulled out a tarot card. 'This,' she said, 'is yours.'

İkmen took it. The Six of Swords, it depicted a woman and a child, backs turned, on a small boat along with six silver swords. A man, his back also turned, was pushing the boat along using a pole. İkmen looked up at Büket Teyze.

'You're grieving,' she said. 'But your life is not static any more.'

The owner of the café, unbidden, brought them both cups of coffee.

Büket Teyze cleared her throat. 'The Ferry of the Dead.' She tapped the card with one long red fingernail. 'Goes from Beşiktaş to Moda at midnight on Kadir Gecesi.'

İkmen shook his head in shock. 'There is no ferry stage at Moda, it's closed.'

She lit a cigarette and then offered him one, which he took.

'Look, love,' she said, 'when you're dead, those things don't matter. You're looking for answers and the Ferry may provide some. It may not. But it's where you need to be.'

'How do you know about the Ferry?' he asked.

She looked at him as if he were mad. 'How? How do I know the yalı of Admiral Tonguç is haunted by his children's nanny? I just know,' she said. 'Don't ask foolish questions. It's unworthy of you and of your poor mother.'

He felt cold. This was his world, as it had been his mother's, but it provided no comfort. He said, 'How will I know I've got the right ferry?'

'Oh, you'll know,' she said. 'Just like you'll know when to get off.' She whipped the tarot card out of his hand and put it back in her bag. 'That'll be ten lira,' she said.

Chapter 10

He'd remembered the policeman's name had been Inspector Süleyman. He'd been in plain clothes, had been a mature man, and so Imam Metin felt that he probably wasn't some ordinary beat cop. He'd also been confident, arrogant even – he'd certainly given Selçuk a drubbing when he'd hit that beer-drinking man – and that was why Metin had decided to go straight to police headquarters. He probably had some high-ranking job, so where else would he be? If anyone could help Metin find out about Cengiz Bey, it had to be someone clever, like Süleyman, or so he felt. At the very least he might be able to allay his fears, which were not inconsiderable. Metin felt guilty for thinking that Cengiz Bey was lying when he said he had cancer. But he couldn't help it. He just didn't believe him. And if he didn't believe him about that, then what else was the man lying about? And why?

Predictably, the front-office staff had known Inspector Süleyman. Some very young officer in uniform had told Metin to wait, and so he had. But that had been hours ago. Looking at the Directorate of Security's website on his computer had given him the impression that things tended to move rather more rapidly than they had in the past, but official delay still seemed to be the order of the day. And it was Ramazan.

Back in the old days, before mobile phones and the Internet, neighbours had looked out for each other in İstanbul. Often the reason for this was nosiness, but it was also to do with caring about one's neighbourhood or mahalle. But had that always applied in the more upscale districts?

Çetin İkmen had never lived anywhere posh, and although buying property in Sultanahmet was now something that only millionaires did, he didn't and couldn't relate to any of his new well-heeled neighbours. He lived in an expensive apartment by default.

Bebek, however, had always been exclusive. When İkmen had been a child, the yalıs had been lived in by mainly middle-class secular types, with a small smattering of old Ottomans. Generals, doctors and lawyers made up much of the population. The Tonguç family had been typical. But who had been their neighbours? And who, if anyone, had noticed that blood-soaked body in the garden back in August 1976?

When the Tonguçs had sold up, they'd had no servants. The names Halide Tonguç had given İkmen of previous retainers had drawn a blank. But the issue of the neighbours had not come into his consciousness until now. And that only happened because he saw one. He waved to her, expecting the elderly lady to be somewhat appalled, but instead she said, 'Hello, are you the new owner of the Kara Lale Yali?'

'No,' he said. 'I'm helping a friend do some research on the place.'

'Oh,' she said. 'Then maybe I can help. I've lived here for years. My name is Berfu Hanım.'

İkmen bowed. 'Çetin İkmen. May I come over?'

'Please do,' she said.

Once she'd settled İkmen down with tea and cakes at her garden dining table, Berfu Hanım said, 'Admiral Tonguç had a wonderful little garden back in the seventies. Palm trees, a lovely fountain. Quite enclosed, but then we liked our privacy back then. And the admiral had a lot of power.' She looked down at the floor. 'Not as it is today . . .'

113

Eighty-five years old, she'd lived in the house next door to the Tonguçs for sixty years. İkmen thought she looked not unlike a tiny songbird.

'All I can recall about that awful day is when the police arrived,' she said when he asked her about Deniz's death. 'Rauf Bey had just come home from his business in Taksim and he was very clear that we should not stare. I remember him telling the girls.'

'Your daughters?'

'No.' She smiled. 'Rauf Bey and I were never lucky enough to have children. No, the servants. We had two, they worked mainly in the kitchen.'

'Do you know whether they saw anything?'

'Oh, I doubt it,' she said. 'They were just village girls. I read later that when Deniz Tonguç was found, she was wearing a bikini. I think our girls would have said something about that, had they seen it. They would have been shocked. We moved in different circles to the Tonguç family. They were more privileged and modern than we were.'

'Military service attracted huge benefits back in those days,' İkmen said.

'Oh, indeed! Fine salaries, excellent social facilities. But then quite right for protecting the fatherland from all the madness that has come back again in this part of the world.'

An old Atatürkist, İkmen felt that of course she would have been in awe of Alaaddin Tonguç. That was how it had been back then, when the Turks loved their soldiers.

'I didn't know the Tonguçs well,' Berfu Hanım said. 'Although they did invite Rauf Bey and myself to Deniz's wedding. It took place in the Kara Lale Yalı. Beautiful. Tasteful too, classical European music and not a headscarf to be seen.' She sighed. 'Mind you, those boys of theirs were not well behaved. The little one, Ateş, just ran about everywhere, knocking people's drinks

114

over. Timur was his usual moody self, although I have to say he looked lovely in his uniform. The little girls – the poor things found their sister dead, you know – they were sweet. One of them, I can't remember which, clung on to Deniz's arm, all the time looking at her new husband with stars in her eyes. Teenagers are such funny little creatures!'

'Berfu Hanım,' İkmen said, 'do you remember anyone coming to the Tonguç house earlier in the day that she died.'

'I'm afraid I don't,' she said. 'Back in those days, when Rauf Bey was alive, I would first go shopping, then meet him for lunch in Beyoğlu. Then I'd go and play bridge at the Pera Palas. It was a lovely time for me, the seventies. I know there was political trouble, but at least our eyes were still set on the West back then.' She smiled, and with no sense of irony at all said, 'Have you seen Aliki Xipias's ghost, by the way?'

Suzan put her phone in her pocket and ran out into the garden. Çetin Bey had been smoking outside, but now he was nowhere to be seen. His car was still there, so he hadn't left the district. What was he doing? She called out, but no one answered. Where was the man?

In spite of leaving messages for days, Aylin Tonguç had failed to get back to Suzan about whether she would meet İkmen. Then suddenly, five minutes ago, she'd rung to say that if they could come now, she would see them.

But now İkmen had wandered off.

The girl, Rosarita, could only talk to Ömer Mungun. Although she and her mother had left their home in Syria in 2013, the little girl hadn't learned any new languages along the way. Their home, the Christian town of Maaloula, was one of the last Aramaic-speaking places in the country. It had been devastated by the militant Al-Nusra Front and then rebuilt by Syrian government forces since the family had left. Ömer hadn't managed to find out where they had been, but a voyage by sea had been one of the features of their travels. Rosarita's father, it seemed, was currently fighting alongside the Kurdish forces of the YPG. It was well known that there were some Christians in their ranks. It was also Turkish government policy to oppose the YPG, whom they viewed as terrorists.

Alone in his office, Mehmet Süleyman thought about what the child might have witnessed in three and a half years on the road. What had her mother had to do to survive? And how had the child managed to slip into the house in Tarlabaşı unnoticed? The obvious answer was that everyone in that house was either on something or drunk and wrapped up in their own affairs. Surviving as an intravenous drug-user, even in Tarlabaşı, was a full-time job. You had to get money to buy your gear, take it, get high, come down and go out again to get money for more. There was no time for anything else, *and* your natural habitat was under threat, which had to be worrying.

Almost an entire terrace across the road from the three houses supposedly owned by Haluk Andıç had collapsed, and the developers were already clearing the site and putting in footings. If the new properties were constructed as quickly as those in some other parts of the city, they'd be ready for sale in a matter of months. Andıç's properties, two of which were already empty, could all soon be vacant if some of the residents took flight after the murder. Then the whole lot could fall down, or be encouraged to do so. But that wasn't Süleyman's concern. Or was it?

Forensics so far had been copious. Samples taken from the woman's corpse, prints and fibres from the crime scene – many of which could be explained. The kapıcı had gone into the room when he broke the door down because of the flood; he'd also presumably been inside when he rented the room. There were prints from the woman, the girl; some of the other women in

116

the house had touched the outside surface of the door. Some prints were as yet unknown . . . What there wasn't a lot of was paperwork, but then that was standard for a place like that.

Checking to make sure his office door was closed, Süleyman lit a cigarette and leaned back in his chair. The cleric who'd helped him to restrain some religious nutcase in the street a week ago had come to see him about something, but he really couldn't get his head together enough to care. He'd see him in the fullness of time, but at the moment he wanted to think about the real owners of the house on Kalyoncu Kulluğu Caddesi: Tayfun Yıldırım and an Armenian family called Khachaturian.

An official from Beyoğlu council had told him that the house had been bought by and lived in by a man called Mesrob Bey, family name Khachaturian, in 1900. As far as they were concerned, the family still owned it. This was not uncommon in Tarlabaşı, which had once been a largely Greek and Armenian enclave. But what did it mean in terms of Süleyman's victim? Possibly nothing. And yet what Kerim Gürsel had discovered about Yıldırım's illicit sexual activities over in Üsküdar was troubling. What if Yıldırım himself had come to the house on Kalyoncu Kulluğu, seen the woman, then raped and killed her?

Would anyone have seen him, and if they had, would they tell? Was it possible that Yıldırım was diabetic? He'd have to ask Çetin İkmen if he knew or could find out from Yıldırım's niece.

'He called himself Cengiz Bey,' the imam said.

Süleyman looked up at him. 'Surname?'

'Either he didn't say or I didn't hear it,' Metin Demir said. 'He told me he'd been in Maltepe prison with my father.'

'Really?'

The imam shrugged. 'Oh, but it has to be said. My father, Regep Demir, was a thief. He specialised in breaking into people's

117

houses and taking small items like watches and jewellery, although he'd also take cash and later credit cards. Sadly for him, and luckily for you, he wasn't very good at it and was sent to Maltepe five times between 1970 and 1999, when he died.'

'And you don't think this Cengiz Bey was genuine?'

'Although whenever Dad was in prison I lived elsewhere, he always took me back when he got out,' Metin said. 'So I got to know his old friends. Most of them had been inside; many of them were also unemployed and often drunk. This Cengiz Bey didn't look at all like any of them. Really well dressed and fit looking. He said that last time he'd got out he'd gone to the country and made a healthier life there, and he may well have done so. But then he told me he was dying, and I felt sorry for him, of course, but also manipulated. I don't know whether he's really dying or not. He may be, but . . . I just have a bad feeling about this.'

The only reason Süleyman had deigned to see this cleric was because Metin Demir had helped him contain an incident in the street involving a religious zealot and a man with a bottle of beer. Why on earth had he asked for Süleyman by name? Probably because it was the only name the imam knew. But this, his problem, was so . . . paltry. And Süleyman was waiting for İkmen to call him back about whether Tayfun Yıldırım was diabetic.

'He was asking around the mahalle about Dad,' the imam continued. 'People told me and so I went to speak to him, which was when he told me his name and how he'd known my father. He said he couldn't remember where we lived, which may be true. He wanted me to tell him, but I didn't.'

'Do you think he may have wanted to rob you? Or extort money?'

'If he *is* one of Dad's old friends, then yes, he might, and if he isn't, what does he want? As far as I'm aware, Dad never hid any money or valuables anywhere. He left me a few sad objects, which I think probably once belonged to other people,

118

but I don't suppose they're worth anything. Then there's his watch, and the house. My mother left us when I was a child. Dad could be violent to women. I'm sorry, you probably think this is trivial, but I didn't know what else to do. I don't know any policemen, and although my friend Selçuk behaved very badly when you met him, I felt that you were as fair as anyone could be under the circumstances.'

In reality, Süleyman had wanted to hit Selçuk, but he didn't say anything.

'So here I am. Sort of insurance, I guess, in case I get attacked or robbed.' The imam laughed nervously.

Süleyman's phone beeped to say he had a text message.

Where the imam lived, in Karayolları mahalle in Gaziosmanpaşa, wasn't the safest area of the city. Süleyman knew it well. There were a lot of religious tensions around there, mainly centred on the Alevi community. There were also a lot of young people, specifically and particularly young men. Not that the mysterious Cengiz Bey was young, by the sound of him. The imam, a tailor by trade, was around forty, and so this man, if he'd known his father, had to be in his sixties. But Süleyman didn't have time for something as trivial as a shady man hanging around in a shady district looking for an old lag.

He smiled. 'I will make a note of what you've told me in case anything happens. Things like this rarely come to anything.'

When he left, the imam appeared to be satisfied. Süleyman looked at his phone. The text was from Çetin İkmen: *Suzan says Yıldırım is not diabetic.*

And so that was that.

'You don't see a lot of smack round here these days. It's all that fucking bonzai,' Güneş Sağlam said. 'Same effect, though, they still walk around like zombies. Mind you, they're not all shooting up in the streets.'

119

Bonzai, the synthetic cannabis substitute that had taken hold of so many people in the poorer parts of İstanbul, was smoked rather than injected. It was easier and cheaper to obtain than heroin and, addicts reported, had much the same effect. Although bonzai was more likely to make users vomit. And it was rarely used by dyed-in-the-wool heroin addicts.

'But you do have heroin users in your building,' Ömer Mungun said.

'Oh yes,' Güneş agreed. She lowered her voice. 'This won't . . .'

'We're not interested in arresting drug-users, Güneş Hanım,' Ömer said. 'The murder of the Syrian woman is all we care about.'

Güneş looked around to see whether anyone was listening. Sitting in a bar on Nevizade Sokak, she was away from her usual Tarlabaşı stomping ground. But she was still afraid, even though Ömer had been plying her with beer for half an hour.

She said, 'There's him in the basement, with the Armenian name.'

Ömer frowned. 'Armenian name?'

'Branko,' she said. 'His surname's Armenian. Trust me, my dad came from the Black Sea, and I know. Anyway, he uses. There's a little tart on the top floor does. She only came a few weeks ago. I've found her shooting up in the toilet.' She took a swig of Efes. 'Kanat, that's the little rent boy who comes and goes depending on whether he's got a sugar daddy or not, he dabbles. Oh, and of course there's Numan Bey, the old man who lives on the first floor opposite Ali Bey. I've no idea how old he is, but he's been living in the house for years. Longer than me, and I've been in that shithole for ten years. He uses.'

They'd taken statements from everyone who lived in that house – twenty-one in all. Ömer had a dim recollection of a man with long hair who apparently practised yoga.

'People say he was English originally,' Güneş continued. 'I don't know. But he's been on the gear for ever.'

120

The person Rosarita had seen injecting into his leg had been a man. That was all she knew. She hadn't seen his face and couldn't remember anything about his clothes except that he had been wearing boots. But this person, after injecting, had gone on almost immediately to rape and then kill her mother. And although Ömer knew that the child wasn't lying – he'd gained her trust and she spoke freely to him now – he also knew that he couldn't square the act of rape with someone who had just shot himself up. Junkies didn't work that way. The hit relaxed them, taking away all other desires. Had Rosarita maybe got her timings wrong? Had the man and the girl's mother both shot up and then had sex some time later? Or had the assailant been diabetic? But if so, why inject before sex? Surely they injected before food?

Çetin İkmen didn't wear glasses very often. He hated the way they made him look as if his face was disappearing behind them. But he needed them in this gloomy apartment. He needed them to see the tiny, pinched features of the woman they were visiting.

'I went to hospital,' Aylin Tonguç said in answer to his question about what she did after her sister's death. 'In Switzerland.'

Of course, back in the day there was no way someone like Admiral Tonguç would have sent his daughter to Bakırköy psychiatric hospital. That would have been embarrassing.

'They gave me a lot of pills, but then I had to come home and live here with Grandmama. My father's mother. She's dead now.'

'And you've been here, on your own, ever since?'

'I have a girl,' she said. 'She works in the kitchen and does the shopping. I've always had a girl. I can't manage alone.'

İkmen wondered whether the girl who had let him in had a name, and if she did, whether Aylin Hanım knew it.

'I know my family think I'm crazy,' Aylin said. 'They don't visit because they don't want to hear what I'm thinking or feeling. But I can't stop it and I can't help it.'

'My understanding is that you fear you will die.'

'All the time,' she said. 'I can think of nothing else. Zeynep laughs at me. But you would have to have been there to appreciate it.'

'At the seance?'

'The message was very clear.'

'From Princess Fawzia?' He wanted to know whether Aylin would perpetuate her mother's story or side with her siblings.

'No,' she said. 'Aliki, our nanny. I know Mother has always told people otherwise, but it's not true. No princess came through. But Aliki did, and she told us our fate.'

'You believe that?'

She sighed. 'There are things in this world that don't comply with modern values,' she said. 'We ignore them at our peril.'

'Like the Ferry of the Dead?'

Even through the gloom he could see her face blanch. 'How do you know about that?'

'I know you were told about it by Aliki,' he said. He'd decided not to tell her he was going to look for it.

She gazed into the distance. 'It will come tomorrow night.'

'It may.'

She looked up. 'It will.'

'And so it will come.'

'For me,' she said. She was shaking.

İkmen leaned forward. 'It hasn't come for you so far.'

'But it will!' she said.

He could have offered her more sympathy, but he chose to ignore her. He still had more questions. 'Aylin Hanım,' he said, 'do you remember what happened on the day Deniz died? You and Zeynep found her.'

She twisted a handkerchief between her fingers. 'Zeynep went to touch her . . .'

'Did Zeynep see Deniz before you?'

'No.' She looked up. 'We found her together. We washed our dresses in the bathroom because we had cake on them, and then we went down to the garden.'

'Together?'

'Together.'

This did not reflect what Zeynep had told him. But then crime-scene accounts, even from recent times, were notoriously subject to inaccuracies. And this was underlined by what Aylin said next.

'You know my sister Zeynep was a little in love with Mustafa Ermis, Deniz's husband, don't you?' she said. 'When she found Deniz's body, she just stared at it as if she didn't care.'

Aylin started to cry, and Suzan went over to comfort her. But in reality, there was no way to make her fear and the horror that had become her life go away. She'd had a terrible experience when she was little more than a child, and it had consumed her. It was therefore easy, İkmen felt, to slip into the notion that it was Aylin and not Zeynep who was telling the truth about the events of that day and who had lusted over Mustafa Ermis. He reminded himself to be wary.

'I thought you were finished,' the old man said.

Süleyman looked down at him. 'No.'

Ali Ok turned his attention to Ömer Mungun, who appeared more sympathetic. 'Eh?'

Ömer said nothing.

'I don't have to tell you why I'm here,' Süleyman said. He pushed past the old man and walked into the house with Ömer Mungun in tow.

He remembered talking to an elderly man with a slightly odd

accent, and when Numan Osman came to the door of his room, he recognised him immediately. The man had a thick white beard that was almost as long as his hair, which reached down to the middle of his back. He wore a multicoloured shirt and khaki shorts. His legs were stick-thin and he had sores on his wrists and ankles. He was very obviously a user.

'Mr Osman, we have a few more questions,' Süleyman said.

He shrugged. 'Come in.'

His room, which was bigger than most, was dominated by a large and very tattered poster of Che Guevara, an unmade bed and a selection of bongs scattered across the floor.

Süleyman and Ömer Mungun went inside.

'As I told you when I interviewed you before,' Süleyman said, 'I'm not here about your drug use, but about the murder of the woman upstairs.'

'Yeah, that was bad. How's it going?' Osman flopped down on his bed like a teenager, leaving his guests standing.

Süleyman said, 'We've reason to believe that the woman's killer was a man who uses intravenous drugs.'

'How d'you know that? You got blood or something?'

'I'm not at liberty to say.'

'So you thought of me,' the old man said. He sighed. 'Listen, like I told you at the time, I was here, and in the spirit of full disclosure, I was alone and off my face. I've no alibi, but if you want me to give you a blood sample, or semen – I'm guessing the poor lady had sex with this character – I will. I'll do it now if you want. I mean, I get your problem.'

'My problem?'

'Well, there's a few of us in this house, and even though I'm ancient, I'm probably your best bet,' he said.

'What do you mean?'

'Well, Branko downstairs uses – I know you know that because he told me. But he was at his mum's when it happened. The only other man in that particular frame is the rent boy upstairs, and it's not likely to be him.'

That was precisely what Süleyman himself had thought when Ömer had told him about his conversation with Güneş Hanım.

'Women come and go all the time,' Osman continued. 'It's got worse in recent years with all the Syrians. But then how else are they supposed to make money? I'm not judging. Their customers come and go too. To be honest with you, there are people in and out of here all the time. Your killer could have come, done what he did, and left, and no one would even know. There's a lot to be said for hearing, seeing and speaking no evil.'

'I'm aware of that,' Süleyman said.

'I know I'm a hopeless case,' Numan said. 'I'm a junkie. That's why my marriage failed, why my kids won't see me and why I can't go home to my own country.'

Ömer Mungun said, 'Are you British, Numan Bey?'

'I was,' he said. 'I was studying to be a doctor in London until I decided to go to India and find myself in 1972. I got as far as İstanbul, where I fell in love with a local woman and, sadly, heroin. That was that. This city eats you up, as I'm sure you both know. Everyone knows everyone, but no one knows anybody. You know these buildings are very valuable now, not as they are, but for the land they're built on. A lot of bad people come into this area, and I don't mean people like me. I mean the straight ones, in the suits, with the nice neat beards.'

125

Chapter 11

'Darling!'

Suzan was glad to see her aunt Nalan, less so her uncle Tayfun. Wrapped in her aunt's considerable arms, she looked at Yıldırım and said, 'I thought you were out of town.'

He shrugged. 'I came back.'

They'd turned up at the Kara Lale Yalı just as Suzan was about to go home to Galata.

'So what have you found?' Aunt Nalan said. 'Now I have been looking for one of those traditional dark-wood Ottoman beds for years. You know the kind I mean? With the carved headboard and footboard? I've been meaning to ask you, dear . . .'

Suzan felt embarrassed. There was a bed like that in the yalı, the Tonguçs' own bed. She said, 'There is one here, but it belonged to Admiral Tonguç and his wife.'

'Belonged, yes,' Yıldırım said. 'Now it's mine.'

For a moment, her aunt looked stunned, and then she laughed. 'Well, maybe not . . .'

'Why not?' her husband asked. 'When I buy something, it becomes mine. You are my wife and so such things belong to you too.'

He walked into the yalı, mobile phone in hand.

Aunt Nalan took Suzan's arm. 'I know he seems agitated, but really he is being very patient with all this,' she said.

'All what?'

'You looking into this house.'

'He said I could!'

'Yes, of course he did.' Nalan smiled. 'I'm just trying to explain his bad mood.'

Why? As far as Suzan was concerned, Yıldırım was always in a bad mood.

'He's having trouble with his business partners,' her aunt said. 'He was in Antalya, on business, when it all happened. They want more money from him or something, I don't know. But he had to come back. They're foreigners.'

It was a dump, but Filiz needed the money and whoever she'd come to see needed the anonymity. Or the filth? Some men liked degradation. She kicked a couple of used condoms into a corner and leaned against the wall. Were she a superstitious girl, she might have been frightened. But she wasn't. She was beautiful, clever, on the verge of making it in modelling, and one day she was going to be rich. She didn't really like making her rent like this, but what else could she do?

The man, when he arrived, wasn't anyone she recognised from the television. But he was smartly dressed and slim, even if he was probably well past sixty. He did have a beard, but not a great big straggly thing; it was nice and neat. He was embarrassed. Filiz hoped he wouldn't say 'I don't usually do this.'

But he didn't. Filiz smiled and so did he, and then he gave her an envelope and squeezed her breast. She opened the envelope and counted the money.

It was only after that happened that Filiz and her client were placed under arrest. Kerim Gürsel and his colleagues had been required to be patient until money actually changed hands. That way, there could be no misunderstanding about what the couple had been about to do in the Findik Yali in Kanlica where, less than a week before, the body of Fatima Akopoğlu, another wannabe model, had been discovered.

'Will you be there tomorrow night?' İkmen asked. 'On the Ferry of the Dead? Or are you doomed to be here with the djinn in the kitchen for all time?'

In the early-evening light his wife was almost transparent.

'Bülent calls it "Tarkan", you know, the djinn,' he continued. 'After that singer you always found a bit suggestive. He can see you, Bülent. He just chooses to do so from a distance. Çiçek had another interview today, but I don't know how she got on.'

He lit a cigarette. 'I know, not yet sunset,' he said. 'But what can you do? I'm a sinner.' He looked out on to Divanyolu, at the tourists strolling, the carpet dealers scuttling, the police watching.

'There's something missing from this Deniz Tonguç story. One maybe quite small element that I need to unlock. I've still not met the elder son, Timur. I don't know whether that would help or not. It was Timur who claimed his father was having an affair back in the seventies. Then there are the sisters, Zeynep and Aylin, with different accounts of what happened when they found Deniz's body. Aylin had a bit of a thing about Deniz's husband . . . As for the father, I can't exactly get to speak to Alaaddin Tonguç myself, can I? Where he is . . . well, buried alive was how one old thief I used to know described prison. What I do know is that Deniz Tonguç didn't kill herself. But like Arto, I can't make up my mind whether old Dr Sağlam was being leaned on to call suicide for some reason or whether he was just negligent. He was a terrible drunk.'

He leaned back in his chair and sighed. 'I know I need to try and get some time with Deniz's ex-husband, Mustafa Ermis, but he doesn't return my calls. No reason why he should, I suppose.

But if that were me, I think I'd want to know how someone I once loved died. The Tonguç family, you know, I feel they've never been really happy. I think we forget sometimes these days that when the military held so much power, life was restricted, as much for them as for us, in some ways.'

A place that was both a booming mega-city and a village at the same time might seem to be a contradiction in terms. But Arto Sarkissian knew that in the case of İstanbul, that was the only way to really catch the soul of the place. He was always bumping into people he knew in the most unlikely and often populous places.

On this occasion, he was strolling amongst the food tents erected in Sultanahmet Square for the nightly İftar. The sun had set some time ago and so people were sitting around tables drinking tea, smoking and checking their mobile phones. He didn't pay anyone too much attention until a man, probably in his fifties, who was vaguely familiar walked up to him and said, 'Dr Sarkissian?'

'Yes?'

The man bowed slightly, hand on heart. A movement typical of Muslims who preferred not to use the Western handshake.

'Hüseyin Sağlam,' he said. 'You actually called me recently. I'm sorry I didn't get back to you, I've been very busy.'

Arto smiled. Of course. He looked like a younger version of his father on those few occasions when he wasn't drunk.

'No problem.'

Hüseyin looked a little embarrassed. 'I've just celebrated İftar.'

'Of course.'

Multicoloured light from the many booths selling food, drink and children's toys splashed across Hüseyin Sağlam's face, making him look at once green, yellow and blue. Weirdly, he took Arto's arm.

'Come and have tea with me,' he said.

Once they had both sat down with their drinks, Hüseyin said, 'A man like me has to be careful. When you attain a certain position in any political organisation, you make yourself a potential target for those who disagree with that party.'

'Your politics are irrelevant to me,' Arto replied. 'I don't belong to any political organisation. The only reason I contacted you was to try and find out what, if anything, you remember about your father's involvement in the Deniz Tonguç affair.'

Talking to Hüseyin Sağlam made Arto very glad he wasn't active politically. If a simple request to discuss an incident long ago involving his father made the man anxious, he dreaded to think how something that affected him personally would make him feel.

'If it helps, I always liked your father,' Arto said. 'When I returned from university in London, he was very good to me.'

'You know he was a . . . He had problems.'

'He had a drink problem. It's a disease,' Arto said. 'Pretending alcohol doesn't exist doesn't help. Your father was a good man, but on this particular PM he messed up and I want to know why.'

Hüseyin Sağlam shook his head. 'I don't know.'

'But you remember the girl?'

'Oh yes,' he said. 'A suicide.'

'Except that it wasn't,' Arto said.

They were sitting away from the main area of revelry, at a table in the open air on the edge of the Hippodrome. Birds, lit up by the lights from the food booths and the mosques, wheeled above their heads like white handkerchiefs.

'I've read your father's report, looked at the photographs and talked it over with police officers. I'm sorry, Hüseyin Bey, but there is no way Deniz Tonguç killed herself. It's just not possible.'

Hüseyin Sağlam looked down at the ground.

'Your father was a good pathologist,' Arto continued, 'and so I think there are two possibilities. Firstly, that he was too drunk to know what he was doing, and secondly, that someone put him under pressure to deliver that result. You and I both know that the military were very powerful in this country back in the seventies, and Deniz's father was Admiral Tonguç, an extremely important man.'

'Yes, but what good would it have done Admiral Tonguç to have his daughter's death declared a suicide?'

'I don't know,' Arto said. 'Unless . . .' He wanted to say 'he killed her himself', but he didn't. 'I was never happy about military rule in this country and I don't, very deliberately, take any part in politics today. All I want to know is the truth about Deniz Tonguç's death. Your name will not be mentioned by me, you have my word.'

Hüseyin looked unsure. He fiddled with the spoon in his tea glass.

'Hüseyin Bey?'

He looked up. Then he sighed. 'Of course Dad was drunk,' he said. 'By that time he was always drunk. But I also know that he was under pressure.'

'Pressure from whom?'

'I don't know. He performed the PM as soon as he could.'

'Most of us do.'

'But . . . Look, this was a long time ago.'

'I know. One has to try, though.'

Hüseyin shook his head as if attempting to sift memories to the front of his mind. 'If I remember correctly, he said that they hassled him for the report.'

'They?'

'I don't know who. But I do know that he agonised over it, and that wasn't like him. What exactly he agonised over, and why, I don't know. Once the verdict was given, I never heard him speak of it again.'

'Do you know him?' Kerim Gürsel asked.

'No,' Süleyman said.

He was accustomed to the assumption that people who came from old Ottoman families all knew each other.

'Mr Killigil is not someone I have come across.'

The two men watched as a late-middle-aged man was led into one of the interview rooms by Kerim's sergeant, Elif Arslan.

'I have Ömer Bey to thank for this,' Kerim said. 'When he went over to Üsküdar and spoke to that bonzai addict about Tayfun Yıldırım, it got me thinking. Much as those who, let us say, are of a rather more conservative nature seek to limit the public's opportunities to sin, they also limit their own. Where better than a wrecked old house to have a bit of really dirty sex with a pretty young girl? Especially if the owner of the place is a like-minded individual who, for a small fee, will find you a girl and let you use his yalı.'

Süleyman shook his head. 'The girl told you all this?'

'Yes,' he said. 'Poor kid from the back of beyond trying to make it in the big city. I don't blame her.'

'And the client?'

'Local government official,' Kerim said. 'Covered wife, eight kids, pillar of the community. Doesn't make him the killer of Fatima Akopoğlu, of course. But Abdülmecid Killigil, the owner of the Yali, may know something.' He shook his head. 'What people will do for sex, eh?'

Süleyman smiled. He hadn't been with a woman for months and was beginning to feel sad and uncharacteristically agitated.

Kerim patted him on the shoulder. 'Amazing how sometimes these things just suddenly fall into place.'

* * *

132

'Your brother was a liar. He lied about your father because he wanted to hurt him.'

'Why?'

Halide Tonguç looked at her daughter with incredulity. 'Because he blamed him for putting him in the naval academy,' she said. 'How your father was supposed to know he wanted to leave, I don't know.'

Zeynep Tonguç had taken her mother to a small restaurant in Nişantaşı. Halide liked it there because it was quiet, tasteful and discreet. And it served alcohol during Ramazan.

'He used Deniz's death as an excuse to drop out,' Halide continued.

'So why accuse Daddy of infidelity if that was what he intended to do anyway?'

'Quite.'

Zeynep leaned across the table and lowered her voice. 'He said Daddy tried to bribe him to keep quiet.'

'I've told you, Timur lied,' Halide said. 'Your father never took a mistress, and even if he had, now is not the time to bring such a thing up. He has enough trouble . . .'

'I know you're lying to protect him,' Zeynep said. 'And I understand that.'

Halide shook her head. 'No. No!'

'Mama, do you know where Timur is? He never picks up.'

'No.'

'Look, I know you've kept in touch with him. I know you always have, even before Daddy was arrested.'

'He will deign to speak to me occasionally, yes,' Halide said. 'But don't forget he rejected all of us when he left home, and that included me. He was nowhere near the yalı when Deniz died.'

'So who was?' Zeynep said.

'That is what Dr Tan and the inspector intend to find out.'

133

Chapter 12

It had been in the 1970s when large numbers of Kurds first started to arrive in İstanbul from the east. They tended to move into districts depopulated by other groups of non-Turkish citizens – Greeks, Jews and Armenians. Tarlabaşı was one of these districts.

Ömer Mungun had been trying to follow up on Kerim Gürsel's research by looking for any more information about the Deniz Tonguç case for Çetin Bey. But then he'd come across a very detailed set of notes about a body that had been found in Tarlabaşı in 1979.

Written by an Inspector Altınbaş, the notes concerned the discovery of the body of a young Kurdish woman called Emine Doğan. Lately arrived from Anatolia, Emine had been sixteen, and married, when she had disappeared from her husband's family's apartment on Çatık Kaş Sokak in March 1977. Her decomposed body was found two years later in a disused cellar; identification had only been possible by the jewellery found on the corpse. She had died by strangulation, possibly via ligature, which was interesting given the investigation in which Ömer was currently involved. Her murder had never been solved. More chilling than that, however, was that her body had been found on Kalyoncu Kulluğu Caddesi.

Finally, his daughter Çiçek had a job. It was only a waitressing job at a cafe in Cihangir, but after being out of work for a year, to Çiçek it was like a blessing. Çetin İkmen left his apartment that morning walking on air. Now that his daughter was going to be earning again, she could, hopefully, start to rebuild her life.

Then he received a call from Ateş Tonguç.

'I spoke to my brother-in-law Mustafa for you, as I said I would,' Ateş said. 'But he didn't seem too keen to help. However, I am meeting him for coffee today at eleven.'

'So you'll ask him again?' İkmen said.

'No. But if you have some time around midday, he will speak to you.'

'He's changed his mind?'

'It would seem so, yes. I think he wants me to publish something he's written about tea. He's been threatening to do it for years. But anyway, look, I'm meeting him at the bar of the Büyük Londra. Why don't you come and join us at midday? Then I can leave you with him.'

'His name is Inspector Süleyman.'

Not so much as a flicker crossed Constable Kiliç's expressionless face.

'He works out of headquarters . . .' The imam's voice faded. What was the point?

Supposed to be a community-focused officer, Constable Kiliç was about as interested in the community as they were in him, which was not at all.

'You said yourself nothing's been stolen,' he said. 'I don't know what your problem is.'

Imam Metin Demir made himself calm down before he spoke. 'Someone has been in my house without my permission. I noticed it last night when I got home. The lock on my back door is broken. There . . .' He pointed. 'It's been forced.'

'Looks normal to me,' Kiliç said.

'But it's not normal,' the imam persisted. 'It's been forced. I didn't force it. Someone has been inside my house.'

Kiliç chewed the inside of his mouth. 'So what's this got to do with some inspector?' he said.

Metin could feel his blood pressure rising. He took a breath. 'I told Inspector Süleyman about a man called Cengiz Bey who turned up out of nowhere saying that he knew my father. I had no knowledge of this man and so I questioned his motives. I feared he might wish to do me harm in some way. Or steal from me.'

Kiliç shrugged.

'Inspector Süleyman told me to report any suspicious incidents to my local police, should such a thing happen, and so I have.'

There was a pause, and then Kiliç said, 'So you've reported it and I think it's nothing.'

The imam rolled his eyes. But Kiliç was unaffected.

'Look,' he said, 'if you're worried, report it to this Süleyman and have done with it. In this district, what do you expect? You're lucky whoever broke in didn't rip out your kidney to sell on to some diseased American.'

Metin sat down on his bed and watched the officer leave. Since when had Turkey become a country where people sold their organs? And yet he knew it happened. He shook his head. Even his father hadn't been that desperate.

Halide trembled. Even as she watched that tall, unbowed figure walk confidently towards her, she still feared for him. Her husband, Admiral Alaaddin Tonguç, was being held in solitary confinement, and although Halide knew, because he had told her, that he had not been tortured, there was still doubt in her mind. One heard stories, even if the prison was one of the quietest places she had ever experienced.

After walking through a metal detector and subjecting herself to a retinal scan, Halide had walked across an eerily silent concrete yard to this hot room and the sight of her husband standing between two guards. Where were the screams of pain? The faces of despair one always imagined haunting the periphery of prison complexes? The smug, cruel leers of the men who beat other men?

There had been nothing but politeness and silence. And that was terrifying.

Alaaddin sat on the far side of the table that would separate them and bowed his head.

'Halide.'

She wanted to touch him, but touching wasn't allowed.

'Alaaddin.'

She hadn't even known this visit had been approved until just before she'd left her sister's apartment in Karaköy. Her phone had rung to the sound of the Orthodox Christians in the church above singing without accompaniment. The terse official voice from the prison had contrasted sharply with the basso profundo tones of the Russian priest.

And then all the way out to Silivri she had wondered. Did she tell Alaaddin about this renewed interest in Deniz's death, or didn't she?

He'd spoken barely a word about his eldest daughter since her death. As soon as her body had been taken away for analysis, he had spent all his time pressurising the doctors for a result. It wasn't even as if he was religious. In Islam, a dead body was supposed to be buried within twenty-four hours of demise. Failure to do so might result in the soul of the dead experiencing pain. But Alaaddin had never believed such rubbish, as he'd always considered it. No.

At the time, Halide had wondered whether Deniz's death was so hard for him to bear that he just wanted the post-mortem done and out of the way as if it had never happened. His grief had been hot; she had been able to see it burning him up inside, but he'd never openly expressed it.

'I brought you some honey cake, but . . .' she began.

He nodded his head. They both knew the cake would be confiscated.

'How are our children?'

'The same,' she said. 'Ateş's business continues. He's taken to specialising in cookery books.'

This was a new departure for someone who had once published foreign novels.

'Good.'

'Zeynep is visiting. She wishes she could come and see you, but . . . Aylin remains the same.'

He shook his head. He'd become wearied by Aylin's antics a long time ago.

'And you?'

She knew she had to tell him.

'Alaaddin Bey,' she said, 'there is some interest in Deniz . . .'

He looked up. It was as though his great grey head was emerging from the sea, like a whale. 'What do you mean?'

'The people who bought the house,' she said. 'They . . . Alaaddin Bey, this is not anything of an official nature . . .'

'Then what?'

'They're interested in the history of the house.'

'What? That philistine, Yıldırım?'

'No, it's his niece, she's an historian. She's no one,' she said, meaning that Suzan Tan had no connection to anyone in power.

'Then tell her to mind her own business,' he said.

Halide said nothing. It was impossible to converse freely with her husband under these circumstances, with guards looking on and listening in, but she also knew he had to be made aware that, much as she supported him, what had happened in the past had been left unresolved.

138

'Alaaddin Bey, it is unfinished,' she said.

His eyes narrowed. 'The girl killed herself. What else is there to say?'

She took a deep breath. 'There is some doubt about that now . . .'

'Doubt!'

One of the guards put a hand on his shoulder, which Alaaddin Tonguç pushed away. The guard reacted immediately. He looked at Halide and said, 'This visit is over.'

They pulled him out of the chair. As he left, he shouted, 'It is not unresolved, it is over!'

Kerim Gürsel put his feet up on his desk. It was a habit he'd developed whilst working for Çetin İkmen, who liked nothing better than to rest his feet on his paperwork.

Talking into his phone, he said, 'Mr Killigil admits he set up the meeting between Filiz Güdül and her red-faced punter, but he categorically states that he knows nothing about Fatima Akopoğlu.'

He heard Dr Sarkissian sigh on the other end of the phone. 'No DNA matches at this end,' he said.

Kerim put a hand up to his head. Although he did eat during Ramazan, he tried to keep it to a minimum for the sake of those around him, but he was hungry now and his head hurt.

'Erdal Akopoğlu, Fatima's brother, arrived this morning,' he said. 'He's completely bewildered. The family come from a village outside Artvin. Up in the mountains, making honey and growing tea – the sort of place no one ever leaves.'

'Except Fatima.'

'She wanted to be a model, apparently,' Kerim said. 'When, I wonder, will young people stop seeing this city as some sort of utopia where their dreams can come true?'

'As long as there are cities, people will come to seek their fortunes.'

'So I had to tell this man, basically a subsistence farmer, not only that his sister had been raped but that she'd also probably been on the game,' he continued. 'He looked at me as if I'd just slapped him. Only good thing is that Filiz Güdül has proved to be an excellent witness. She's a bright girl considering she comes from Nowhere, Anatolia. Gave me the inside track on Abdülmecid Killigil, who, it seems, has been running a nice little business out of his old yalı for years.'

'You may well end up with some big names in your net,' Arto said.

'Hopefully.'

There was a pause, then the doctor said, 'One thing I can still do is run DNA comparisons for Fatima Akopoğlu against unconvicted prisoners on remand.'

Kerim frowned. He knew that happened, but he felt uncomfortable about it because it involved treating those who had yet to be tried as guilty. Many such people were detained for political reasons.

'Mmm.'

'I don't like doing it either,' the doctor said. 'But for the sake of completeness . . .'

İkmen could tell that Mustafa Ermis had been a good-looking man in his youth. Now middle aged, he was still as slim as a boy, and his hair, though grey, was thick and stylish. On the down side, he looked furtive, but then so did the man sitting opposite him, Ateş Tonguç.

In a most un-Turkish fashion, İkmen had arrived at the bar of the Büyük Londra on the dot of midday. Maybe the two men looked taken aback because he was on time?

Ateş Tonguç quickly recovered his composure. 'Ah, Çetin Bey, come and join us.'

The lobby bar of the Büyük Londra Hotel in Beyoğlu had a

noble history. Not only had Ernest Hemingway taken the odd drink or twelve there, but Agatha Christie and Mustafa Kemal Ataturk had been patrons too. In more recent years it had achieved a reputation as a repository of dusty *fin de siècle* camp. But after a refit it was now cleanly opulent, with only a vestigial campness, which İkmen felt was a shame. A couple of old parrots in one corner did not, he felt, really cut it. Luckily the old gramophone was still *in situ* and some of the things that crowded the various sideboards looked a little grubby, which was a good sign.

Ateş Tonguç introduced his brother-in-law, and İkmen and Mustafa Ermis shook hands.

'Can I get you a drink, Çetin Bey?' Ateş said.

'I'd love a Virgin Mary.'

Ateş smiled. 'That's a Bloody Mary without the vodka, right?'

'Now that I'm officially retired, I try to keep alcohol for the evenings,' İkmen said. 'It would be far too easy to get into the habit of drinking in the day.' He knew old officers who had travelled just that route. Drinking beer all day, slumped in front of the television.

Ateş called over one of the waiters and ordered.

After a moment of slightly awkward silence, Mustafa Ermis said, 'Ateş Bey tells me that you would like to speak to me about Deniz.'

'Yes.'

'It all seems like such a long time ago now. I've married twice since and have children. But I was in love with Deniz.'

'I remember,' Ateş said. 'I used to wrinkle up my nose in horror whenever you kissed. As kids will do.'

Mustafa Ermis smiled.

Ateş rose to his feet. 'I must get back to my office,' he said.

'You'll consider my proposal?'

'Of course. I'll get back to you.' He turned to Çetin İkmen.

'Please do order whatever you want from the bar, I have an account here.'

İkmen smiled. 'Thank you.'

Ateş left just as İkmen's drink arrived.

'So . . .'

'Ateş tells me you are reopening the investigation into Deniz's death,' Mustafa said.

İkmen took a long, cool slug of spiced tomato juice. He ignored the fact that he'd left messages for Mustafa about just this subject. 'Not officially,' he said. 'Although that may come eventually. A pathologist who has re-evaluated the post-mortem on Deniz's body is convinced she couldn't have killed herself.'

'I can understand that,' Mustafa said. 'I had doubts myself. Which I expressed at the time.'

'You were questioned by the police, I understand.'

'Yes,' he said. 'I was in İstanbul the day Deniz died but I was over at our warehouse in Üsküdar. I'm a tea producer.'

'Yes,' İkmen said. 'Kızıl Ağaç Tea, yes?'

'Yes,' he said. 'My father started the company in the fifties. We have land around Rize . . .'

'Which is a tea-producing area.'

'Indeed. And since the industry was liberalised, we've done very well. Things were still awkward with Caykur in the seventies and so my father had many other business interests then. Trying to live on tea alone would have been impossible. I ran the tea operation, such as it was, from here in the city. A consignment of product had arrived and I had gone over the water to receive it.'

'Did you know that your wife was going to be at her parents' house that day?'

'Yes,' he said. 'She spent a lot of time away from our apartment in Şişli, not because she disliked it, but because I was always busy and she was used to being with her family. She missed them and I understood that. I had no problem with it.'

142

'Why were you under suspicion if you had, I imagine, witnesses to your visit to Üsküdar?'

Mustafa sighed. 'You won't like this, Çetin Bey, but I was the husband, and police then – or some of them at least – were lazy.'

İkmen nodded. Yes, many of them had been. Back then, they'd been poorly paid and the proportion of officers with anything beyond primary education had been low. He'd been one of the exceptions.

'They pulled me in and knocked me around while asking me questions about my relationship with my wife,' Mustafa continued. 'They wanted me to say that Deniz and I had had problems, that she was cheating on me – mainly because she was found in a bikini. But she wasn't, and I said so. I kept on saying so until they released me, which, I believe, was when the pathologist's report was presented declaring her death a suicide. I know I didn't kill her, but I don't believe she killed herself.'

'Do you have any idea who might have done?'

'None,' he said. 'She came from a loving family. My family approved. She didn't always see eye to eye with my mother, but that's not unusual with mothers and daughters-in-law. My mother would never have harmed her.'

'Was she happy?' İkmen asked.

'Yes. Of course, moving from her family home wasn't easy for her. I know she missed her sisters particularly. I had to work, and so she was often alone with my mother and the servants. It wasn't ideal, but what marriage is ever ideal?'

'True.'

İkmen's had been. There had been issues around religion for Fatma, but the two of them had always loved each other and their children.

But then Mustafa Ermis's face darkened. 'Except . . .'

'Except?'

He moved his head closer to İkmen's and said, 'There were two personal issues.'

İkmen frowned.

Mustafa took a drink from his glass – gin and tonic by the smell of it.

'Çetin Bey, I have never told anyone these things I'm about to tell you, and to be honest, I have pondered long and hard about it ever since Ateş told me you wanted to talk to me.'

'Mustafa Bey, this will be just between ourselves . . .'

'Before Deniz and I were engaged, I had a . . . What would one call it? A one-night stand, I suppose, with her sister,' he said.

'Aylin?' She had apparently been sweet on him.

'No, Zeynep,' he said. 'All very embarrassing, and of course worrying for both of us in case she became pregnant. She didn't.'

'Did you love her?' İkmen asked.

'No. Nor she me, to my knowledge. It was just sex. We were both curious and attracted to each other. I did love Deniz, even then, but . . .' He shrugged. 'That brings me on to my second revelation.'

'Which is?'

He took a deep breath and then said, 'Deniz would never let me make love to her. Not even after we were married. She was too nervous. I didn't force her; I'm not that kind of man. She died a virgin.'

Except that İkmen knew she hadn't.

'And no, I didn't tell the police about that at the time, because I was too humiliated. I remain so if the truth be told.'

'And what about Zeynep?' İkmen asked. 'Did you tell the police about your one-night stand with her?'

'No,' he said.

'Why not? Because she was underage? If you cared for Deniz so much, surely you understood that the police would need as

144

much information as they could get from everyone, including you. Whatever the cost.'

Mustafa looked a little riled by this.

'Well?'

'Well the truth, if you must, is that I was being brutally beaten by policemen on a daily basis when I was in custody and I wanted no more of it. They would have killed me. And I was afraid of Deniz's father. If you had ever met Admiral Tonguç, Inspector, you would know how sensible my actions were. He was at the height of his powers back then and he would have killed me had he known I had deflowered Zeynep.'

'But that investigation was of a murder . . .'

'I know!' He leaned forward and reiterated, 'But Tonguç would have killed me.'

And you, İkmen thought, are apparently a coward.

Sugar Barışık had been in conversation with greasy Cenk the pornographer when Ömer Mungun arrived. But he'd scuttled away almost immediately.

'He's old school,' Sugar said once she'd thrown several cats off the chair she offered the sergeant. 'I tell him, you want to get your stuff on the Internet, but he won't. Says he doesn't know how to use it. I said, "Ask your son," but he prefers his son doesn't have anything to do with his business. Ridiculous. I don't know the Internet myself but I know everyone uses it to watch sex movies. That said, Cenk's stuff is probably way too tame by modern standards. The things you hear! Things even the most depraved wouldn't have done in my day! Where's Prince Mehmet today?'

Ömer was used to Sugar's questionable furniture and so he sat down in spite of the layer of something strange, but mercifully dry, that covered the seat. 'He's interviewing,' he said.

He didn't elaborate. Süleyman had in fact been drafted in to assist Kerim Gürsel while he interviewed elderly aristocrat Abdülmecid Killigil, for the second time, about the murder in his yalı at Kanlıca. Playing on the class angle, they hoped that Süleyman would be able to shame the man into opening up.

'So to what do I owe the pleasure of your company?' Sugar asked.

Ömer said, 'I've been looking at some old reports about Tarlabaşı. Murders.'

'Oh, plenty of those these days!'

'But not in the past,' he said. 'One that caught my eye happened on Kalyoncu Kulluğu Caddesi, almost opposite our current murder scene, in 1979.'

She shrugged.

'The body of a woman was found in a disused basement, badly degraded and only identifiable from her jewellery.'

Sugar frowned. 'Was she a Kurdish girl?' she said.

'Yes, called Emine Doğan. She'd gone missing two years earlier. Died by strangulation, possibly via the use of a ligature. The investigating office was an Inspector Altınbaş. He died back in the eighties, so I can't speak to him . . .'

'So you thought you'd come to me.' Sugar smiled. 'Well, I don't recognise the name, but I do remember a girl getting murdered back then. Really shocked the neighbourhood. And I do remember Inspector Altınbaş, or Rauf, as I used to call him.'

'He was a . . .'

'Punter, yes,' she said. 'Lovely man. Liked shoes, but no rough stuff. Always used a condom. Don't think there *is* a condom in this part of town these days. All the men want to "feel".' She shook her head. 'Maybe they should stop using bonzai. Anyway, one of the things I remember Rauf saying at the time was that he thought the girl's killer was local.'

'Why?'

'Don't know,' she said. 'I never asked. But I don't think he ever went public with that. This area used to be just one big quiet, orderly knocking shop with a few artists thrown in for colour. You didn't have to step over piles of junkies or clear away the bodies of bonzai addicts who'd collapsed on your doorstep. A lot of our punters were police and military – establishment. No one wanted anyone scrutinising these streets too closely.'

'And so the case was dropped?'

'No DNA or CCTV or any of that technical stuff back then,' she said. 'Unless there were fingerprints or someone was seen, that tended to be that. And the corpse of that girl was little more than a mummy, as I recall.'

Ömer leaned forward and rubbed the head of a slightly scabrous cat at his feet. 'Sugar Hanım,' he said, 'do you know whether anyone still living on Kalyoncu Kulluğu was living there when this murder occurred?'

She thought for a moment. 'I think that old hippy was there.'

'Which old hippy?'

'Don't know his name. But he's a foreigner of some sort.'

'English?'

'Or American, Australian, something like that,' she said. 'Have you met him?'

'Yes,' Ömer said.

'She was definitely not a virgin when she died,' Arto said. 'Although whether that was simply because she had been raped on the day of her death, I can't definitively tell you. As far as I'm aware, no blood was discovered inside her bikini bottoms.'

'Not every woman bleeds when she loses her virginity,' İkmen said.

'I know.'

Tales about women cutting their fingers to provide evidence of their virginity on their marriage bed sheets were legion.

'But using what I now know to be a very unreliable PM report, we can't be sure of anything,' the doctor continued. 'So Deniz Tonguç may have been a virgin when she got married, but she may not have been.'

İkmen groaned. 'Well, if Mustafa Ermis is telling the truth, then she didn't want to have sex with him. He did have sex with her sister Zeynep, though. A minor at the time. Rumour was that it was Aylin who had the hots for him, which she may have done. Wonder if she knew about Zeynep? It also makes me wonder about the two sisters' conflicting stories about when they discovered Deniz's body. According to Zeynep, Aylin preceded her into the garden that day and was screaming when she arrived. Aylin had them both arriving together. It may just be faulty old memories . . .'

'Or something more sinister . . .'

'Possibly.'

He heard Arto clear his throat at the other end of the line. Mustafa Ermis was long gone, but İkmen still haunted a distant corner of the Büyük Londra's lobby bar, swilling down Virgin Marys. Soon he'd have to make his way home and try to have a nap before what could be either a very disturbing or disappointing night.

The doctor said, 'It makes you realise just how vital an accurate post-mortem is. Old Orhan Sağlam was always treated as a bit of a joke, but in fact his drunkenness was a real problem. And when I spoke to his son, he remembered that his father was put under pressure to deliver a swift verdict on Deniz.'

'By whom?'

'Hüseyin didn't know and claims his father never told him. But we know already that the admiral was keen to bury his daughter as soon as he could. Hüseyin also claims his father never spoke about the case again. So whatever happened must have affected him.'

* * *

148

Ömer stood in front of the house and looked up at its filthy windows. Mainly closed, in spite of the heat, they were large, once venerable, sash-cord ones that did nothing to screen out the smell of dope smoke from the street.

Ali Ok, the kapıcı, sat on the stone steps in front of the building, no doubt counting down the hours to İftar. He looked up at Ömer Mungun. 'Back again?'

Ömer hadn't come back just because of what Sugar Hanım had told him about the discovery of the Kurdish girl's body in 1979, but also because he'd learned of another murder that had taken place in Tarlabaşı, this time in the summer of 1973. Again it was of a girl, not on Kalyoncu Kulluğu Caddesi, but further down the hill towards Kasımpaşa. There were no details this time, just that she'd been Armenian. She must, he thought, have been one of the last Armenians to live in Tarlabaşı. She'd also been killed after the Englishman, Numan Osman, had come to live in İstanbul.

Ömer said, 'How long have you lived here, Ali Bey?'

'In this house or in Tarlabaşı?'

'In this house.'

He shrugged. 'I came with Osman Bey,' he said.

Osman Güler, the previous landlord, had taken possession of the house in 1969, even though the deeds had still been and remained in the name of the Khachaturian family.

'When did Numan Bey move in?' Ömer asked.

'In the seventies.'

'Do you know when?'

He shrugged. 'No.'

'Anyone else in this street you remember from those days?'

Ali Ok looked up. 'How should I know?' he said.

'Well, friends . . .'

'I don't have time for friends. Not with this place. Where's Mehmet Süleyman Efendi today?'

If Süleyman had been there, Ali Ok would have been falling over himself to answer his questions.

'None of your business,' Ömer said.

'Anyway, Numan Bey is out if you wanted him,' the old man continued.

'I didn't say that I did.'

'Then why are you here?'

But Ömer kept that to himself. He had wanted to see Numan Osman if he could, but not officially. Not yet.

Chapter 13

Beşiktaş ferry stage held memories that only İkmen kept now that Fatma had died. Although they had both lived in Üsküdar as teenagers, Fatma had had an aunt who lived in Beşiktaş. Sometimes she would stay with her for a few days, which was when Çetin would meet her at the tea garden that used to be on the waterfront. Fatma was generally supposed to be shopping for her aunt, but she'd take a few minutes to stop for a glass of tea and some furtive hand-holding underneath the table. He remembered it with tears in his eyes as he looked across the dark waters of the Bosphorus to the place where he had been born. With Fatma dead, his father long gone and very little contact with his brother, only the Sarkissian brothers, Arto and Krikor, remembered old Üsküdar now. It made him feel momentarily irrelevant, as if he was falling off the edge of the world.

İftar had come and gone and now the city was celebrating Kadir Gecesi, the Night of Power, with fireworks that burst over the black waterway in showers of red, green, silver and yellow. Music played and kids skipped along pavements waving glow-sticks they'd hassled their parents to buy in Sultanahmet Square or Taksim. The last ferry from Beşiktaş to Kadıköy had left almost two hours ago, and the booking hall was shut and shuttered for the night. Only the mad, the borderline bad and the possibly dangerous to know were in evidence now. And İkmen.

Watching drunks piss up against walls wasn't something he enjoyed, but he put up with it. Where else were the homeless supposed to piss? He even helped a wobbly junkie to his feet when he fell over while looking for a dry place to sleep. It was a little thing, as was the ten-lira note he gave him with instructions to buy himself something to eat. He wouldn't, he'd spend it on gear, but what the hell? He smiled when İkmen pressed it into his hand, and just that made it worth his while. The world was heartless enough without adding to its horror by denying a poor addict who couldn't even afford a bed in a Tarlabaşı flop house.

İkmen lit another cigarette and scanned the broad waterway in front of him for a Bosphorus ferry. Nothing. But then why would there be? The Ferry of the Dead was superstitious nonsense. Yet still he waited. His mother had peddled superstitious nonsense all her short life; he had to give it a chance.

Suzan placed the two small figures in a padded box, which she sealed, wondering whether she'd ever see them again. Professor Kemal Bey at the archaeological museum had been thrilled when she'd sent him the photographs. Two Armana Period figurines, one of which he thought was possibly an image of the heretic pharaoh Akhenaten. They must have belonged to the Egyptian princess Fawzia, for whom the Kara Lale Yalı had been built.

Suzan had just finished wrapping the parcel when Tayfun Yıldırım appeared.

'What have you got there?' he asked.

She knew he'd disapprove of her actions, but she also knew she couldn't hide anything from him. Even if she wanted to.

'Some Egyptian figurines,' she said. 'I'm taking them to the archaeological museum to be dated.'

'Why?'

'Because they may add something to our knowledge of Ancient Egyptian culture,' she said. 'I think they must have belonged to Princess Fawzia.'

152

'And now belong to me.'

She looked into his cold, pale eyes and inside she shivered. He'd left her alone all day. Why had he suddenly appeared in the middle of the night?

'So you're giving my property to some museum?'

Suzan wasn't going to back down on this one. She'd let the gold cross go, but these were possibly priceless Egyptian figures.

'Yes,' she said. 'They are important cultural artefacts. They don't belong to anyone.'

'They belonged to that princess.'

'In those days, people looted ancient sites. We're more enlightened these days.'

He put his hand out. 'Give them to me.'

'No,' she said. 'They'll appear in the museum as items donated by you. Think of the kudos you will gain.'

'Think of the money they'll make me if I sell them to a collector.'

'Where they'll spend eternity in some vault in Switzerland? No!' she said. 'It's my duty as an historian to expand historical knowledge. Private collection stifles that!'

Tayfun Yıldırım didn't answer. He just hit her face so hard that her lip split.

Mehmet Süleyman lay on his bed and smoked. So many fireworks were going off outside, he didn't need to turn any lights on, and so he lay in occasionally orange-, green- and white-lit darkness.

Kerim's suspect Abdülmecid Killigil had been, for him, the worst kind of old aristocrat. Entitled, slimy and opportunistic. When he'd thought that Kerim might be religious, he'd plied him with religiously inspired rhetoric designed to exhibit his allegiance to Islam, and when Süleyman himself got involved, he became a 'royal brother'. They'd both slapped him down – hard.

153

Killigil had 'rented' his yalı out to men he refused to name and what he described as high-class prostitutes that he himself engaged. But he still claimed no knowledge of Fatima Akopoğlu. He was insistent in fact that none of the men who used his service would want a 'foreigner'. When asked what he meant by that, he'd said, 'That is a Hemshin name. Why would men other than her own want her?'

The Hemshin were a group of people who lived in the mountainous district of Artvin. Descendants of Armenian Christians, they had been Muslims and loyal citizens of the Republic for generations. Fatima's crushed brother, Erdal, had confirmed that his family were Hemshin and refused to be ashamed of it. And why should he be? Süleyman considered himself a Turkish patriot, but the sometimes virulent racism that was on occasion used against minority communities made him feel sick. His Ottoman ancestors had prided themselves on what they considered to be their fair treatment of minority groups. So why did people who said they admired and sought to emulate the Ottomans behave like this?

But was Killigil telling the truth? Kerim felt he probably was, which led them back to square one. A woman had been killed in his yalı and they had no idea as to the identity of the killer. Apparently Dr Sarkissian was going to try and match the DNA found at the site to that of political prisoners and those on remand. But Kerim felt bad about it. So many people currently on remand were innocent, although one dared not say such a thing in public. And so treating their most sensitive data as a viable source of information felt wrong.

But what if a political prisoner or someone on remand had committed this crime?

It came silently, and quickly. He'd turned around to look at a group of boys playing football in the road, and when he turned back, there it was. A standard, full-sized Bosphorus ferry with steam up. In complete darkness, it docked to one side of the booking hall, and as he watched, he saw a man throw a gangplank to the shore. It was the kind of elderly ferry one didn't see much these days.

The man with the gangplank neither looked at him nor spoke. But İkmen nevertheless knew that it was for him and jumped on.

The gangplank was being withdrawn when another man ran towards it. The ferry was already under way when he jumped the gap between the shore and the vessel. It wasn't inconsiderable.

For a moment İkmen thought the newcomer might speak to him, but the man was out of breath and, because he clearly wasn't young, İkmen decided to let him get on with his recovery.

The ferry was old, scuffed and battered. Built before plastic became ubiquitous, everything that wasn't metal was made of wood. It was one of the old stagers İkmen recalled from his childhood, but with one difference: everyone was seated. Row upon row of men, women and even children sat in complete, unmoving silence. Even at night there was generally a çaycı serving glasses of tea, for a small consideration, and people selling cheap toys or shonky kitchen implements was almost de rigueur. And usually the passengers talked.

İkmen found a place to sit at the end of a bench and lit a cigarette. He hadn't smoked on board a ferry for years, but he doubted whether anyone would stop him, and although he couldn't see anyone else smoking, the whole vessel reeked of smoke. No one even looked in his direction.

So, were these fellow travellers dead? Apart from the fact that they neither spoke nor, it seemed, moved, they all looked normal enough. Headscarfed aunties in vast, dusty black coats; thin-moustachioed fishermen, brown as nuts; elderly men leaning on

155

sticks; sad-eyed kids trying to hide behind their hands. The types were all there. But with no soundtrack.

The man who had jumped on to the ferry came into the cabin and sat down about as far away from İkmen as he possibly could. As he lowered himself on to the bench, he cleared his throat. It was the only noise, apart from the vessel's engine, that could be heard.

It had been many years since İkmen had taken a ferry so late at night. A lot of the routes no longer operated services beyond 10 p.m. Ever since the first Bosphorus road bridge had been built in 1973, ferry traffic had been dwindling. Now, with two more bridges spanning the great waterway, even more people chose to cross by road.

As the ferry steamed out into the middle of the oil-black strait, İkmen looked back at the first of these bridges, which until 2016 had been called the Bosphorus Bridge. It had been renamed the 15 July Martyrs Bridge in memory of the victims of the 2016 failed coup. Strictly that included Fatma. But İkmen had never considered his wife to be a martyr, mainly because he knew she would never have given herself that title. She'd died because she'd been in an accident. Wrong place, wrong time. And so he still called it the Bosphorus Bridge. The dead, he thought as he looked around him, didn't care whether they were martyrs or not.

The ferry steamed along the Asian coast to the accompaniment of celebratory Kadir Gecesi fireworks and the occasional burst of music. Nearly every mosque in the city sparkled with light as the faithful gathered to pray on the most auspicious night of the year. The dead, if they were dead, looked uninterested. But then if they were indeed dead, could they even see what was going on around them?

İkmen knew he was disorientated. This was his mother's world, not his. He had only ever been partly immersed in it, although

156

in recent years he had felt as if the traditionally unreal was closer than he had ever really imagined. His continued relationship with his wife represented the most extreme manifestation of this. But he also knew that something far deeper was at play here too, and that it was in no way spiritual. The notion he had of the ground constantly shifting underneath his feet at the behest and to the orders of people he didn't know was purely political. What the hell was 'the truth' anyway, and how did he think he was going to find it in relation to the death of Deniz Tonguç?

The old man eventually turned up just past midnight. Ömer Mungun hadn't planned on staying in Tarlabaşı to wait for him quite as long as he had, but one hour had drifted into two, which had bled into three and then four . . .

Since Çetin İkmen was a connoisseur of unofficial Tarlabaşı drinking dens, mention of the inspector's name had smoothed Ömer's path into one such establishment, which had a fine view of the house where Numan Osman lived. And using İkmen's name as an entree had allowed him to sit nursing just a single glass of rakı and a lot of water for a very long time.

Ali Ok, the kapıcı of the building, had disappeared into his apartment when the sun had set and not reappeared. Word was that he drank, but only in the comfort of his own home. Outside, he was too ostentatiously pious to do so.

Ömer followed Numan Osman into the building and knocked on his door. The old man answered immediately. His eyes half closed, he was clearly high, but he let Ömer in and then flopped down on his bed as was his custom.

That said, it was still late and he was pissed off. 'What do you want?'

'I'd like you to cast your mind back to 1979,' Ömer said. 'You were here . . .'

'I came here in the early seventies,' Osman said. 'December

157

1973, if you want me to be precise. The wife threw me out just before New Year. I've been here ever since, on the gear, as you know. What is this?'

'In 1979, the body of a young Kurdish girl called Emine Doğan was discovered in a house opposite . . .'

'And you think that was me?' The Englishman shrugged. 'Tying that in, no doubt, to the murder of the woman in this house.' He shook his head. 'Yes, I was here in '79 and yes, I remember the murder. But I didn't do it.'

'I'm not saying that you did.'

'Whatever.' He waved a hand in the air. 'Look, I'll tell you what I know, OK?'

He motioned for Ömer to sit down, then lit a cigarette.

'The basement where she was found has gone,' he said. 'Demolished. It was, I think, number eight. Owned back then by a Greek, one of the last. But all the tenants were European pot-heads. It was a cheap flop house for kids on the road to Kathmandu. One of them found the body. Before the police could even get here, they had it out in the middle of the street.'

'What?'

'It looked like a mummy. I know you Muslims are really queasy about things like that. But remember, these were European and Australian and American kids. They were fascinated. I was less so, but I went out to see what was happening, and there it was, not much more than a skeleton wearing a necklace. I admit I was curious.'

Ömer, though not a Muslim and so not bound by their strictures surrounding dead bodies, was, nevertheless, appalled.

'I just looked at it,' Numan Osman continued. 'Then the cops came.'

'The police removed the body from the street?'

'Yeah, by which time everyone was out looking. Some kid was even selling sherbet – you know how it is in places like

158

this, gotta make a profit. Only one missing was old Ali Ok –not that he was old in those days.'

'He was kapıcı here back then?'

This confirmed Ok's story.

'Yes. How he's lasted so long, I'll never know.'

'Why?'

'He's always ill,' Numan Osman said. 'He was ill the day the mummy turned up. Whenever something big's happening, you don't see him for dust. It's either his stomach or his head or he can't leave his bed. I was amazed he was here when you lot turned up for that woman.'

'He found her,' Ömer said.

'Trouble with him, if the truth be told, is that he drinks when he shouldn't.'

'He shouldn't?' Ömer asked. 'Why?'

'He's diabetic,' the Englishman said.

There was a bump as the ferry came alongside the jetty. A voice called out, 'Kadıköy!' through the ferry's loud-hailer system. İkmen had spent the entire journey in silence, almost in a trance. Mesmerised by faces that looked straight at him in a way that he rarely saw amongst those on ferries in the daylight, he had fallen into a meditation of absolutely nothing. He didn't move.

The ferry was supposed to go on to Moda, and yet he knew he had to get off because Moda had no ferry terminal; it hadn't had one for years. But still he couldn't move. It was only when a man sitting opposite touched his knee that he finally got to his feet, although he didn't know why that should have made him do so.

He got off, and as he stepped down on to the dark, silent shore beside the Kadıköy ferry terminal, he noticed that he was entirely alone. Silence inside had been replaced by silence outside, and he began to shiver, as if he'd just gone into shock.

What had that been about? And why had the fortune-teller back in Beyoğlu been so keen for him to have that experience? He'd learned, as far as he could tell, absolutely nothing. Certainly nothing about the death of Deniz Tonguç. And if that ferry, which was now pulling away from the terminal and heading out into the channel once again, had been full of dead people, how could he know that for certain? They'd all looked grey and said nothing, but hadn't that simply been because they were tired? Had the ferry itself not just been put into service because it was the night of Kadir Gecesi, when of course more public transport would be needed? In spite of who he was, he ached to call it all nonsense.

'Taxi!'

And then he was suddenly himself again, watching the man who had run to catch the ferry after him climb into a yellow cab on the road outside the terminal.

Then he knew what he should do.

Such a lot of people had come to pray, it made Imam Metin Demir's heart sing. Places like Karayolları had a bad reputation for crime and disorder, and he was glad to see so many people he knew to be less than perfect in his small mosque. He could see two men who, like his father, had been in and out of prison all their lives. One of them was crying. If this Kadir Gecesi could turn his life around, that would indeed be a blessing. But Metin knew that there was also a shadow over the proceedings, for him, personally.

He'd not seen the man who had come to find his father again. But he still couldn't shake the conviction that in spite of his professed ill health, the visitor had meant him harm. His house had been broken into, and although nothing seemed to have been taken, he felt violated. Also, although he hadn't admitted as much to the police, he couldn't be sure that nothing *had* been taken. That old tin full of bits and pieces his father had stolen over the

160

years wasn't something he had ever paid much attention to. He hardly ever looked at it, let alone inside it. If anything had been taken from there, how would he know? And if it had, would that actually matter?

Old Regep had been a failure. In and out of prison all his life. If he'd ever had anything of any value, he would have sold it long ago. Occasionally he'd told stories about some of the great houses and apartments he'd supposedly got into and robbed back in the day. But he usually told these tales when he was drunk and, Metin had always thought, they'd probably had more to do with James Bond films he'd seen than his actual life. But pondering on these things didn't make the imam feel any more secure. On the Night of Power he should be joyful, but he wasn't.

The taxi driver was one of that dwindling cohort of old İstanbullus who didn't stop smoking in spite of the ban in all cabs, and who talked incessantly. Usually the sort of man İkmen liked, on this occasion he irritated him.

'There is no ferry stage at Moda any more and I think that restaurant they've got there now is shut,' the old man said as he drove through the quiet middle-class streets of Moda.

'Yes, I know, but just take me there anyway,' İkmen said.

The other person who'd got off the ferry, the running man, had also climbed into a taxi, but İkmen hadn't caught where he was going. That was his problem. For himself, İkmen had decided that the only thing he could do now was to go to Moda and see what happened. If the ferry docked and disgorged a plethora of wraiths, then he'd know that the Beyoğlu fortune-teller, not to mention the Tonguçs' old Greek nurse, had been right. That or he'd gone mad. And if nothing happened, well then nothing happened and the status quo of normal life would have been retained. Or not . . .

'I don't know what's happened to this place lately,' the taxi driver continued. 'All coffee shops and posh restaurants. There's nowhere round here these days where you can just get a glass of tea. It's all special in some way. Tea from Russia, or with milk like they have it in India, and all costing the earth.'

İkmen was caught between the urge to let the driver's words wash over him or to wait until he almost inevitably blamed the demise of Moda on secularism, and then challenge him. But then the man changed the subject to football, and so İkmen zoned out.

Moda ferry terminal had been built in 1917 in full ornate Ottoman style. Now a restaurant, the little building was accessed via a pier, which, by not much more than the light of the moon, İkmen walked out upon. Below him, the Sea of Marmara glittered just as blackly as the Bosphorus he'd recently traversed. Except that this body of water was untroubled by any shipping close to the shore.

He looked and looked, but nothing came. Straining his ears to try to catch any telltale sounds of churning water, he stood without moving for four cigarettes, which in his case meant almost twenty minutes.

As he walked back along the wooden pier, he saw that someone else was leaving too.

Chapter 14

Mehmet Süleyman looked down into the street. All the residents of the house were gathered out front, corralled into a tight knot by a cohort of armed officers. Those that weren't complaining were sitting on the steps with hopeless but resigned expressions on their faces.

The raid, backed up by a hastily acquired search warrant, had come about after Ömer Mungun had called Süleyman in the early hours of the morning. The investigation into the death of Rosarita's mother, Takla Elias, had taken a new and potentially fruitful turn.

Down in the street, Numan Osman was swearing and pacing and showing all the signs of an addict in dire need of a fix. One of the old whores was only partly dressed and so was displaying far more varicose-spidered leg than Süleyman imagined she would have wanted.

Ömer Mungun emerged from the room occupied by Güneş Sağlam and said, 'A joint and a bottle of codeine linctus.'

'Painkillers,' Süleyman said. 'Put them back.'

'Yes, sir.'

Some of the old girls were in their seventies. Still on the game in their dotage, they needed something to dull the agony of day after day of sexual punishment by the dregs of the city. Ömer moved closer to his boss so that he couldn't be heard by anyone else. 'Sir, do we have to go through the women's rooms?'

'Yes,' Süleyman said. 'Until and in case we find something.'

'Yes, but those we've identified . . .'

'The whole house has to be searched again,' Süleyman said.

Suzan wasn't picking up her calls. She should be at the Kara Lale Yalı, but with her phone off, she could be anywhere. İkmen settled back into his chair and closed his eyes. A hot wind was blowing off the Sea of Marmara and it was making him want to go back to bed and resume the paltry three hours' sleep he'd managed to get when he'd returned home from Moda.

What had that Ferry of the Dead business been about? In spite of what the fortune-teller Büket Teyze had said, he was none the wiser. And it had unnerved him. Once he'd got off the ferry at Kadıköy, it had seemingly disappeared. What did that mean? He opened his eyes, hoping to see Fatma sitting in her chair on the other side of the balcony, but she wasn't there.

İkmen went into his living room and gathered all the paperwork he possessed about Deniz Tonguç's death. If pathologist Orhan Sağlam had indeed been put under pressure to declare the girl's death a suicide, then who could have done that, and why? Back in 1976, the military had been the supreme power in the country, and so the sort of person who could easily have exerted pressure on a public servant would have been a member of the armed forces. Logically, this seemed to put Admiral Alaaddin Tonguç clearly in the frame. But why push for a quick result? Religious observance had been suggested as a reason. But the admiral wasn't a believer, and at the time, it had been unwise to be overtly religious. Many people were, it had to be owned, embarrassed by suicide, but he hadn't hushed that up. Everyone had known about the verdict.

At the time of Deniz's death, the admiral had been at the Gölcük naval base in Kocaeli. But he had returned home not long after Zeynep and Aylin had discovered their sister's body. As İkmen understood it, the girls hadn't called their father. So why had he come back? Had someone called him at the base? Back in those days, there hadn't been mobile phones, so there had to be a record of any call – although whether that still existed or not was anyone's guess.

Ateş had been with his mother visiting relatives the day Deniz died; the girls had attended a party; the admiral had been at Gölcük, and Timur Tonguç had been at the academy on Heybeliada. And yet, at this distance in time, how could any of those alibis be verified?

There was an old adage that stated that whoever found a murder victim was probably the killer. But that was actually rare in practice, although İkmen knew that investigators overlooked it at their peril. He considered Zeynep and Aylin Tonguç and their mismatched stories . . .

Güneş Sağlam had fronted it out brilliantly when Süleyman had taken her back into the house. Laughing, she'd said to her friend Yeliz, 'I think he wants a free one!'

But once inside, she'd become sombre.

'What is it?' she said.

Süleyman, sitting on a rickety wooden chair in the hallway, said, 'Condoms.'

'What about them?'

'I haven't found any.'

'You won't.'

Süleyman looked at his deputy. Ömer Mungun raised his eyebrows.

'None of you?'

'No,' she said. 'Why would we? Women like us? At our age? Here? Inspector, we service the scum of the earth. Someone has to. We fuck slobs so we can feed our habits, buy stuff for our leg ulcers or give money to the grandchildren so they won't have our lives when they grow up.'

'You risk disease.'

She shrugged. 'You ever study biology?' she asked.

'Yes,' he said.

'Darwin?'

'Yes.'

'Well, it's Darwinism in action. Us and our clients as the weakest, ugliest and stupidest in society will eventually die out via the gift of venereal disease. It's perfect.'

But Süleyman shook his head. 'Stupid is not an appellation anyone could apply to you, Güneş Hanım,' he said. 'How do you know about Darwin?'

But she said nothing. If she was indeed an educated woman, she certainly wasn't the first, and wouldn't be the last, to end up on the game.

Süleyman dismissed her and then said to Ömer Mungun, 'I want to supervise what remains in person.'

Was the supposed curse Aylin Tonguç now lived under in fact a smoke screen for the guilt she felt at killing her sister Deniz? And if that assumption was correct, what about Zeynep? She'd been there too. Why hadn't she hidden herself away afterwards? Zeynep Tonguç had seemed perfectly normal when he'd met her. Whatever normal constituted. Did that therefore translate into the possibility that Aylin was more likely than Zeynep to have killed Deniz? According to Zeynep, she had entered the garden shortly after her sister. Even so, she would surely have known whether Aylin had killed Deniz, because the latter would still have been dying when she arrived. Or was Zeynep the real killer, hiding behind her sister's apparent insanity?

İkmen sat down again. Admiral Tonguç had come home at what had turned out to be just the right time. It could have been a coincidence, but İkmen didn't really believe in those. However, in order to find out whether the admiral really had been at Gölcük on the day in question, and when he had left, he would have to contact the base. Which, though possible, was difficult in view of the fact that the admiral was now a prisoner of the state. This left Timur Tonguç.

As yet uncontacted, Timur was a sort of hippy New Ager, if his siblings were to be believed. He too had come home on the day that Deniz was murdered, and had used his sister's death as an excuse never to go back to the naval academy. This had left his disappointed father with no option but to banish him. And a man like Admiral Tonguç would have taken such a step with comparative ease. İkmen knew some of these old military families, and they were completely unbending. Had Timur killed his sister to get out of military school? That was too extreme, İkmen felt, even for an İstanbullu. Or was it?

But none of this answered the question about why the admiral might have encouraged the pathologist to declare his daughter's death a suicide. Unless he had killed her himself. But he was at Gölcük. Or was he? And was it even going to be possible to find that out?

İkmen picked up his phone again and dialled Suzan's number. But there was still no response.

'Nothing to do with me. I'm just the kapıcı.'

'And yet the money people make in this house pays your wages,' Süleyman said.

'Haluk Andıç runs this place.'

'On behalf of others.'

Ali Ok shrugged. 'I don't know about that,' he said. 'Anyway, I thought you were interested in Numan Osman.'

'We are,' Süleyman said. 'But we're also interested in you.'

'Why?'

'You were living here when two young girls were murdered,' Süleyman said. 'One in 1973, and the other whose body was discovered in 1979.'

'Numan Bey was here too.'

'Not in the summer of 1973,' Süleyman said. 'And if you thought Numan Bey was a killer, why didn't you tell someone?'

'I didn't think he was a killer – then.'

'Why do you now?'

'Because he was here.'

'Ali Bey, you are diabetic.'

'Yes. Why?'

'How often do you have to inject yourself with insulin?'

'Three or four times a day.'

'And where do you inject yourself?'

'Why?'

'Just answer the question.'

Behind them, in the kapıcı's room, officers including Ömer Mungun opened drawers and emptied cupboards.

Ali Ok said, 'At the moment, in my thighs. But you have to rotate it. Arms, stomach, legs. I've been diabetic since I was a teenager. Type one. That's why I do this job. I'm not well enough to do anything else. It's a disability.'

Süleyman leaned back in his chair. Rosarita Elias had seen whoever killed her mother inject a substance into his leg before he had sex with her.

'I inject and then I can eat,' the old man said. 'If I don't do it, my sugars go mad.'

'What about exercise?'

'What, me? Exercise? I don't do it,' he said.

'You must have to take deliveries from time to time. You use gas bottles.'

'Years since I took those in,' he said. 'I get the gas man to do it these days.'

168

'So you only inject yourself before a meal?'

'That's right.'

'And we can check all this with your doctor?' Süleyman asked.

The old man laughed. 'Only if you can dig him up. I've not been to the doctor for years.'

'So where do you obtain your insulin?'

'Off the Internet,' he said.

'Halide Hanım?'

'Yes.'

'It's Çetin İkmen.'

He heard her say, 'Oh.'

There was a pause.

'Hanım, if you have time, I'd like to talk about Deniz . . .'

'Would you.' She sounded stern – and tense. 'Well, Çetin Bey, I do not want to talk about her.'

She had been nervous when he'd gone to see her with Suzan, but this time she sounded more than nervous. She sounded afraid.

'Has something happened?' he asked.

'No,' she snapped. There was another pause.

'Hanım?'

'I want you and Dr Tan to stop,' she said.

'Stop?'

'Let my daughter rest in peace. This may be an interesting project for you, but—'

'An interesting project?' He was incensed. How dare she! 'Madam, Dr Tan and I want to find the truth! As much for your daughter Aylin—'

'Aylin is beyond help.'

'I disagree. Her quality of life—'

'Is zero at the moment,' she said. 'Please leave us alone.'

'But madam, you told me yourself that you believe Deniz was murdered.'

'Murdered? Committed suicide? What is the difference? My daughter is dead, Çetin Bey. Let her rest in her grave.'

She put the phone down.

Ömer Mungun thanked Dilek Osman for calling him back so quickly and then whispered what she had told him in Süleyman's ear. He also placed a package in his hand. Süleyman glanced down at it and then showed it to Ali Ok. The kapıcı looked confused. 'What . . .'

Süleyman smiled. 'Sergeant Mungun, please find a chair and join us.'

'Yes, sir.'

It was hot and smelt of piss in the corridor between the kapıcı's room and the communal lavatory. Ali Ok looked sweaty. But then, Süleyman thought, so did Ömer. It was that kind of day.

'Condoms,' Süleyman explained as he looked down at the box in his hand. 'Found in your room, Ali Bey.'

'So?'

'So why just in your room?' he continued. 'Are they for you?'

'No! I've never been married . . .'

'Married men usually want children and have no need of condoms,' Süleyman said. 'Do you go with the women in this house?'

'No!'

'Why not?'

'You've seen them,' he said. 'They're old whores. Who'd want them?'

'Their customers?'

'So I keep a few condoms for the old women's customers,' he said. 'So shoot me. I don't charge.'

'Just as well considering I have been informed there would be no takers,' Süleyman said. 'You and I both know what kind

170

of house this is, Ali Bey, and so I ask again, who are these condoms for?'

Ali Ok looked down at his hands.

'For you?' Süleyman said. 'You can tell me; I'm not a prude.'

The kapıcı shrugged.

'Although I must say I find it odd that a man of advanced age like yourself, and diabetic to boot, should still be having sex . . .'

'There are ways.'

'So enlighten me.'

Still looking down, Ali Ok said, 'You just use more insulin.'

'Why?'

'It helps.'

'How?'

'I don't know.' He looked up. 'But it . . . it does.'

'Has a doctor ever told you to do this?'

'No. I worked it out for myself.'

'Interesting.' Süleyman turned to Ömer Mungun. 'Sergeant, can you please tell us what Numan Osman's ex-wife told you about the time she threw him out of their house back in the seventies?'

Ömer cleared his throat. 'Yes, sir. It was on New Year's Eve 1973.'

'Which means that Mr Osman would not have been here in Tarlabaşı in the summer of that year?'

'No, sir.'

Süleyman looked at Ali Ok, who shrugged again. 'Doesn't mean he didn't kill that girl in the late seventies.'

'No.'

'The little Armenian kid in 1973—'

'How do you know she was Armenian?' Süleyman asked.

There was a pause, and then Ali Ok said, 'I remembered.'

* * *

İkmen went and sat out on his balcony again. He put his head in his hands, and when he took them away, he hoped to see Fatma. But she was stubbornly invisible.

Suzan Tan had finally got back to him, and İkmen had given her the edited highlights of his conversation with Halide Tonguç. Then Suzan had stuck the knife in. Not horribly or with malice, but she'd done it nevertheless.

'Çetin Bey,' she'd said, 'I'm so sorry, but I have to agree with Halide Hanım. I think that in view of her husband's detention, we should do as she asks.'

And of course on one level, she was right. But that didn't mean that İkmen didn't feel deflated – and angry. Deniz Tonguç hadn't killed herself; someone had murdered her, and now no one would ever be held to account. And they should be. But how? If Halide Tonguç didn't want any further action taken and Suzan was out, that just left Zeynep and Ateş – not that the publisher was really that interested. Deniz had died when he'd been a child. That family convulsion had barely affected him, unlike the situation now with his father. Zeynep? Well, she was open to question . . .

Was Admiral Tonguç a traitor? İkmen didn't know. Instinctually he was always on the side of what had once been called the 'secular elite'. But was that right in this case? He'd never met the man. He knew his type – stiff, unyielding, often very attractive to women. He'd even, allegedly, had a mistress.

İkmen began to wonder who knew about that apart from Timur and Zeynep Tonguç, whose number he now tapped up on his phone.

It was all circumstantial. There was no forensic evidence to tie old Ali Ok, the kapıcı, to the murder of Takla Elias, no one had seen him go into or come out of her room on the day she was murdered, and the fact that he had a packet of condoms in his room meant nothing. Not on its own.

'Do you know how Rosarita Elias saw the man who killed her mother inject himself?' Süleyman asked Ömer Mungun.

'She was under her mother's bed,' Ömer replied.

'Ali Ok said he injected himself in the thigh,' Süleyman said. 'That great source of all knowledge, the Internet, tells me that the thigh is the favoured placed for diabetics to use. I looked it up. By the way, I do hope that the fact Ok gets his insulin on line made your blood curdle too.'

'Yes, sir.' Although, were he to be honest, Ömer knew a lot of people back in Mardin who bought their medication on line because they couldn't afford to go to the doctor.

'What I was wondering,' Süleyman continued, 'is how the girl saw the man who killed her mother inject into his thigh while she was underneath the bed. Surely she would have needed to put her head out in order to do so. And if that is the case, wouldn't she have seen his face too?'

'She didn't say he injected into his thigh,' Ömer said. 'She just said his leg.'

Süleyman nodded. 'Go back and see her and try to get some clarification – but without leading her,' he said.

'Yes, sir.'

Arto Sarkissian checked the DNA results three times. He even called up the forensics laboratory to speak to the assistant who had run the comparison. But there could be no doubt. He looked again at the results on his screen and wondered who he should contact first, Kerim Gürsel or Çetin İkmen.

Chapter 15

'You want the truth?'

'That would be good,' Çetin İkmen said. Again his phone buzzed to let him know he had a message, and so he switched it off. It had only taken him five minutes to get from his apartment to Zeynep Tonguç's hotel, but he was out of breath. He lit a cigarette. It was cool in the shade on the terrace of the Four Seasons and he had a glass of ice-cold tonic water. Life, on one level, was fine.

'My mother has always been conflicted about Deniz,' Zeynep said. 'She was always harder on her than she was on the rest of us. Deniz was by far and away the prettiest of us girls. She was, I've heard relatives say, very like our mother had been when she was young.'

'You think your mother was jealous?'

'Yes. She'd lost her youth, her husband was away most of the time and she was saddled with all these kids.'

İkmen sat back in his chair. 'You told me before that your brother Timur told you he thought your father had a mistress. Do you think your mother knew?'

'I don't know,' she said. 'My mother has always kept up a front, and continues to do so. Anything unpleasant is not allowed in. And there's always a reason. At the moment, it will be my father's detention. I think she does, deep down, want to know the truth about Deniz, but she doesn't want that to jeopardise my father's case.'

'How could it?'

'Oh, come on, Çetin Bey! You know how it is. Alleged traitors are blamed for all sorts of things. Why not murder?'

'There's no evidence that your father killed your sister.'

'There's no evidence for a lot of things that are treated as truth,' Zeynep said.

And yet Admiral Tonguç had got back to the Kara Lale Yalı at a very convenient moment the day that Deniz died.

'About your father's arrival home that day,' İkmen said. 'Was he expected or did someone call him?'

Zeynep shrugged. 'He was due home that day,' she said. 'But at that time? I don't know. Aylin and I called no one, that I do know. When we found Deniz, we both, well, we fell apart.'

'You know when I spoke to your sister she told me that you found Deniz together. You, on the other hand, said that you went to the toilet and so therefore arrived after her. Can you account for that?'

'That's what I remember,' Zeynep said. 'If she remembers it differently, I can't do anything about that. It was only a few minutes. Do you think Aylin killed Deniz?'

'I don't know,' İkmen said.

'Why would she?'

He sighed. 'I've spoken to Mustafa Ermis . . .'

'Really?' Zeynep looked away.

'Aylin was sweet on him.'

'Listen, I know she's a bit odd, but I don't think Aylin would have killed Deniz to get her hands on Mustafa. I mean, look at what it's done to her!'

'And you,' İkmen said. 'What did your association with Mr Ermis do to you?'

'Me?' She laughed. 'He was my sister's husband.'

'With whom, according to Mr Ermis, you had a one-night stand before he married Deniz.'

She didn't say anything for a while, but her face became red. Eventually she shrugged. 'A drunken fumble.'

'You had . . .'

'We had sex, I became pregnant and got rid of it,' she said. Then she turned on him angrily, 'Satisfied?'

İkmen shook his head. 'I didn't say that to humiliate you, Zeynep Hanım.'

'I know.' Deflated, she shook her head. 'Mustafa . . .'

'He told me you didn't get pregnant.'

'He doesn't know,' she said. 'No one does. Inspector, like the rest of my siblings I wanted to live my own life and be loved and get away from our parents. Mustafa was handsome and he spun a good line back in those days. We were stupid kids.'

'It must have been hard for you organising an abortion on your own back in the seventies,' İkmen said. 'You were a child.'

'I was and it was. But it was better than facing my father with a baby in my belly.'

They sat in silence for a few moments, and then İkmen said, 'Do you have any idea who this mistress of your father's might have been?'

'None,' she said. 'You'd have to ask Timur.'

'I've been trying to.'

Zeynep Tonguç lowered her head.

İkmen said, 'Unless I speak to your brother, I can't get a complete picture of what happened.'

She looked up. 'My mother keeps in touch with him. She always has, even when my father forbade it. But I don't think she's seen him for years. She certainly wouldn't want him here now that Father's in prison.'

'Why not?'

'Because he's a square peg' Zeynep said. 'He always was. Father so wanted him to be a military man like him, but he just wasn't. Been hiding halfway up a mountain in Artvin for years, supposedly running some sort of pansiyon. I suspect he's probably getting stoned and having sex most of the time.'

'Did he get stoned and have lots of sex when he was at home?'

'No,' she said. 'Father was far too strict with all of us. But I knew Timur had a wild side. He hated the academy and claimed that he used to take dope in there that he bought from foreigners in Sultanahmet. My mother still refuses to believe that ever happened. But even so, she won't have him in İstanbul, in case someone digs something up about him.'

'What about the rest of you?'

'Oh, we're boring,' she said. 'Except for Aylin. But how much damage can she do, locked away in the dark? I called her this morning, given that it was Kadir Gecesi last night, and surprise, surprise, she is still alive.'

İkmen smiled. 'I caught the ferry your old Greek nurse was talking about,' he said. 'It appears to be an extra service put on for people returning home late from the festivities.'

Not that he knew this. He'd been unable to find out anything about an extra ferry service. But he'd also had no ghostly revelations while on board. How else could such a strange and yet also banal experience be explained?

'Well of course it is!' Zeynep said. She shook her head. 'In spite of all the nonsense one sees on TV and the Internet these days, I still only believe what I can actually see. Ostensibly ours was a secular household when I was a child, but we all still lived in thrall to that ridiculousness. What with Mother's spiritualism and Aliki's superstition. And we girls all had to be good and quiet and pure. No going out unchaperoned with boys for us.'

'Your parents would have been choosy about who your brothers married too?'

'Oh yes. God knows who, if anyone, Timur married, but Ateş did as he was told. Married a nice girl from a military family, had a couple of kids and then divorced her because he was unhappy. I'm not saying we had a dysfunctional family life, but it was contradictory and often confusing, and I think that we're the rather odd and diverse people we are today because of it.'

'Diverse is good,' İkmen said.

'Yes, but odd isn't.'

'Maybe not.'

She lit a cigarette. 'Well, anyway,' she said, 'I would like you to continue to look into my sister's death even if my mother doesn't. I know you suspect me . . .'

'I suspect everyone,' he said.

'I'll pay you, and Dr Tan.'

İkmen told her that Suzan was no longer involved. Zeynep frowned and said, 'That's a shame. You don't know why?'

'Because of your mother,' he said. But he felt that wasn't the only reason. When he'd spoken to Suzan, something had broken in her voice that made him think there was more than just Halide Tonguç's dismissal at play.

'Well, I want you to continue.'

'But I do not need payment . . .'

She waved his comment away. 'Let me be the judge of that,' she said. 'Now, where do we go from here?'

He took a deep breath. 'I really need to speak to your father or your brother, or both.'

'Oh,' she said.

'And anyone who was at the naval academy with your brother.'

She thought for a moment. 'Timur didn't really do friends at the academy. But I do remember one young man coming home with him. I can't recall his name, but Aylin might. He was quiet, like her. Another oddball.'

The old man shuffled uncomfortably in his seat.

'Can I have some privacy?' he asked.

The food he'd requested, which turned out to be a plate of cheese and spinach börek, had just arrived.

'No,' Süleyman said. 'Eat while we talk.'

'While I inject myself!' Ali Ok countered.

'Oh, yes. I can go out for a minute, I suppose.'

Süleyman had brought the old man into headquarters while Ömer Mungun went to see if he could get any more information out of Rosarita Elias about her mother's killer. The search of the house on Kalyoncu Kulluğu Caddesi was now over, but Süleyman had decided to hang on to the old man. He couldn't keep him for long.

He left the interview room and went into the viewing area next door. While he could see the old man, Ali Ok couldn't see him. Süleyman sat down and watched as the kapıcı went over to the door, opened it and then closed it when he saw the guard outside. He sat down again.

Kerim Gürsel shook his head.

'Could it be a false positive?' he asked the doctor. 'One hears of such things.'

'There's always that possibility,' Arto Sarkissian said. 'And given the admiral's high profile . . .'

'Yes.'

'With a familial match this close, it's rare,' he said. 'That's why I want Çetin Bey to see it too.'

DNA harvested from semen samples taken from the body of Fatima Akopoğlu, the Fındık Yalı victim, had matched closely to those of imprisoned alleged traitor Admiral Alaaddin Tonguç. This meant that the assailant was a level 1 or close blood relative of the admiral.

'There are, I believe, two sons,' Arto continued.

Kerim sighed. 'A visit to the prosecutor's office beckons. Dr Sarkissian, do you think Admiral Tonguç was a member of this shady, religiously inspired . . .'

179

'Tonguç was always a devout secularist,' the doctor said. 'But who knows? Maybe such people are involved in some hellish alliance with certain religious types to bring down the government. The military have lost much of their power in recent years. It depends whether you believe they would stop at nothing to regain it. We live, it seems, in a world dominated by smoke and mirrors.'

Kerim shrugged.

'Not that Admiral Tonguç's case has any bearing, we hope, upon your own,' the doctor said. 'If one of his sons killed that girl, then what his father may or may not have done is irrelevant.'

'Yes,' Kerim said. 'But you know as well as I do that as soon as this gets out, it will be a circus.'

The doctor nodded.

'It could also encompass what Çetin Bey is doing,' Kerim continued.

'I know,' the doctor said. 'I've been trying to call him, but he just won't pick up.'

Ali Ok pulled the right leg of his baggy shalvar trousers up to his thigh and then got down on the floor. Sitting back on his heels, he put his hand in his jacket pocket and took out a disposable syringe. This he laid on the floor beside him. He looked, Süleyman thought, as if he were about to pray. Then, clearing his throat, he picked up the syringe, took the cap off and injected himself in the top of his thigh. As the needle went in, he winced with pain.

Ömer Mungun, who had joined Süleyman in the viewing room, said, 'Do you think he sometimes injects in conjunction with prayer?'

Süleyman looked up. 'What did Rosarita Elias say?'

'She described something like this,' Ömer said.

'Makes sense. If you were underneath a bed, you'd be able to see something.'

Ömer watched the old man stand up and return the syringe to his pocket. 'Why does he do it like that? I'd just put my leg up on a stool or something.'

'You don't have skinny legs and wrinkled skin,' Süleyman said. 'This way he can stretch the skin and get the needle in without losing it. Will Rosarita make a statement?'

'As long as I translate, yes.' Ömer smiled. 'She's a lovely kid, you know, sir.'

Süleyman stood up. 'She's safe now.'

'But not with her father.'

'He's in Syria,' Süleyman said. 'She can't be with him while he's there. It's too dangerous.'

'You know her carers say she asks about her father all the time.'

'She may do,' Süleyman replied. 'But at the moment, to be with him would put her at risk. Sometimes amongst family is the most dangerous place a person can be.'

The imam stopped short in his tracks, his heart hammering. It was that wretched man again. Cengiz Bey. His father's so-called friend from Maltepe.

'Good afternoon, Metin Bey.' The man bowed. 'I remembered where your old house was.'

Of course he did, he'd already been inside! But then Metin didn't know that for sure. He suspected it, but without evidence, he could hardly accuse this man of breaking and entering.

'Hello,' he said.

'Are you on your way home?'

He was. It was hot and he was in need of a nap. But he wasn't about to tell Cengiz Bey that.

In the end he said, 'You're still in town.'

'Yes. There was a lot to see. But I'm catching a bus out tonight.'

'Oh.'

'I stayed for Kadir Gecesi, but now I must go home.'

'For Şeker Bayram.'

'Yes. One must be with one's family for the end of Ramazan. It is so important.'

What did he want? And why did Metin feel so uneasy in his company? Was it simply because Cengiz Bey, like his late father, had been to prison? Was it because he was dying? If that were to be believed . . .

Cengiz Bey smiled. 'I know you don't remember me, but I wondered whether I might spend İftar with you on my last night in İstanbul. I would consider it an honour.'

Metin had been invited to break his fast with his assistant Selçuk Çeviköz's family. Old Ahu Hanım, Selçuk's mother, always invited him in spite of the fact that she had never been able to cook. It was a trial. Dry pilav and gristly mutton. He'd already suffered it three times this Ramazan. But to go to dinner with a man he suspected of trying to rob him . . .

'I was thinking it might be uplifting to take İftar with all the people in Sultanahmet Square,' Cengiz Bey continued.

Metin had wanted to go to that. It was usually a very lively affair and the food on the stalls always looked delicious.

'I'll gladly pay,' Cengiz Bey said. 'My bus leaves at midnight and so I can't afford to take up much of your time. Let us meet at sunset beside the German fountain.'

Metin knew it. The fountain had been built for the last Ottoman sultan by Kaiser Wilhelm II of Germany. A sort of thank you, some felt, for the support the Ottomans had given the Germans in World War I.

He hesitated. At least it would give him a chance to quiz Cengiz Bey further, and maybe even find out why his presence made him feel so uncomfortable. And they'd be in a public place. He could even, if he chose, see Cengiz Bey on to his bus to . . . No, he didn't know where he lived, apart from in the country. And then there was the prospect of Ahu Hanım's awful food.

'That would be very nice,' he said eventually. 'I look forward to it.'

His name was Burhan Aksoy and he was dead. Even İkmen, who wasn't a connoisseur of modern art, knew the name. Aylin Tonguç had followed his career from inside her living tomb until his death in 2014. She had been attracted to him when her brother had brought him home from the naval academy one weekend.

Shouting into his ancient phone beside the queues waiting to go into the Ayasofya, İkmen had told her he'd been aboard a ferry from Beşiktaş to Kadıköy at midnight and survived. But all she said was that of course he had; the Ferry of Death was not coming for him.

Burhan Aksoy's legacy lived on in the shape of his old studio in Cihangir. For a small consideration, one could view his work, talk to the people who ran the place and buy books about his philosophy.

It wasn't İkmen's kind of thing. There seemed to be a lot of daubing going on, as well as some small stick figures in the distant background that were faintly sinister. It had said on the website that Aksoy's gallery was run and curated by his widow, and indeed, a very attractive middle-aged woman had taken his money and given him a leaflet when he arrived. Now, drinking from a bottle of water, she smiled when she saw him looking at her and said, 'Can I help you?'

Nobody else was in the gallery and so İkmen and Burhan Aksoy's widow, Angela, went outside to sit at the smokers' table on the pavement. Angela, who came originally from Italy, poured them both glasses of water. And, this being trendy, liberal Cihangir, nobody stopped to question them about why they weren't fasting.

'I knew of Timur Tonguç but I never met him,' Angela said.

İkmen had been entirely candid with her about who he was and what he wanted to know. She had smiled and said she'd help if she could.

'I didn't meet Burhan until I came on holiday to İstanbul in 1982,' she said. 'He was easy to fall for.'

İkmen smiled. From his photographs, Burhan Aksoy had been a handsome man.

'We'd been together for a few years when he told me about his time at the naval academy. He hated it. For the first year he was in despair. But then Timur, a fellow square peg in a round hole, came and the two of them took on the place together. According to Burhan, they were always being beaten or placed on a charge for some misdemeanour or other. Being improperly dressed, drinking, not taking care of their kit.'

İkmen lit a cigarette. 'Why did they lose touch?'

'I don't know,' she said. 'It was after Timur's sister died back in the seventies – what you have talked about. I'm sorry, I never really asked Burhan about it.'

'Why would you?'

She shrugged. Then she said, 'My husband died in a road accident. One minute he was here, the next he was gone. There are so many things I wish I'd asked him before he died. So many things I wished I'd said.'

İkmen knew what she meant. He hadn't even managed to tell Fatma's ghost everything that was in his heart. He doubted whether Angela even had that luxury.

'But life goes on, and so must we.' She smiled. 'I have two lovely sons to remember my husband by, and, of course, his work.' She drank some water. 'I feel Burhan's art is not your kind of thing.'

'Oh, does it show?' İkmen said. He smiled. 'No, Angela Hanım, I'm afraid it isn't. I am a simple man who likes his art to show him things his small brain can understand.'

'I appreciate your candour,' she said. 'We get a lot of people coming in here more simply to be seen than anything else. They tend to pontificate, too, which Burhan always hated. He used to call such people "fakes" – long, long before Donald Trump used that word.'

They both laughed, and then Angela said, 'You know my husband was writing his memoirs when he died. His work was much more popular in America than it was here or in Europe, and so the publisher who engaged him was American. Of course that all fell apart when he died. I'll be honest, I've never been able to bring myself to look at what he wrote. I've no idea how far he even got with it. But it's on my system, and so . . . well, if Burhan can help you find out the truth about Timur's sister's death . . .' She shrugged. 'I can send it to you as a PDF.'

İkmen was truly taken aback. 'Are you sure?' he said. 'I mean, I could be . . .'

'Anyone? No,' Angela said. 'This is İstanbul, Çetin Bey, the city of a thousand villages where everyone knows everyone. And of course I've seen you on television when you were with the police.'

Books had been written about how, when offenders were presented with evidence of their own guilt, sometimes they confessed. Keeping secrets for many years, if not decades, was stressful, and it was this release of tension that eventually burst the dam of pent-up anxiety.

'I was an ugly child who grew into an ugly adult,' the old man said. 'My mother was Roma, my dad a Kurdish hamal. He drank and she sold herself on the streets. I did finish elementary school. I could've gone on to high school if my parents had let me. Then I got this illness.'

'Diabetes?'

'Yes. One day I collapsed in the street. Couldn't do my military service. I was apprenticed to a builder, but I couldn't do that

185

either, so I took a job as a kapıcı with old Osman Bey. I was just a boy, but I looked old for my age. My parents were dead by that time and my only sibling was in Cyprus. I think he died some time ago . . .'

Mehmet Süleyman hadn't grown up in an apartment block, but he knew that people who had often speculated about the lives of the men who kept their buildings secure. The kapıcılar who nosed into the lives of their tenants and who sometimes acted as the eyes and ears of the local gossips as well as the city constabulary. It was said they knew everything. It was also said that the only reason they did was because they didn't have lives of their own.

'I knew I'd never marry,' Ali Ok continued. 'Not someone I fancied. One of the old whores would've had me for the air of respectability it would have given her. But I didn't want one of those. I don't know what it is about very young girls . . .'

'Takla Elias was in her twenties,' Süleyman said.

'She looked like a child,' he said. 'Had I known she had a child herself, I wouldn't have been interested. She came to the house begging for work. Not the first refugee to do that, won't be the last. As soon as I saw her, I wanted her. I said she could come and live in the house and I'd look after her. She was up for it.'

'What? Sex with you?'

'Yes,' he said.

'So why did you kill her?'

'I don't know,' the old man said. 'It just doesn't feel right unless I kill them. Not finished.'

Ömer Mungun said, 'You killed them to silence them?'

'Not consciously, I don't think,' Ali Ok replied. 'I mean, who's frightened of a little girl or a refugee?'

'You were.'

'No, I wasn't.' He shook his head, as if trying to clear it. 'No, it was just unthinkable. I had to kill them.'

'Was the Armenian girl in 1973 your first?' Süleyman asked.

The old man was so normal and rational it was frightening. But then that was, the inspector knew, in the nature of someone who was sociopathic. Strictly according to the law, they were 'normal' – normal and highly dangerous. Süleyman's ex-wife had been a psychiatrist, and her words rattled around in his memory now. *Sociopaths are OK provided they're not thwarted. They're intelligent and feel the world owes them. If the world doesn't deliver, then watch out.*

And the world hadn't delivered to Ali Ok. Clearly no fool, he was ugly and poor and his diabetes had probably been the last straw.

'No,' the old man said. 'My first was a little girl called Sisi. I didn't think I would ever be able to get an erection. Since I got ill, I never had. Then I saw her.'

'When was this?'

'I can't remember exactly: 1969, 1970? Before Natalia.'

'The Armenian girl?'

'Yes, I remember all their names,' he said. 'Sisi was playing in the street. She was one of the Roma kids. I'd always envied their freedom – and she was beautiful.'

'What happened?'

'I offered her money. I said I needed a fit little child to run and get me some cigarettes. She went. When she came back, I took her inside to give her a cold drink – it was a hot day – and then it happened. She didn't make a noise.'

'She was probably terrified.'

Ali Ok's face was completely blank.

'What happened to her body?'

'I wrapped it up and put it on my cart,' he said. 'I had a little two-wheeled barrow I used to collect the water back then. I dumped it in the Golden Horn.'

Süleyman looked at Ömer Mungun and then said, 'Was she ever found?'

'I don't know.'

'What about her parents? Didn't they come looking for you?'

'No.' Ali Ok leaned forward. 'Back in those days if people went missing, they just went missing. Especially if they were poor. Not like now.'

And in a sense he was right. People moaned about surveillance in modern İstanbul, but it did make events like little Sisi's death far less likely.

'There was some trouble with Natalia, she made a lot of noise, so when Emine came into my life I had to be more careful,' the old man said. 'As soon as she aroused me I knew I'd have to plan. I knew that number eight no longer used their basement because it was unsafe, and so we made love there. It was where I left her, as I'm sure you know. I only ever took the ones who aroused me. I would never take an innocent.'

Süleyman saw Ömer Mungun's face redden. He was angry too, but giving in to it would get them nowhere. He said, 'So tell me how Takla Elias, desperate refugee, aroused you.'

'Well that came out of nowhere. As I said, she looked very young and she was very pretty and polite. She said she'd do things . . .'

'Probably cleaning or odd jobs.'

'Yes, but she meant more than that, I know. I'd not had sex since, well, a girl called Sara, a tourist I think, but that was back in the nineties and had been most unsatisfactory. A bunk-up against a wall and then she walked away. It haunted me.'

'That she lived?'

Ali Ok didn't respond. When Süleyman had first met him, the kapıcı had been a snivelling, servile, apparently religious old man who had almost prostrated himself before him. Was it talking about his past sexual triumphs that now made him seem so confident, almost contemptuous? It was like speaking to another person, which maybe, in a way, it was.

188

'I had to plan Takla,' he continued. 'I knew that you would expect to find my fingerprints in her room, since I am, after all, the kapıcı. But I'm not stupid and so I took precautions against DNA. I bought condoms, which I used when we made love.'

His use of the phrase 'making love' was turning Süleyman's stomach.

'No one saw me go into her room or come out. Even if they had, they're always drugged. What do they know? If all that water hadn't poured into the room below, I would have just let her make herself apparent and then called you.'

'Make herself apparent?'

'Smell,' he said. 'It's hot. It wouldn't have taken more than a few days. It's always better to do these things in the winter for just that reason.'

'These things . . .'

The old man smiled. 'In the eighties, between my relationship with Emine and that disaster with Sara, I had many affairs.'

Süleyman leaned forward in his chair. 'You're confessing to other murders? Who were they?'

But Ali Ok didn't reply.

'You said you remember all their names . . .'

He looked away.

'Where . . .'

He looked back again. 'Wouldn't you like to know?'

It was then that Ali Ok took the reins of control out of Süleyman's hands – and the policeman knew it.

Chapter 16

Ateş Tonguç liked having his office on the top floor of his publishing business. Up there he had a large space all to himself and his own private bathroom. He could also smoke his pipe in peace. He was reading a manuscript submitted by a woman from Kayseri about Yörük cuisine, when the police marched in.

'Ateş Tonguç?'

Surrounded by a squad of men in police uniform, the man who spoke was in plain clothes.

'Yes.' Ateş stood. 'Is this about my father?'

The man said, 'You must come with us.'

So they've finally decided to drag the rest of us in, Ateş thought. But he wasn't going to go easily. That was something he'd always promised himself, ever since the old man was taken into custody.

'No,' he said. 'You tell me what this is about first. You tell me whether you've got my mother and my sisters.'

One of the young uniforms stepped forward, but the man in charge held him back.

'Your mother and your sisters are of no interest to us,' he said. 'Only you and your brother.'

They were going after the men. Ateş thought about what Zeynep would say: *Typical patriarchy!*

'Why?'

'We can discuss that down at headquarters.'

He picked his pipe up and puffed. 'I'd rather we discussed it here,' he said.

190

He saw the plain-clothes officer sigh, while the men behind him almost ground their teeth in anticipation of getting their hands on him. For a few precious years, this sort of behaviour amongst the police had all but disappeared. That said, the man in charge seemed almost human.

'Sir, don't make me have to arrest you,' the almost-human said. 'All I can tell you at this stage is that this matter has nothing to do with your father.'

'I see.' Was he telling the truth? Probably not. 'So what *is* it about?'

The officer sighed. The men behind him exchanged what Ateş interpreted as contemptuous looks.

When he spoke, his words came out at Ateş like a bolt from the blue.

'You're *walking* home! From here?'

Arto Sarkissian had come across Çetin İkmen on İstiklal Caddesi where Hamalbaşı Caddesi crossed over into Yeni Çarşı Caddesi. He was in his car and, oddly for him, İkmen was on foot.

İkmen bent down so he could speak through the window of the doctor's new, very black Mercedes.

'Walking allows me to think,' he said. 'It's a new hobby. Anyway, they won't let you smoke on public transport.'

The doctor groaned. 'Get in,' he said. 'I've been calling you for hours. What have you been doing?'

İkmen got in and told him. Then the doctor dropped his bombshell.

'So let me get this straight,' İkmen said. 'The DNA sample taken from the semen found in Fatima Akopoğlu's body is a close match to that of Admiral Tonguç?'

'Yes,' the doctor said. 'Too close to be simply down to chance. Kerim Gürsel is going to question Ateş Tonguç about

191

his whereabouts on the day the woman was murdered, and there's an alert out on his brother and a male paternal-line cousin who lives in Malta.'

İkmen shook his head. 'I have an address for his pansiyon in Artvin and a mobile number that he fails to answer. But apparently that's quite normal for him.'

'You'd better pass those details on to Kerim Bey.'

'I will. As far as I am aware, it's only the mother, Halide Tonguç, who has any contact with Timur,' he said. 'They're a very difficult family. They all claim to want to know the truth about Deniz's death but appear unwilling to face up to what needs to be done in order to do that.'

'With Admiral Tonguç in prison, that's understandable,' the doctor said. 'Any intimation of further scandal could make his situation worse.'

'I know.'

'And I can't think of anyone who could have put pressure on old Orhan Sağlam apart from Admiral Tonguç.'

İkmen asked if he could light a cigarette in the doctor's car, and Arto, as usual, let him. 'But open the window,' he said.

İkmen lit up. 'I wish I could speak to him,' he said.

'The admiral? Not a chance.'

'I know. But maybe at the end of his life, now he's in so much trouble . . .'

'You think he'd confess? To what?'

'I don't know,' İkmen said. 'If he did kill his own daughter, I can't imagine why. Or how. But there was something rotten in that family. The younger sisters both infatuated with Deniz's husband – Zeynep had sex with him and became pregnant. Timur at the academy, miserable as sin, Ateş needy and neglected. Deniz had just got married to a man she claimed to love, but she wouldn't consummate the marriage. Why? And if she wasn't a virgin . . .'

'Which we can't prove or disprove.'

'. . . then who was she sleeping with?'

'You think it might have been her father?'

'Who knows?' İkmen said. 'The way the day she died developed makes me wonder. If only I could contact Gölcük naval base about this, and confirm whether Tonguç was there that day, without plunging myself into a pit of suspicion! Why does contact with people like Tonguç instantly put one in the traitor frame?'

'You know why.'

He sighed. Ever since the attempted coup of 2016, Turkey had operated under a state of emergency, which meant that anyone suspected of holding views that might have their genesis in shady religious organisations or philosophies could be subject to arrest.

'Admiral Tonguç had a mistress,' İkmen said. 'Or rather that was the belief – or the fabrication – of his son Timur. I don't know who she was, but assuming she lived in the city, maybe the admiral was with her the day Deniz died. But even if he was, that doesn't explain how he managed to get home just after Aylin and Zeynep found Deniz's body.'

'Coincidence.'

İkmen gave the doctor a sour look. Then he said, 'OK, assuming he was due home that day, why just at that moment? We didn't have mobile phones back in 1976, and anyway, my understanding from my own military service, back when dinosaurs roamed the earth, was that trying to contact someone in the forces was a bit like trying to phone abroad. Almost impossible.'

'You're right,' Arto said. 'It was a nightmare back then. But, I reiterate, coincidence.'

İkmen shook his head.

Mehmet Süleyman looked at Ömer Mungun's tired, strained face and put a hand on his shoulder. Not one to mollycoddle his officers, he nevertheless knew that the prospect of finding the dead bodies of little girls was pushing his deputy to his limits.

But here they were, back in Tarlabaşı, this time accompanied by officers with picks and spades.

Addressing his team, Süleyman said, 'Half of you start excavating the back yard; the rest of you into Ok's room to pull up the floorboards. If necessary, I want this whole place ripped apart.'

Now that Ali Ok had confessed to the murder of Takla Elias, on the one hand Süleyman had done his job, but on the other he had just apparently entered the world of a serial killer. And although Ok refused to name the five girls he claimed to have murdered in the 1980s, a search had to be conducted for their bodies. Süleyman tried not to think about how the old man was probably loving the way he had manipulated and taken control even from a cell at headquarters. He was probably laughing at the thought of his old neighbours being pushed out of their rooms by police. He'd hated all the junkies and old whores he'd looked after for the last forty years.

'Sir . . .'

Süleyman looked at Ömer Mungun.

'Over there.' The sergeant tipped his head at a group of smartly dressed people watching what was happening from the building site opposite.

Süleyman scowled. What were they? Architects? The owners of the site? Investors? Whoever they were, he didn't like the way they looked at the house and its neighbours with hungry, acquisitive eyes.

'I have not been to Kanlica for decades! The only time I ever go over *there* is to visit one of my authors who inconveniently lives in Kadıköy.'

Unbeknownst to him, Kerim Gürsel knew what Ateş Tonguç

194

meant. He too had been born and raised on the European side of the city, and he too only went over *there* when he had to. A lot of Europeans felt the same.

'Where were you on the seventeenth of this month?'

Ateş sighed. 'In my office,' he said. 'I've given you my diary; see for yourself. I can't remember exactly what I was reading that day, but I imagine it was probably some drivel about molecular gastronomy or how pomegranate juice can cure death.'

He was an angry man. But then not only was his father in prison; he also, it seemed from what he said, hated the books he published.

'What about the evening? Did you attend any of the İftar—'

'My father's in prison. Why would I flaunt myself in public? Anyway, I don't fast, and you can make of that what you like.'

'So what did you do?'

He crossed his arms over his chest. 'I can't rightly remember, but if I did what I've been doing relentlessly for the past three years, I went back to my small and lonely apartment in Teşvikiye and watched Netflix. I imagine I probably bought something to eat at home, mainly because, like a lot of divorced men, I can't cook.'

'So you can't—'

'No, Inspector Gürsel, I can't give you an alibi. And don't think for a moment that my belligerent attitude towards you is in any way real. You frighten me. This whole situation terrifies me. My father is in prison and I'm a single middle-aged man who may well have gone with a young woman in Kanlica one day when I was feeling horny. But I didn't. I behave myself scrupulously, because if I don't, I have nothing. My ex-wife already has the house I bought for us both to live in, and my children take up any paltry sum I might earn from publishing inane cookbooks instead of the cutting-edge fiction I once produced. I'm playing the game, and it's hard, but I am not the kind of man who lets off steam with prostitutes, and I certainly don't kill people.'

Kerim Gürsel nodded. Underneath his stern exterior, he hid quite a regard for this man, and he hoped that the DNA cheek swab they had taken from him would indeed prove his innocence. If it wasn't an exact match, he was safe.

The inspector said, 'Do you know where your brother is?'

'Timur? I've not seen him for years. I have an address in Artvin.'

'I have that.'

'Then you know as much as I do,' Ateş said. 'Timur left our family after falling out with my father.'

'What about?'

'Father made him take up a place at the naval academy on Heybeliada. Timur hated it and left, so my father cut him off. He travelled for years and then ended up getting this pansiyon in Artvin.'

'How do you know this if you don't see him? Do you talk on the phone?'

'No,' he said. 'But I know my mother does. I am loath to involve her as she has enough to contend with, but I also know that if she knew I was in trouble, she would want to help. If my brother is not at his property in Artvin, then I have no idea where he might be. My mother may or may not know his whereabouts.'

It was tiny. A metre and a quarter at most. The skeleton of what had to have been a child. Mehmet Süleyman put one gloved hand into the cavity in the wall and touched it very lightly. He had seen many terrible things during his career, but this made him despair. This was the sort of crime the mass surveillance of citizens was meant to prevent, and if the old man was telling the truth and he had killed most of his victims prior to the installation of CCTV cameras, to some extent they could be counted as a success. But Süleyman also knew that preventing crime was only part of their purpose. Things like this would always happen while poor people and those outside the norm were just ignored.

A young constable had found it when he broke into a cavity he found in the wall between Ali Ok's bedroom and his kitchen. It had turned out to be a cupboard the old man had papered over. The little skeleton, Süleyman now saw, was stacked against another one behind it.

He stood up and said to Ömer Mungun, 'I'm sealing the whole building.'

'Sir.'

'Get the forensic team up here and then go to the community centre on Zerdali Sokak and ask them if they can organise accommodation for these residents.'

'Shouldn't the owner of the building do that, sir?'

Süleyman gave him a look.

'The man who officially owns this building is probably out of his mind on heroin, and those who actually own it will simply use what is happening here as an excuse to evict the tenants when we have gone. My aim is to get the place searched and put back together as quickly as we can.'

'That won't be easy,' Ömer said.

'Then we'd better get on with it.'

Burhan Aksoy's book had no title. But he'd written quite a lot before his death. Sixty thousand words, which was surely, İkmen felt, quite enough for any but the longest, most vibrant life.

Çiçek came in and flopped down on the sofa. She'd just completed her first day at the café and looked exhausted.

İkmen looked up from his computer screen. 'Busy day?'

She shook her head. 'Honestly,' she said, 'there are parts of Beyoğlu where you wouldn't know it was Ramazan. I didn't get a minute to myself. Not that I'm complaining. Just being back at work makes me so happy. Exhausted, but happy.'

'I can remember a time when no one in Beyoğlu knew what Ramazan was,' İkmen said.

When he was a child, Beyoğlu had been largely a Greek and Jewish district. There had also, in those days, been a sizeable Italian Levantine community. He wondered whether the Tonguçs' nanny, Aliki, had come from that area, and whether the fortune-teller Büket Teyze had grown up listening to old Greek tales about ferries taking dead people across the Bosphorus. That nothing had happened on his own journey across the strait hadn't made him disbelieve what either Büket or Aylin Tonguç had told him. What was living, what was dead, what was real or unreal were concepts that had always had a fluid nature in a city as old and deeply rooted as İstanbul. And that applied to every ethnic group who had ever settled there. Time moved differently in a place so thick with past, present and future.

'Did you get paid?'

'At the end of the week,' she said. 'It's a proper job, not some gig thing.'

'I know.'

In spite of her difficulties, he hadn't wanted her working in what was known as the gig economy. Being paid by the hour and arriving for work only to be turned away if you weren't needed that day were not things Çiçek needed in her life.

He said, 'Do you know anything about the artist Burhan Aksoy?'

'There's a gallery in Cihangir,' she said. 'Modern art; you wouldn't like it. Didn't he die?'

'Yes, his widow runs the gallery,' İkmen said. 'Do you like his stuff?'

She sat up. 'Not really. A bit splashy for me.'

'Splashy?'

'Like the American Jackson Pollock,' she said. 'He used to stand in front of canvases and throw paint at them. I get it; it's just not for me.'

İkmen, who really hadn't got it, said, 'Get what?'

'The anger and the passion,' Çiçek said. 'Pollock was a tortured alcoholic.'

'Why?'

'I don't know,' Çiçek said. 'But he went into therapy, in that way Americans often do. Aksoy's breakdown I can understand.'

'I didn't know he had a breakdown.' His wife hadn't said anything about it.

'I don't know much,' Çiçek said. 'Only what I read in the papers. Aksoy was in despair over the political situation. He'd been part of the whole Gezi Park protest movement in 2013, but when that didn't last, it's said he lost hope. Like Pollock, he died in a car accident, although Aksoy was alone where Pollock wasn't. Aksoy also wasn't drunk, although there are those who believe he may have crashed his car deliberately.'

'Because of the political situation?'

'Yes,' she said. 'He was one of those who initially supported the AK government back in 2002 when they first came to power. I guess he was fed up with the secular elite and the military.'

'Like a lot of us.'

'But then for him it went sour,' she said. 'Again, like a lot of us.'

There had been times when İkmen had despaired of his daughter ever being employed again. Accused in the wake of the attempted coup of 2016 of involvement with a shady religious organisation, she had fallen foul of the religiously inspired government, which many now believed to be more dangerous than the old secular elite.

'I've got a copy of his incomplete memoir,' İkmen said.

'Really? Why? Wouldn't think that would be your sort of thing.'

'It's work,' he said. 'By the way, have you spoken to Hülya recently?'

'No. Why?'

'Just wondering whether she knows anything about her friend Suzan Tan,' he said.

'I'll ask her. But don't you see Suzan? For this investigation?'

'Not any more,' İkmen said. 'She quit. I don't know why, but I'd like to.'

Her mother cried. Zeynep put her arm around her shoulders and said to the police officer sitting opposite, 'She doesn't know anything.'

'Your mother admitted she called your brother when this unofficial investigation into your sister's death began,' Inspector Kerim Gürsel said.

Zeynep shook her head. What a mess this was all turning out to be! 'To tell him to keep away,' she said. 'Look, you have to understand that with my father in prison, this is all very difficult for us. We want to know who killed Deniz . . .'

'And so why warn one of your surviving siblings to stay away?' Kerim Gürsel said.

The older woman, Halide Tonguç, raised her head. 'Timur leads an unconventional lifestyle,' she said. 'How would it look having a man who lives like a hippy around our family? With my husband in prison? My husband disowned Timur many years ago. Alaadin Bey doesn't need all that raked up now!'

'But if you're trying to piece together what happened in 1976, and Timur was there . . .'

'He had nothing to do with Deniz's death!' Halide Tonguç said. 'He loved her, just like the rest of us.' She looked at her daughter. 'I should never have let that Tan woman into our lives. I should have kept the door between the living and the dead closed.'

The policeman broke through her misery.

'Look,' he said, 'let's put all of that to one side. I need to find Timur. So far his mobile phone rings out, the same for the land-line at his pansiyon. The local police have been to the pansiyon and found it empty. Your other son Ateş has given me what must be an old mobile phone number, which is dead. Halide Hanım, this is urgent: when did you last contact your son?'

She didn't look at him. 'A few days ago.'

'On which number?'

She showed him; it was what was believed to be the current mobile number. 'What did you say to him, Halide Hanım?'

'To Timur? I didn't speak to him, I left a message. I told him to keep away.'

'Because you didn't want his appearance to jeopardise your husband's case?'

'Yes.'

'Do you have any reason to believe that Timur may have ignored your advice and come to the city?'

'No,' she said. 'He's not been in touch.'

Inspector Gürsel turned to Zeynep. 'And you?'

'I've not spoken to Timur for years,' she said.

'What about your other sister?' He looked at his notes. 'Aylin Tonguç?'

Zeynep felt her heart sink. 'Inspector, I don't think Aylin has seen Timur since Deniz died in 1976. She's a recluse who lives in a fantasy world. He wouldn't even get through the door.'

Chapter 17

Finally, İftar! Metin didn't usually have a problem making it through to sunset without eating or drinking, but today had been hard. Maybe it was because he'd been nervous about meeting the man sitting opposite. As he put the traditional break-fast fare of three dates into his mouth, an awkward silence lay between them. Was it because he still wondered what Cengiz Bey wanted? Because he found accepting that such a healthy-looking man was actually dying was stretching his credulity? Or was it simply because the food tent Cengiz Bey had chosen was packed with so many people of all ages, races and states of hunger that the noise was terrific. Or at least it had been until everyone began eating.

Dates finished, Metin tucked into the fragrant mutton stew and pilav that was the speciality of this particular establishment, occasionally dipping bread into the sweet thick gravy.

Cengiz Bey, not nearly so ravenously hungry as everyone else, sat behind his half-finished meal and said, 'As I recall, your father wasn't a religious man. What brought you to Islam, Metin Bey?'

Metin told him about the old widow Tansu Hanım who had looked after him whenever his dad was in prison, and how she'd instructed him in the Five Pillars of Islam.

'To work for the good of everyone just seemed like a rational choice,' he said. 'All Dad ever did was cause chaos, and it never brought him happiness. I've come to realise that the only real happiness life has to offer is through service to others. And that is what Islam is.'

'I am pleased for you.'

'Not that I can really be categorised as a traditionalist,' he continued. 'Our mahalle was very mixed back in my youth. We didn't just live alongside our Alevi brothers and sisters; we also still had a few Christian and Jewish residents back then, though they all died years ago. I always found their beliefs fascinating. Dad, as you probably remember, didn't have much time for minorities.'

'I don't know,' Cengiz Bey said. 'I never discussed such things with him.'

Metin took this not as proof that he was who he said he was, but not as proof that he wasn't either. Old Regep had always liked İstanbul's minorities, mainly because they drank without guilt.

Music began, and it was deafening. Every year the local municipality put on a huge nightly show of events ranging from performances of the Ottoman military band, the Mehter, to Karagöz puppet shows and recitals of religious music. This was the latter, and consisted of the haunting music of the nose flute, or ney. But because it was amplified to such a ridiculous extent, the sound was distorted. Not that anyone else seemed to be bothered by it, and that included Cengiz Bey. He shouted, 'You've done very well for yourself, Metin Bey.'

'I had the benefit of learning tailoring from an old man from Kayseri,' Metin said. 'A Pontic Greek called Aristotle Bey. He was full of all the old pre-Christian Greek myths and he was a very good teacher. And of course Dad left me the house.'

'Oh.'

'Just a shanty, as you know. But he built it with my grand-father and there are deeds.'

'Lucky for you.'

'Yes.' Metin winced at the screeching music and then became silent. Güllaç, the traditional dessert of pastry and pomegranate often served at Ramazan, was beginning to appear in the tent, and he hoped that he'd be able to somehow eat it in peace.

Had Timur Tonguç loathed the naval Academy as much as his friend Burhan Aksoy? It was difficult to know without speaking to the man, but according to Aksoy's memoir, it was very likely they had both equally loathed the place.

He had written: *I was and have never been a cold shower sort of a person and neither was Timur, although he was rather more used to it on account of the fact that his father was an admiral. When at home Admiral Tonguç ran his family like a ship. Timur also knew why he was at the academy – to fulfil his father's ambitions for him – whereas I did not. Quite why my old man sent me there I never found out.*

Aksoy's father had been a jeweller in the Grand Bazaar. According to earlier chapters, a lot of Burhan's peers at elementary school had thought he was a Jew because of it. He wasn't, but had his father been trying to make a point about being a full-blooded Turk when he'd sent his son to the naval academy?

Çiçek was asleep on the sofa. Neither of them had eaten an İftar meal, but that was all right because apparently she'd eaten at work. Outside, in the city, somewhere among the music and the red-, green- and blue-lit streets, Samsun sashayed and shimmered her way from pastane to coffee house to bar. Later she'd come home carrying a bag of doughnuts or a carton of tripe soup or some other weird and incongruous foodstuff. İkmen would eat then. He lit another cigarette and read on.

Now that it was dark, the men were flagging. They'd all missed İftar, even though a whole load of them had lit cigarettes as soon as the cannon fire signalling sunset had finished.

204

Süleyman said to Omar Mungun, 'I'm going to call it a night. Post guards, on overtime, front and back and tell the rest of them to go home.'

'Yes, sir.'

They were all exhausted. The two bodies behind the walls in Ali Ok's room had been the first and last corpses they'd found. But the basement and half the back yard had still to be investigated.

What made a man do such things? Was it just loneliness combined with unrequited sexual urges? No, of course it wasn't. A quarter of all the men in the city probably fell into that category. What made Ok different was that he had a sense of entitlement. Psychopaths did. He couldn't get sex and so he took it because it was his right. Then he'd kill his victim to 'finish'. Was that his way of saying that he couldn't actually ejaculate after sex? The kill obviously fulfilled a function not only connected to hiding what he'd done. But what?

It took Süleyman a while to realise that he'd driven in quite the wrong direction to reach his own home. As a brightly lit and very loud Sultanahmet Square came into view, he realised that he had been unconsciously heading for Çetin İkmen's apartment.

They'd let Ates Tonguç go home with instructions not to leave the city. That wasn't difficult. He didn't know anyone much beyond İstanbul. Even his authors these days tended to be city-bound. No more cannabis-addled, magic-obsessed experimental writers waiting to metamorphose into alcoholics in the back streets of Bodrum. Those days had gone.

Ateş switched his television on and pulled his curtains. Yet more Ramazan fireworks were not something he needed. He picked his favourite programme, *Resurrection: Ertuğrul*, and slumped down in front of it. He didn't usually enjoy TV shows with nationalist messages, but this one set in the early days of the Ottoman Empire was at least entertaining. Not that his mind would let him rest.

He'd never heard of the woman who'd been murdered over in Kanlica. Fatima Akopoğlu was someone he had never met and now never would. And yet what would he do if his DNA matched exactly that found on her? And how did the police even know he could be a close match? And Timur? And of course his cousin Genc in Malta, though he was well into his seventies. Inspector Gürsel hadn't been exactly free with his information.

All he really knew was that he hadn't murdered anyone. He couldn't believe that his brother had either. Even though Ateş had almost forgotten him. He'd even been in the habit, for years, of telling people that he just had two sisters. Not that Aylin was exactly out and about, but he did see her at least once a year.

No, the only member of his family he could imagine killing anyone was his father, and he'd been in Silivri for almost a year so that had to be impossible. But if he'd been out and suspicion had fallen on the family, what would Ateş have told the police?

Çiçek got up off the sofa and, almost without opening her eyes, made her way to her bedroom.

Mehmet Süleyman, standing in the middle of Çetin İkmen's vast, shabby living room, said, 'I'm sorry it's so late. I just sort of ended up here . . .'

İkmen smiled. 'I'm glad you did,' he said. 'Are you tired?'

'Yes, but not sleepy.'

'Good. We need to talk.'

'Oh yes, we do.' Süleyman sat down. 'I imagine you've heard that the Tarlabaşı murder is no longer a mystery.'

'I spoke to Kerim Bey briefly and I've listened to the news. A good result for you.'

'Is it?' He shook his head. 'The kapıcı did it. Sounds like a Turkish version of an Agatha Christie novel. But sadly that's where the similarities end.'

'What do you mean?'

'It seems the kapıcı, an elderly, seemingly mild-mannered example of the species, is a serial killer. Of little girls.'

İkmen drew in a breath and then exhaled slowly. 'God.'

'As well as the Syrian woman, Takla Elias, who was his only adult victim, there are two more historical victims he says are his, plus two very small bodies we found earlier today hidden behind the walls of his room. We have no idea how many more we might find because he's now taken charge.'

'He's enjoying your pain.'

'As such offenders do.'

İkmen offered his friend a cigarette and they both lit up.

'I know these people surface from time to time, but that doesn't make it any easier,' Süleyman said. 'And I know that I could approach the problem the old-fashioned way . . .' He meant beating the old man up. 'It goes on, and I'm pretty sure that our new commissioner wouldn't have a problem with it.'

Commissioner Ozer, unlike his two predecessors, was the sort of man whose focus was very much guided by crime clear-up figures and an unquestioning devotion to higher authority. How those clear-up rates were achieved was not, he felt, his problem. In addition, if his officers fell foul of the methods they used to get those results, that wasn't his problem either.

İkmen said, 'But you would.'

'You taught me well,' Süleyman said. 'As you know, I've been down that road once and I wouldn't do it again.'

'But this stance your kapıcı has taken, you feel, puts him in control?'

'Yes.'

'Well then, I would take him to the house,' İkmen said. 'Not with a view to making him talk; just let him walk around. If he is, as he seems to be, a sociopath, he will be proud of his handiwork, and if you watch him carefully, you may find that he even gives away the position of any further victims. Of course he may also know that you are watching him for any potential tells, but it will put him on his guard and it will help you to take back control.'

Süleyman nodded. 'That's true.'

'It's a game with people like this, don't forget,' İkmen said. 'You could probably beat him to a pulp and he'd still not talk, because winning is all that interests him now that he's lost his liberty.'

'He confessed. I was pretty certain it was him by that time, but . . .'

'Confession can be control, as you know,' İkmen said. 'No, you now need to assert yourself, the best way to do this, I think, is by walking him around that house and watching his reactions. If he steers you in the wrong direction, then so be it. But knowing that you can interpret his responses, whatever they are and whenever they occur, will put him on the spot. It will make him realise that you are the one who is really in control.'

Süleyman smiled. 'I can't tell you how much we miss you, Çetin.'

Güllaç, warm sheets of rose-flavoured pastry soaked in milk and decorated with pomegranate seeds, was one of the true delights of Ramazan. Metin's surrogate mother, Tansu Hanım, had always made it in vast quantities, knowing how much he loved it. But unlike his childish self, he now ate it slowly, savouring every bite. He smiled at the man opposite him, who confessed that güllaç was one of his favourite things too.

'Prison food either makes you disregard eating or become obsessed with it,' Cengiz Bey said. 'For me it was the former. I can be quite indifferent to it. And yet I have a sweet tooth.'

Regep Demir had always been indifferent to food – and not just savoury dishes.

Now that the music had finished, they could talk more easily. Quite a lot of people had eaten and left, and so the atmosphere was less charged.

'You said,' Cengiz Bey said, 'that your father left you his house.'

'Yes. He used to say that the house was the only honest thing he'd ever done, apart from this . . .'

He put it on the table and saw Cengiz Bey frown.

'That's a Rolex,' he said. 'It must be worth . . .'

'Not a lot,' Metin said. 'Dad gave it to me shortly before he died. But then I sat on it by accident a few weeks later. Smashed the glass and buckled the case.'

'May I look at it?' Cengiz Bey asked.

'Of course.'

He picked it up and peered at it.

'I think the back opens up somehow,' Metin said. 'I don't know. Ever since I sat on it, I've not attempted to do anything with it. I just carry it around because if Dad did get it via honest means, then it's important.'

'Absolutely.'

Apparently fascinated, Cengiz Bey turned the watch over.

'Do you want me to try to get the back open?' he said.

Metin did and he didn't. He still didn't really know who this man was.

But then the waiter arrived with their bill, which Metin insisted upon taking.

'Let me pay for your last meal in the city,' he said. 'It will be a blessing.'

He turned to face the waiter and began counting out money from his wallet.

'Of course he could have done it,' İkmen said.

'Kerim Bey told me he couldn't imagine it,' Süleyman countered.

'Well, without wanting to cast aspersions on Kerim Bey's abilities as a police officer, I have to disagree,' İkmen said. 'Ateş Tonguç is a very personable man, but as you and I both know, anyone is capable of murder. Let's look at the facts: Tonguç is middle aged, divorced, by his own admission bored with his life, prevented from publishing the books he'd like to publish by prevailing societal norms and he's got no alibi. He's a perfect candidate for a moment of madness with Fatima Akopoğlu.'

'And killing her?'

'Who knows?' İkmen said. 'Maybe she tried to blackmail him?'

'And yet Fatima Akopoğlu was unknown to Killigil, the owner of the Fındık Yalı, or so he says.'

'Quite,' İkmen agreed. 'But having said all of that, I must confess I am pleased that Kerim is now looking for Timur Tonguç. He's the only member of the family I haven't been able to reach so far – apart from the admiral.'

'You think Deniz Tonguç's murder was committed by a member of her family?'

'Yes. At the moment, I can't put anyone else at the scene at the time of Deniz's death. To be honest, I can't actually put any family members there either. The original police reports I have seen exonerate the husband. His alibi stood up then, and if I'm honest, it probably stands up now, in spite of the fling he had with Zeynep Tonguç. I don't think it was a serious thing for either of them. But I may yet be wrong.

'The main line I've been following so far actually concerns the admiral. Dr Sarkissian is convinced the PM on Deniz's body was deeply flawed, which you know. And although we have no evidence, it seems to both the doctor and me that the only person who could have put pressure on poor old Dr Sağlam to call a suicide in the face of all evidence to the contrary was Admiral Tonguç. But why?'

'Why indeed?'

'To cover up murder or to make a nod towards religion? And things become even more potentially problematic when you consider where people were, or said they were, on that day.'

'What do you mean?'

'Admiral Tonguç turned up just after Aylin and Zeynep found their sister's body. Was his appearance, in full dress uniform no less, a coincidence, or . . .' İkmen shrugged. 'According to Timur, the admiral had a mistress. Had he been with her? Who was she? I don't know. As for Timur himself, I'm reading a post-humous memoir written by a man with whom he attended the naval academy in Heybeliada. So far I've learned that Timur was indeed his friend and they were both rebellious. You may know of the writer.'

'Oh?'

'The artist Burhan Aksoy.'

'Yes,' Süleyman said. 'Wild, splashes. I rather like his stuff. I didn't know he was dead.'

'In 2014, a car accident,' İkmen said. 'And of course you like his stuff, you're posh.'

Süleyman laughed. 'What?'

İkmen smiled. 'You're supposed to be cultured. We working-class oiks just know what we like.'

'Oh Çetin.' Süleyman yawned. 'God, I do miss you.'

'Well then, if you care so much, let me get on with reading Aksoy's memoir. Don't try and drive home; you're exhausted. Bülent's old room is still made up. There's a range of incompre-hensible male grooming things in there that you're welcome to use. I'll even make you breakfast in the morning. Go on! I won't take no for an answer.'

Süleyman rose stiffly to his feet. 'Thank you, Çetin. You know you really are something of a saint.'

'Oh, get to bed!' İkmen said. And then he looked back at his computer screen.

Was it a sin to do something good and then, albeit unconsciously, congratulate yourself? Imam Metin Demir thought it probably was, but he consoled himself with the fact that paying for Cengiz Bey's İftar meal was harmless. He took his change from the waiter and turned back to his guest. But he wasn't there. He quickly asked the waiter if he'd seen where his companion had gone, but the man just shrugged and said, 'No.'

Metin looked around the tent, and then ran outside and into the brightly coloured throng of people milling around the stalls in the Hippodrome.

So the watch was broken, but it was still, as Cengiz Bey had observed, a Rolex, and they were worth money. What had he been thinking when he had allowed a self-confessed thief to handle it? It was surely meaningless to anyone but Metin. And then he remembered that someone had been inside his house and taken nothing.

Had it been the watch that this man had been looking for all along? And if so, why? Did it hold the key to some secret that Metin's dad had kept even from him?

And then he realised. Maybe if the watch had been intact, if he hadn't sat on it, he'd know what it meant. Then he felt guilty. Villain though his dad had been, Metin had let him down, and that was unforgivable.

Pushing his way through the İftar crowds, he raced towards Divan Yolu and, if he could get one, a taxi. He couldn't see the man anywhere! Cengiz Bey had said he was due to catch a bus out of İstanbul, which probably meant going from the city's biggest bus station, at Esenler. The only problem, apart from getting there, was that Esenler was massive and Metin didn't have a clue where Cengiz Bey might be going.

Chapter 18

When she woke up, Zeynep Tonguç was as stiff as a board. Spending the night at her aunt's apartment in Karaköy, with her mother, did not make for a restful night's sleep. As soon as the police had gone, her mother had become hysterical. Ateş was possibly in the frame for the murder of that woman over in Kanlica, and now they were looking for Timur. Why? He'd left town decades ago! And he was a peace-loving hippy type!

Neither Zeynep nor her mother understood. How could either man be involved in such a thing? Zeynep had thought about calling Çetin Bey to see whether he knew anything, but then decided against it. One heard such things these days, about the police tapping people's phones, listening to their most intimate conversations.

Zeynep, who had slept beside her distraught mother, sat up and looked out of the window. It was barely light, but she could see the seagulls wheeling on the fresh early-morning air. Up underneath the Orthodox church, her aunt's apartment had the feeling of a place nearer to heaven than most. Not that Zeynep felt anything like the presence of God at her side.

Pursuing her brothers was just the latest in what could become a long line of incidents guaranteed to break her father's spirit and make him confess to things he hadn't done. Clearly those who opposed him didn't know him. He'd throw the world to the wall to save his honour.

* * *

'Mehmet?'

Çiçek, washed and dressed, was walking across the living room towards the kitchen when she saw him.

Süleyman put his finger to his lips. İkmen had fallen asleep at his computer and was snoring. Süleyman followed Çiçek into the kitchen and shut the door.

'Did you stay the night?' Çiçek asked as she fired up the samovar for the morning tea.

'In Bülent's room, yes,' he said. 'Your dad invited me.'

'It's OK,' she said. 'I don't mind. Just wondered if you were woken up by Samsun too.'

'No, what happened?'

'Drunk – again,' Çiçek said. 'Dad had to put her to bed and she wasn't happy about it. I think she wanted to go back to the bar.'

Samsun, though mostly a homebody these days, still liked to paint the town red whenever she did go out.

'Looks like Dad pulled an all-nighter,' Çiçek said. 'I've not seen him do that since he retired. I bet he loved it.'

Süleyman knew what she meant. İkmen was at his happiest when he was up against a problem. Cornered, he always fought and he always loved it.

'Cigarette?'

Süleyman took one and they both sat down at the kitchen table to wait for the samovar to boil.

'How is your new job?' he asked her.

She shrugged. 'I'm a waitress, but in a place where the hip and the happening go. I'm just so pleased to be working.'

He smiled. 'When people get to know you . . .'

'Oh, I'm not looking towards the future,' Çiçek said. 'No way. As long as I can pay my way, that's good enough for me.'

She'd travelled all over the world as a flight attendant, learned three languages so she could do just that when she was at school;

215

it was so strange to hear herself talking about just clinging on. But that was the reality.

So what now? After almost all night spent ranging around the vastness of Esenler bus station, Metin had only just been able to make himself a couple of eggs for Suhoor and feed Sara the cat before he'd fallen into his bed. Now, still exhausted, he was awake and very anxious.

Cengiz Bey, or whoever he really was, still had his dad's old watch. He was probably hundreds of kilometres away by this time; the chances of anyone catching up with him were slim. And even if Metin did go to the police, what could he tell them? A man whose surname I don't know, who is a bus driver, but I don't know where, has stolen a broken watch from me that may or may not be worth something? That local so-called community officer would laugh at him and do nothing. Yet if he went back to head-quarters and asked for Inspector Süleyman again, they'd probably throw him out. News bulletins were reporting that the police had found the man who'd killed that woman over in Tarlabaşı, and that they feared he may have killed others. What they'd think about Metin's broken watch situation was probably not repeatable. But that didn't stop him feeling sad. That old watch was the only thing his father had ever really worked for, and its loss made him feel that his memory of poor old Regep had been violated.

He could hear Samsun snoring, but otherwise the apartment was empty. Çetin İkmen took his laptop out onto the balcony, where Fatma was waiting for him.

'Well, that was a hell of a night,' he said once he'd sat down and lit a cigarette. 'Mehmet turning up like that, Samsun waking all the neighbours when she came home with some story about being propositioned by Johnny Depp. She should never drink Southern Comfort and she knows it. And then there's this . . .'

Fatma's expression didn't change. It rarely did, but she always looked interested. It was disconcerting in a way because she'd never been interested in his work when she was alive. When she'd first appeared, this sudden curiosity had confused him. And because he didn't know any Muslim divines he could talk to easily, he had gone to see a Catholic priest from the church of St Anthony in Beyoğlu. Father da Mosto was not a friendly man and he had no social skills whatsoever, but he always told it as he saw it. He'd told İkmen that he didn't believe in ghosts and that 'Fatma' was just a projection of his grief. She wasn't evil or sinister in any way; she just was, and one day, when İkmen was ready for her to leave, she would. Then he'd told him to go home and concentrate on his children and grandchildren.

İkmen didn't point to what he could see on his computer screen; that would be ridiculous. But he referred to it. 'This is that memoir of Burhan Aksoy. God, but the man goes into detail! Writing about painting competitions at primary school, his father's drug addiction, memorable meals from his youth . . . A bit self-absorbed for my liking.' He shrugged. 'Anyway, amid the endless interruptions of yesterday, I finally got to the bit where Aksoy goes to the naval academy on Heybeliada. It involves a litany of accusations against his instructors as well as almost fifty pages of deathless prose about how the hardship he endured inspired him, how he started to use his anger, blah, blah. Then we get to Timur Tonguç. Another rebel, the only other young man Aksoy felt he could relate to. Aksoy is extremely frank. It would seem that Timur seduced him. He's dead and so we may never know if this is true or not. But it's very graphic and so I will spare you the details. What I have to say, however, is that Timur Tonguç, if all of this is true, was very sexually experienced for such a young boy and really, well, violent.'

According to the artist, Timur had liked his sex rough, with Aksoy assuming a decidedly feminine, almost victim-like role.

And yet, although claiming that since his early twenties he had been entirely straight, Aksoy admitted that he had been very much under Timur's thumb.

İkmen read from the laptop. "'In retrospect, Timur knew how to manipulate. At the time, I thought that what I was experiencing was love, but it wasn't. I was just there, and because he was physically attracted to me, I would do. I was besotted. I remember being so happy when he agreed to stay at the academy during the 1976 summer vacation, just, as I thought, to be with me. My father was dying by that time and my mother wanted all of us to be as far away as possible, to save us the horrors she chose to endure alone. Later I found out that Timur didn't want to go home to his family. During the early days of that vacation he told me how much contempt he felt for them. It made me feel cold.'"

Dominant, seductive and contemptuous – Timur Tonguç wasn't coming out of this well. İkmen thought that he must have been spectacularly attractive as a young man to make up for so many negative qualities. But then teenagers could be notoriously shallow.

However . . .

'And then,' İkmen said, 'one day suddenly Timur just ups and goes home. This is early August 1976, which is the month in which Deniz died. He returns, according to Aksoy, the following lunchtime. Aksoy, by his own admission, was worried in case Timur was going to see another lover. So they had an argument. And then Timur was off again mid afternoon. Called away. Aksoy says he didn't know at the time why he left again, but later he learned that Timur had been called home because his sister had been found dead. So I reckon he must have left school on the fifth. Stayed over, at home? Who knows? Then Deniz, we know, died on the sixth. Now I ask you, Fatma, how does that work? Hold that thought.'

218

Of course she said nothing. He went into the kitchen to get more tea. The djinn hissed at him and he hissed back. When he returned, he said, 'That thing needs to learn some manners.' He sat down. 'Anyway, the upshot of all this is that someone called Timur mid afternoon on the day his sister died, whereupon he left the island. But Aylin and Zeynep hadn't yet discovered Deniz's body by that time. And where was Timur the night before Deniz died? According to his family, he wasn't at the Kara Lale Yalı – unless they're all lying.

'It takes over an hour to get from Heybeliada by ferry. Then probably another hour to Bebek by bus. So if he left the academy at, say, three, he could have been at the yalı by five. But apparently he wasn't. So where was he? And why, if he left the island the day before, did he return? Was it just to see his lover, Aksoy? Or was there a more sinister reason? The academy authorities stated that he was on the island at the estimated time of Deniz's death. Did he go back so that people could see him and make an assumption about his whereabouts that wasn't true? I mean, there were no classes taking place over the holidays. The boys who remained at the academy were there because either their parents were abroad or they wanted to be there to work . . .' He shook his head. 'These posh schools also act as babysitting services for the rich who can't be bothered to entertain their own children in the summer. But I doubt the remaining staff pay too much attention. It is, after all, their holiday too. Anyway, if we assume that Aksoy is telling the truth, then Timur Tonguç could have killed his sister. The question is why.'

They got the old man a chair. It was only ten o'clock, but already the sun was hot and he complained that his legs ached.

'This yard has always been a disgrace,' he said to Süleyman as he sat down just in front of the back door.

He wasn't wrong. If the house on Kalyoncu Kulluğu Caddesi

was a mess, its back yard was an outrage. In spite of frequent rubbish collections by the municipality, people used it as a dumping ground for old mattresses, clothes and bags of general rubbish they couldn't be bothered to put out for collection. Of course, dealing with this should have been part of the kapıcı's job, but Ali Ok freely admitted he hadn't done that for years.

'If people wish to live in their own squalor, then who am I to make them do otherwise?' he said.

Süleyman said, 'It was your job.'

Ali Ok shrugged. Süleyman, for his part, said no more. He didn't want to antagonise the old man. That would be counter-productive. Ok had come back to the house without complaint.

Süleyman ordered the group of uniforms in front of him to dig up the remaining unexplored half of the yard. Ömer Mungun watched the old man, who appeared to stare into space with a smile on his face.

The only photograph the Tonguç family had of Timur was twenty years old. It showed a tall, distinguished-looking man in his early forties. His mother said he'd had it taken for one of her birthdays, as a present, which was why his hair was short and 'he doesn't look like a hedonist'. Fair skinned but dark haired, he'd been good looking in a classic sort of way, like his father the admiral. Ateş Tonguç, by contrast, was clearly a man who didn't bother about his appearance more than he had to.

Kerim Gürsel's phone rang.

'Good morning, Inspector Gürsel, I am Yarbay Mevlüt Halişdemir of Şavşat Jandarma in the province of Artvin.'

It wasn't unknown for the city police to be contacted by members of the paramilitary gendarmerie force based out in the country, but it didn't happen every day.

'Good morning, Mevlüt Bey,' Kerim said. 'How can I help you?'

'It's how I may be able to help you, sir,' the man replied. 'I

220

was contacted early yesterday by officers at police headquarters in Artvin regarding an individual who owns a pansiyon eight kilometres from the town of Pazar where I am based. Officers from Artvin went to seek this individual, one Timur Tonguç, but found the premises deserted.'

'Yes. Do you know where he is, Mevlüt Bey?'

'Sadly, no. But you may wish to know that one of his neighbours is already known to you.'

'Who?'

'Erdal Akopoğlu,' Halişdemir said. 'He is the son of local honey producer Cengiz Akopoğlu. By neighbour I mean, in these parts, their homes are two kilometres apart, but—'

'You do mean Erdal Akopoğlu, brother of Fatima Akopoğlu?' Kerim's heart hammered.

'That is correct. She ran away from her family last year and I believe you recently found her dead.'

'Yes.'

Erdal Akopoğlu was still in the city, waiting for his sister's body to be released for burial.

'The Akopoğlu family don't know Tonguç well,' the jandarma continued. 'They were not friends. They are Hemshin, they tend not to mix.'

The Hemshin people of the Black Sea region were a very distinct group. The descendants of Armenian converts to Islam, they were famous for their cultivation of tea and maize and their prowess at keeping bees.

'I will speak to Erdal Akopoğlu,' Kerim said. 'Thank you.'

'I can't let you in.' Zeynep Tonguç closed the front door of the apartment behind her. 'My mother's having a breakdown over all this.'

İkmen said, 'Look, just a couple of questions.'

'About where Timur is? I don't know.'

'No,' he said. 'About how Timur came to be at the Kara Lale Yalı on the day that Deniz died. And when.'

'What do you mean, how did he come to be at the yalı? He arrived.'

The divine liturgy service in the church of St Panteleymon above their heads began. Unaccompanied bass voices of unearthly richness.

Zeynep lowered her voice. 'My aunt is up there but my mother is in the kitchen. What's this about?'

'I think your brother Timur may not have been on Heybeliada all day when your sister was killed.'

'What? No, that's not possible,' she said. 'Timur arrived after my father. He'd come straight from the academy.'

'Not according to his old friend Burhan Aksoy,' İkmen said.

'Burhan? What did he say? Where did you find him?'

'I didn't. He's dead,' İkmen said. 'But he wrote a memoir, which his widow let me see. Burhan Aksoy places your brother at home the day before Deniz died as well as during the morning of the day in question.'

Zeynep flung her arms in the air. 'He wasn't!' she said. 'And I should know because I was there. We all were except for my father and Timur. Deniz had come over the night before; she stayed with us in her old room. She did that sometimes.'

This was the first time İkmen had heard anything about Deniz staying over.

'So your sister was at the yalı when you and Aylin went to visit your friend in Yeniköy?'

'Yes. She was having a day in the garden, sunbathing. She didn't just turn up and go into the garden while we were all out. But my brother wasn't there,' she said. 'I didn't see him until he came home that evening.'

'At what time?'

'I don't know!'

222

'Do you know who contacted him?'

'I assume it was my father.'

'But you didn't hear him call the academy.'

'I was hysterical,' she said. 'I'd just found my eldest sister dead. I don't know what happened.'

Çetin İkmen experienced the unique feeling of both despair at her answers and elation at what could possibly be in the gaps in her knowledge she had now exposed.

The three young constables leaned on their spades while they drank from water bottles. The ground in the back yard, baked hard by the sun, was difficult to shift.

Ali Ok looked up at Süleyman. 'I'm not saying anything.'

'I know,' Süleyman said.

'So why am I here?'

'Why shouldn't you be?'

The old man shrugged. 'Good point, but I'm not going to help you.'

'It will go better for you when it comes to court if you do.'

'I don't care.'

Süleyman looked across at Ömer Mungun, who shook his head. The old man wasn't revealing anything about the whereabouts of more victims, if indeed they existed, via either his body language or his behaviour.

'Who were the two bodies we found behind your wallpaper?' Süleyman asked.

'I don't remember,' Ali Ok said.

'You told me you remembered all your victims' names.'

'Did I?'

He was still playing games, all but one of which was entirely under his control. Sadly for Süleyman, the one element that wasn't under his control, the old man didn't care about. But he said it anyway.

'Carry on like this and you'll go away for ever.'

Ali Ok shrugged again. Then he looked up and said, 'At least in prison I'll get fed.'

'You think?'

The old man looked uncertain for just a moment, then he smiled. 'And I'm too old to be some gang boss's girlfriend.'

'Yes, but you will be incarcerated for the crime of sex with minors as well as child murder. A lot of our prisoners don't like people who do those things. Even murderers, provided they have only killed adults, hate twisted bastards who rape children.'

'I didn't rape—'

'I don't want to hear your crap,' Süleyman said. 'Just know that under current circumstances, your incarceration will not be comfortable.'

'People in Silivri are put into solitary confinement . . .'

'Those convicted or awaiting trial on political grounds are another matter.'

The old man didn't reply. He just smiled. Did he know his face was all over the newspapers and on the Internet?

Süleyman tried another tack he knew was doomed to failure.

'My officers, these young men here, are tired,' he said.

'They're young.'

What had he expected?

He looked up at the two constables who served as Ali Ok's escort and said, 'Take him back.'

They pulled the old man to his feet.

Süleyman addressed the search team. 'And you men, stand down. We need equipment here.'

The three young men looked relieved.

As he was taken back into the house, Ali Ok said to Süleyman, 'You won't go far in your job if you're soft on people.'

When he'd gone, Süleyman said to Ömer, 'Organise digging equipment. I'm leaving you in charge of the site. I'm going off for an hour. I got very little sleep last night.'

'Yes, sir.'

'Call me if you find anything or need me for any reason.'

Ömer was perfectly capable of managing a crime scene, and Süleyman himself was, for the moment, done. Sick to his stomach, he left the house and made his way back to his car.

There was a police car outside Aylin Tonguç's block. Was it something to do with her – or rather her missing brother – or something else entirely? İkmen had been calling her ever since he'd left her mother's apartment in Karaköy, but she wasn't picking up. Was she out? No, that was ridiculous.

He walked into the entrance hall and was immediately accosted by the building's kapıcı.

'Who are you? What do you want?'

He was a small middle-aged man with the frightened eyes of a street cat in the middle of a busy road. İkmen wondered what he had to hide.

'I'm here to see Aylin Hanım,' he said.

'Oh, you can't go up there!' the kapıcı said. He lowered his voice. 'Police.'

'I am police,' İkmen lied.

'Oh.' The man bowed. 'Bey effendi . . .'

İkmen mounted the stairs. Thank God Aylin Tonguç lived on the first floor. He'd actually arrive, hopefully, hardly out of breath at all.

The first person he saw at the top of the stairs was Kerim Gürsel's sergeant, Elif Arslan. Tall and blonde, she rested back on the banister rail, one skinny-jeaned leg crossed over the other. When she saw İkmen, she smiled.

'Çetin Bey,' she said. 'Wow, are you—'

He put a finger to his lips and went over to her. 'What's going on?' he whispered.

'Why?'

That annoyed him. He suddenly realised he wasn't accustomed to being questioned about his motives, particularly by members of the police.

'I was coming to see Aylin Tonguç,' he said. 'About her brother.'

He could see from Arslan's face that she was about to question this, but then she remembered. 'Oh yes,' she said. 'You're looking into the death of her sister.'

'Yes,' he said. 'I should speak to Kerim Bey. Can you tell him I'm here?'

'What, now? He's with Aylin Hanım . . .'

'Look, if he's angry, I'll take full responsibility.'

She sighed. Then she pushed herself away from the banister and walked towards Aylin Tonguç's door.

'I know this is all part of the case against my father. I won't say any more. But my brothers have nothing to do with it.'

Kerim Gürsel sat down without asking permission. Sometimes, as a working-class İstanbullu, he could see what people from the countryside meant when they described the city's middle classes as rude and high handed. It was hot, the apartment was airless and Kerim felt just about to drop. Unlike Aylin Tonguç, dressed entirely in what appeared to be black velvet, who wasn't even breaking a sweat.

'Hanım,' he said, 'we need to speak to your brother Timur in order to rule him out of an ongoing investigation. Your younger brother, Ateş, has already submitted himself to DNA testing, which at this stage is simply a precautionary measure.'

'But why my brothers?' she said. 'Why our family?'

'I'm not able to tell you that at this time,' Kerim said. 'But if you know where he is, I would urge you—'

Elif Arslan whispered in his ear. 'Inspector İkmen is outside.'

Normally, and much as he loved the former inspector, Kerim would have asked İkmen to meet him back at headquarters. But he too had been involved with this family, albeit on what might or might not be a cold case.

'OK,' he told Arslan. 'You wait here.' He stood up and bowed to Aylin Tonguç. 'I'm sorry, Aylin Hanım, someone needs to speak to me. I'll be back as soon as I can.'

She said nothing, but she looked offended.

Out on the landing, which was considerably cooler than Aylin Hanım's apartment, Kerim found İkmen walking up and down. He probably needed a smoke.

'Çetin Bey,' Kerim said.

The two men embraced. Once İkmen's sergeant, Kerim still felt an intense sense of loyalty to the man who had taught him almost everything he knew.

'I came to see Aylin Tonguç,' İkmen said. 'Because I, too, need to find her brother Timur. I kept on ringing, but neither she nor her maid picked up.'

'Oh, the maid is off,' Kerim said. 'Why the sudden urgency to find Timur? Have you discovered something new on your cold case?'

'Yes,' İkmen said. And he told Kerim about what he had found in Burhan Aksoy's memoir. Then he said, 'And you?'

'Still need to get hold of Timur Tonguç's DNA,' Kerim said. 'Between ourselves, there is some evidence that he may have known my victim, Fatima Akopoğlu, back in Artvin.'

'Do you have any evidence he's been in İstanbul?'

'No. No family members have seen him, and that includes Aylin Tonguç. Was that all your business with her?'

'Not quite,' İkmen said. 'I wanted to go over with her the

timings of what happened on the day her sister died. I want to see whether her memory is any better than her sister Zeynep's.'

Kerim sighed. 'Well I can't let you in there while I'm questioning her,' he said. 'I'm sorry. But my investigation is live.'

'Of course.'

'That said, if you have simply arrived here at the same time by chance . . .'

'Which I have.'

Kerim shrugged.

Unlike İkmen's previous visit to this dark, stifling apartment, Aylin Tonguç was not still. Moving, albeit slightly, in her seat, she was not the ravaged-faced idol of inaction he had seen before. Rather, something was moving inside, something she didn't want anyone to see. What was it?

As he watched her speak to Kerim Gürsel, İkmen couldn't make up his mind whether she knew the whereabouts of Timur Tonguç or not. A brother she kept on saying she hadn't seen for decades; what was he to her?

He was her brother. İkmen looked around him into the darkness that gathered in every corner.

Chapter 19

He walked from Gaziosmanpaşa down to the Golden Horn. It had proved impossible for him to work with the theft of his father's watch on his mind. And yet Imam Metin Demir berated himself for it. It was just an old watch; it wasn't as if anyone had died. If it had been so precious to him, why had he let Cengiz Bey examine it while he paid for their food?

The truth was that old Regep's watch didn't really mean that much to him any more. It hadn't done for years. He'd carried it around more out of habit than anything else. His trouser pockets felt light without it.

Metin had always liked to be by water if he was upset. Even as a child he'd wandered down to the Horn, popping out between the old Greek houses of the Fener quarter, dodging the cars to cross Mürselpaşa Caddesi and then settling himself down in the small park beside the Orthodox Church of St Stephen. It was while he was peering hopelessly into the distance looking for a break in the traffic on Mürselpaşa that he saw Inspector Süleyman sitting in the small garden outside the Hotel Troya.

A nineteenth-century wooden house, the Troya had once been the home of a Greek merchant and his family and had some years ago been called the Hotel Daphnis.

Clearly enjoying a quiet coffee, the policeman looked as if he could be half asleep. Should Metin disturb him? He watched the traffic build up again and almost, but not quite, grind to a halt, then speed up again. He looked from the road to Süleyman and then back. Now that he'd seen the man, he couldn't un-see him, and he really should tell someone about the watch. But then again, was Süleyman even on duty?

Metin looked at the road, back at the hotel, glanced at the church, and then suddenly a voice said, 'Imam Metin?'

'Dad.'

'Hülya?'

İkmen put his coffee down and leaned back in what was a very squishy leather chair. Modern, so-called American-style coffee joints were big on large, supposedly comfortable chairs. This one made him feel as if his arse was on the floor.

He spoke into the phone as softly as he could. He hated people who shouted into them at the tops of their voices.

'What's up?'

'Have you seen Suzan?' his daughter asked.

'Suzan Tan?'

'Yes. Have you?'

'No,' he said. Keeping the front of Aylin Tonguç's apartment in view wasn't easy from an almost prone position. İkmen wished he'd never moved. 'Why?'

'I saw her this morning and she looks as if she's been in a fight.'

'A fight?'

'Someone hit her – hard. She'd put on make-up and tried to hide it, but her nose is crooked and her face is swollen and bruised. I instantly thought of her new uncle . . .'

Tayfun Yıldırım. Yes, it wasn't a giant leap.

'Did you speak to her?'

'Yes,' Hülya said. 'She reckoned she'd fallen down some stairs. I wanted to say, "Look, I'm a policeman's daughter, don't even try to kid me," but I didn't. Could be the reason why she didn't want to work with you any more. Maybe that pig warned her off.'

'Mr Yıldırım does have permission to demolish the Kara Lale Yalı and then rebuild,' İkmen said. 'But I'll look into it.'

'Please. I hate to think she's being bullied by that man.'

'Me too.'

But it would make sense. Yıldırım was a ruthless man who had a reputation for getting his own way. Painstaking historical research would not impress him. And although he owned sites all over the city, the land underneath the old yalı was probably one of his most valuable properties. Suzan had said he'd only given her permission to investigate on sufferance.

İkmen sat forward in his uncomfortable chair and looked at the apartment block across the road. Aylin Tonguç had simply reiterated her original story. Her brother had been at the naval academy all day, and although she didn't know who had called him after she and Zeynep found Deniz, she did say it might have been her father. But that still didn't explain why Timur had left Heybeliada mid afternoon.

The entire family had to be nervous because their father was in prison. But even with Zeynep Tonguç, İkmen couldn't shake the conviction that they were all covering up for something. Maybe not the same thing in every case, but they each had a reason to hold something back. But what?

Aylin Tonguç had been a wreck. Eyes darting everywhere, she'd looked at Kerim Gürsel, surely one of the most mild-mannered officers, as if he were a devil. Something was rotten and it was something that affected each member of that family in a different way.

'I was having a few moments to myself,' Süleyman said. 'I'm working on a case that is disturbing, to say the least.'

'Oh, then don't let me stop—'

'Sit. Sit,' Süleyman said. 'You are not my problem, Imam Demir.'

The little garden in front of the Troya was one of the places Süleyman liked to come in order to be alone. But on this occasion, he didn't mind talking, provided it was to someone who had nothing to do with that house of horrors in Tarlabaşı. Ömer had called five minutes ago to let him know that another small body had been found behind a pile of timber in the attic.

'I need to finish my coffee,' he said.

The imam smiled. Here was a man who was honest about his position on fasting, and he respected that. It was the people who pretended who annoyed him.

'Not many people come here, unless they're staying in the hotel,' Süleyman continued. 'And there are not a great many of them.'

'Balat is rather off the tourist trail,' Metin said.

'Yes. Pity.'

'I agree.'

'So what brings you here?' Süleyman asked.

'Oh, it's one of my happy places, if you must know. When I was a child, I found that being near water always calmed me down during times of trouble.'

'You're troubled? About the man you think broke into your house?'

The imam hung his head. 'I have been so stupid,' he said. 'I saw him again.'

'When?'

'Yesterday.'

A man came and sat at one of the other outdoor tables and opened a newspaper.

'What happened?'

'Well, I was taken aback,' Metin said. 'There he was in front of my house. He asked me to join him in Sultanahmet Square for İftar.'

'And you . . .'

232

'I went. I was curious. What if he had known my father? That was what I kept thinking. If I rejected him, I would feel bad. I am the son of an ex-offender; I know all about the kind of rejection a criminal record can bring. And I thought, maybe he really is dying . . .'

'And?' Süleyman lit a cigarette.

'And he robbed me,' the imam said. 'He took a watch, my father's . . .'

He wasn't looking at Süleyman any more, but at the man sitting at another table with his newspaper.

'That's him!' the imam said. 'There!'

The man who had been quietly reading his newspaper found himself a spectator in a drama about which he had no knowledge.

Metin pointed at the photograph on page four of the man's newspaper. 'That's him,' he said. 'A few years ago, I should imagine, but it's definitely him. I sat and talked to him for over an hour.'

Mehmet Süleyman said, 'Are you sure?'

'That is a picture of the man who called himself Cengiz Bey,' the imam said. 'I would stake my honour on it. Why is his picture in the paper?'

'Because a colleague of mine needs to speak to him to eliminate him from his inquiries,' Süleyman said.

'Inquiries into what?'

'A murder in Kanlica.'

People arrived and people left Aylin Tonguç's apartment block, called the Nice Apartments. Built in the 1920s, when many Turks still felt that the French way of life was the acme of high culture, it was the sort of place where residents wore designer clothes. The only exceptions to this were their servants. İkmen realised that sitting in the coffee shop was pointless. He either went back in and tried to talk to Aylin Tonguç again, or he went home. Her maid hadn't appeared, and so he had to assume she was alone now that Kerim Gürsel had gone. This meant she might not open the door to him. But he had to try.

He walked into the building and was instantly accosted by the kapıcı.

'You again?'

'Yes,' he said. Then he had a thought. 'Is there an entrance to the building that the servants use?'

'There's a back way, yes,' the man said. 'But everyone has to pass through the entrance hall. I couldn't do my job if people just came in and out as they pleased.'

'Do you know if Madam Tonguç's maid is here today?'

'No,' he said. 'Went this morning.'

'Where?'

'I don't know. I don't pry. My residents' privacy is safe with me.'

İkmen wanted to laugh. Since when did kapıcılar not know everything that went on in their buildings?

'Madam Tonguç is alone,' he said. 'Is the girl on her day off?'

'I don't know. She doesn't usually have a day off. Girls like that don't.'

He meant uneducated girls from the country. In spite of everything politicians claimed to have done for the rural poor, country people, particularly girls, were still looked down upon by many city dwellers. Mainly because the sorts of jobs they could expect to get were so low-status.

'Has Madam Tonguç had any other visitors?' İkmen asked.

'Only you and your colleagues,' the kapıcı said.

İkmen walked up the stairs and stood on the landing. Aylin Tonguç's apartment was at the end of a short corridor. As he drew closer, he saw that her front door was ajar. He could just see the hallway beyond, which was, as usual, in half-light.

'Madam Tonguç?'

A faint sound that he couldn't identify came from inside.

'Aylin Hanım?'

The silence was complete. İkmen pushed the bottom of the door with his foot. But opening it just a few more centimetres showed him nothing. Just more darkness, and now the faint sound of a ticking clock. He took a breath before he opened the door completely.

What was revealed to him this time, at the entrance to what he knew was the living room, was a heaped-up blacker darkness on the floor. It made no sound, but İkmen knew in his bones what it was, and he ran down the corridor and fell to his knees, which became immediately soaked in her blood.

Aylin Tonguç didn't make a sound. İkmen took out his phone and called for an ambulance before using his torch to find her head, which was covered in blood from a wound to her forehead. She appeared to have stopped breathing.

It was while İkmen was clearing her airways and putting her in the recovery position that he heard the sound of running feet, and then a crash as whoever had been in the apartment slammed the door behind them.

Inspector Süleyman left the imam with a slightly younger man who was investigating the Kanlica murder.

'I am Inspector Kerim Gürsel,' the officer said. 'Thank you for coming in, Imam Demir.'

'What else could I do?' Metin said. 'If this man who called himself Cengiz Bey has murdered someone, I want to bring him to justice. And I'd like my dad's watch back.'

Gürsel said, 'Of course.'

He began to question Metin about Cengiz Bey's appearance, what he had talked about at İftar and the few details the imam had about his background.

'Most of my dad's old friends are dead,' Metin said. 'Some

died in prison, some of alcoholism, drugs. The world is unfor-
giving to ex-convicts. My dad drank himself to death, and
although it pains me to say it, I can understand that. There was
nothing for him.'

'But this Cengiz Bey was different?'

'Yes,' he said. 'Smart, not on anything as far as I could tell.
He claimed to be a bus driver somewhere in the country. I wish
now I'd asked him where, but as I told Inspector Süleyman, I
had a bad feeling about him. It was only when he told me he
was dying that I sort of changed my mind.'

'Sort of?'

'I couldn't shake the feeling he was manipulating me. That
only lifted at last night's İftar. He was really easy to be with and
he did appear to have known my dad. Not that if he is this Timur
Tonguç he could have done. Dad didn't know regular people –
only to steal from them.'

'Maybe your dad stole from this man? Do you know anything
about the watch Cengiz Bey took from you?'

'No,' Metin said. 'Only that Dad always said it was one of
the few things he'd come about legitimately.'

'Did he ever tell you how?'

'No,' he said. 'And then I broke it.'

'A Rolex.'

'Yes. Not that it made any difference to me. It was just Dad's
watch. He wore it until he was on his deathbed, when he gave
it to me. I should have got it repaired. As Cengiz Bey said, a
Rolex is a Rolex even if it's broken, which must be why he stole
it.' He leaned forward. 'Who is this Timur Tonguç, Inspector?'

'A man I want to interview in relation to a murder,' Gürsel
said.

'So . . . he's not committed a murder?'

'I don't know.'

'And yet he's running away?'

'I think so. But there may be other reasons for that.'

'What?'

'I don't know.'

'Stop him!'

İkmen glanced at the man's figure disappearing down the staircase and then ran back to Aylin Tonguç, yelling as he went, 'Stop that man!'

Whether the kapıcı answered or not, he couldn't hear. But what he did know was that no one stopped the man as he ran across the entrance hall and flung the front doors open so that they crashed loudly against the outside wall.

Thankfully he'd managed to get Aylin Tonguç breathing again, but those breaths were only shallow. Completely unconscious, she didn't even groan. Had whoever had attacked her damaged her brain? And who had assaulted her so viciously, and why? The kapıcı had said she was alone, so had her attacker been a burglar? And if so, had he only just broken in or had he been in the apartment, hiding, when İkmen had visited before with Kerim Gürsel? They had not, after all, searched the place. Had the man been someone who knew Aylin or, maybe even more crucially, her maid?

İkmen put a hand on Aylin's neck to feel the faint pulse beneath the skin, assuring himself that she was still alive. He found himself asking himself where the ambulance crew were, but he knew the answer. Stuck in or battling with traffic. The city grew bigger ever day; it was ridiculous.

Footsteps made him look up. The kapıcı said, 'What happened?'

'She was attacked,' İkmen said.

'Robbed?'

'I don't know. I've been busy keeping her alive. I yelled down at you; did you not hear me?'

'Er . . .'

237

'Well never mind,' İkmen said. 'You didn't stop him.'

'No, I was, er, I was in the um . . .'

'Why not just say the word "toilet"?' İkmen said.

'Well, it's not nice . . .'

İkmen wanted to exclaim 'May God save me from prudery!' but he didn't, because now he needed to bend down to hear what Aylin Tonguç was trying to say.

Chapter 20

Beyond the police cordon lurked the vultures. Armed with long-lens cameras and attitudes they had worked to hone into the kind of poisonous judgemental moralising that certain readers liked, the men and women from the gutter press, the ghouls and the weirdos of the Internet.

Mehmet Süleyman and Ömer Mungun looked at them from inside the 'House of Death'. Süleyman said, 'Wonder how many of that lot are being paid by Tayfun Yıldırım and his silent Armenians to suggest this house is razed to the ground.'

Since Süleyman had returned from Balat, yet another small body had been found in the back yard.

'Maybe they have a point,' Ömer said.

'Oh, they do. But for the wrong reasons.'

'You don't think this was engineered in some way, do you, sir?' Ömer said.

'By Yıldırım et al.? No,' he said, 'but it is a gift to them and they may have known that the old kapıcı had a liking for little girls, though we'll probably never know. When Commissioner Ozer chairs the press conference tomorrow, no doubt many unhinged theories will be created by the ladies and gentlemen of what we are still obliged to call the press.'

Ömer said nothing. With a few notable exceptions, the Turkish press had become ever more conservative, to the point where, some like Süleyman believed, truth was almost entirely non-existent.

'Our job will be to try to make sure these victims are named, that their deaths are attributed to the right person . . .'

'You don't think Ali Ok killed all of them?'

'I don't know,' Süleyman said. 'And until and unless we can get the old bastard to talk, we *won't* know. That will depend upon whether he stops enjoying himself and decides to do something decent for once in his life. Tragically for us, because he is a sociopath, that is unlikely.'

'I wonder how he got to be like that, sir?' Ömer said.

Süleyman lit a cigarette. 'I don't know and nor do I want to know,' he said. 'You know my second wife was a psychiatrist. Her job was all about finding the "why" behind acts like those of Ali Ok. I used to be much more interested in that myself. But now I only want to get to the truth and lock these people away. I imagine it's probably something to do with getting older.'

It was his old office, the one he'd once shared with Mehmet Süleyman, Ayşe Farsakoğlu and latterly with Kerim Gürsel. Though it was now cleaner, tidier and very obviously Kerim's domain, Çetin İkmen nevertheless felt a wave of nostalgia as he passed through the door.

In front of Kerim, Elif Arslan and İkmen, three members of the Tonguç family sat in a line on ancient chairs İkmen remembered using as footstools.

'I've got you all here because of what Aylin said to Çetin Bey before she was taken to hospital,' Kerim said.

'We should be with her.' Halide Tonguç shook as she spoke. 'I should be there, I'm her mother.'

'Your daughter is in surgery,' Kerim said. 'There is nothing you can do to help her. She's in the best hands she can be.'

It was unusual to hear Kerim being so direct, if not brutal. But then İkmen remembered that, in part, that was the role. He too had assumed the mantle of brutality from time to time when he was in Kerim's shoes.

'She might die!'

Zeynep Tonguç put a hand on her mother's shoulder.

Kerim said, 'And she may not. As I understand it, Halide Hanım, your daughter has a fractured skull, which has caused some bleeding on her brain. This needs to be arrested, which is what the surgeon is doing now. There is nothing any of us can do.' He folded his arms on his desk. 'I have brought you here in order that we can all be honest with each other.'

Ateş Tonguç shuffled uncomfortably in his seat.

'For my part,' Kerim continued, 'I can tell you that as of an hour ago, you, Mr Tonguç, are cleared of any suspicion in the murder of Fatima Akopoğlu. The DNA sample we harvested from Fatima's body does not match yours. However, your brother, Timur, is another matter.'

'Why are we under suspicion?' Ateş said. 'Why do you think my brother and I . . .'

'When your father was arrested, a DNA sample was taken from him,' Kerim said. 'When we obtain DNA samples from scenes of crime, we match them against those of past and existing felons as well as those taken from people on remand. Your father's sample was close, but not a match to the one found at Kanlica. Like yours, Mr Tonguç. We have yet to obtain a sample from your cousin in Malta, but the authorities there have told me he hasn't left the country in over a year.'

'And Timur?'

'We need to find him in order to exonerate him – or not.'

'Or not?'

Kerim looked at Halide Tonguç. 'Madam,' he said, 'can you explain to me why your son is running away? Can you further explain to me why, according to your daughter Aylin, he attacked her so viciously?'

'It wasn't him, it can't have been!'

'That is what she said to me,' İkmen said.

It had been a moment that would live with him for a long time. Aylin had struggled to get the words out through the blood that had oozed from her mouth.

Halide Tonguç shook her head.

Kerim continued. 'I don't know whether Aylin and Timur argued or whether what happened was an accident. I can't even speculate.'

'But you want to get him in to do a DNA test,' Ateş said.

'That too.' Kerim looked at all of them. 'It's important. Whatever has happened, he has questions to answer. Did any of you know he was in İstanbul?'

'No,' Zeynep said.

'I told him to keep away,' Halide said.

'So you were in contact . . .'

'Mother was always in contact,' Ateş said. 'When Father fell out with Timur after my brother refused to go back to the academy, that was it for him. But for the rest of us . . . I heard from him very occasionally. Not lately. Zeynep?'

'Rarely,' his sister said. 'It was Mother who kept in touch. I don't know if our father knew.'

Kerim looked at Halide Tonguç. 'Hanım?'

She sighed. 'Yes, I did keep in touch occasionally,' she said, 'and no, my husband didn't know. Timur just drifted. He lived on the coast for years, then he acquired that place in Artvin. I thought he might settle down, but he was rarely there in recent years. I told him when his father was imprisoned, but I also told him not to come home. At first I didn't want to upset him. Seeing our house being sold off to that monstrous property developer, experiencing the pain of being a social outcast . . .'

'Do you think that would have upset him?'

'I don't know,' she said. 'He never had a great deal of feeling

242

for his father. Alaaddin Bey was always harder on him, as the elder son. And Timur, well, he knew things about his father . . .'

'What things?'

Ateş placed a hand on his mother's arm. 'Mama . . .'

'He knew his father had a mistress,' she said.

Zeynep echoed her brother. 'Mama . . .'

'We must tell the truth. We have no choice,' Halide said. She looked at Kerim. 'I didn't want Timur to come here dragging all that up again. Not with my husband in prison. It would blacken his name still further if it got out.'

'And yet you initially encouraged Dr Tan and myself to investigate a very dark period in your family's history,' İkmen said.

'Yes, it was stupid,' Halide said. 'But Dr Tan was so persuasive, and also I wanted to know. My eldest daughter died in 1976 and it has always conflicted me. Conflicted all of us. I convinced myself for many years that she committed suicide, but I also always knew that had to be wrong.'

'Why?'

'Because . . .' Her eyes began to water. Zeynep gave her a handkerchief. 'She'd just got married,' she said. 'And . . . and I was completely cut out of any investigation into her death. We all were.'

'What do you mean?' İkmen asked.

But Halide Tonguç said nothing. Her daughter continued for her. 'We were never really interviewed about what happened.'

'Why not?'

'Daddy said we were too distressed. He answered all the questions on our behalf. Ridiculous, I know.'

'But he wasn't there,' İkmen said. 'And why didn't you tell me this before?'

She looked at the floor.

Kerim sighed. 'All right,' he said. 'This is very interesting, but for the moment we just have to find Timur. We know for sure now that he's been in the city, because he attacked Aylin. Can any of you think where he might be? People and places he had some attachment to?'

'He left in 1976,' Ateş said. 'I was a kid, I hardly knew him. As far as I was concerned, he was either at home or at college. The academy moved some time ago, didn't it?'

'To Tuzla,' İkmen said. 'I believe it is now part of the naval training school. Would he go back there?'

'No,' Ateş said. 'Why would he? He hated it there.'

'Why did he go to Aylin's apartment?' Kerim asked. 'Did he get on well with her?'

'No,' Zeynep said. 'Not that I know of. I'm surprised she even let him in. She doesn't always agree to see me. Gets that girl of hers to turn me away.'

But the girl hadn't been there, according to the kapıcı. Indeed, now he came to think about it, İkmen wondered how, and when, Timur Tonguç had got in. Why hadn't the kapıcı seen him?

'I think he used to like to go to the cinemas in Beyoğlu,' Ateş said. 'When they showed the old Yeşilcam movies.'

Before Hollywood dominated the visual life of the nation, the local film company Yeşilcam had made much-loved comedies, tragedies, science-fiction epics and even some soft porn. Their films made older Turks like İkmen a little misty eyed.

'Those cinemas have gone,' Zeynep said. She threw her arms in the air. 'I don't know what he liked to do. That friend of his who came to the house . . .'

'Burhan Aksoy is dead,' İkmen said.

She shrugged. 'Then . . .'

And then her mother, who had been listening and saying nothing, spoke.

'I know where he might be,' she said.

* * *

244

'You should've let me beat him up,' Selçuk Çeviköz said to Imam Metin Demir.

Metin closed his eyes. Why had he spoken about Cengiz Bey to Selçuk? Because he had no one else he could tell.

'It's over now, Selçuk, let it go.'

'He stole your dad's watch.'

'Yes.'

'He needs to be punished.'

Metin put down the almost completed suit jacket and said, 'I can't concentrate. It's no good. I'm going home.'

The strain of talking about his encounter with Cengiz Bey to the police coupled with lack of sleep had given the imam a headache. He knew he had work to do, but he also knew that if he didn't lie down for a while he'd feel sick by the time İftar came round, and he couldn't afford not to eat.

Selçuk, as was his wont, begged to stay on in the workshop to tidy up, but Metin made him go home. Let loose on his own, who knew what inadvertent damage he'd do, or where he'd put things, never to be found again?

Metin walked back to his house, opened all the windows to get rid of some of the stifling heat, lay down on his bed and went to sleep.

'You still pay her rent?'

Ateş Tonguç was beside himself. The stem of his pipe, gripped between his clenched teeth, juddered.

'You lost your home, *our* house, and yet you pay rent on an apartment for our father's mistress?'

Halide Tonguç couldn't meet her son's gaze. Nor her daughter's.

'Your father made me promise,' she said.

Her daughter stood up, 'Unbelievable!'

'So Timur was right,' Ateş said. 'How did he know?'

'You'd have to ask your father . . .'

245

'But *you* knew?' Zeynep said.

'I did.'

'All along?'

'He met her in the early seventies,' she said. 'He set her up in a small apartment where she lives to this day.'

'The one you pay for!'

İkmen looked at Kerim Gürsel. This family was falling to pieces, but his investigation was still ongoing.

Kerim held up a hand. 'The rights and wrongs of this are not issues for the present time,' he said. 'I have to find your son, Madam Tonguç. Now where does this mistress of your husband live?'

He knew she'd seen him, and although he was both tired and depressed, Mehmet Süleyman was glad. He smiled.

'Hello.'

Çiçek İkmen smiled back.

'Just finished work?'

'Yes,' she said.

'Are you preparing İftar for your dad?'

'He's out,' she said. 'And let's face it, we don't really do İftar, do we?'

'No.'

'But I am going to Nevizade for a drink,' she said. 'If you fancy joining me . . .'

'That would be great,' he said.

She took his arm and propelled him into Beyoğlu's principal drinking street.

'Any idea where you want to go?' he said.

'No. Just any old bar that serves gin.'

Chapter 21

Years ago, back in the 1970s, people had lived on Nevizade Sokak. There had always been bars, but there'd also been apartments too. Once, at the beginning of the twentieth century, they'd been the residences of some of İstanbul's louche demi-monde; by the seventies, they had mostly been tenanted by the poor.

Hayrünnisa İnce, though originally the daughter of a water carrier from Mersin, had not been one of them. Back in 1974, when she had walked into her high-ceilinged apartment, complete with French-style balcony, she'd been the most well-dressed and well-fed inhabitant of Beyoğlu. Everyone had known what she was. But everyone had also treated her with respect. She was the admiral's woman, and you didn't mess with one of those. Now, however, things were different. Now she had to make money by telling fortunes in cafés and bars, and if Madam Tonguç didn't carry on paying her rent, she knew she'd be destitute.

She put her empty beer bottles in the bin outside the meyhane next door to her apartment and was just about to go back inside when a man's voice said, 'Hayrünnisa Hanım?'

'Dad has always found ways to position himself at the centre of the action,' Çiçek said. 'When Mum died, he stopped doing that, which was terrifying.'

'He'd also retired,' Süleyman said.

Çiçek took a sip of gin and tonic. 'Not through choice. But then I don't have to tell you that.'

She didn't. İkmen's wife had been asking him to retire for years, but it was only when he realised he couldn't work with the department's new commissioner, Ozer, that İkmen finally left the police. Ozer was never going to allow him the scope for independent thought and action that had characterised his predecessor's tenure. Commissioner Hürrem Teker had encouraged her officers to use their initiative – an aspect of her practice that had eventually brought her into conflict with her superiors.

'So this Tonguç man is connected to that death over in Kanlica?' Çiçek asked.

'Possibly,' Süleyman said. 'Although quite where Metin Demir and his stolen watch fit in, I don't know. The timepiece came from the imam's father, who was an habitual thief and so not really the most obvious companion for the son of an admiral. Tonguç claimed that he knew Regep Demir in prison, but we know that Timur Tonguç has never been to prison.'

'Perhaps he made friends with him because he wanted to explore the rough side of life. Rich people do that sometimes.'

'Possibly . . .' Süleyman drained his beer, then asked the waiter for another and lined up a second gin and tonic for Çiçek.

'I don't want to get drunk,' she said.

'No, I'm not . . .'

'I don't *want* to get drunk, but I may end up doing it anyway.' She smiled. 'What am I doing waiting at table in my forties? God knows I'm no snob, and I'm more grateful for this job than you will ever know, but working with people young enough to be your children is a challenge. I'm sure they see me as some sort of fossil.'

'I'm sure they don't.'

The drinks arrived and he changed the subject. 'So I imagine your father is working with, or at least consulting, Kerim Bey.'

'To be honest, I'm leaving him to it. This is the first time he's been animated in months. When Bülent came for İftar the other evening, he said Dad seemed like a different person. It's amazing, and not a little creepy, the way the deaths of strangers animate that man.'

Süleyman suddenly looked grave. 'People who do what we do are not regular men and women,' he said. 'I don't know how we stand it, but then maybe that is why we can, because we have no deep self-awareness. Maybe we lack something that others do not or maybe we are simply people who constantly crave excitement – to use a very inappropriate word.'

'You missed him.'

Hayrünnisa Hanım wasn't the sort of woman, İkmen thought, that one could imagine having been beautiful in her youth. But then again the cheap knock-off Beşiktaş football club tracksuit she was wearing did her no favours. It was a little too small and made the rolls of fat on her back, particularly, look lumpy and uncomfortable.

'Missed him when?' Kerim Gürsel asked.

'I don't know.' She lit a cigarette. 'Couple of days ago.'

Her apartment smelt of cigarettes, although the principal aroma on offer was beer. And given that the place looked as if it hadn't been cleaned up since the 1980s, it was not a giant leap to suppose that Hayrünnisa Hanım had a drink problem.

'Do you know where he went after he left here?'

'No.' She shrugged.

'How did you know Timur Tonguç?' İkmen asked.

She looked at him as if he was mad. 'He's the admiral's son,' she said.

'Do you know any of the admiral's other children?'

'No.'

'So how and why do you know Timur?'

She scowled. 'What's this all about?'

'Just answer the question,' Kerim said.

She threw him a look so dark it made İkmen shudder. What had Admiral Tonguç seen in this woman? Especially with a sober and attractive wife at home. Then he remembered that Halide Tonguç had also been, in her youth, really rather odd. What with the spiritualism and the weird beliefs and, he had to admit, a certain formality and coldness to her nature.

'He followed Alaaddin Bey here one day,' she said. 'He must've been sixteen. Came right up here, knocked on the door, and when I answered, he pushed past me and went for his father.'

'Because the admiral was seeing you?'

'Course,' she said. 'I could understand that. I thought the admiral would kill him. I had to pull him off the boy. I told him not to be so hard on him, of course he was upset. Timur, bless him,' and here she softened a little, 'threatened to tell his mother. But of course she knew.'

'Madam Tonguç knew about you?'

'I've never known Halide Hanım, never wanted to, but I've always respected her. Met her once back in the dim and distant past. Alaaddin Bey loves her, in his way. He loves us both. It's why he let her do all that spiritualist stuff, because he loves her.' She looked up. 'He loves me because I love sex.'

'You're sure Madam Tonguç always knew about you?' İkmen said.

'Yes,' she said. 'She still pays my rent, for which I'm grateful.'

'I think the admiral has instructed her to do so.'

'Whatever. I don't care,' she said. 'It gets paid.'

'What was Timur Tonguç doing here two days ago?' Kerim asked.

'I let him stay,' she said. 'When he comes to the city, he stays with me. Can't stay with his family, can he? And before you say anything, there's never been anything sexual between us. He was a kid when I met him. He still is to me.'

'Does his father know?'

250

'No,' she said. 'Alaaddin Bey has always been good to me, don't get me wrong, but I know he's a harsh man and I know that over the last twenty years he's seen other women. And I don't mean his wife. He and I have always practised give and take. So when he cut Timur out of his life when the boy wouldn't go back to the academy, maybe he knew I still looked out for him.'

'Timur didn't resent the fact that you had in effect replaced his mother?'

She smiled. 'He's a nice boy, is Timur, but he's an acquired taste. He ended up liking me, I think, and I became useful to him. His whole family rejected him really. He says he's always been different, but I think he's just like his father. And that's why they don't get on, too alike. Why do you want him?'

Kerim said nothing.

Hayrünnisa Hanım shook her head. 'You know,' she said, 'he was visiting me the day his sister died. Neither of us knew then, of course.'

İkmen said, 'Deniz?'

'Yes, he was here,' she said. 'Came over from Heybeliada the night before, said he had to get away from that awful place.'

İkmen looked at Kerim, who shrugged.

'When did he leave you on the day that Deniz Tonguç died, Hayrünnisa Hanım?' İkmen asked.

'In the morning,' she said. 'No one ever asked me about it, though. I thought they might, but it never happened.'

'Çetin!'

Was that Çiçek Mehmet Süleyman was with? He put his glasses on and saw that it was. The two of them were sitting outside a bar, drinking.

He walked towards them. 'What are you two doing here?'

Süleyman stood. 'In my case, attempting to relax,' he said.

Seeing Kerim Gürsel behind İkmen, he added, 'Kerim Bey, what are you doing here?'

Together with Kerim's sergeant, Elif Arslan, they gathered at Süleyman and Çiçek's table.

Çiçek said, 'Get some chairs.'

'We're not staying,' Kerim said. But when Elif brought chairs, he sat down.

'Are you still looking for Timur Tonguç?' Süleyman asked.

'Yes.'

İkmen and Elif sat.

'We had a lead here in Beyoğlu, but . . .' Kerim shrugged.

'Nothing?'

'No.'

'And yet we've learned that Timur was staying with this lead, the admiral's mistress, the night before his sister died back in 1976,' İkmen said. 'That supports his old friend Burhan Aksoy's memoir, which stated that he left the academy on Heybeliada the day before Deniz was killed.'

'So someone was lying?'

'More than one person, I think,' İkmen said. 'I should like to talk to the admiral, but . . .' He waved a hand.

'In the meantime, I have to get hold of Timur,' Kerim said. 'At the very least, he attacked his sister Aylin in Şişli. She's still in surgery as far as I know . . .'

'Well, my imam positively identified him,' Süleyman said.

'For which I'm grateful,' Kerim said. 'I can't think he's got any more to tell us, can you?'

'No, but that doesn't mean he hasn't,' Süleyman said. 'Tonguç stole his father's watch for some reason. He has no idea why.'

'Are you sure?'

'That's what he said.'

'And yet I wonder,' İkmen said.

'About what?'

'This imam's father . . .'

'He was a thief, by all accounts,' Süleyman said. 'I struggle to understand how he would have known Timur Tonguç. He had a record you could see from Russia.'

'And yet Tonguç wasn't the perfect military brat,' İkmen said. 'He wanted to drop out. Why wouldn't he have friends in İstanbul's seedier streets? He probably found that exciting.'

'How does the watch come into it?' Elif Arslan asked.

'We don't know,' İkmen said.

Çiçek stood up. 'Well, it's been fascinating,' she said. 'But I really think I should leave you all to your work now.'

Süleyman stood too. 'I'm sorry, Çiçek.' He looked at his colleagues. 'We were having a drink . . .'

'You're off duty,' Kerim said.

'Yes, but . . .'

Of course he wanted to continue this conversation; perhaps he even wanted to get involved in the case. Çiçek knew that and she smiled. 'I'll see you soon, Mehmet. Dad.'

And then she left.

The look on Süleyman's face did not escape İkmen. Disappointment mingled with relief. He knew it well. When Fatma used to leave him to his work, he'd always felt the same way.

Süleyman sat down. 'So what now?' he said.

They'd been told that she couldn't eat, speak or even breathe without assistance. And although the hospital staff had washed off the blood, her face was heavily bruised, her lips hanging in purple lumps around her breathing tube.

Halide Tonguç put a hand up to her mouth. Her son, Ateş, moved to support her.

'God! Is she going to die?' she asked the doctor who had ushered them into the room.

'We don't know,' the doctor said. 'We've removed a blood clot from her brain. Now we have to wait.'

Zeynep Tonguç cried. The doctor ushered the family back into the corridor. Other patients' relatives moved around aimlessly, occasionally sitting down and then standing up again without apparent thought. Such was life on an intensive care unit, where death peeped over everyone's shoulder.

The doctor left and the two women sat down.

Zeynep looked at her mother. 'Why did you tell him? He didn't need to know that Deniz's case was being looked into again.'

'I had to tell him in case he decided to come here,' her mother replied. 'I did it to keep him away. For your father's sake!'

'But it didn't work, did it. He came, and now we're here!'

Ateş crouched down between them. 'Arguing amongst ourselves will do no good,' he said.

They both looked at him, and then Zeynep said, 'What do you know? You were a child when Deniz died.'

'What's that got to do with anything?' he said. 'Deniz has been dead for forty-one years; our brother has just attacked our sister today.'

'Exactly,' Zeynep said.

'What are you saying?' he asked.

But it was Halide Tonguç who replied. 'She's saying nothing,' she said. 'We all know nothing.'

'Except that isn't true,' Zeynep said. 'Because you've hidden the truth, haven't you, Mother?'

Halide said nothing.

'You've lied. You lied about that woman, Daddy's mistress, you lied about Timur not being here . . .'

'I didn't know he was here. I didn't! I told him not to come. I don't know how Deniz died. I wasn't there. You were.'

'I didn't kill my sister.' Zeynep began to cry again. 'Why do you think I wanted Dr Tan and Çetin Bey to get involved? I want to know the truth.'

'And so do I,' her mother said. 'Because I don't know why I lost my daughter. I don't know. I don't know . . .'

She curled into her son's arms and sobbed.

The whole family had started eating. Selçuk's brother, Teoman, had laid a rug out on the pavement on which his mother had arranged a massive break-fast platter of dates and Ramazan pide plus bottles and bottles of fizzy soda. When he saw the imam walking towards him, Selçuk jumped to his feet.

'You came!' he said. 'Are you feeling better, Imam Metin?'

'Yes, yes.'

But he didn't look it. He was still white in the face and his clothes looked rumpled.

'Come and sit . . .'

Metin moved close to Selçuk. 'I need to take the van,' he said.

'My van? But it's—'

'Yes, it's İftar, I know. But I need to go somewhere. Give me the keys to the van and I'll be on my way.'

Selçuk thought the imam looked a bit mad. He certainly didn't seem his usual self. Also, he'd never asked to drive the van before. Why now?

'Of course you can have the van,' he said, 'but you don't like to drive. That's why I do it. Can't I take you to where you want—'

'I can drive.' The imam bit his bottom lip. 'Just give me the keys.'

The imam had bought the old Citroën H van fifteen years ago so that Selçuk could pick up cloth from his suppliers and, if necessary, deliver orders to customers. And although Selçuk loved the ancient gunmetal-coloured crate, even he had to admit that driving it wasn't something that someone with minimal experience should attempt.

'Yes, but you don't—'

'Selçuk, I have a driving licence. Just because I don't use it doesn't mean I can't drive. Also, I own the van. Give me the keys.'

Selçuk put his hand in his pocket and took out his keys.

İkmen ordered coffee for everyone. Süleyman didn't want any more alcohol, and Kerim and Elif were technically still on duty. Once the drinks had arrived, he said, 'If we assume that Timur Tonguç did kill that young woman in Kanlica, we have to ask ourselves why.'

'The local police believe he knew of her,' Kerim said.

'In Artvin?'

'Yes.'

'Were they . . . close?'

'That is unknown.'

'Why come all the way to İstanbul to rape and then kill her?'

Kerim shrugged.

'There's something we still don't know about this man,' İkmen said. 'Although to be honest, I believe there's still a lot we don't know about his family.'

'What do you mean?'

'You said yourself, Kerim Bey, that Halide Tonguç is probably still being economical with the truth in order to protect her husband, and I have uncovered some anomalies about the movements of the family on the day Deniz died that make me feel most uneasy.'

'And why attack Aylin Tonguç?' Elif said. 'What was he even doing at her apartment?'

'Hiding?' Süleyman suggested.

'But why there? And why attack her like that?' İkmen shook

his head. 'This all goes back to 1976. Think about it. Halide Tonguç is contacted by Suzan Tan and, under some pressure from her daughter Zeynep, agrees to allow us to try and find out what really happened to Deniz. Halide tells her estranged son, Timur, to stay away, ostensibly because he is at odds with his father, who he may compromise in some way. But compromise how? The admiral is in prison, so what could Timur say or do to make that situation worse? Well, there's his affair with Hayrünnisa Hanım . . .'

'In this climate, that could be problematic,' Elif said.

She was right. Proof of sexual impropriety would do Alaaddin Tonguç no good at all.

'And yet would it make anything that much worse?' İkmen asked. 'I don't pretend to understand what constitutes a political crime in this country now, but it seems to me that the admiral is not going to see daylight for a very long time, whatever is discovered about him. No. There's something more, and it's something to do with the timing of events on the day Deniz Tonguç was murdered.'

He didn't know what he was doing. How he had even got to the bridge was a mystery to him. He'd driven the wrong way down at least one one-way street. People had shouted at him, but not the man sitting at his side. He hadn't said a word.

The traffic was nightmarish. Of course it was! It was always bad, and on the last night of Ramazan, it was even worse than usual. People were trying to get home for İftar, and now that the sun had set, they were late. Volleys of horns blasted into the night sky, and he felt the car behind nudge the van forward.

The imam looked at the man in the passenger seat and tried not to let the gun he was holding make him descend into full-blown panic. Why did he want Metin to get him out of the city? The imam could barely drive, and he'd told him so! As the traffic began to move, he ground the gear stick into second, and the van protested by juddering forward before eventually settling into gear with a grunt.

To get out of the city meant, as far as Metin was concerned, somehow getting to the Bosphorus Bridge, which ran from Ortaköy on the European side to Beylerbey on the Asian shore. At Beylerbey, Metin knew, there were toll booths. Maybe that was the point at which he would be able to jump out of the van and make a break for it. If he wanted to do that . . . But did he?

He was scared. This man, Cengiz Bey, Timur Tonguç, whoever he was, had broken into his house while he slept and threatened him with a gun. He'd have to be mad not to be terrified. But why him? And why had this same man stolen his father's old watch? OK, it was a Rolex, but it was also broken. There had to be more than just money at stake here, surely?

Ataturk Bridge now behind him, Metin coaxed the van onto Refik Saydam Caddesi. If he could get to Taksim, there were all sorts of tunnels underneath the square. One of those had to lead eventually to the Bosphorus Bridge, didn't it? He hadn't driven since well before the square had been redeveloped, and with no map or satellite navigation device, he had no idea about how one even got into the right lane for the tunnels. It didn't help that he was shaking. He opened his mouth to speak, so that he could tell this man he was totally at a loss here, but the man silenced him with, 'Shut up and drive.'

Easing forward, centimetre by centimetre, taking his foot off the brake and stepping on the gas to try to make the ancient van go uphill, was making his leg ache. How did people do this every day? And more to the point, why, when the city had so many public transport options these days? Everybody knew that the municipal buses were awful, but there were trams, ferries, the metro . . .

A man in a big black SUV pulled level with the van and Metin saw him laugh at the vehicle. Time was when almost everyone had old cars and no debts. Now the reverse was true, and Metin felt, not for the first time, as if people had lost their souls to consumerism. His van was forty years old, but it was paid for.

And now the van, the imam and his frightening passenger were on Tarlabaşı Bulvarı and the approach to Taksim. Metin looked around for a sign that might give him a clue as to how to approach the square. If he got it wrong, he could end up going deeper into the city, and he didn't know how much longer he could drive under duress like this. What with the shaking, the pounding heart and the sweat that was pouring out of him, he felt light headed and sick. Driving wasn't natural to him, and so he had to keep on reminding himself to put his feet on the brake and the clutch to stop the thing, put it into neutral, then move off in first, accelerate and . . .

He didn't know how it happened. A foot that should have been stopping the van slammed onto the accelerator, and then he was inside the boot of the car in front with the steering wheel jammed into his stomach. As he threw up over the windscreen, a man from the vehicle in front came running over, opened the van door and punched him in the side of the head.

Horns blared and there was the unmistakable sound of crunching metal as the car behind the van ploughed into it, followed by another crash behind that. Then there was what sounded like an explosion. People began to scream.

Although not Metin's passenger, who, it seemed, had gone.

Chapter 22

The four of them ran. Süleyman knocked his coffee cup to the ground, where it smashed, but nobody cared. There'd been an explosion on Tarlabaşı Bulvarı and everyone feared the worst.

As he pulled a puffing İkmen along after him, Kerim Gürsel said, 'Hasn't our city suffered enough?'

Even if he could have answered, İkmen would not have needed to. İstanbul had soaked up punishment for years, always coming back – be it from terrorism, accident or even a coup – to its bruised, battered and beautiful self. But would this be too much?

As the four officers reached Tarlabaşı Bulvarı, they could see flames, and a multiple pile-up of vehicles all the way back almost to Refik Saydam Caddesi.

So there was a fire down on Tarlabaşı Bulvarı . . . So what? Why did everyone always have to go and watch these things? Was it just a Turkish trait or something universal that made otherwise sane people want to look at things burning? Ateş Tonguç sat down on one of the many now vacant chairs outside the first meyhane he came to and ordered half a bottle of rakı. He needed it.

He'd left his mother and Zeynep at the hospital. Aylin was apparently stable, but his mother wouldn't go home, so she said, until his sister opened her eyes. Such lack of realism was typical. What could she possibly do for Aylin that wasn't already being done?

Ateş poured a large measure of rakı into his glass and topped it up with a minimal amount of water. He lit his pipe and leaned back against the wall of the nameless meyhane he had chosen. There was a smell of burning fuel, if he wasn't mistaken, on the air, mixed with the aromas of rakı, fish and grilled meat. The waiter who had served him had said people were talking about the fire resulting from a bomb. But even if that were the case, what could Ateş do about it? He could hear people screaming, but then people always screamed whenever anything like this happened because everyone's nerves were on edge. İstanbul was not the quiet backwater where he had been born.

Ateş was about to close his eyes for a few moments when he saw a face pass in front of him that made his whole body shake.

'Can't work out whether the SUV slammed its brakes on suddenly or the old Citroën couldn't stop,' the traffic officer said. 'Doesn't help that the SUV driver's run off.'

Not that he was surprised. Drivers ran away from crash sites on a regular basis.

'What about the driver of the Citroën?'

'Oh, he's over there.' The officer pointed to a slumped figure by the side of the road.

'What about the fire?' İkmen asked as he pulled fragments of what appeared to be scorched paper out of his mouth. It was everywhere.

'I don't know,' the officer said. 'But word is it's not a bomb.'

Elif Arslan, sniffing, said, 'Diesel.'

'Diesel, petrol, gas – it's all here,' İkmen said as he watched people in cars light up cigarettes and cigars.

'Mehmet Bey . . .'

But Süleyman had gone. İkmen looked over his shoulder and

saw that he was talking to the man who was sitting by the side of the road.

'What are you doing here?'

Ateş took his brother inside the meyhane and sat him down in a dark corner. Sitting next to him, he lowered his voice. 'You know the police are looking for you?'

'Yes.'

'They think you murdered some girl over in Kanlica.'

Timur said nothing. Ateş didn't need this demonstration of what had always been a feature of his brother's behaviour to make the past come crashing into the present. Whenever Timur hadn't wanted to answer a question, he had simply remained silent. Ateş was five years old the first time he could actually remember him doing this.

'You did it, didn't you?' he said. 'Why? And what did you do to Aylin?'

Timur Tonguç was taller than his brother. In spite of having lived away from cities for most of his life, he was also more stylish. A 'peacock' was how their mother had once described him. She'd also used the same word for their father.

'Aylin?' Timur said. 'What of her?'

'You almost smashed her skull in!'

He looked away. 'You're insane.'

Ateş pulled his arm. Timur looked down at his brother's hand with distaste.

'I know what you did with Deniz,' Ateş hissed.

His brother's face reddened. 'Will you help me or not?' he said.

Ateş got to his feet and walked towards the street. When he reached the door of the meyhane, he yelled, 'Police!'

Which was when Timur shot him.

* * *

262

Mehmet Süleyman wasn't the sort of person who indulged in open displays of emotion, but he felt sorry for the imam, and so once the paramedic had given him a blanket, he put it around the man's shoulders and then placed his arm around him. Imam Metin Demir was as cold as snow, his face a taut grey disc. But he could talk and he wanted to.

'I can't be sure, but I think he went right,' he said.

'Into Beyoğlu?'

'I think. I . . .' He coughed.

İkmen leaned down and touched his arm. 'Don't try to talk.'

Flight into Beyoğlu seemed most likely simply because it would have taken Timur Tonguç longer to thread his way through the traffic to get to Tarlabaşı. Either way, he was armed and clearly dangerous.

Kerim Gürsel said, 'I'll take Beyoğlu. Sergeant Arslan, Tarlabaşı.'

'Yes, sir.'

'Call for backup.'

'Yes, sir.'

Elif Arslan left, her phone already at her ear, stepping through the gaps between the stationary vehicles, passing the wounded and the shocked sitting or lying in the road. Traffic officers had now arrived in force, but paramedics were still thin on the ground. It only took one accident on a major thoroughfare to force the entire city into a state of gridlock.

İkmen said to Gürsel, 'I'll come with you.'

'No. He's armed.'

'So are you.'

'But you're not,' Kerim said. 'And you're not a serving officer now, Çetin Bey.'

That was true. It meant that if anything did happen to İkmen, it would be down to him. But what of it? He had no debts, and he'd made a will leaving everything to be divided equally amongst his children.

'And so?'

'And—'

'I'm armed,' Süleyman said.

'You're off duty.'

He repeated İkmen's phrase: 'And so?'

He stood up, leaving Imam Metin to one of the paramedics.

There was a moment of silence, and then they heard the imam say, 'I still don't know what he wanted with me.'

'We'd best find out then, hadn't we?' İkmen said.

Kerim Gürsel gave in to what had become inevitable.

'Come on,' he said.

'What's taking them so long?'

Muharrem was a waiter, not a doctor, and yet, under supervision from Devrim, who was also a waiter but was training to be a doctor, he was doing his best. When he put pressure on the shoulder wound, the man groaned.

'Sorry! Sorry!'

'Don't let him bleed out!' Devrim said.

If only Devrim had got to him first, but he hadn't, and so Muharrem just had to hang on as best he could.

'Are you all right?' he asked the man, whose face was the colour of ash.

'My brother just shot me.'

'Your brother!'

Devrim said, 'Sir, try not to get upset. Keep calm.'

He ran to the open door and looked out into the street. There had been a multiple pile-up on Tarlabaşı Bulvarı, and although sirens were blaring all over the city, none of them seemed to be moving in the direction of Nevizade Sokak.

An old woman the boys often saw about the street came out of a doorway and said, 'What's going on?'

'Some man's been shot,' Devrim said.

'Have you called an ambulance?'

'Yes, but there's been an accident on the Bulvarı. I don't know when they'll get here.'

Muharrem saw his friend begin to tremble. Did that mean he feared the man might die?

What was it with people? Why did they always have to run towards trouble? Making their way back into the streets of Beyoğlu, the two officers and İkmen found themselves having to fight through crowds of people moving in the opposite direction. They also had to make sure that none of those individuals was Timur Tonguç. Backup was on its way, but when it would arrive was anyone's guess. In the past, Çetin İkmen had always thought badly of people who went to look at accidents. With the exception of his mother, who claimed to be able to see the souls of the dying leave their bodies on long silver threads, he had always considered their interest prurient. But post 9/11, his view had changed. Although ghouls still existed, a lot of people now checked out loud noises and plumes of smoke from a desire to know what they were up against this time.

On the corner of Yeni Çarşı Caddesi and İstiklal, they stopped.

Kerim said, 'All right, let's split up. He's not a young man and so he can't have got too far. Çetin Bey, do you think he might have gone back to Hayrünnisa Hanım's?'

'It has to be a possibility,' İkmen gasped. Even slowed down by the crowds, making his way up the hill from the Bulvarı to Beyoğlu had taken it out of him.

'I'll head up to Tünel,' Süleyman said.

Tünel, İstanbul's funicular railway, was a very quick way to get from Beyoğlu down to the Galata Bridge. And from Galata, there were many opportunities to escape via tram, bus or water.

Kerim took hold of İkmen's wrist and pulled him along into the almost empty Balık Pazar. They noticed that the local cats were helping themselves to the fish that was on offer in nearly every shop and restaurant, and also that the kokoreç seller had left his grill on. The smell of charred lamb's intestines was almost overwhelming. Heading down along the uneven pavement towards Nevizade Sokak, they had to avoid small piles of ice that the fishmongers had thrown into the street, as well as other fishy hazards such as discarded heads, scales and tails. They saw one woman, a tiny blonde who was clearly drunk, but no one else.

When they turned into Nevizade Sokak, they saw Hayrünnisa Hanım standing in the middle of the narrow alleyway talking to a young man dressed as a waiter.

'Let me on and then close the doors, but do not allow the carriages to move,' Süleyman said.

The funicular railway operator wanted to ask the policeman what he should do with all the people who wanted to get on the little train but couldn't. But he didn't. And although when he opened the doors, briefly, for Süleyman to board, there was a surge forward, people soon backed away when they realised the barriers had been shut.

However, the operator wasn't as quick in shutting the doors as he had been in opening them, and someone hurled himself out.

Kerim Gürsel requested assistance from any medical staff currently engaged in the emergency on Tarlabaşı Bulvarı. In the meantime, the young man who had been putting pressure on Ateş Tonguç's gunshot wound allowed Çetin İkmen to take over.

'You're sure it was your brother Timur who shot you?' Kerim said.

'Absolutely,' Ateş said. 'I don't know whether he just meant to wound me . . .'

'Thank God that's all that happened,' Kerim said. 'How are you feeling?'

'I'm in pain, but I've had worse.' Ateş winced.

Hayrünnisa Hanım reached down and touched his face. 'If I'd known that Timur was going to do this, I would never have let him stay,' she said. 'I'm so sorry . . .'

Kerim's phone rang. It was Süleyman. When he'd finished the call, he said, 'Mehmet Bey thinks it's possible a man seen running from Tünel in this direction is Timur Tonguç.'

Backup officers still hadn't arrived, although one of the young waiters at the meyhane's front door called out, 'Paramedics are here!'

İkmen passed the tablecloth he'd been using to staunch Ateş's wound to Hayrünnisa Hanım and said, 'I'll go and look.'

Kerim, who had gone to greet the paramedics, said, 'Head for the top of the Balık Pazar. I'll meet you in a minute.'

İkmen headed off.

Süleyman hadn't been able to definitively identify the man the Tünel operator had seen jumping out of the train. Now, jogging along İstiklal Caddesi, he thought about Timur Tonguç and wondered what had made him shoot his own brother. Kerim had told him that Ateş was not badly wounded, but even so, he'd still shot him.

He passed the Catholic church of St Mary Draperis, recalling with horror its lifelike and sometimes bloody statuary. Dark and what his ex-wife Zelfa, a Catholic herself, always described as visceral, it was a reminder in the modern world of the agony that could accompany death. And although his mind was searching for a tall, distinguished-looking middle-aged man, his thoughts were also on Ali Ok's little victims. There was a chance there were still more bodies to discover, maybe all over Tarlabaşı, maybe all over the city. Keeping any secrets that still remained was now the old man's principle and only pleasure.

Süleyman wondered how Ali Ok had kept himself going during those long periods of time when he didn't kill. Had just the thought of what he had done in the past been enough, or had he visited his victims from time to time? Serial killers were rare, and Ok could, possibly, be Turkey's most prolific. If they ever got to the bottom of his crimes.

People were beginning to return from the crash site to get on with their lives, coming out of shops they had locked themselves inside only half an hour ago, thanking God the explosion they had heard hadn't been a bomb. The old man who sometimes walked along İstiklal playing his violin was scraping out his version of 'Hava Nagila', while a group of young gypsy girls played pipes and drums. Timur Tonguç was disappearing into a street regaining its normality, which, Süleyman knew, would make finding him all the harder.

'I tried to be kind to him because I felt guilty,' Hayrünnisa Hanım said.

One of the paramedics tried to place an oxygen mask over Ateş Tonguç's face, but he pushed it away.

'And the rest of us?' he asked. 'What about the admiral's other children?'

She shook her head. 'I never knew you,' she said. 'He sought me out. Your father went berserk.'

'My father was and always will be a hypocrite.'

'Can you be quiet for a minute?' the female paramedic said. 'I want to take your blood pressure.'

Ateş, in an attempt to calm himself, closed his eyes. The paramedic performed the test and then said, 'It's a bit high.'

'Is that surprising?'

'We need to get you to the hospital.'

'I should hope so,' Ateş said. 'I have been shot.'

'You've been lucky,' she replied.

'Really?'

Hayrünnisa Hanım said, 'Timur was a lost boy. I shouldn't have encouraged him, but he was such a sad child, and your father was so—'

'You slept with my father; you are implicated in his behaviour,' Ateş said. 'And don't imagine my brother was such an innocent either. I know what he did with my sister.'

'What? You don't mean Deniz? He didn't kill her; he loved her. He told me.'

The paramedics lifted Ateş onto a stretcher. He said, 'Oh, he loved her. Just not in the right way for a brother to love a sister.'

It hadn't struck İkmen before, probably because he'd never knowingly seen Timur Tonguç in the flesh. But now that he was looking at him, he could see that he was the man who had jumped onto the Ferry of the Dead at the last minute. At the time, and from looking only at old photographs, İkmen hadn't seen the resemblance. Now that he did, he couldn't un-see it. Although whether Tonguç recognised him or not was another matter. İkmen didn't even know whether he'd seen him.

He watched Tonguç disappear right off İstiklal Caddesi into a tiny opening known as Hazzopulo Pasaj. Once a centre of Greek İstanbul, the Pasaj now consisted of a vine-draped tea garden surrounded by antique shops, tattoo parlours and hat emporia. It had always been popular with students and intellectuals, but as İkmen followed Tonguç through the dark cobbled entrance, he could see that it was almost empty. He called Kerim Gürsel.

'He's in Hazzopulo Pasaj,' he whispered. 'Just gone in at the İstiklal end. I'm behind him.'

'Backup's arrived,' Kerim said. 'I'll cover Meşrutiyet Caddesi and send some muscle behind you.'

Hazzopulo Pasaj was open at both ends: one onto İstiklal, the other out onto Meşrutiyet Caddesi opposite the British Consulate. There was also a third exit, through the meagre grounds of the church of Panaya İsodyon via an almost invisible door onto Meşrutiyet Caddesi. As a child, İkmen had always considered this little thoroughfare a magical place. In those days, back in the fifties and sixties, Hazzopulo had been an incredibly raffish place, where intellectuals rubbed shoulders with strippers, and the gypsies and witches of İstanbul plied their fortune-telling trade amongst the vines, heavy with grapes and the smell of old wine. His mother, the Albanian witch Ayşe İkmen, had worked the pasaj many times, and had sometimes taken her two boys with her. Çetin could still remember how she had once produced a kitten out of thin air for a child who had been crying. The little girl had laughed and then, due to a trick of the light, he assumed, his mother had quite disappeared. He had found her outside the pasaj, smoking in a shop doorway. She had been, she told him, to see a prince of the fairies.

People appeared to be drifting back from Tarlabaşı Bulvarı, sitting down on the small wooden stools underneath the vines. For a moment, Timur Tonguç appeared to think about leaving, but then he pulled up a stool too, and when a waiter walked over to him, he ordered tea. He was sitting slightly apart from the main group of drinkers in the middle of the courtyard, alone in front of the entrance to the church.

İkmen took the decision to join him.

'He's armed,' Süleyman said into his phone. 'And there are people in there.'

Four uniformed officers stood to the side of the entrance to Hazzopulo Pasaj, waiting to be told what to do next.

Kerim, who was at the Meşrutiyet Caddesi end with Elif Arslan and three more uniforms, said, 'We can't alarm him. He's a way

270

away from other people, but we need to limit those at risk. Close the pasaj from your end and I'll close up here.'

'Çetin Bey's in there.'

'Yes,' Kerim said. 'We have to trust he knows what he's doing.'

Süleyman watched as İkmen sat down opposite Timur Tonguç and opened a newspaper. He wasn't armed. He'd rarely carried a gun when he was on the force. But back then, he hadn't also been bereaved.

After instructing his officers to cordon off the pasaj, the inspector walked towards the tea garden.

Chapter 23

Çetin İkmen had seen Kerim briefly when he'd walked from the church to the top of the stairs into the tea garden and then back again. Now Süleyman was looking in the window of a tattoo parlour near the İstiklal Caddesi end of the pasaj.

And people had stopped arriving.

İkmen pretended to read his paper while wondering how long it would take Tonguç to realise he was trapped. It felt eerie sitting opposite him like this. Seemingly oblivious to anything except his tea, Tonguç stared into space like a man entirely at peace with himself. İkmen's brain, by contrast, churned. What had Timur Tonguç been doing catching the Ferry of the Dead on Kadir Gecesi? When the vessel had docked at Kadıköy, only İkmen and this man had got off. The others had gone on. If indeed there had been others . . .

The waiter brought İkmen's tea. Did he also give him a knowing look as he set it down? He heard what sounded like the shutters coming down over one of the shop windows behind him. He watched Timur Tonguç look up.

The hairs on the back of Timur Tonguç's neck were rarely wrong. Now standing proud from his flesh, they were reacting to the fact that the pasaj appeared to be closing. And yet, unless he had grown completely out of touch with İstanbul and its ways, Hazzopulo was always, Ramazan or no Ramazan, heaving with people. The incident on Tarlabaşı Bulvarı had come and gone, and the city had moved on, as it did. He looked down at his right wrist, which still bore the bruise it had sustained when the imam's van had been hit by the vehicle at its rear. Already old news.

And yet what of it lingered? What had Imam Metin told the paramedics, the police or both about him? What could he have said? Had the imam known who he was and why he'd been so interested in him? They hadn't exactly chatted. Metin was very different from his father. There had been a man open to possibilities. There had been a flexible man.

He touched the weapon that was in a holster underneath his left armpit.

He finished his tea and looked around for a waiter to get him another. But there were none. For the first time, he looked at the man sitting opposite reading *Hürriyet*. Two men who had been drinking tea down by the tattoo parlour got up and walked away. Did they pay? He thought not.

The man sitting opposite rustled his newspaper and then put it down and smiled. Did Timur know him? And if he did, how? Where from?

Süleyman took his phone out of his pocket and put it to his ear. At first, all he could hear was a rustling noise. Now was not the time to get a handbag call from his mother. But then he began to hear a voice he recognised.

'. . . took a very late ferry on Kadir Gecesi,' İkmen said. 'Beşiktaş to Kadıköy. I noticed you because you, unlike the other passengers, didn't look ill.'

And then he laughed.

Süleyman looked over at İkmen's back, and beyond that, to the face of Timur Tonguç.

* * *

273

'The other passengers were dead. I thought you were too.'

İkmen smiled. 'No,' he said, 'I just look as if I've died. It's a lifestyle choice.'

'What do you mean?'

İkmen's formal psychological training had been scant, but one thing he had observed over his long years in pursuit of those who killed was that they rarely had a sense of humour. He put his hand in his pocket and touched his phone. Hopefully Süleyman was getting this.

Another shop closed its doors.

'Do you really believe that all the other passengers on that ferry were dead?' he asked. He lit a cigarette. 'You seem like an educated man . . .'

'You look like a peasant.'

Having absolutely no sartorial ego had held İkmen in good stead for most of his life. He smiled. 'You have me,' he said. 'Working class I was born and working class I remain. Doesn't mean that I'm ignorant, though. That ferry was put on to help people who wished to spend time in the imperial mosques. You know how auspicious the Night of Power is deemed to be . . .'

'It's nothing to do with that,' Tonguç said.

This man had just been a shape on the ferry. İkmen had been entirely engulfed in his own surprise that the vessel even existed. Aliki had been a crazy old woman; what had she known? But if she'd known so little, then why had he gone to find the ferry? What did that say about him?

'So, assuming we both boarded the Ferry of the Dead to meet with those we have lost, who did you hope to see?' he said.

'You first. Who did you hope to find?'

'Me?' He left it a little while before he continued, knowing that if he said what he wanted to say, there would be no way back. 'I hoped to see your sister, Deniz.'

He leaned towards the other man. 'We know you are armed,

Mr Tonguç. So we know what a terrible mess you could make of me and anyone in my vicinity. But if you do that, you will die.'

Tonguç put his hand inside his jacket and Süleyman drew his pistol. Above the tea garden, on the steps up to the church, Kerim Gürsel also removed his weapon from its holster.

İkmen had apparently stopped speaking. So what would Tonguç do now?

Çetin had always been the sort of officer who faced his adversaries head-on. Even before Fatma had died, he'd been inclined to gamble with his own mortality. Süleyman caught Kerim Gürsel's eye. They would both watch and wait, because they both knew that was what İkmen would want.

'The Americans,' İkmen continued, 'have a word for that process of finally knowing something that has been obscured for a long time. They call it closure.'

There was a gun pointed straight at his nose and he didn't know how to feel. Partly because he realised his body wasn't playing its usual game. There was no increase, as far as he could discern, in his heart rate. No breaking of sweat. Did this mean he didn't care?

'I think that you, at the very least, know how Deniz died.'

Tonguç said nothing.

'And if I were to put money on who ended her life, I think I'd put it on you,' İkmen continued. 'I'd do that because your reported movements on the day of Deniz's death don't add up. I don't know how you did it, but I believe your father may have helped you – although I'm not *so* sure about that . . .'

Timur Tonguç, İkmen now realised, had very pale blue eyes. Almost translucent, and extremely unnerving. He wanted to look away from them but found that he couldn't.

'I could get away if I shot you,' Tonguç said.

'No you couldn't.'

The tea garden was empty now, save for Süleyman at the İstiklal Caddesi end and Kerim at the Meşrutiyet Caddesi exit.

'My colleagues would kill you.'

'Maybe that's what I want.'

'You don't believe that any more than I do,' İkmen said. 'If that were the case, why are we here? We're here because you wanted to get out of the city so badly that you chose to kidnap a man with a van that looks older than I am. That, Mr Tonguç, is desperation.'

'That man,' Tonguç said, 'is part of my story.'

'Which you have to decide whether you want to tell,' İkmen said.

'Why would I want to do that?'

'Because if you don't tell your own story, then someone else will make something up. I know you don't give a damn about closure for your family. But I do think you need people to know the truth, because I believe you are frightened of stories that people make up.' He leaned forward. 'Stories, you know, once entrenched, can take on lives of their own, like your sister's supposed suicide . . .'

Kerim Gürsel wanted to speak to Süleyman, but his phone was engaged. He was listening to İkmen's side of a conversation with a man whose pistol was now in plain sight. What now?

His sergeant, Elif Arslan, whispered in his ear. 'We must hold our nerve.'

Although younger than Kerim and junior in rank, Arslan seemed to be able to read him. İkmen had taught him well, but he was still new in the job and realised that he lacked confidence.

'OK,' he murmured.

İkmen and Tonguç were conversing in whispers now and

Kerim felt the sweat on his skin go cold. Looking at them sitting on those low stools, their heads almost touching, made him feel as if he was eavesdropping on a desperately private conversation between lovers, or between two men who planned to explode the world.

'I will tell you now,' Timur Tonguç said.

'And then you kill me and they kill you?'

'No!'

'Then what?'

But that was what he had meant and so he stayed silent.

'Surrender your weapon to me and then we can talk,' İkmen said.

'I can't.'

'Yes you can.'

İkmen had forty years' worth of experience with almost every situation the criminal world could throw at him. He recognised that Tonguç was stuck. Trapped, unable to go forward or back, he could very easily put his pistol in his own mouth and pull the trigger.

Çetin knew what he was doing, but Mehmet Süleyman nevertheless felt his heart begin to race. Tonguç had stopped talking and his shoulders had become slack, as if he had given up. İkmen was probably one of the best officers at talking people down – or he had been. But then he wasn't the man he'd been when he was still on active service, before Fatma Hanım had died. And although his mood seemed to have improved since his involvement with the Deniz Tonguç case, Çiçek had confided to Süleyman that she was still worried about him.

'As soon as he gets in, he's out on the balcony talking to Mum,' she'd told him. 'And as for the thing in the kitchen . . .'

The İkmen apartment's djinn. Süleyman couldn't see it, but

that didn't mean much. He wasn't even on nodding terms with the things Çetin and his family routinely saw and heard.

'If Dad were to truly accept Mum's death, then the djinn would go and I'd stop having to look at its ugly face every time I want a glass of tea,' Çiçek had continued. 'But he won't let her go. He wants to be with her.'

Tonguç could put that gun in his mouth or he could just shoot İkmen. Süleyman looked over at Kerim Gürsel standing on the steps up to the church and wondered what he was thinking.

Then he heard İkmen say, 'Do you have children, Mr Tonguç?'

İkmen saw Timur's face change.

Searching for something positive to say had proved difficult. This man had potentially killed his own sister as well as a woman he had known back in Artvin; he'd also attacked another of his sisters and shot his own brother. İkmen didn't know whether he had children or not. No one had ever mentioned the subject to him. It was a gamble.

Tonguç took a deep breath. 'My son lives in Ankara,' he said. 'With his mother. I don't see him.'

'Does he bear your name?'

'No,' he said. 'His mother's.'

'Does he know you are his father?'

'Yes. He is twenty-three.'

He was talking.

'What does he do?' İkmen asked.

Tonguç smiled. 'He is a clown,' he said. 'He entertains children. Travels all over.'

İkmen understood. This travelling lifestyle was what Timur himself had always wanted. Had he deserted the boy, or had the young man and his mother left him? İkmen didn't have time for such questions.

'Think of him,' he said.

'He doesn't think of me.'

'Because you don't want him to,' he said. 'Because you cut him out of your life.'

He didn't know that. Time was ticking on. He thought about Süleyman and Gürsel's superior, Commissioner Ozer, and imagined him shrieking at his underlings to get his officers to end this stand-off immediately.

But then Tonguç said, 'Well, wouldn't you cut your child out of your life? If you were me?'

And suddenly, just the thought of his children made İkmen want to weep. Why was he gambling with his life like this?

Timur Tonguç raised his pistol.

İkmen didn't want to die. It was as if the sun had just come out. He said, 'Think of your boy. Stop this now and you can tell him the truth. Your truth. Shoot me and you're just another cop killer. What is more, you'll be a cop killer who did all of these terrible things for no apparent reason.'

The danger to İkmen was clear and imminent. Süleyman sought the eyes behind Kerim Gürsel's raised gun and nodded once. He had the clearer shot, the one less likely to endanger Çetin İkmen.

He heard Kerim take off the safety catch.

'It was my father.'

Tonguç handed the pistol over to İkmen, who held it in the air for his colleagues to see.

'Get down on the ground, hands out to your sides,' he said.

Suddenly Timur Tonguç looked confused. No one was whispering any more, and what looked like a flood of police officers was running towards him.

İkmen yelled, 'On the floor! Hands to your sides! Do it!'

Shakily Tonguç slid off his stool and onto the ground. It felt dusty, and small stones rasped against his face. Then there was an explosion, and he screamed. But it was just fireworks overhead signalling the end of the Holy Month of Ramazan. A police officer patted him down, while another one cuffed his hands behind his back. When they stood him up, everyone in the tea garden was staring at him.

Everyone.

Chapter 24

Aylin's sister Zeynep was the only member of her family who was with her at the end. Despite being on life support, she simply stopped breathing. Halide Tonguç, asleep in a chair in the corridor outside, didn't even wake up when Zeynep pressed the alarm bell and medical staff came running.

Zeynep let her mother sleep. She tried to ring her brother Ateş, but he had his telephone off. Eventually she sat down beside her dead sister and told her how sorry she was that she hadn't believed her. The Ferry of the Dead had finally come for Aylin, as she had predicted. Would it now come for Zeynep? No. She pulled herself together. That was ridiculous.

İkmen had to be in the room. That was the deal. Tonguç wouldn't talk otherwise. Commissioner Ozer could go on about the inappropriateness of having a civilian in an interview with a suspect, but Tonguç wasn't budging.

'That man faced me down when he could've simply let me kill myself,' he told Kerim Gürsel. 'He deserves to know the truth from my mouth.'

But he refused the offer of a lawyer. 'What's the point?'

If he was guilty of so many crimes, Kerim Gürsel was tempted to agree. And yet he was uneasy with Timur Tonguç's choice. Without the suspect's lawyer on hand, he felt exposed. Due process was not being done. It often wasn't, but not when Kerim Gürsel was involved.

Tonguç stated his name, his age and his address in Artvin province. Now where on earth did he begin?

Bruised ribs were nothing in the scheme of things. More to the point was that the van was completely wrecked and the man in the car who had smashed into the back of him was blaming him for the accident. Technically he was right, but the fact was that the imam was being threatened at the time the accident happened. He had told his side of things as he saw it, including the fact that he had been effectively held against his will. Now, at last, he was home.

He hadn't expected anyone to be up now that there was no need to eat before dawn, but there were always exceptions.

'Imam Metin!'

He might have guessed Selçuk would still be rolling around. If Metin hadn't known him better, he would have thought his assistant was drunk, but he was too pious for that. He was just simply elated, God bless him.

Selçuk embraced him. How was he going to tell him about the van?

'Selçuk . . .'

Metin's phone rang. He answered it eagerly. It only put off the inevitable, but he knew how Selçuk's eyes would look when he told him about the accident. Like a whipped puppy.

'Hello?'

'Imam Metin Demir?' It was a female voice.

'Yes?'

'This is Sergeant Arslan from police headquarters. I am glad to be able to tell you that we have apprehended the man who kidnapped you.'

It was a relief. Even though he hadn't thought about it since he left the hospital, he felt his muscles relax. 'Oh, that's good. Thank you,' he said.

'He is being interviewed now,' she said. 'We will need to speak to you in the morning. Can you come and meet Inspector Gürsel here at ten?'

'Well, er, yes . . .'

He had hoped to go to bed and wake at about midday, but so be it.

'I will come and pick you up at nine thirty,' she said.

He hadn't expected anyone to come and get him. 'Oh, that's—'

She cut the connection.

'So, Imam Metin,' Selçuk said with a smile on his face, 'how did you get on with my van?'

'We fell in love.'

People convicted of sexual abuse often suffered from the delusion that the object of their desire reciprocated their feelings. To call it just sex was too painful – and too true. But İkmen was glad that Kerim Gürsel let it pass. Whatever one's own feelings, the job was to allow the suspect to speak.

'We couldn't help ourselves,' Tonguç said. 'Whenever we were alone, we touched each other. Then one day Deniz asked me to . . . It was beautiful.'

Two Turkish virgins in the 1970s? İkmen doubted that. The only reason that his own first time with Fatma hadn't been an unmitigated disaster was because his father had been progressive and had made sure his sons knew what to do.

And what of Timur's later affair with Burhan Aksoy? The artist had described the man he had loved back then as 'experienced'. Had that just come about via the incest with his sister?

'We knew it couldn't last. We'd have to marry other people one day. Father chose our friend Mustafa Ermis for Deniz. There was only a year between Deniz and myself and so we had a lot of friends in common. I know why Father did it. He needed the money, and Mustafa's father was a gangster back then. Smuggling drink and cigarettes in and out of Rize. I learned a lot about Ermis senior when I lived in Artvin. The north-east of this land is another country. But anyway . . . Unlike my father, who just saw money whenever he looked at Mustafa, I liked him. Aylin was besotted with him for a while, but she was just a kid. And I think he loved Deniz. And then our father discovered our secret.'

'How?' İkmen asked.

'Aylin,' he said. 'Deniz had been married for a month when he took me to one side. I don't know how Aylin knew. Only Ateş ever saw anything to my knowledge, but he was only five. He knows now, but—'

'Since when?'

'Since he grew up and realised what we had been doing that day.'

Ateş Tonguç was still in hospital.

'So everyone knew?' Kerim said.

'Not Zeynep,' Timur said. 'Not that I know. Mother?' He shrugged. 'I think she may have.' He shook his head. 'Father's problem with it wasn't moral. I don't know what he thought about what we did. When he took me aside, we talked of a problem that he had learned about from Mustafa Ermis's father. My sister Deniz wouldn't consummate the marriage. Of course, I knew that already.'

'Your sister was afraid her husband would reject her if he discovered that she wasn't a virgin?'

'Partly,' he said. Then he smiled. 'But mainly it was because she didn't love him; she loved me. She would never have betrayed me.'

The look on Tonguç's face, a self-satisfied leer almost, warranted at the very least a slap, but İkmen sat on his feelings.

'What happened?'

'Father said that the family honour had to be protected at all costs. And then he told me to kill my sister. It was my punishment.'

* * *

284

If Çiçek İkmen woke up and found that her father was still not home, she would worry. So Mehmet Süleyman called her, and in spite of the fact that it was three o'clock in the morning, she asked him to come round. She'd heard about the fracas in Hazzopulo Pasaj and wanted to know what had happened. Samsun was still apparently celebrating the end of Ramazan somewhere.

His mind already on the problem of how many murders he could charge Ali Ok with, Süleyman couldn't sleep anyway. When he arrived at the İkmen apartment, Çiçek took him into the kitchen and made tea.

As he sat down at the kitchen table, she offered him a cigarette and then joined him. Süleyman told her about her father's part in the capture of Timur Tonguç.

She ran a hand through her hair. 'God, he's incorrigible,' she said. 'What can you do with him?'

They went into the living room so that Çiçek could recline on the sofa. She was clearly exhausted and worried.

'Mehmet, be honest with me,' she said. 'Do you think my dad wants to die?'

He didn't know and he told her so. But she just shook her head.

'I wish I shared your ambiguity,' she said. 'Even now he's out and about again, all I see is him coming in every evening and talking to Mum. Samsun and I just about get five minutes of his time.'

Süleyman put a hand out to her, which she took. He had known Çiçek since she'd been a teenager. Once, long ago, before her abortive marriage, she'd had a crush on him.

She put her other hand up to her face and cried.

'I stayed with Hayrünnisa Hanım the night before I went home,' Tonguç said. 'I made several journeys back and forth to the academy over those two days.'

'To create doubt?'

'Yes.'

'Although your friend Burhan Aksoy suspected there was more to your travels than just restlessness,' İkmen said. 'That said, he was in love with you at the time . . .'

'Burhan is dead,' Tonguç said.

That was cold. İkmen wondered how Burhan Aksoy would have felt had he been able to hear how Tonguç spoke about him now.

'His wife gave me access to his papers.'

Timur looked down at the floor, momentarily cross. 'She had no right . . .' He shook his head. 'Doesn't matter. I knew my family were all going to be out that day. Everyone would be accounted for, except possibly me, but my father would make sure that was taken care of.'

'You're saying that your father instigated your actions?'

'Yes. He needed a way out of Deniz's situation with the Ermis family. If she was discovered to be damaged goods, old man Ermis could insist his son divorce her and take back the large sum of money they had paid my father to secure a marriage to a prestigious family like ours. My sister's dowry was her name; that was it. My father would lose both face and money if this happened.'

'Are you telling us that your father ordered you to kill your sister?' Kerim asked.

Timur paused for a moment and swallowed hard. 'Yes. He was the last to leave the yalı, which he left unlocked for me. But someone got there first.'

İkmen hadn't been expecting this. 'Who?'

'Deniz had told me she was going to be in the garden all day, sunbathing and reading. She was. Well, actually she was asleep, but . . . Someone had got into the house. I didn't know until it was all over.'

'By that you mean until you had killed your sister?' Kerim said.

Timur looked away. He swallowed again. 'He'd pushed the front door and it had opened. He'd been upstairs helping himself to my mother's jewellery. He didn't know I was there and I had no knowledge of him until we saw each other through the open French doors into the garden. I was holding the knife I'd just used.'

'I know it's hard for you and your siblings to watch, but your dad needs to be occupied,' Mehmet Süleyman said. 'There's no way he's going to drift into becoming a little old man sitting in a corner of a coffee house.'

Çiçek, who had stopped crying, squeezed his hand once and then let go. 'I know,' she said. 'And at first I was glad that he was busy again. Now I don't know . . .'

Süleyman sat on the floor in front of the sofa. 'You're going to have to trust him,' he said. 'When he was on the force, you had to have faith in his judgement.'

'He had all of you at his back then,' she said.

'He still does.'

'You know what I mean.'

He did. Officially İkmen was on his own. But Süleyman and Çiçek knew that the reality of the situation was rather different.

'While people like Kerim Bey, Ömer Mungun, Sergeant Arslan and Dr Sarkissian are still employed . . .'

'I know you take care of him,' Çiçek said. 'But I also know what a stubborn old goat he is. He always does his own thing . . .' She shook her head. 'I left my cigarettes in the kitchen. Would you mind getting them for me, please, Mehmet?'

'No, of course not.'

He stood up.

*   *   *

'My father took control,' Tonguç said. 'With the police who came to the house, with the pathologist . . . He just shut it down, as he knew he could.'

'But what about this man?' Kerim asked. 'The one you saw through the French doors?'

'He was robbing us.'

'But he saw you with a bloodied knife.'

'Yes.'

'What happened?'

'He ran, but I stopped him.'

'With the knife? Did you kill him?'

'No,' he said. 'I held him up against the wall until he dropped my mother's jewellery. I didn't know what to do with him. I was a kid and he wasn't that much older. His ID was in the name of Regep Demir, and he told me he was a thief.'

Kerim said, 'And so Imam Metin Demir . . .'

'Is his son,' Tonguç said. 'I never told Regep what I'd done, he never saw the body, but I gave him my watch.'

'To buy his silence.'

'It was mutual,' he said. 'An agreement between a thief and a murderer. I told him it was valuable, which it was, and he said he'd keep it to give to his son when he grew up.'

'And you believed him?'

'What choice did I have?'

'You could have killed him.'

Tonguç said nothing. What was going through his mind?

Eventually he said, 'When he left, I followed him. I'd never been to Gaziosmanpaşa before. He lived in a shack, a gecekondu, where his son lives now.'

'Did he see you?'

'I made sure he did, so he would know I knew where he lived.'

İkmen frowned. 'What time was this?' he asked.

'One p.m., two . . .'

288

'And then later, you went back to the house.'

'I went back to Heybeliada first, as we'd agreed. My father took things from there. He organised everything. People like him could do that back then.'

İkmen remembered the days of the all-conquering military very well.

Timur Tonguç put his head down. 'The only thing he couldn't sort out was my watch,' he said.

'You wanted it back?'

'No,' he said. 'But it was special. As well as being a Rolex, it also had my name engraved into a panel in the back. My name and the date that I entered the naval academy. My father had given it to me.'

'And did he know you'd given it to Regep Demir?'

'No,' he said. 'And he still doesn't.'

He helped her to her feet.

'You should go home and I should go back to bed,' Çiçek said.

Mehmet Süleyman nodded. 'Indeed.'

She smiled. 'Thank you for coming to tell me about Dad. If I had woken and he wasn't here, I would have lost my mind. You're a good friend.'

'It's my pleasure.'

He bent down as he always did to kiss her on both cheeks, but then he saw a look in her eyes he hadn't seen for a very long time.

'When my father was arrested, I knew there was a possibility of information coming out about Deniz,' Tonguç said. 'The gutter press had already unearthed my mother's interest in spiritualism. Then Mother told me that an historian was looking into Deniz's death, and so I knew that I had to secure my old watch. It was a loose end that could come back to haunt my father's case. And much as he and I didn't see eye to eye, I didn't want my family to suffer.'

'Your mother and your siblings assisted with the investigation,' İkmen said. 'How much did they know?'

'I left home after Deniz's death.'

Could he not bring himself to say the word 'murder'?

'That was the deal,' he added.

'You killed your sister in exchange for your father buying you out of the academy and letting you make your own life.'

He didn't answer.

'How could you do it?' İkmen asked. 'Although I hate the idea, I can at least understand the social and religious thinking behind so-called honour killings. But this was for money.'

'And honour,' Tonguç said.

Kerim Gürsel said, 'If you love someone, how—'

'She was going to have to have sex with Mustafa if I didn't.'

'Yes, but you knew that when she got married.'

'She promised me she wouldn't,' he said. 'And she never would have. Not unless he raped her, which in the end I knew he would do. He'd have to, in order to save face with his own family.'

İkmen turned away. How could a family with access to the best education money could buy, to the best homes, the best food, the best life chances – how could they become embroiled in something so barbaric? But then something similar had happened to his own mother, killed by members of her family in order to preserve their precious Albanian code of honour.

'I killed Deniz because I loved her,' Tonguç said. 'I hesitated. But she . . . she begged me. She let me do it.'

Neither of them had wanted it to be like that. She'd never slept with anyone except her ex-husband, who had been lazy to the point of torpor when it came to sex. For his part, Mehmet

290

Süleyman hadn't wanted to expose his own neediness, especially not to Çiçek.

And yet what had happened was undoable. As they lay naked, side by side on her bed, they both contemplated their frantic coupling with a mixture of satisfaction, anxiety and horror. They were friends! She had gone through a phase of being besotted with him many years ago, but that had long passed. Or so she'd thought.

Eventually he took a deep breath. 'I'm—'

'If you say you're sorry, I will hit you,' she said.

He looked at her, all wild, tangled hair and unruly great breasts, and had to stifle a smile. She'd thrown herself on top of him. His body was covered in bite marks from her overenthusiastic mouth. He'd never come so quickly in his life. But then he hadn't had sex for almost six months.

She put one long, slim hand up to his cheek and stroked his face.

'I loved it,' she said.

He kissed her palm.

'I don't know what it means, if anything, but I loved it,' she reiterated. Then, because she'd always been a forthright person, right from very young, she added, 'I know women have always fancied you because of how you look, but I didn't realise you were so big.'

'Ah.'

Automatically he put his hand over his penis. Then they both laughed.

'She wanted to die,' Tonguç said. 'She looked up at me and she smiled, her eyes beseeching me. In a way, the verdict of suicide was correct. She would rather die than be without me.'

İkmen imagined the confusion that poor, bewildered girl must have felt.

'And only your father knew that it was you who killed her?' Kerim asked.

'Yes.'

'So why did you attack your other sister Aylin yesterday?'

'When I realised that you were looking for me in connection with Fatima Akopoğlu, I had to find somewhere to stay until I could get out of the city.'

'You had stayed with Hayrünnisa Hanım, hadn't you?'

'Yes. But I couldn't go back there. Whatever she did with my father, she's a good person. She loves me almost like a son. If she knew what I'd done, it would have put her in a terrible position. She knows nothing. I went to Aylin's because I knew that she knew.'

'Knew what?'

'About Deniz and me. I'd always wondered whether she also suspected that I'd killed Deniz.'

'And did she?'

'She said nothing until I was about to leave. Then she accused me. You hadn't long left her apartment and she felt guilty for lying to you and hiding me. She told me that she was sick of all the years she'd wasted being afraid of me.'

'She was afraid of you?'

'Yes,' he said.

'So why did she let you into her apartment?'

'I've no idea. You'd have to ask her. Maybe she finally wanted to confront her fear.'

'What about the Ferry of the Dead?' İkmen said.

Timur Tonguç smiled. 'That old story. That was what she told people to explain the fact that she was hiding from life because she didn't want to tell anyone what was really in her mind.'

'That you might have killed her sister.'

'Yes,' he said. 'There is no Ferry of the Dead; it's pure fantasy.'

'And yet you and I boarded an unscheduled ferry from Beşiktaş to Kadıköy on the night of Kadir Gecesi,' İkmen said. 'And whilst the ferry was full, only you and I got off at Kadıköy.'

'No.' Tonguç shook his head. 'Everyone got off; it was the terminus for that service.'

İkmen felt momentarily wrong footed. Could he have possibly been wrong about the Ferry of the Dead? But then he remembered something.

'So why did you, just as I did myself, take a taxi to the old Moda ferry stage and look out into the Sea of Marmara?'

'I don't know,' Tonguç said. 'A moment of weakness? Like you, I boarded on the off chance that Aliki's old story might be true. But of course it wasn't. Such things don't exist. There is no magic, no God, no spirits of the dead. A man writes his own story and takes care of his own business. That's why I came to the city when I knew Deniz's case was being reinvestigated. If I wanted to survive, I had to get my watch back from old Regep and I had to do it in such a way that no one would ever know.'

'Hayrünnisa Hanım knew you were here.'

'She knows no one and will do nothing, even now, to endanger me or my family. But Fatima Akopoğlu was a different matter. When I first arrived in İstanbul and saw her – and more significantly, she saw me – I knew I couldn't just let her loose with that knowledge. She'd be telling all her relatives back home where I'd gone.'

'And so you killed her.'

'Yes,' he said. 'The venue wasn't my choice, but it proved to be very quiet and very secluded. And she told me she'd taken men there before.' He shrugged. 'Like so many country girls up in the big city to seek their fortune, she'd become a whore.' Then, suddenly and incongruously, he smiled. 'I was glad to know that she didn't have a pimp, however. They are such dreadful people, don't you think?'

Chapter 25

Zeynep Tonguç kissed the top of her brother's head. In the space of twenty-four hours, he'd been shot by his elder brother, undergone surgery, and now Zeynep had told him that Aylin was dead.

The ward he'd been placed in was heaving, but a sympathetic nurse had put a screen around his bed so that Ateş and Zeynep could have some privacy.

'It was definitely Timur who attacked her?' he asked his sister.

Zeynep, who had neither slept nor eaten for over a day, held a cup of water up to his lips and said, 'Have a little more.'

He sipped. He knew he was dehydrated after his operation, but he was almost beyond feeling in light of this latest item of news.

'The police say he admitted to it,' Zeynep said. 'As well as admitting to the murder of that girl over in Kanlica.'

'They thought that was me at first,' Ateş said.

'The DNA sample.'

'Yes.'

'Well it was Timur.' She took the cup away once it was empty. 'Inspector Gürsel also said we must be prepared for some news about Deniz's death. What do you think that is? Do you think Timur . . .'

'I don't know.'

Was now the time to tell his sister what he knew? What he'd known since he was a five-year-old child?

'And now the police are questioning Father too,' she continued.

'Mother is in pieces. Another daughter dead, a son in custody, you here—'

'Zeynep,' he cut in. It really was now or never. 'I need to tell you something . . .'

She smiled. 'And I have something to tell you too,' she said. 'About Mustafa Ermis and me . . .'

'He's playing the madness card,' Ömer Mungun said.

Süleyman put his head in his hands. He didn't do sleep deprivation well, whatever the cause.

'In what way?' he asked.

'Refuting his earlier statements, pleading no knowledge of his victims one minute, calling them his children the next.'

'Are you sure the strain of arrest hasn't affected his mind? He is old,' Süleyman said.

Ömer smiled. 'This is Ali Ok, sir.'

And he was right. Someone who had hidden his monstrous crimes for over forty years wasn't easily going to lose his mind. He'd even hidden some of his victims almost within touching distance. No. The old kapıcı was still playing games.

'Any more discoveries?' Süleyman asked.

Ömer had been at the site for most of the previous night.

'No,' he said.

'So the residents are still in the community centre?'

'Yes. Although in spite of the cordon, we've had a couple of visits from one of the apparent real owners of the property.'

'Tayfun Yıldırım?'

'The same.' Ömer sat down opposite his boss.

'Out from behind the shabby coat tails of local junkies.'

'With his invisible Armenian original owners in tow,' Ömer said. 'That building will be razed to the ground as soon as we say we've finished with it. I feel sorry for all the old ladies, the Englishman, even the little rent boys.'

295

'Me too. But what can be done?' Süleyman said. 'By taking the place apart to look for Ok's victims, we are part of the problem. An historic building cannot be demolished, but we have wrecked what was already a very fragile house and the road is now clear for Mr Yıldırım and his cronies.'

'The long march of development continues.'

'It does,' Süleyman said. 'And if I were a cynical man, I would say that Mr Yıldırım and his colleagues probably knew more about Ali Ok and his activities than they will ever let on.'

'You think so, sir? Really?'

Süleyman leaned back in his chair. 'Ömer, my dear friend, anything is possible in this city. Always has been and always will be. Why do you think people come from all over the country to seek their fortunes in İstanbul?'

'No comment.'

Kerim Gürsel had been afraid his visit to Silivri prison would end up like this. Admiral Tonguç was much thinner than he appeared to be on television. But he was no less angry now than when he had first been arrested in the full glare of multiple TV camera crews.

'Your son Timur alleges that you instructed him to kill his sister Deniz in 1976,' Kerim continued. Tonguç had already no-commented his way through his previous questions. Now they were at the nub of the matter, he was sticking to that line.

'No comment.'

'He further alleges that it was you who shut down the criminal and pathological investigations into Deniz's death and that it was directly upon your instructions that the matter was finally judged to be suicide.'

The admiral turned his head away. Kerim looked at Elif Arslan and indicated that if she had any questions, now was the time to ask them. What she said didn't come as a surprise, but it did shock everyone in that room, including the admiral's guards.

'How could you hold the value of the lives of your children so unequally?' she said. 'If your son is to be believed, they were both involved in an incestuous relationship, and yet you clearly saw Deniz as the problem. Was it just because her sexual preferences, if that is what they really were, could cost you money? Or was it because she was a girl and you are the sort of man who believes that women are always to blame for sexual indiscretion? Because women tempt men, don't they? Even their own blood.'

Infuriated, his face red with anger, the admiral rose from his chair, only to be pushed back down by the guards. He looked at Kerim Gürsel, clearly expecting the policeman to rebuke his female colleague. But he didn't.

'I'd answer the question if I were you, Admiral,' Kerim said. 'Because this is not going to go away. The investigation into Deniz's death is now live once more, and as I know you have been told, your son Timur is also charged with killing a prostitute as well as your daughter Aylin.'

The old man stared down at the table in front of him. 'I am bereaved,' he said.

'Yes, and so is your wife, your son Ateş and your daughter Zeynep. I am sorry for the loss of Aylin,' Kerim said. 'She was a very sad lady, and more sinned against than sinning.'

The admiral said, 'You met her?'

'When we were trying to track down your son, yes,' Kerim said. 'It was your DNA sample, Admiral, that gave us a clue as to who might have killed the prostitute Fatima Akopoğlu. When Ateş was cleared we turned to Timur, who ran.'

But if Kerim and Elif were waiting for the admiral to ask who Fatima Akopoğlu was, and why Timur had killed her, they were to be disappointed. He turned his face away and stared at the wall.

* * *

Selçuk knocked on his door three times before he finally got the message that Metin wanted to be alone. The imam just couldn't face the inevitable flood of questions, not to mention the other queries Selçuk still had regarding the van. No matter how many times Metin explained it to him, he couldn't understand why it was beyond repair. He had, he said, many friends who could repair it – by which, of course, he meant his brother and a couple of his semi-criminal mates.

The police had said Metin could have the watch back once they'd completed their investigation. But he didn't want it. Just thinking about it made him go cold. What the police had told him about his father's involvement with Timur Tonguç had sickened him. All these years he'd thought of old Regep as a kind of harmless thieving loser, when in fact he'd colluded in a murder. How could he have done such a thing?

The inevitable conclusion he came to was clear – he'd done it for his son. Tonguç had told him the watch was valuable, and Regep had taken it as a legacy for Metin. He'd never considered selling it for his own profit; he probably imagined that by the time Metin himself sold it, the whole Deniz Tonguç affair would have been forgotten. Timur Tonguç had clearly taken a similar gamble.

But then the past had caught up with both of them, and with Metin.

Çetin İkmen had just woken up from a restless sleep when he saw Çiçek attempting to creep past his chair and into the kitchen.

'Dad,' she said. Weirdly, she looked guilty, although he couldn't imagine why.

'You home from work?' he said.

'It's nearly eight o'clock,' she said. 'How long have you been back?'

'Since two, I think.' He rubbed his eyes with the back of his hand. 'Mehmet Süleyman said he told you where I was last night, which is why I didn't call.'

'Yes,' she said. 'Dad, I've got stuff to put in the fridge . . .'

'Oh, go, go,' he said.

He closed his eyes again. Whatever she was putting in the fridge wasn't his affair, even if everything else was. The Tonguç family represented everything that was both rotten and amazing about families. Rotten because the father had elevated his own status and financial security above the safety of his children, and in doing so had created a copy of himself in Timur. Amazing because of the love and resilience İkmen had seen when he'd visited Ateş, his sister Zeynep and their mother at the Florence Nightingale Hospital in Şişli. He didn't know whether Halide Hanım had been aware of her children's incestuous relationship or her husband's deal with Timur, and in a way, he didn't want to know. She hadn't, as far as he could tell, done anything wrong, and if she had suspected anything, well, she was paying for her neglect now.

What he did want to know about was the Ferry of the Dead. Because although Kerim Gürsel had told him that sometimes extra night ferries across the Bosphorus were put on during Kadir Gecesi, he knew what he had seen and they hadn't been the living. Also, Timur Tonguç had lied. İkmen had got off the ferry at Kadıköy and had gone on to Moda to see whether he could spot it. But it had disappeared. Just like Fatma, who, when he'd finally got home that afternoon, had been nowhere.

Chapter 26

One week later

'I wish I could help you,' Ömer Mungun said to the two old women carrying their shopping back to Tarlabaşı community centre.

Güneş Hanım shrugged. 'You got us into the community centre; what more can we ask?'

'It's the city who should rehouse us,' her friend Yeliz said.

'I know,' Ömer said, 'but . . .'

'We're old whores and so no one gives a shit,' Güneş said. And when she saw Ömer struggling to know what to say next, she said, 'It's all right, Sergeant, we do know.'

He laughed.

'I'm just shocked, although I shouldn't be, at how quickly the old place has been torn down,' Yeliz said. 'Yesterday it was there, today it's gone.'

Nothing except a pile of rubble remained of the house on Kalyoncu Kulluğu Caddesi.

'That developer will have his way.'

'Yes,' Güneş said, 'although I blame that old bastard Ali Ok for all this. I always knew he was a wrong 'un.'

'You never—'

'I never said because he was our kapıcı,' Güneş said. 'What was I supposed to do? He'd've thrown me out.'

They all continued walking in silence. Then Ömer said, 'And you? What will you ladies do?'

'Same as ever,' Yeliz said. 'Just somewhere else.'

'Where?'

'I don't know,' she said. 'But we'll survive, Sergeant. Old whores do.'

And Ömer Mungun could only agree with that. In spite of everything, the old whores, trans girls and rent boys of Tarlabaşı would always be with their city, no matter what anyone else thought of them.

'Hülya told me you were leaving town.'

Çetin İkmen stood in the middle of a hallway crowded with boxes. A thin and strained-looking Suzan Tan put a label on one of them and then stood up.

'Yes,' she said. 'I have a job in Antalya.'

'The coastal sunshine will do you good,' he said.

She smiled.

He thought about not addressing the problem of Tayfun Yıldırım, but then decided he had to.

'I hear Mr Yıldırım is busy with his properties in Tarlabaşı,' he said.

She turned away. 'And the demolition of the Kara Lale Yalı.'

'It's down?'

'Yes.' She looked at him. 'Who would want to live in a place of such infamy?'

She had a point. Ever since the news about Timur Tonguç had broken, the campaign against his father had intensified. Now not just a traitor but also a murderer, albeit by proxy, the admiral had no friends left and neither did his old home. In a way, it was understandable. But İkmen still felt sorry for the family. He'd seen terrible footage on the news of Halide Hanım, dressed in black, weeping hysterically. How would she hold up now, he wondered; would she retreat back into the spiritualism and super-stition of her past?

'You know,' he said, after a pause, 'if you ever have trouble with Tayfun . . .'

'I won't.' She looked him straight in the eye.

'Because people like—'

'I'm going to make a new life in Antalya,' she said.

Were there still shadows of old bruises around her eyes? Even if there were, what could he do?

'Tayfun Bey is no longer a problem for me,' she said.

'Good.' He smiled. 'But if he ever touches you again, you know where I am.'

But she just carried on packing, and didn't answer him.

Heading up the hill towards Tünel, İkmen thought about paying a visit to the woman who had recommended he take the fabled Ferry of Death across the Bosphorus. But when he drew level with the coffee shop, he saw that it was closed.

Maybe he was meant never to know what the truth about the Ferry of the Dead might be. He wondered whether Timur Tonguç was left with questions about this too, but then decided that he probably had other, greater worries on his mind.

Mehmet Süleyman leaned out of his living-room window and looked down into the street. As regular as clockwork, there she was, walking back to Tünel on her way home.

He called down to her.

'Çiçek Hanım!'

She looked up and frowned. It had been a week since they'd slept together, and not a word had passed between them.

'Mehmet Bey?'

'Can you spare a moment?' he asked.

'Why?'

'I have something for you.'

She made a face, which was typical of Çiçek when she was mildly annoyed.

'Come up!'

She sighed. 'If I must.'

He saw her enter the building and say something to the kapıcı, who would, no doubt, be angry with him later for shouting out of the window. He heard her climb the stairs, slowly. It was hot again, and she was tired after a whole day on her feet.

He opened his front door and stood leaning against the door frame. When she saw him, she said, 'What?'

'Come in,' he said.

'It better be good.'

She entered the apartment and he closed the door behind her. Anxious now that she was actually here, he looked her up and down and then said, 'Hello.'

'Hello to you too,' she said. 'What do you want, Mehmet? If it's about—'

'Yes, it is about that,' he said.

'Oh well, get on with it then. But just to put your mind at rest, I've not read anything into what happened between us, I've not told my dad anything. No harm has been done.'

He'd had a speech all ready. It had been about how impetuous he'd always been, how it had always got him into trouble, but how for once he'd done something he didn't regret. But then the way she was looking at him was making him sweat, and so he just resorted to action rather than words. He grabbed hold of her shoulders, took her in his arms and kissed her.

When he'd finished, eliciting a less than enthusiastic response from Çiçek, she said, 'I suppose that means you want to carry on where we left off?'

'Yes . . .'

'Mmm.' She stood back from him and crossed her arms over

her chest. 'Well, let's see, shall we? Don't forget, Mehmet, I know all about you. So you mess me around like you've done to the women in your life before, and there will be consequences.'

And then, to his amazement, she left.